LERZA'S
LIVES

ST. MARTIN'S PRESS   NEW YORK

LERZA'S
LIVES

John Danica
AND
Lucy Freeman

A THOMAS · DUNNE
BOOK

This is a work of fiction. All names, places, characters, and incidents are entirely imaginary, and any resemblance to actual events, or to persons living or dead, is coincidental.

Library of Congress Cataloging-in-Publication Data

Danica, John.
  Lerza's lives / John Danica and Lucy Freeman.
    p. cm.
  "A Thomas Dunne book."
  ISBN 0-312-05976-0
  I. Freeman, Lucy. II. Title.
PS3556.R392L47 1991   90-27082
813'.54—dc20   CIP

First Edition: August 1991
10 9 8 7 6 5 4 3 2 1

This book is dedicated to the Vietnam veteran. Gordon, Ray, Nicky and Joe—we were young and naive . . . but we learned quick. And to my fallen brothers who didn't make that return trip to C.O.N.U.S. I miss you Al, Eddie, Leroy, and all the other marines of Alpha Company.

SEMPER FI
'67–'68

Acknowledgments

I would like to thank my partner and co-author, Lucy Freeman, whose encouragement always came during my deepest doubts. Her optimism was contagious and her unselfishness a goal. This book and any future works exist because of Lucy.

I want to thank Ruth Cavin, senior editor at St. Martin's Press, who took a big chance on a first-time writer. She always found the time to answer my persistent questions with witty and supportive letters from New York.

Thanks also goes to our agent, Jane Dystel, who sold this book because she believed in it. Thank you, too, Karen Smith, for transferring my scribblings into neatly typed pages and, finally, thanks to my wife and two daughters, who allowed me to pursue my dream. I love you, Mom.

John Danica

Some of us live in a world of blacks
and whites shaded by grays;
   Others in a world of maybes;

I have seen that thousand-yard stare
in your nineteen-year-old face;
   Immediately before and right after
those firefights where people die;

We shall not rest until *all* are
accounted for; but—
   How do we account for those who came
home, but didn't?

—A poem by a marine named Smith

PROLOGUE

The Lance Corporal walked point. The point was the lead man on patrols. It was his job to look for ambushes and booby traps. Points in Vietnam had a life expectancy of twenty-seven days.

Few men volunteered for point—the Lance Corporal did. His cover man was the ex-Sergeant, now a private. The cover man walked directly behind the point and protected him, because the point often kept his eyes to the ground looking for punji stakes and trip wires.

Nobody liked the ex-Sergeant. He talked only to the Lance Corporal. The ex-Sergeant had been in Nam before receiving numerous decorations on his first tour. When he returned to the States, he punched a commissioned officer in the mouth and was given six months of hard labor. It wasn't the first time. He hated being a peacetime marine, with his spit-shined shoes, marching, and saluting. He hated officers. He liked the Nam.

While in the brig at Camp LeJeune, North Carolina, he volunteered for a second tour in Vietnam. They reduced him in rank to private, he forfeited six months pay, and was given orders for Wes Pac—Vietnam. He and the Lance Corporal were both assigned to Alpha Company, First Battalion, First Marines. That had been seven months before. It was now January 1968.

In Vietnam grunts (the infantry) never slept a complete night. If you weren't on an LP (a listening post), you were on night ambush or perimeter watch. Two hours of watch, four hours sleep. Grunts usually did their two-hour watch on a buddy system. Two men stayed awake for two watches or four hours. They did this for two reasons—to help keep each other awake and because it got lonely. During those long nights, men talked. You got so close to your buddy that you could quote his girlfriend's dress size or the name of his first-grade teacher.

None of the men of Alpha Company would stand watch with the ex-Sergeant. He didn't engage in conversation and, if he did, it was one-word snarls.

Two months after the Lance Corporal and the ex-Sergeant arrived "in country," the ex-Sergeant saved the life of the Lance Corporal.

They were on a night ambush several clicks from the airfield. As usual the Lance Corporal led the squad-size ambush past the perimeter into the night. Those first few steps into total darkness after leaving the relative safety of a perimeter were exhilarating. "Snoopin' and Poopin'," the grunts called it.

Lieutenant Smith had briefed the squad about the nearby village, which turned into a Vietcong supply center after dark. The ambush team carried M-16s, a shotgun, an M-79 grenade launcher, and an M-60 machine gun set up near the road leading to the village. The night was hot and sticky, and the heavy Marine Corps flak jacket had caused a painful rash under the Lance Corporal's arms.

Firing orders were simple. The village had a sundown curfew; anyone entering or leaving would be killed. Free-fire zones eliminated decisions. The Lance Corporal didn't see the Vietcong approaching from his rear, the ex-Sergeant did. When it was over and they were safely back inside their perimeter, the Lance Corporal tried to thank the ex-Sergeant. The ex-Sergeant repeated two words: "Fuck it."

From that night on the Lance Corporal and the ex-Sergeant were together. True, the Lance Corporal did most of the talking, but he didn't care. They stood watch every night and shared their C rations. The Lance Corporal gave the ex-Sergeant the four cigarettes issued in each C-Rat carton, and the ex-Sergeant gave the Lance Corporal his cocoa and cookies.

The Lance Corporal found out a lot about the ex-Sergeant over the next few months. Like the wife and child he'd lost in an auto accident, and his childhood in an orphanage. They occasionally shared a bottle of Silver Fox whiskey. When they got real drunk, the ex-Sergeant talked about his past and cried. The Lance Corporal would tell the other marines the ex-Sergeant wasn't so bad; eventually he referred to him as "my best friend."

It was a hot, clear day, right after the monsoons, when the company-size patrol left Fire Base Julie. The Lance Corporal led the three platoons through the canopied jungle. The ex-Sergeant walked five paces behind. The Lance Corporal had his M-16 on automatic, finger on the trigger. The ex-Sergeant carried a shotgun, a practical weapon in the thick jungle. Two bandoliers of 5.56-mm ammo crisscrossed the Lance Corporal's chest, and two grenades were carefully snapped to his cartridge belt.

It was supposed to be a routine patrol—just a walk in

the woods. The ex-Sergeant had almost smiled that morning when a new guy lit a gaseous heat tab in his hooch and ran out gagging. Everyone was in a good mood. The patrol came to a creek bed, forty yards of shallow water between two tree lines. The Lance Corporal signalled for Lieutenant Smith, who told him to cross.

The Lance Corporal was midway across the creek when he heard it. The snap of a bolt closing, followed by a sharp *crack* echoing along the water.

The bullet from the AK-47 hit the fleshy part of the Lance Corporal's thigh. He fell facedown into the water; it covered half his body. He saw his blood mixed with the running water and rolling downstream. The Lance Corporal had been wounded before and knew he wasn't hit bad this time. An experienced combat vet was aware of the degree of the danger.

As the Lance Corporal lay in the creek bed, the men of Alpha Company retreated to the tree line and returned fire. The two tree lines now were exchanging fire, with the Lance Corporal in the middle of the killing zone, unable to move. The rounds flew across the forty yards of creek, inches above the Lance Corporal's head.

Suddenly the ex-Sergeant appeared. The Lance Corporal wanted him to go back and screamed that he was fine. As the ex-Sergeant reached the Lance Corporal, he was hit three times in the chest. The ex-Sergeant fell prone alongside his only friend, face to face.

The ex-Sergeant spoke clearly and strongly in spite of the three hits. He asked, "Are you okay?"

The Lance Corporal nodded. With that, the ex-Sergeant died.

The Lance Corporal looked at the three small bullet holes in his friend's chest and thought how neat and precise they appeared. He placed his arm under the ex-Sergeant's head and lifted it out of the water. The two men lay in the creek bed for several moments, oblivious to the firefight.

Slowly the sounds of battle returned to the Lance Corporal's ears. Anger replaced fear. He unsnapped a fragmentation grenade from his cartridge belt, pulled the pin, and threw it from his prone position. After the explosion he pulled himself to his feet, M-16 in one hand and a second grenade in the other.

From a standing position he threw the second grenade toward the NVA tree line. Because of his adrenaline, the grenade carried well within the jungle. The men of Alpha Company then heard a strange, animal-like scream erupt from the Lance Corporal as he charged the NVA tree line with his M-16 blazing on automatic.

A second bullet hit the Lance Corporal's head, leaving a two-inch crevice along the right front top of his skull. This only seemed to anger him more. He reached the enemy tree line, shouting profanities and bleeding severely.

The marines of Alpha Company, first battalion, first Marines, witnessing this bizarre scene, suddenly rose from concealment and followed the Lance Corporal into the deadly tree line. When it was over the body count was twenty-two enemy dead, an unknown number of wounded, and four prisoners. The remainder of the crack NVA regiment had scattered into the woods. The marines suffered one dead— the ex-Sergeant. Five were wounded; only one was in need of stateside medical evacuation.

The Lance Corporal lost consciousness. Hours later, perhaps even days, he tried to open his eyes, sensing someone standing near. He could feel the clean sheets, smell the hospital. Though he still had a headache, the morphine had dulled the pain. He forced his eyes open and saw the star of a brigadier general and the railroad tracks of two young captains. The three surrounded his bedside.

The General spoke. "How you feeling, Marine?"

The Lance Corporal put up a thumb, and said, "Okay, sir."

The General's voice turned formal. He read from a sheet of paper he held before him:

"From, Commanding General, USMC, Wes Pac Vietnam, to Commanding Officer, Alpha Company, First Battalion, First Marines. Subject, Purple Heart, third award, and Silver Star. It is with pride that the President of the United States of America and the Commandant of the Marine Corps presents the following:

"On January 31, 1968, the insurgent Communist forces attempted a threefold attack in the vicinity of the vulnerable Quanq Tri Airfield. This was the beginning of the Tet offensive, and enemy success at Quanq Tri would have significantly weakened the entire I Corps Sector of South Vietnam. While on routine patrol, men of Alpha Company, First Battalion, First Marines, encountered the advance NVA regiment for the Tet offensive. Although severely outnumbered, they successfully and courageously defeated the enemy.

"This encounter saved the lives of numerous South Vietnamese allies and American service personnel at the Quang Tri Airfield. Performing in the highest traditions of the Marine Corps, a grateful nation presents the Purple Heart, third award, and the Silver Star to Lance Corporal Joseph Lerza."

PART I

Lend me five President Grants?" Reginald (Bubba) Nite asked.

Joe Lerza laughed. He knew Bubba was up to no good; Bubba was *always* up to no good.

"Only got twenty George Washingtons," Lerza said, pulling his last twenty-dollar bill from an old wallet. "Whatta' you need it for?"

Bubba Nite eased up next to Lerza and whispered, "A sure thing. A mare named Mrs. Ed running tonight at Garden State."

"Thought you were on a gambling wire tap."

"I am." Bubba winked like a co-conspirator. "Worked the graveyard shift last night. Overheard the fix on this nag."

Lerza waved the twenty enticingly under Bubba's nose and said doubtfully, "Don't know. This is my lunch money for the week. Besides it's unethical, immoral, and probably even illegal to give it to you."

"When did *you* get religion?" Bubba sneered. Then, pleadingly, "Twenty'll get you eighty."

"Here." Lerza released the bill and handed it to Bubba. "You keep the juice." He chuckled. "Just pay back the twenty so I won't get my ass chewed by Father Nick in the confessional."

Joseph Anthony Rico Lerza did not look like an FBI agent. Everyone told him that. It was more than his physical makeup that distinguished him from other FBI agents. It was those sensitive hazel eyes. They showed he had been places and seen frightening things most people hadn't. The ghetto where he was born, the jungles of Vietnam where he bled, and the endless back alleys where he later earned his paycheck. Within the small world of the FBI Lerza had a "rep." The other agents used words like "different," "unorthodox," and "hot dog" to describe him.

At forty his five-eight frame did not hold the midlife bulge gracefully. He no longer worked the dangerous streets and left the all-night surveillances and search warrants to the younger agents. He was now out to pasture as the Philadelphia office's public-relations officer. One of those created positions to stick old war-horses like Joe Lerza in. A dead end.

The hands on the wall clock pointed at eight-fifteen as the old black rotary desk phone rang. He picked it up before the second ring. "Lerza."

"Hi, Joe." The familiar sound of the telephone operator. "The boss wants to see you."

"I'm on my way, Betty."

He pushed away from the low-bid government desk and maneuvered around the wall-to-wall FBI agents who filled up the squad room. It was a three-ring circus, with the agents screaming into the phones at each other, and into dictating machines.

As Lerza entered the outer office of the Special Agent in Charge, the "SAC," his face broke into a smile at Betty Northrup, a pleasant, middle-aged widow. One of those genuinely nice souls every office should have but rarely does.

He leaned toward her and asked, "Hey, gorgeous, when are we gonna run off to Tahiti and dance naked in the sun?"

She smiled and said, "Don't tempt me, Joe. I'm in a weakened condition."

He sighed. "I can't stand this constant rejection."

"All right, Joe, you talked me into it. But I won't strip naked 'cause I'm too fat."

"Who says?" He deadpanned. "You're perfect, darlin'. Just perfect. Now, before you and I get into some serious trouble, tell me why the boss wants to see me."

"Don't know."

"Aw, come on, Betty. You know *everything* that goes on in this office."

"Everything 'cept this." She smiled again. "He's had the door closed since he got in. And I haven't seen any paper with your name on it recently."

He shook his head, a thoughtful expression on his face. "Don't like it, Betty, don't like it at all. Last guy went in there under mysterious circumstances got transferred to Butte, Montana."

Lerza's mind was racing, trying to figure out what he had done wrong. Or, more accurately, what he had been caught at. The Bureau had so many rules and regulations, a cloistered nun could break a page full before lunch. Let's see, he thought, I left my desk unlocked last week. Didn't put a file away two weeks ago. Forgot to submit an itinerary last month. Oh yeah, a biggie, I missed firearms the last three shoots.

He laughed. "Probably a promotion."

"Sure." Betty ran a comb through her hair. "One thing

'bout you, Joe, you got a good sense of humor. Mr. Keenan said to go right in."

Lerza blew her a kiss as he entered the inner sanctum of the SAC. Bosses were queer creatures. Before they became bosses they were regular guys—a few beers after work, an occasional beer during work, and constant complaints about their bosses. Then *they* became bosses and started using words like "interfacing," "no," and "you're on your own if you get caught."

Brad Keenan did look like an FBI agent. Tall, lean, graying temples, steel-blue eyes, and an endless supply of dress-white shirts. If Darryl F. Zanuck had called central casting for a G-Man, Keenan would have showed. He sat behind a desk large enough to land a 747, framed by the American flag and J. Edgar Hoover's photograph. Personally inscribed: "To Brad. You are the finest agent in my Bureau. Best Personal Wishes, J. Edgar."

The SAC looked up as Lerza entered. "Have a seat, Joe."

Lerza took the chair opposite Keenan and waited.

A few seconds later Keenan asked, "How are things going?" He sounded earnest, as though he really cared.

"Couldn't be better, boss."

"Good to hear, Joe. Good. What's the latest in PR?"

"The usual. I issued a press release on the Reems arrest. Channel 3 is running a special on drug trafficking, and I'm doing some training with the new agents."

"You enjoy that kind of stuff, Joe?"

"Love it, boss."

"Really?" A slight skepticism in his tone.

Lerza hesitated, on guard now. "Yeah, sure."

"Ever miss the streets?"

"Sometimes. But it passes."

"You speak Sicilian, don't you?"

"Yeah." He tried to figure out where this conversation was heading.

Keenan looked at a paper on his desk and recited, "Vietnam, 'sixty-seven to 'sixty-eight. War hero, three Purple Hearts and two Silver Stars. Weapons expert. Psychologist six years after returning home and getting a degree at the University of Pennsylvania. Ten years working organized crime. Five years narcotics."

Oh, shit, Lerza thought, he's reading from my jacket, he's got my personnel folder, what is this all about?

Keenan went on, "Two long undercover assignments. One with the La Coso Nostro. Bureau pilot. Ten citations for bravery and four disciplinary censures." A moment's silence, then, "Like the edge, don't you, Joe?"

Lerza did not know what answer his boss wanted, so he just shrugged.

"We got a very serious problem, Joe," Keenan's most ominous voice. "*You* could help. That is, if you wanted."

Lerza's Italian mother, bless her soul, had used the same line on him, and it always worked. He sat there feeling guilty and did not know why.

Finally the words emerged, "I'll do whatever I can, boss."

"Good!" Keenan sounded greatly relieved, as though he had expected to be opposed.

Lerza slumped in the hardback chair and prepared for a case briefing. He had heard a thousand of them.

"It involves a major organized crime family and the Satan Motorcycle Gang. The Philly mob is about to split right down the middle, and the Satans are planning to pick up the pieces. The Young Turks feel the commission has gone soft, and the elder statesmen feel the youngsters don't understand the way crime should be conducted."

He sighed and went on, "The Satans are using the rift and moving into the mob's most profitable business—narcotics. The young Italians want retaliation. *War*—all-out war! They're being barely restrained by the commission, but it can't last very—"

Lerza interrupted, "Don't sound like a problem to me. Let 'em whack each other off and we just sit back and ID the bodies."

"I almost agree with you, but it's not that simple. If the wrong side wins, the city could return to the kind of senseless violence of the Twenties and Thirties. We know what we got with Don Amato. The old man keeps a lid on the rough stuff while conducting his business—loansharking, gambling, prostitution, and narcotics. Sounds bad, but it's controlled. We do our thing trying to catch him, he does his thing, everybody goes home at night to dinner. If this young mobster, this Miceli, or worse yet, the Satans, win out, we'll all be zipping up body bags and some of them will be filled with innocent people."

"Who *is* this guy Miceli?" Lerza asked.

"Anthony Miceli controls the narcotics end of the family business. A violent man who took a dirty, third-rate piece of their action and turned it into their shining star. Along the way he bought a lot of nasty friends he now owns. Miceli's goal is to be the *capo de tutti capi*—boss of bosses. And he's not far away from making a move. Amato's old and sick, barely able to control Miceli."

"Why doesn't Amato just name his successor, then retire alive?"

"Source tells us Miceli would kill him before Amato got his gold watch."

"Source?" Raised eyebrows.

"We got an inside person," Keenan admitted, then let

it drop. "Amato's limited in his options. Name Miceli as boss, then retire. Die of old age. Have Miceli kill him. Or fight it out."

Lerza controlled a yawn. "Somehow I can't get all emotional about some aging gangster."

Keenan's eyebrows rose. "Forget about the Satans? Right now they're making their move on every major mob customer. They have a network set up that rivals Miceli, and they got the muscle to back it up."

Lerza felt uncomfortable and said, "This motorcycle gang ain't exactly living up to my image, boss."

"Oh? And what's that?" Slight sarcasm.

"Fifteen drunks on motorcycles terrorizing Mr. and Mrs. Jones from Ames, Iowa, on their camping trip at Yellowstone."

"Unfortunately, that's what the public thinks, too." Keenan picked up a magazine. "Let me read you something from the last O.C. digest. 'The newest threat to American society today is the Outlaw Motorcycle Gang. Highly organized on a national level, they have a chain of command similar to the military. The more sophisticated gangs are in the same stage of development as was the American Sicilian Mafia of twenty years ago, in terms of numbers, range of illegal activities, counter law-enforcement techniques, and ruthlessness. If allowed to develop at its current pace, it will surpass the LCN within the next ten years.' " Keenan looked up. "I'd go on but you have the picture."

Lerza said thoughtfully. "So it's a lot more than some meth labs and hookers."

"A lot more." Keenan expanded. "Chapter president is a mysterious person, street name of Lu. The frightening thing about him is the knack this guy has for the business. Looks like the rest of them. Tattoos, long hair, glazed eyes.

But operates the Satans like a senior VP from E. F. Hutton. Drug profits go into silent real-estate holdings, bearer bonds, and Bahama banks."

Lerza sighed and said, "The Hell's Angels, Bandidos, and Pagans are all into drugs, laundering their profits through legitimate businesses. What's so different about the Satans?"

"Two things. They're located in Philadelphia, making a move on the Italians. And their worship of Satan and the occult."

"How come?"

"It's rumored that Lu was a marine in Nam, 'sixty-eight Tet offensive. Story goes that he won the Navy Cross for saving the lives of half his platoon by charging a fortified NVA position with a bullet in his chest. He goes into a field hospital, successful surgery. Anticipated complete recovery but a week later comes up AWOL. Supposedly walks into Cambodia and hooks up with the mountain people and—"

Lerza interrupted, "Interesting fellow."

"It gets better." Keenan smiled. "The mountain tribe Lu hooks up with practices Palo Mayombe, a cult that stresses evil for evil's sake. A cult that allegedly has perfected a mind-control technique."

Lerza tried to downplay what he was hearing. "Hell, boss, the Marine Corps practices mind control, too."

"I've researched this in the Bureau archives, Joe," Keenan protested, "and there's documented cases that would curdle even your blood. A kid cuts off his hand in South Dakota in the name of Satan. A father in Vermont sexually abuses his three- and six-year-old daughters before cutting out and eating their hearts. A mother in—"

Lerza interrupted. "Enough. I get the message, boss."

Keenan sat back in his chair, allowed the mental pictures of his morbid examples to fade slowly. Finally he said, "All has to do with mind control, Joe. The leader brainwashes his members into believing that living sacrifices will protect them from anything—bullets, narcotics, and FBI agents. The killing supposedly protects them."

Keenan paused in his monologue; it reminded Lerza he was not there for chit-chat. But he was going to let Keenan earn his eighty-eight thou a year.

"So?" Keenan broke the silence.

"So?" Lerza played dumb.

"I want you to go under." Keenan had finally said the words. They hung in the still of the room as Lerza formed a reply.

Finally he said, "I'm flattered, boss, I really am. But deep undercover is seven days a week, and one of my kids ain't real sure I'm her daddy because of my last undercover. Calls me Mr. Joe."

The SAC almost smiled. "We both know undercover is voluntary, but I want you to reconsider," he said; it was almost a plea. "The Judge is extremely interested in the outcome of this case."

He's certainly pulling out all stops, Lerza thought. The euphemism "Judge" meant the current FBI director and former judge, William Sessions.

"Why me, boss?" he protested. "There are a lot of young single guys out there who'd love to go under. Usually means fancy car, high-priced address, and enough bullshit to dazzle any cocktail waitress for years to come."

Keenan sighed. "Last thing we need is some accountant-type out there with three pounds of gold on his neck trying to talk tough and fit in with these mopes and bikers. They'd make him before he said, 'Pass the sugar, please.' "

Lerza smiled inwardly at the image, knowing Keenan was right. Most FBI agents came from Middle America. They were serious, educated people who worked the bank frauds better than anyone else could, but would come up seriously short trying to convince some guido that they grew up with housing rats as pets. This type of criminal had his own language, a whole different way of communicating, and "I'll break your fuckin' kneecap" just did not naturally roll off the tongue of every Princeton graduate. First time he got tired or scared or drunk he would revert back to suburban babble.

Lerza still tried to sound uncommitted as he asked, "What's the plan?"

"Source introduces you to Miceli as a Class One, Grade A coke distributor. Order up and take delivery as many times as you can. Every delivery adds up to five to fifteen."

"He that dumb?"

"No, but he trusts the source. Actually, Miceli will never make a delivery. Just meet you one time, to negotiate price and arrange for delivery. But if we record that first meeting, it's all we'll ever need."

"I get it, boss." Lerza leaned forward. "Old RICO'll jump up and grab their ass. Racketeering Influenced Corrupt Organization, Title Eighteen, United States Code. The lawman's law. Miceli just has to meet and discuss that first time, then every delivery after, whether he's there or not, means it's his five-to-fifteen, too."

"It gets better, Joe. The statute also specifically provides that not only is Miceli criminally liable for every subsequent drug deal, but also every person in his enterprise. In this case it's the entire Philadelphia crime family. As if Amato and every last member and associate delivers those drugs. Whether they know about it or not." Keenan sounded enthusiastic, rare for him.

"How does that jam up the Satans?"

"After a few deliveries from the Italians, the Satans will approach *you*. Offer a better deal. You take it."

"Sneaky, boss, very sneaky." Lerza laughed. "Then they're in the same trick bag as the mob, even have the enterprise. The whole motorcycle gang gets sent to trade school at Lewisburg for remedial license-plate making without even the pleasure of meeting me."

"Right, Joe." Keenan smiled. "The bikers have colors," he went on. "Tattoos, live in a common clubhouse, and keep records of paying dues. They make it very easy to prove they're all members of the Satans, and that's the enterprise. Buy drugs from one Satan, it's like buying from every last one of them."

"God bless conspiracy." Lerza realized somewhere during the conversation he had become more than just a listener.

If he went under, Laura Lerza would kill him, yet he knew he would do it. Keenan was right; he liked the edge. Maybe it *was* the danger he craved—almost needed. Perhaps that was why he had quit being a psychologist who sat in a chair day after day, not speaking but listening, not actively moving, but prostrate, like a corpse.

And he had to admit that doing public relations for the Philadelphia FBI sucked. Becoming even more involved, he asked, "What's the snitch's motivation?"

"Best there is." Keenan paused. "A woman scorned."

Lerza smiled; Keenan almost returned the smile. They both knew Lerza was going under.

"My new name?" he asked.

"Joe Vitali."

He sighed. "Just once I wanna name without a vowel on the end."

Keenan tossed an envelope in his direction. Lerza opened it, found a Pennsylvania driver's license, social-security card, MasterCharge card, and video-club membership in the name of Joseph Vitali, 415 South Third Street, Philadelphia, Pennsylvania, 19103. The address clicked. Lerza realized he was about to move to Society Hill—at least two grand a month with a swimming pool somewhere on the roof.

Keenan watched as Lerza inspected the documents. "You're going to need a control agent and another undercover agent," he said finally. "Someone to open doors for you, drive the Mercedes, and cover your back. All the best drug dealers have a flunky. Your choice."

After a quick mental rundown of people he knew who would fit the bill, Lerza said, "Patricia Masters for the control agent."

"Never heard of her." Keenan seemed noncommittal.

"Former New York homicide detective. A looker. Tough yet competent. Black belt in karate, gourmet cook. Bottles her own wine, and if you get out of line she'll break the bottle over your head."

"Sounds like your type." Keenan almost smiled again, a record number for one meeting, Lerza thought. "How about the second undercover?"

Lerza knew what Keenan's reaction would be but said the name anyhow. "Special Agent Russell Yablinski Knepp."

Keenan loud. "The Pittsburgh Moose? Last I heard he's under suspension!"

"This one wasn't his fault," Lerza lied. "And besides, no charges were pressed."

Keenan moaned. "Knepp should come complete with a warning label. Why him?"

Lerza resorted to his most sincere voice. "Moose and I once worked a fugitive case, boss. Bad guy had already killed four convenience store night clerks and word was he'd hit the one on Lindbergh Boulevard. After a five-night stakeout the supervisor called it off, chalked it up to bad info. The

Moose stayed out there on his own time seven extra nights. Peed in a coffee cup and ate beef jerky sticks till the bad guy hit. Saved the life of a seventeen-year-old girl with freckles and a ponytail. That's why I want the Moose."

Keenan waved his right hand in the air. "Touching, but the thought of you two running loose out there scares the bureaucracy out of me. I only hope Control Agent Masters can control."

Keenan was semiserious, Lerza thought. A control agent in an undercover case fulfilled many functions. Some were mundane, like getting the undercover's paycheck to his family, some more serious, like passing on updated intelligence. But the main function of a control agent was to be the UCA's only link with the world he was leaving.

Undercover work wreaked psychological havoc. You were outside the system—no bosses, no clocks, no checks and balances. The temptation was always there—sex, money, booze, and drugs. Justified by "for the good of the case." Some UCAs went over the line to the other side; some just straddled the fence.

A good control agent could spot the telltale signs and bring you back before it got too far. Patty Masters, a combination Mother Teresa and Ma Barker, could not be snowed, bullied, or sweet-talked. She was the perfect choice.

"Okay." Keenan gave in. "Contact Knepp and Masters. Then draft a teletype to their SAC assigning them temporary duty here."

Lerza nodded.

"Questions?" Indicating the meeting was over.

Lerza shook his head and stood up to leave.

He was almost out the door when Keenan said warmly, "See you later, Mr. Joe."

Turning, Lerza actually saw the SAC smile. It was a rare sight.

Back at his desk he put a call in to the Pittsburgh office. "Let me talk to Special Agent Russell Knepp, please."

The voice giggled at the mention of Knepp's given name. "You mean the Moose. Yes, sir. May I ask who's calling?"

"Tell that scoundrel it's his Italian cousin."

More giggles followed by, "One moment, please."

Then Knepp's shout, "Joey! The original Eye Talion Stallion. How the fuck you doin'?"

"Whatta you up to, Moose?"

"Before your rude interruption I was giving a neck massage to the lovely Miss Karen Sue Wycowski, our hunky switchboard operator."

"Wanna take a break from harassing bureaucrats and massaging Croatian necks?"

"Whatta you got in mind?"

"Pack up all your obnoxious polyester suits in the brown paper grocery bags you call luggage and get your butt on the next plane to Philly. You're going undercover."

"I ain't going to Philly, Joey."

"Why?"

"There's no I and I. And besides, I'm still on suspension."

"You're back on the books as of ten minutes ago," Lerza said. Then, already regretting the next question, "What's I and I?"

"The perfect boilermaker, Joey," Moose said, his voice serious. "Iron City beer and Imperial whiskey."

"We got some good booze here, Moose."

"I've tried it, tastes like toxic waste."

"Call me when the plane lands." Lerza ignored the Moose's protest.

"What's the case?"

"Mainly covering my back."

"I'll come then." For the first time Moose sounded amenable. "A helpless midget like you needs my protection."

"Thank you and good-bye." Lerza hung up, smiling.

He made a similar call to Special Agent Patricia Ann Masters in Manhattan. Eventually he tracked her down at Kung Sook Yoon's martial arts studio, where she had just completed requirements for her sixth-degree black belt by thumping three guys armed with bamboo sticks. He asked her to join him in Philadelphia. The dojo's sensei screamed something foreign at her as she agreed to join Moose and him. She hung up before he could tell her much about the case.

His Springfield, Pennsylvania, home was a split-level, complete with finished basement and outrageous mortgage. It was a widely held myth that special agents of the FBI made big money. Lerza maneuvered his 1988 Granada, with its terminal case of rust, around the little red wagon and a Strawberry Shortcake Big Wheel.

His two daughters spotted him halfway up the walkway. They ran to him, screaming, "Daddy! Daddy!"

Maria, age seven, was tall for her age, sophisticated beyond her years. She attended ballet class, art class, and the accelerated class at the elementary school. In sharp contrast, Angelina, nicknamed Rocky by the neighborhood children, was built like a vending machine and led with her head. At any given time she had a minimum of one cut, two bruises, and three scrapes on her little body.

Lerza stepped out of the Granada and gathered the girls in his arms, always amazed they had emerged from the same womb.

"Dinner in twenty minutes," he said. "Don't leave the yard."

As he opened the front door, Laura Lerza entered his arms. She pulled him close, saying "I need a Joe Lerza hug. Bad day in Dodge."

"Wanna tell me about it?"

"Nothing a vacation and a referee wouldn't cure." She laughed. "The toilet's leaking, and the kids drove me crazy."

He kissed her lips, thinking back in time. He had just returned from Nam, complete with crutches and a chip on his shoulder. He met her one ice-cold night and she literally saved his life, this pretty freshman from Ohio. She cleaned his vomit—brought on by the excessive cheap booze—soothed his anger, forced his death wish away.

Holding his wife tightly, he tried to form the words in his brain, words that would tell her he would be leaving soon. Words that forecast a half-empty bed for months, perhaps even a year, and a vacant seat at the breakfast table.

They walked arm-in-arm to the front bay window and watched their daughters playing on the lawn. He postponed the moment as long as he could.

Suddenly he said, "The vacation's gotta be put on hold for a while. I'm on a case."

"You're off public relations?" Laura's lovely face showed mixed feelings.

She knew from years of experience that her husband's heart was on the streets. The desk job had been his way of making up for the years of late nights, lost dinners, and postponed vacations. She knew it could not last. Besides, she loved him now more than ever, wanted him to do work he liked, rather than tolerated.

He said softly, "I'm going under." Waited for her reaction.

"When?" Her voice accepting.

"Soon."

After a moment of silence, she turned and kissed him on the lips.

Then she said, "I'm glad. Do good, Joseph. Do good."

2

Forty limousines lined the driveway to the main building of the exclusive country club. Drivers gathered in small groups, exchanging stories and drinking hot coffee from Styrofoam cups. Two large men stood, silent and motionless, at the front door. They talked to no one, not even each other.

The large dining table inside the main banquet room was colorfully and professionally set with imported bone china, French crystal glassware, Portuguese silver, and fifty dozen red roses. The food sat in stainless-steel serving pans heated with Sterno. No employee of the Swarthmore Country Club was anywhere in the building. In fact, no employee or member of the Swarthmore Country Club was within ten miles of the front gate.

The fifty-three men in the banquet room all wore conservative business suits, with one exception. They were all elderly gentlemen, with the same exception. The exception was a young man in his mid-twenties, wearing a flashy imported Italian suit. His hair was a little too long, his nervousness hidden with a loud, aggressive voice. The other men spoke in somber tones, all awaiting the start. The young man drank wine in large gulps as he quickly moved from group to group.

A communion bell chimed from somewhere within the room, and conversations ended. The old men silently formed themselves into two neat rows facing each other, near the front wall of the room. Each held the hand of the man next to him.

The bright lights suddenly dimmed, dramatically blackening the large room. For several moments the room was so silent that only the breathing of the elderly men echoing off the high banquet-room ceiling was audible.

Michael Amato stood alone at one end, centered between the two rows of men. The young man in the imported suit stood alone at the opposite end. They faced each other. Behind Amato was a table covered with a wide black cloth. On the table was a statue of the Madonna with eight candles burning before it. There was also an antique parchment covered with script and an old silver knife. The handle of the knife was intricately carved with a rare design. The blade had recently been sharpened and glistened in the candlelight.

Amato spoke, the words a mixture of Latin and Italian. His voice cued the young man, who began a measured walk down the center of the aisle toward him. He stopped as he reached the Don, and extended both arms out, palms up.

Amato addressed the younger man. "Are you aware of what is about to take place?"

"I am, Don Amato," the young man replied.

Amato looked him directly in the eye as he said, " 'I enter this family willingly.' "

≡ 20 ≡

The young man repeated the words and waited for the next ones.

" 'This family comes before everything.'

" 'I would accept death for the family.'

" 'I will never betray the family.'

" 'I give obedience to Don Amato.'

" 'I vow *Coda Omertus.*' "

Amato then took the faded parchment with the ornate Italian writing. He placed it in the young man's left hand. He lifted the silver knife with the carved handle and cut the man's right palm. The young man looked as if he wanted to flinch, but he didn't.

As a trickle of blood appeared, Amato turned and picked up one of the eight candles on the table. He placed it beneath the parchment in the young man's left hand. As the old parchment ignited, Amato pressed the young man's palms together—mixing the blood and fire. He held them firmly together until the fire went out. Then, placing his hands on the young man's shoulders, he kissed him fully on the lips.

The young man turned and faced the other men in the room. One by one they approached him, repeating Don Amato's kiss.

When it was over, Anthony Miceli was *made.*

Michael Amato was tired. At seventy-one, he had trouble concentrating. The doctor used some fancy term, but it came down to old age. Amato leaned over the armrest of his worn recliner and reached for one of the several prescription bottles on the table. If he didn't hold the brown vial six inches from his eyes, the words would be a blur.

What was *this* pill supposed to do, thicken his blood or thin his glands? He didn't care any more; he swallowed the pink tablet down with the remains of the espresso coffee the doctor forbade him to drink. It was easier to take the medication than argue with Angelina, who counted his pills each day.

He heard her footsteps before he saw her. "Michael, did you takea your pills?" she asked.

Turning toward the doorway, which Angelina filled, he saw his wife of thirty-nine years. All two hundred and ten pounds, in a flowing red-and-white flowered dress.

"Thatsa good, Michael. Do whatta the doctor says and you feel better." She smiled approvingly.

"Yes, Angie." Just to say something.

"I makea the raviolis, you favorite. Come'n eat."

"Can't, Angie. Got a meeting at the club."

"Eat first. Then meet. You worka too much." She waved a fat hand. "When you gonna retire, Michael? Lika other people."

After forty years in Philadelphia, Angelina Amato, born in Venice, still spoke broken English. She talked only to other chubby Italian ladies who had also come to America forty years ago. Her whole existence was the grocery store, the kitchen, and bingo on Tuesdays.

"I'll be home around eight," Amato said. "Heat it up then, Angie."

He heard her grunt of acquiescence. She returned to the kitchen to add to and subtract from the pots and pans on the white stove. He thought, She is right, I should retire. He had been a success by any standard. Enough money not to have to look at prices on menus, enough to own houses in Miami, New Jersey, and a condo in Bermuda. What the hell did it all mean, anyhow? Miami was all Cubans, Jersey smelled, and the water in Bermuda gave him diarrhea. If there was only someone who could take his place. The men he trusted couldn't do the job and the ones who could were not to be trusted. They did not understand "the old ways."

As a young man he had been consumed by his work and had built a reputation as an honorable man: shrewd, fierce, but fair. Even now, his five-foot, eight-inch, one-hundred-and-ninety-pound frame showed little fat, and his hazel eyes could still strike terror in anyone. He lived in the same neighborhood of South Philadelphia where he had first settled sixty-three years before, when he arrived from Calabria. His home looked like the other row houses on Snyder Avenue, at least from the outside. But if someone looked closely at the photographs on the dining room wall, they would see a young Amato dining with Marilyn Monroe, arm in arm with Babe Ruth at Yankee Stadium; one even showed President Harry Truman shaking his hand.

Not too bad for an immigrant who came to the United States without a penny in his pocket. He had made the long boat ride to Ellis Island when he was only eight. Uncle Salvatore got him a job at a restaurant in South Philly. He scrubbed the floors, cleaned the toilets, and graduated to busboy. That took five years, and it was five more before he became a waiter. Five years later he owned the restaurant.

Amato slowly rose to his feet, stood until the light-headedness passed, and put on his suit jacket. His driver would be waiting.

"Hello, Daniel," he said as he shut the front door behind him.

"How you feelin' today, Mr. Amato?" the tall, gray-haired chauffeur asked.

"As good as I can, Daniel. Ready?"

"Yes, sir." The chauffeur pushed his bifocals back to meet Amato's eyes.

Daniel Di Sipio had been Amato's driver for the last thirty years. No youngster himself, Di Sipio was sixty-three, had poor eyesight, mild diabetes, and a heart murmur. Not your classic bodyguard.

The black Cadillac was waiting on the street with its back door open. Amato had said, when he first saw the Sony TV in his automobile, "Who'd a thought the inside of a car would be bigger and nicer than my first two houses?"

The neighborhood kids always surrounded the limo, and Amato rarely disappointed them. He let them file into the bulletproof, three-hundred-thou luxury limo, handed them a dollar or two, called each by name, and laughed as they filed out the opposite door. They all knew him, were familiar with what he did, and loved him. One day, when he was younger and in better health, he had played stickball with them. He even hit a home run over the St. Thomas Aquinas School roof and became so excited he gave the boys twenty dollars for a new pimple ball.

Di Sipio pulled out slowly, careful to avoid the kids running alongside. The Cadillac rolled down Snyder, making a left on Broad Street, passing row after row home that made up South Philly. The attached houses boasted white marble steps, scrubbed every day by little old Italian ladies who then carefully swept the cement sidewalk. They showed great pride in their work. On the outside the homes were not particularly attractive, but the insides were showplaces. Plastic covers on every chair, floor-to-ceiling mirrors behind the parlor couch, crystal chandeliers in the dining room, a crucifix over every bed. South Philadelphia had more Italians in residence than any place on earth except Italy.

The limo stopped on the corner of Broad and Tasker, and William Averone stepped in. Billy "One Punch" Averone had earned his nickname after six pro fights. Now, One Punch was seventy-four, suffering from terminal stomach cancer. Six months at the outside was all he had left. He was Amato's closest friend; in the last forty-eight years they had often been drunk together, chased girls together, prayed together, had even killed together. All the things best friends did.

"Ciao, Miguel." Averone was happy to see his friend.

"And a good day to you, William."

"Another meeting, eh?" Averone said, as though to himself. "Don't seem like a month."

"It doesn't, and today, well, I'm just not in the mood."

Averone coughed, Amato licked dry lips, and in the front

seat Di Sipio squinted as he drove. Three sick old men in a big black Cadillac driving through South Philly.

"Have you given any thought to what we discussed?" Averone asked.

"Some."

"Well?" Averone pressed.

"Something has to be done, I agree, but *what* I don't know yet."

"He's out of control, Michael. We both know it."

"Yes, he's dangerous, he's crazy but—he's also smart."

"Then do it! Kill him, Michael, before it's too late."

"It has to be done right," Amato said calmly. "Because if it's not, there'll be a bloodbath. You must remember, my friend, Miceli doesn't play by our rules, the old rules. He has *no* rules."

"I can't understand." Averone looked puzzled.

Amato turned to face his dear friend. "Miceli is powerful, very powerful," he explained patiently. "He has built his own power base within the organization. He has many people loyal to him, people I can't control. Also, he has financial leverage in his favor."

"Why do we allow this?" Averone was asking.

"It was I who let it all happen," Amato said. "I allowed Miceli to get too far. It would have been easy to control or eliminate him in the beginning, but I was distracted. By his smooth tongue, promises, fancy clothes. Hypnotized by the kind of money his narcotics made. Impressed with this tough-talking, capable young man. And then, when he shed his skin and the snake appeared, it was too late. If we kill him now, openly, terrible things will happen."

"What could happen to *us?*" Averone asked.

"I told you Miceli was smart, but I never dreamt of the kind of money narcotics could bring. *Never!* And with that money comes power. Miceli controls our narcotics, and both the importers and distributors are known only to him, will deal only with him. Our casinos are merely places to wash the massive narcotics profits. Our prostitution merely a method to further drug sales. Our loansharking, only money borrowed by addicts and low-level distributors to buy *more* drugs. *Everything* centers around narcotics, and Miceli understood this years ago. He understood power, and while we were drinking our wine and marrying off our daughters to accountants, Miceli was building his power base."

Averone looked defeated. Michael Amato was more than just a friend. He was a man Averone had admired and respected, a man seemingly invincible, who had always made the right decision, afraid of nothing and no one. But now Amato was telling him that some Young Turk was smarter and tougher than he was.

Averone insisted, "Michael, let me call Tommy. He's a pro, he'll be careful. Miceli will just disappear."

"If it happens like that, we all lose."

"Why?" In puzzled tone.

"First off, Miceli's people will seek revenge and many of our friends will die. Secondly, we cut off our nose to spite our face, we lose our best source of income. And lastly, the Satan Motorcycle Gang will move in and could be worse than Miceli."

"Come on, Michael," Averone disagreed. "The Satans are a bunch of unwashed bums with oversized bicycles."

"I wish that were so, William." Amato's solemn voice went on, "They're highly organized and waiting for us to weaken. In the end they could be a greater threat to us than Miceli. Especially if we have internal war."

The Cadillac pulled to the curb in front of a large, three-story building. A canopy extended from door to street with the words "The Italian Club" printed on both sides. The two men were ten minutes early for their business meeting.

Their business was organized crime, and Michael Amato was the capo of the Philadelphia crime family.

"What do we do, Michael?" Averone was reluctant to leave the limo's backseat until the matter of Miceli was settled.

"I will deal with both Miceli and the Satans," Amato said calmly.

"A favor, Michael?" Averone requested.

"Anything."

"Promise me it will happen before I die?"

"I promise, William. I promise." Complete sincerity in the capo's voice.

"W H O the fuck they think they are?" Tony Miceli asked Hard Rock Mastrograrani.

"Ain't shit, Tony," Hard Rock answered. "Tattoed long-hair fags is all." He was driving the white Lincoln as though he were Mario Andretti.

Anthony Giovani Miceli was tall for someone of southern Italian descent, almost six-two. He had wavy black hair and nervous brown eyes. He always dressed to the hilt—six gold chains around his neck, three rings per hand, pointy imported shoes, open silk shirts were his uniform of the day.

Hard Rock was his driver and friend. Hard Rock was also a psycho. He once killed two men with his bare hands because they teased him, called him "fat." He did this while in an Italian prison, serving life for murder.

Miceli took the white plastic straw, shoved it up his right nostril. With his forefinger he pinched his left nostril closed and lowered his head to meet the line of white powder on his briefcase. A slight head movement and the powder disappeared. "Good shit," he said approvingly.

"Uncut," Hard Rock added. "Our Miami friends know what they're doin'."

"Twenty-five a key at ninety-six percent. Step on it twice and resell it at fifty grand. One fuckin' hundred percent profit."

Hard Rock ran a massive hand through his greasy hair. He hit the horn, ran a yellow light. " 'Cept the Satans sell at forty a key. Arny Tomossino switched last week."

"Yeah, remind me to go have a talk with Arny," Miceli said.

He checked his Rolex with the twenty-six diamond chips. "We got two hours before my meeting with the old man and his group of nursing-home rejects. Every month I keep waiting for one of them to seven-out at the table."

"Save us the trouble." Hard Rock chuckled.

The nose candy reached Miceli's brain and he became invincible—Hannibal, Hitler, and Conan the Barbarian all rolled into one.

"We got time to see some titties," he said.

Hard Rock knew what that meant: the Classy Chassis topless joint on Thirteenth Street. Actually a front for Miceli's drug business, a safe place to meet, negotiate, and deliver. Sort of an unofficial office. A place to look at titties.

"You gonna bring it up today?" Hard Rock asked.

"What?"

" 'Bout making me, Tony."

"Oh yeah, Hard Rock," Miceli lied. "I'll bring your name up again, only don't get your hopes up 'cause it only takes one blackball."

Miceli did not want to tell Hard Rock that Amato would not make Hard Rock a member if he were Alfonse Capone reincarnated. Amato thought Hard Rock was retarded. And Miceli did not need the aggravation of the same argument today.

"Fuck, Tony, you're made and I wanna be made," Hard Rock whined.

"Just a matter of time, Hard Rock," Miceli said, telling the truth. "When I'm running the show, you'll be my lieutenant."

Hard Rock smiled, as if thinking of that day. "I can wait," he said.

At forty-two, Miceli was the last guy made in the Philly family, some twenty years before. Now the average age of soldiers was sixty-six. Amato had refused to allow anyone *Coda Omertus*—the code of silence—since Miceli. There were seven associates for every made guy, but they would always be second-team. A wise guy got a ceremony, a better class of chick, the front table at any club and a pension—of sorts. Associates did the donkey work, "go see this guy," "break that guy's thumb," "deliver this," "sorry, this meeting's only for made guys."

The Lincoln double-parked on Lombard Street near Thirteenth. This section of Philadelphia served as the hangout of the city's freaks—gays, transvestites, punk rockers, hookers, and an assortment of other people who had fetishes so disgusting that Miceli would not use public toilets in the neighborhood.

As they entered the Classy Chassis, Wicked Wanda was finishing up her routine with Chico the Monkey. Amazing things, what a monkey could do with a naked lady. Wanda nodded as Miceli strutted past the stage. Chico hissed and had to be restrained. The monkey had hated Miceli ever since the night the Mafia man had tied up Chico and hung him from the fire escape in Wanda's apartment. Seems like a jealous Chico had kept jumping on the bed while Tony and Wanda were trying to "dance."

The back office was newly decorated, with freshly painted walls, leather chairs, a wooden desk. Etchings of naked ladies in chrome frames hung on the walls.

"What's cookin', Stormy?" Miceli asked the lovely woman behind the desk. He sat down across from her.

"Hi, honey." Stormy Monday, a.k.a. Bernadette Sue Rowe, greeted him. "Hi, Hard Rock," an afterthought.

"You beeped last night, kid. What's up?" Miceli wanted to know.

He took a seat opposite her as Hard Rock leaned against the door, looking mean.

"Business, babe. A real high roller with bucks."

"Check him out?"

" 'Course, babe." Stormy said defensively. "I always do. He's legit."

"Run it down, Stormy."

Stormy Monday, exotic dancer, and Tony Miceli, made guy, had once been a hot item. The two had seemed headed for the altar until Tony got a bad case of "the Italians." This included screwing every woman in sight, rubbing Stormy's nose in it, then beating the shit out of her for good measure.

Stormy was now ten years older with a few extra pounds, a few fewer teeth, and a vendetta burning inside. She worked for Miceli, running the club and checking out major drug connections for him.

"Name's Joe Vitali," she started, as if reading from a rap sheet. "He lives near Society Hill. Has a lot of mid-level distributors and buys five keys minimum. Strictly cash, never asked for a front, always pays full boat."

"Why the switch to us?" Miceli questioned.

"Regular importer ripped him off, then got popped by DEA. So Joe's hard up for a regular source who can deal that kind of weight."

"How'd you meet him?"

"Mutual friend, two years ago. The friend is a stand-up guy."

"Know anyone else that's dealt with him?" Miceli pressed. "Ever see shit on him? Ever see him cop or blow? Has he tried to screw any of the dancers?"

Stormy was silent.

"Come on, Stormy," Miceli said impatiently, banging his right hand on the desk. "I gotta be sure the guy didn't just drop out of the sky."

"He's cool," Stormy insisted. "I've snorted with him, and I know two guys he's been dealing with for years. I swear, he's even spent time at the Roundhouse."

"He better be safe, sweetheart. It's your ass if anything goes wrong."

Miceli stared hard at her to see if she shook. She seemed calm.

"Laid down the rules to him yet?" he asked.

"Last night, Tony. He agreed to everything."

"Okay. Set up a meet for him," Miceli said. "Tell your Mr. Vitali I'll just meet with him the first time. Tell him I won't have any shit on me. Tell him I always use delivery boys for actual deals. Tell him I give the ground rules. Tell him once he agrees, he's locked in. Tell him if he breaks a rule he's dead. Okay?"

"I already did, Tony." She lit a long brown cigarette.

He stared hard again as she exhaled a stream of smoke. It used to be, she thought, that stare would make her knees turn to rubber, she would tell him anything he wanted to know, she had loved him. Funny, now the stare seemed almost comical to her, after the humiliations, after the beatings. You could only get knuckle-sandwiched so much, then it did not matter, you could not feel scared anymore, you could only die. He looked now like a little boy trying to frighten someone, but all he had left was the stare. Fuck him, she thought.

"In the meantime, Stormy," Miceli got to his feet, "I'll

run your Mr. Vitali through the computer. If he is who he says he is, we'll meet."

Stormy nodded. "Lenny's waiting for you," she said, changing the subject. "Been here for two hours. Seems nervous."

"Where?"

"Your table."

Miceli went over to the former Miss Bernadette Sue Rowe and took her roughly in his arms. "You done good, baby," he whispered, his lips inches from hers. "If only I was the faithful type." He kissed her clumsily, banging their teeth.

Hard Rock opened the door, and the two of them re-entered the world of topless nightclubs. Loud music and skinny, spaced-out dancers with rose tattoos on their shoulders who put their makeup on with push brooms. Businessmen had replaced derelicts as regular customers; at three dollars a drink it took bucks to get a buzz. About sixteen Brooks Brothers types were taking their long lunches now.

Lenny Pugliesi was working on his fourth Scotch-and-water, trying to steam up as much courage as fast as he could. Pathetic sight, sitting at Miceli's table, with a bad toupee and a worse ulcer. Miceli and the Rock reached the secluded table in the back just as Roxy began her set, dressed as a rodeo girl humping a wooden horse named Trigger.

"Tony, Hard Rock," Lenny said, standing up to kiss Miceli's cheek. "How you doing? Let me buy you a drink."

"Sounds like a winner," Miceli said. "I'll have a Beam, and the Rock'll have some of that battery acid you're drinking." He chuckled.

Lenny asked, "What's the joke, Tony?"

"Battery acid. It reminded me of the time I was eighteen

and used to help collect for the boys. A guy was three weeks behind. I put battery acid in his ear."

Miceli laughed, Hard Rock laughed, but Lenny's laugh was not exactly a laugh, more like a wheeze. He snapped his fingers and waved frantically until a girl came and took the order. It was Wicked Wanda, doubling as a cocktail waitress.

Lenny said nervously, "So, how you guys doin'? How's the main man?"

"Never better, Lenny. Never better," Miceli assured him.

"I got business problems," Lenny said out of the blue.

"Yeah, just tell me and I'll take care of it," Miceli answered, showing renewed interest in the conversation. "You're too good a customer. What's the matter, one of your dealers come up light?"

"No, Tony, nothing like that." Nervously.

Wanda interrupted with a tray full of drinks. Hard Rock tossed a fifty on the tray, patted her bare behind. She started to say something, looked at the expression on Lenny's face, and decided to keep her silent.

Lenny grabbed his Scotch, gulped down half a glass. Then he said, "You been good to me, Tony, no denying that."

"Damn right, Lenny. I made you a rich man."

"So what I gotta say hurts me. Understand?"

Miceli was beginning to understand, recognizing the same tone of voice broads used right before they told you they had met Prince Charming.

Lenny finished off his fifth Scotch, took a deep breath, and plunged ahead. "I got a new source, Tony."

He waited for a reaction, and when it did not come, he started talking as fast as he could. "Nothing personal, believe me. Just that these guys sell it at forty a key. Ninety-eight percent. I can step on it two extra times at that purity, Tony. Make fifteen grand extra every key. See? Nothing personal, just business. Okay?"

"Who's the guy, Lenny?" A hiss.

"They wouldn't like it if I say. You know how close-mouthed I am, Tony. Never dimed on anybody. Good quality, huh?"

His answer came in Hard Rock's left hand, complete with monogrammed brass knuckles. The punch caught Lenny's nose right above the nostril. He went down like the proverbial sack of potatoes.

Roxy watched the action from the stage, detached, never missing a step with Trigger. Some of the customers realized what was happening but chose to ignore it. The price one had to pay for looking at titties during your lunch break.

Miceli leaned over the prone Pugliesi and asked, "One more time, Lenny. Who's the guy?"

Blood seeped from Lenny's nose; the bad toupee was knocked cockeyed. The booze helped reduce the pain a little but not much.

He could only whisper, "The Satans, Tony. I'm sorry. No more, okay? Please."

Miceli grabbed Lenny under the arm to help him to his chair. "Okay, Lenny," he said. "It's a free country. People can do business, who they want. See you later."

Miceli and Hard Rock started for the door. They took a step, then Hard Rock pivoted and once more hit the helpless Pugliesi with a haymaker square on the nose, breaking it again. As they went past the stage, Roxy had Trigger in the missionary position.

Miceli got in his car, so mad he could not speak. The Lincoln reached Broad Street, turned left, and headed toward the Italian Club.

4

A bunch of 1200-cc Harley Davidson hogs kick-started together can cause permanent hearing damage. The bylaws clearly stipulated Harleys only, calling the Japanese motor-cycles "rice burners."

Lu eased the hand clutch on his low rider and cut directly into traffic. He was followed two abreast by guys with names like Acid, Sperm Count, Bunhole, Crazy Mike, Brain Dead, Torture Chamber, Needledick, Killer, and Deranged. You either earned your street name or looked like it. Most of them had the IQ of a head of lettuce and a personality akin to serial killers.

Except for Lu. The president of the Satans was smart, real smart. He was also evil in the true sense of the word. Deep down evil. Most people have both good and evil in their makeup. Lu had only evil.

After deserting his unit in Vietnam, he had hooked up with a Cambodian mountain tribe dedicated to the worship of the Bac Si, or Satan. Always a fast learner, Lu graduated with an advanced degree in devil worship before buying a new identity and coming back stateside. He started the Satan Motorcycle Gang because it was no fun putting on black robes, cutting off little fingers, and dancing around candles alone.

It was a natural marriage—a group of 250-pound robbers who looked as though rats had been chewing on their hair, complete with massive tattoed arms and blind obedience. The public was afraid, law enforcement was wary, and even other criminals gave these threatening young men a wide berth.

Lu pushed the Harley to fifty, enjoying the wind on his face as he went over the "master plan" in his mind. A private daydream that always brought him pleasure.

The Satan clubhouse at Seventeenth and Tasker was an old three-story row home in the middle of Little Italy. Remodeling had taken the form of gun portals in the windows, reinforced steel doors, and a semi-bunker complete with sandbags, and a sentry on the roof.

The scooters rolled to a stop on Seventeenth, and the Satans pushed their kickstands in unison to the ground. Lu turned to check the motorcycles' alignment; it was important to have rules, no matter how petty. His way of control. Mind control, a kind of subtle but necessary brainwashing. Take a bunch of tough guys, society misfits, give them an organization that appeals to their mentality, one with a reputation, a place to hang out. Then direct them into dangerous activities, because this builds togetherness. Keep telling them that they're the toughest and best in the world. Throw in a hierarchy, a chain of command, because most people are followers, and you've built the Satan Motorcycle Gang. It could just as well be the Hell's Angels, Mafia, Marine Corps, or even the FBI.

Lu understood how a group mentality formed. How it eventually overshadows all personal identity.

"Meet me in the office," Lu told Acid, his vice president.

He climbed the steps to the attic office, moving deliberately and in control. He did everything that way, never rushing, never getting ahead of himself. He was tall, an erect six-four, and weighed a muscular two-forty. Dirty blond hair, blue eyes that glared instead of looked. A lot of tough guys had to practice that look, but it came natural to Lu.

A biker's most prized possession is his bike, and he cares for it lovingly. But the gang owned a lot of junk, an assortment of ripped-off and salvaged objects like street signs, posters, gun racks, pinball machines, and old TV's with broken horizontal dials. All in sharp contrast to the third-floor office, which was clean, neat, and color-coordinated. Lu sat behind a metal-and-glass decorator desk, tapping on a digital calculator, when he heard the rap on the door.

"Come in," he called out.

Thomas Bennet Webb actually had attended college, where he discovered that LSD helped him study. The brain cells not pharmaceutically damaged made him some kind of math whiz.

"Sit," Lu commanded. "We'll do club business first."

Acid took a chair opposite Lu, opened a folder, removed papers, straightened them and himself, then told his boss, "I'm ready."

"Membership?" Lu asked.

"Fifty-two full and six probates."

"Finances?"

"Monthly dues and fines paid." Acid went on, glad to be in familiar ground, "Mortgage, taxes, and utilities paid, no outstanding bills."

"Other club business?"

"Needledick got arrested last week." Acid looked up, directly at Lu. "Bullshit traffic stop turned into an assault charge. Out on ten grand bail."

"What did Rosenberg say?" Their court lawyer.

"Probably probation, if he cleans up for court and keeps his mouth shut."

"Tell him I said to do both. What else?"

"That's it." Acid closed his folder.

Lu rose from the desk and approached a painting on the far wall. An original oil of the Prince of Darkness himself, looking down on the room with a glare similar to that of the Satans' head honcho. A quick flick of the frame and the painting swiveled, revealing a wall safe. Lu spun the dial a few times, opened the black door, grabbed a few papers, and walked back to the desk.

"Now on to other business," he ordered.

He removed a pack of unfiltered Camels from a desk drawer, slid one out, and pushed the pack toward Acid. Lu then lit his own cigarette and exhaled deeply. He watched the smoke drift slowly toward the white-tiled ceiling with the recessed lighting.

"The stock market's goin' jackbatty," Acid said, lighting his Camel.

"Sell the utility stuff," Lu said evenly. "Put the money in mutual funds." He did not wait for discussion but went on, "Did our slum landlord partners pay up?"

"A day early."

"Good. What about our off-water bank accounts?"

"Money's been put through the rinse cycle and deposited in our limited real-estate partnerships."

"Good man, Acid." Approvingly. "I scheduled a pickup. Ten keys prepaid from my Asian relatives. Send the dancer, conservative skirt and blouse, with a kid and diaper bag, L.A. airport, the fifth of the month. Flight 910, United, arrives six-ten P.M. The baggage claim check is attached to the ticket."

Lu handed an airline ticket to Acid. He opened it, inspected the Honolulu-to-L.A. one-way, stamped and inked with gates and seating assignments. As if Mrs. Mom and Junior just got back from a grandma visit. All that remained was to pick up the Gucci luggage and book a TWA to the city of brotherly love. Carry-on baggage slid under the seat with enough blow to keep Cleveland high for a month.

Acid uncrossed a leg as if he had suddenly remembered something important. "Lenny called this morning"—a higher pitch in his voice—"from Saint Agnes hospital. We got trouble."

He waited for Lu to ask questions the way most people would when you use the word "trouble." But Lu was never like other people, and Acid continued, "Miceli busted him up bad. Lenny gave us up as his suppliers."

"Good." An unexpected reply.

"Lenny's scared." Acid felt confused. "He may go back to the wops."

"Tell Lenny we understand."

"What?" Surprise in his voice.

"Just say it and mean it."

"Okay, but this fuckin' guy Miceli ain't gonna just disappear, Lu. He's gotta do something about us sooner or later."

"Acid," Lu said softly, "Miceli's got the same problem Hitler had. Can't fight a war on two or three fronts. Spreads you too thin. Win a battle, lose the war. He's got internal problems with his boss. A boss who don't want any part of us 'cause he knows the troops downstairs don't have a bottom line to life. We don't have wives, kids, or grandchildren who could get hurt.

"These mob guys wanted a slice of the good life, nice homes, big cars. These trappings make you unwilling to take risks. You got something to lose and that makes you weak. They brag about how business is business, they don't understand that once you have a weakness you can only hope everybody plays by your rules. If not, you lose."

He was silent a moment, then went on, "Narcotics is the biggest money-making business in the history of mankind. The Satans are in a position to be wholesalers, retailers, and distributors. The cops and feds arrest their ten percent and pat each other on the back while the six o'clock news rolls. The politicians talk tough on drugs, make everybody piss in jars, get reelected, then forget us till the next election. It's a farce, drugs are as American as heart attacks. Nobody understands people, they just don't."

He let the thought hang. Acid could only nod; he had never heard his boss say so much at any one time.

"Miceli's surveillance?" Lu asked, back to business.

"Street surveillance says Miceli hasn't met with any new customers. Girls at the club confirm Lenny's story. No new faces."

"Good. Work on his old sources. Drop our offer another five."

The five-button desk phone interrupted, making the kind of sound you paid AT&T $4.50 a month extra to hear.

Acid picked it up before the second ring. "Nine-six-oh-seven, who's calling?"

"Who?" he repeated, as if to confirm something he merely thought he heard.

"How'd you get this number?" Defensively. "How do I know you are who you say?"

"Right," he said, then punched the red "hold" button. He held his hand over the receiver, looked wide-eyed at Lu. "Guy says he's Michael Amato."

Lu smiled and took the phone from the astonished Satan vice president.

"Hello, Michael," he said, as if expecting the call.

5

The bed was soaked with his sweat. A cold sweat just like Nam. He could not sleep, did not come close. Shut his eyes a couple of times, but his mind would not stop thinking. Even the Roget champagne had not helped.

An overwhelming sadness engulfed him, and he knew why. This was not television. The public demanded their quick video fix, where the undercover cop meets with a major drug dealer after the third commercial. A last-minute shoot-out, and all the bad guys are arrested.

In real life, when a cop or agent went deep, there would be no discussions with the lieutenant back at the precinct. No after-work beers with the other cops *and* no daughters putting their arms around you saying, "I love you, Daddy." Deep undercover meant living it twenty-four hours a day, seven days a week, until it was over. And "over"' could mean many different things.

Joe Lerza lay in bed experiencing that same gut feeling

he'd felt the night before he shipped out to Southeast Asia. He'd been nineteen then, with only himself to worry about. Physically and mentally stronger, the way nineteen-year-old marines are.

Their lovemaking last night had been frantic on Joe's part, but he knew Laura well enough to realize it was a notch higher than a mercy fuck for her. Because she loved him, because it had been anything but natural. Good-bye sex never is. There is always the emotional urgency, like a conjugal visit on death row.

Lerza regretted his decision to go deep but, now made, he wanted to get started. Being an FBI agent was not what he did, it was who he was.

His mind raced like a video game, flashes of his life flickering on the screen of his mind. "Be loyal—be bold," the old policeman, his father, said on his deathbed. Part of Lerza wanted to retreat to his safe, quiet, predictable life as a public-relations gnome. Other people's problems—the same ones over and over, but with different voices.

In PR Lerza went through the administrative motions but something was missing. Vietnam had given him a massive dose of the thing he craved most—the edge. He thrived in Nam, lapping up the exhilaration of every night ambush, every search and destroy, and every firefight. It was his element, but he didn't know why. Couldn't explain it, only relish it.

Maybe it was preordained—the destiny of every boy following in his father's footsteps. Maybe he wanted to be the man in the great police overcoat emptying his weapon each night, and smiling the smile that meant he felt secure, the look of complete control and power. Maybe that's why he had joined the FBI.

Or maybe it was the survivor's guilt that burned a hole in his soul each and every day over the ex-Sergeant's death.

His best friend dying for him in that hot hellhole. Maybe it should be *his* bones disintegrating in Vietnam.

The bedside clock showed 5:30 A.M. Laura stirred beside him, curling her big toe on his ankle, the way she had slept for seventeen years. Her touch made him all the more determined to get going. He had his game face on; any retreat into this safe, loving world would only make it tougher.

After downing four cups of coffee and two bagels in the darkened kitchen, it was time. The first plane would be landing in an hour.

He approached his daughters' bedroom, his tears close to spilling. Marie slept as she lived, neat and concise. The blanket and sheets looked as though the bed had just been made and she had somehow been inserted into them. Angie, on the other hand, dangled one leg over the bed's edge; her pillow sat on the floor; the green water pistol he had given her was tucked into her Big Bird pajamas.

A kiss to the cheek of each and the tears got closer. Laura waited at the front door. Their embrace was brief, only three words spoken: "I love you."

Five minutes later he turned onto I-95, driving a gray Mercedes registered to Joseph Vitali. The tears had come and gone. It was showtime. "Break a leg," as they say. He hoped it would not be literally true for him, a leg smashed or cut off by an angry dope dealer.

The first plane to touch down was the Allegheny commuter from Pittsburgh. That meant the Moose. Special Agent Russell Knepp was a certified public accountant but would not admit it because he believed CPAs were faggot, Communist liberals. He had been fifty pounds overweight by Bureau standards for the last eight years, but nobody had ever had the courage to tell him.

The Moose was also a former Army Airborne Ranger, former Pittsburgh cop, and the former husband of three

Mrs. Mooses. He was a borderline alcoholic and he honestly enjoyed an occasional brawl. Since image was so important to the Bureau, they kept Moose out of the public eye, made him SWAT team leader and Pittsburgh's designated door-masher. He was a walking paradox of brains, brawn, and loyalty.

Lerza spotted the green polyester leisure suit rambling down the ramp. The Moose grabbed Lerza under each arm and lifted him an inch or so off the red carpet in a sort of embrace.

"How the fuck ya doin'?"

"Put me down, you mutant," Lerza hissed, "or I'll tell everybody you sleep with a night-light."

"Good to see you, Joey." Moose released Lerza, a smile on his face. "Still as short as a circus midget, I see."

"Cut the short jokes. I'm your new boss."

"Bottom of the barrel, Joey."

"And quit calling me 'Joey.' "

The two men paused, finished with their opening barrage of insults. It was a typical cop/military ritual, a way of saying "Hi, I missed you."

"Get your luggage and meet me at Gate Fifty-six," Lerza ordered.

"This *is* my luggage." The Moose tapped a black over-night bag with STEELERS emblazoned on it in gold letters—an opening-day giveaway. "What's at Gate Fifty-six?"

"Just as well," Lerza said of the luggage. "We'll go to Chestnut Street this week for new wardrobes. Compliments of the Bureau."

"What's at Gate Fifty-six?" Moose asked again.

"We're meeting two other people, and don't ask any more questions now. You'll get a briefing and game plan later today."

"Hey," Moose protested. "The munchkin's all official. Go Bureau on me, Joey, huh?"

"Fuck you, Moose."

Pan Am Flight 876 was twenty minutes late. More than one male head swiveled when Special Agent Patricia Masters exited the portable jetway. Auburn hair, wide green eyes, and a slender yet muscular figure added up to a devastating combination. She wore a conservative tweed business suit with fashionable high heeled pumps that accented spectacular legs.

Moose noticed that the hello kiss lasted a split second longer than "just friends." Masters and Lerza had been new agent partners in Cincinnati. A lot of late-night surveillances and soul-searching talks. The desire had never been consummated but came close.

"Nice trip?" Lerza asked.

"Sat next to an insurance adjuster," she said, her voice low and husky. "Learned words like supernumerary and double indemnity."

"This is Russ Knepp," Lerza said, and stepped back.

"I know all about the Moose," Masters said, no judgment in her voice.

Moose took a step toward her, and asked, "How the fuck ya doin', Patty?"

Lerza knew what was coming, knew also it had to take its own natural course. Knowing Masters, he felt semi-sorry for the Moose.

She picked up her briefcase, gave Moose one of those looks nuns give second-graders.

"I heard all about Moose," she said, speaking to Lerza alone. "I heard that if you could get past all the macho bullshit, all the sexual innuendos, all the locker-room clichés, and all the unnecessary profanity, that Russ Knepp is the kind of special agent you'd want on your side if things got tough. So," she continued, smiling, "if he does his job and is a good boy, I won't have to drop-kick his testicles up to that double chin."

Moose's mouth fell three inches as he watched Masters spin on her heels and start down the tiled airport hallway.

"That's one tough bitch," he whispered to Lerza, "but I think she likes me."

The DC-9 carrying Dr. Donald Grant Thompson, a board-certified Federal Bureau of Investigation psychiatrist, was four minutes early, compliments of a tail wind. Lerza introduced him to Masters and the Moose, and the unlikely four piled into Lerza's Mercedes, headed toward a rented hotel room for a six-hour head session. The Bureau had recently set up psychological safeguards for its undercover program; today's meeting was one of the requirements.

"How's the weather in D.C.?" Lerza asked Dr. Thompson.

"Typical for this time of year," the psychiatrist replied.

"The Redskins got a sorry-ass team, eh, Doc?" said the Moose.

"I don't follow football," Dr. Thompson replied.

"How's their chess team?" Moose persisted.

The ride mercifully ended at the Bellevue Stratford. Twenty minutes later the group sat in a small circle sipping hot hotel coffee in a room Keenan had reserved for the day so they could hear the warnings of the psychiatrist.

Lerza studied Dr. Thompson, wondered why all psychiatrists looked like him. Oval, oversized eyeglasses, shoes with tassels, long strands of thinning hair combed over a bald spot.

Thompson started formally, "The Bureau has only been in the undercover business since 1972. Which was, not coincidentally, the year Hoover died."

Lerza said, "The old man didn't want his agents under. Too much temptation."

Thompson sipped his coffee and continued, "Mr. Hoover's fear had validity. The Bureau's UC program has experienced serious setbacks recently. Six undercover agents were arrested in the last five years."

"I knew Fasulo," Lerza said. "Good man, but there's no excuse for selling dope."

Undercover Agent Angelo Fasulo had become as much a part of a cocaine importation network in Miami as the subjects he targeted.

"Tommy Duffy was on my squad in New York," put in Masters. "They should have brought him in six months before—"

She could not say the words, but everyone in the room knew Duffy's story. Three years under and everything seemed fine until the day he snapped. Blew away his wife and two small sons before turning the .357 on himself.

"These are the extreme cases," Thompson said, resuming his lecture voice. "There are other, more subtle consequences of deep undercover work. Statistically speaking, in the last five years thirty-one FBI undercover agents have been treated for a myriad of personality disorders. This includes severe depression, multiple neuroses, psychoses, acute alcoholism, extreme paranoia, and other adjustment disorders. Not to mention twelve divorces, eight drug dependencies, and four forced resignations all related to the tremendous pressures of this investigative technique."

"Is it worth it?" Masters got right to the point.

"That's not for me to judge," Thompson replied. "You three would be better evaluators of the practical and legal effects of undercover work. I am here merely to make you aware of the psychological pitfalls awaiting you."

He paused, then went on, "You've been tested and re-tested. You are supposedly mentally fit and able to withstand the severe bombardment to your senses and the attack on your psyche. Two years ago the Bureau ignored any psychological ramifications of its UC program. It had no psychiatrist on retainer, no acceptance that deep undercover work had any negative effects on its agents."

He paused for effect, and went on, "Thank God, they now admit there's a price to pay for undercover work."

Lerza asked, "What you're saying, Doctor, is that the Bureau is sometimes willing to risk an agent to make some arrest?"

"Whoa, Joey," Moose said. "These people who go over the edge would've ended up at the ice-cream factory sooner or later, wouldn't they, Doc?"

"It's a double-edged sword," the psychiatrist said. "The fact is that people attracted to undercover work share common personality traits, such as resentment of authority, big egos, tendency to be loners, predisposition to aggressiveness, the rationalization of rule-breaking. *And* some degree of a death wish, but it's these very qualities that make them successful deep undercover agents."

"I get it," Moose said. "If that bad guy didn't actually believe we were also bad guys, he wouldn't even talk to us."

"Essentially correct," Thompson said. "In short-term UC work you can act or role-play being evil for one, two, or even ten encounters. *But* over an extended period of time you must internalize your role to stay under."

Masters pointed an accusing finger at the psychiatrist, and asked "What you're saying then is that there's a fine line between them and us?"

"Yes." A single-word reply that left no doubt.

Several hours after lunch, four pots of coffee, serious

discussion, and a few lighthearted laughs, the skull session ended. Thompson summed it up with a warning. "When you walk out that door today," he said, "you two men will be leaving your pasts behind. You'll have no clocks, no bosses, none of the checks and balances that normally stabilize behavior. Stay close to each other, and to Miss Masters. One another is all you have to remember the world you are leaving. Good luck!"

The psychiatrist started to say something more, then paused as if deciding against it. The three agents froze, waiting for him. Masters asked, "Something else, Dr. Thompson?"

"Very well," he said, looking directly at Lerza. "Joseph, I have some serious reservations about you going under again."

"Why?" Lerza protested.

"Your Vietnam experiences, your personality, the fact that you've been deep before," Thompson began. "I've reviewed your personnel folder, and it reads like a soap opera. War hero, Bureau hero, family man, plenty of conflicting demands on a person reared in a strict Catholic setting. Vietnam forced you to act in a manner that was repulsive to your basic values. Then the Bureau made similar demands. It's just that a person like you can take only so much. Can resolve these internal conflicts to a point, then—" Thompson didn't finish his sentence; he allowed the others to provide their own doom.

"Yeah, well, Doc," the Moose said, getting to his feet, "we sure appreciate your concern. If Joey starts drooling or wants me to wear my pajamas backward, I'll nine-one-one him before you can say 'Sigmund Freud.' "

Thompson reluctantly chuckled; even Masters could not hold back a smile. The Moose had a way with words.

Lerza took a last sip of cold coffee and grabbed his coat. "Excuse us," he said. "The Moose and I have a household to set up."

"Remember, Joseph," Masters said seriously. "Every Wednesday afternoon, Triangle Bar, Twelfth and Moyamensing. The beeper for emergencies."

"Would I ever pass up a chance to have a drink with you?" Lerza asked.

Masters stood up, unexpectedly kissed Lerza on the mouth, then whispered, "Be careful." She turned to Moose, jabbed his arm, and added, "You, too."

The two undercover agents were silent as they drove down Spruce toward the UC apartment. Lerza worked the last six hours over in his mind. Moose was right, he thought, those other UCAs who crossed the line were weak to begin with. He, on the other hand, had his feet on the ground— good wife, nice kids, things in perspective.

No problem.

6

The Italian Club had been a sweatshop in the Thirties. Amato bought it for a song in '63, gutted the insides, making it the hottest night spot in South Philly. Glass chandeliers, brass rails, silver champagne buckets, and a tuxedoed maitre d' named Salvatore who remembered everyone's name.

Frank Sinatra, David Brenner, and all the aging neighborhood rock 'n' roll stars like Frankie Avalon, Fabian, and Bobby Rydell played the main room. Amato comped them with limos, wine, and women. In turn, they sat at his table, smiled at the paparazzi, treated him the way ambitious Duluth parish priests do Vatican cardinals.

The basement boasted three professional bocce ball courts where Amato drank red wine, screamed at the little balls, and argued with other old Italian men about frivolous matters. It was his favorite place, a spot where business was put on hold. A place where his bocce ball was only as good or bad as that of Tony the barber or Santo the corner butcher.

The third floor held lavish offices where business was conducted. Off-limits to everybody but the boys. Today was the monthly executive session when the capos gave progress reports, just like IBM. It was ironic: the bigger you got, the more money you made, the more you resembled government bureaucracy with its obsession for meetings, paper, and decision by committee.

Miceli looked around the oblong oak conference table from his seat, farthest from Amato. Seating by seniority and it showed. Those at the other end of the table, making small talk, looked at death's door. Slouched in chairs, bifocals the thickness of Coke-bottle bottoms, an occasional hearing aid, one walking cane, four prostates, and two double bypasses. He couldn't believe *these* were the guys he'd heard so much about in his youth—guys who busted heads and kicked ass—and worse. Hard to imagine.

He thought, Let's get this fuckin' thing started, I got real business to conduct.

"Good afternoon," Amato said to the room at large. "Let us begin."

Vito Coliano, capo of gambling and prostitution, stiffened. He was ready to give his report first, as he had done for the past sixteen years.

The frail mafioso began, "Gentlemen, numbers last month grossed one-point-five million. After paying off winners, precincts, runners, bag men, and other incidentals, we netted eight hundred and two thousand. Not bad, not good. End of report."

"Fine." This was Amato's way of saying, "Next."

That meant Rocco Donati and casinos. Donati had turned seventy-seven in July and was bent like a banana since disc surgery.

"Our five casinos had a good month," he said. "All showed net profits totaling two-point-two million. A minor problem with the Jersey Gambling Commission making noise about suspending Plaza's license for minor infractions. Our mouthpiece is on top of it, expects to have it legit soon."

"Excellent work, Rocco," the Don said.

And so it went. Dominic Costa, loansharking. Robert Esposito, vending machines, black market records, and videos. The *consiglieri*, William Averone, overseer of legitimate investments and business fronts. Carlo Cicci, at ninety-five the oldest mafioso alive, allowed to babble each month about the good old days.

Then it was Miceli's turn. He straightened his Gaetano sports coat, twisted a big gold pinky ring, flicked imaginary dust off his sleeve.

"Mr. Amato, men of the commission," he began. "Narco—I mean, our product," correcting himself.

The old mob guys were funny about actually saying words like "narcotics," "heroin" or "cocaine." They had tried for a long time to avoid the drug business. It was dirty and, in their way of thinking, only appealed to the lower class of street criminals. But in the mid-sixties reality suddenly became unfashionable and even kindergarten teachers were "turning on" before breakfast. The strange double standard where it was honorable to choke a guy with a piano wire but immoral if a fourteen-year-old OD'd in a hallway no longer operated in reality, but the distaste for the "product" remained.

Miceli continued, "Our product had a good month, grossing some three-point-eight million. Overhead killed us, what with mules, mix for cuttin', chemist, transportation, and so on. Hit us up for two and a half. We ended clearing a mil three."

"Sufficient," Amato said, knowing Miceli was skimming at least half a million dollars each month.

"I ain't done yet, Mr. A.," Miceli said, before anyone else could take center stage. "We got problems."

"Go on, Anthony."

Miceli stood up. "The fuckin' Satans are killin' us," he announced, a near-scream. "And it's about fuckin' time we act."

"So you tell us each month, Anthony," Amato said coolly. "We'll discuss it, but keep your language civil in this room. This is *not* the streets."

They proceeded with the same conversation of the last ten months, with Miceli insisting, "We gotta go after the Satans, old style."

Amato objected, "No violence."

Miceli asked, "Why?"

Amato said, "The timing is wrong—elections, public opinion, other factors you're not aware of."

Miceli said, "Then let me whack a wholesaler who switched. It'll set an example."

Amato said, "Maybe. I'll give it some thought. In the meantime, cut prices and compete."

Miceli begged, "Aw, come on, Mr. A. That's no fuck— no way to do business."

Amato said, "It's the way I conduct business, Anthony. Any other problems?"

Miceli wanted to talk about initiating four of his guys, about a sixth casino, about opening a disco in Center City, but he did not say a word. The cocaine was wearing off; he did not feel quite so invincible.

He simply said, "Nothing else."

Amato looked away, making it clear discussion was over. Ten minutes later he ended the meeting, finishing it off with, "Anthony, I'd like you to remain."

The old men pushed away from the conference table. A few shared knowing looks; it was about time this punk Miceli was put in his place.

When the room was emptied of the others, Amato fixed his famous stare on Miceli. This, and the old man's silence, made Miceli squirm.

"What's wrong, Mr. A.?" Miceli finally asked.

"This talk's overdue."

"Yeah, maybe it is." Almost defiantly.

"You got something to say about the way I operate, Anthony, now's the time to say it."

Miceli's first instinct was to rip into Amato, give it to him the way he'd done so many times in his mind. Call him a fuckin' scared old man. Tell him new blood was needed. That he should go to Florida and learn shuffleboard. That's what he *wanted* to tell Amato, but something deep within would not allow it.

Part of his feeling was fear, but mainly it was conditioning. Italian kids who had gone to strict Catholic schools did not talk that way to elderly crime bosses. Miceli also knew Amato still had the national commission's backing. If he forced the issue without their okay, three hundred guys named Bruno would be in Philly by evening.

"You know I got nothing but the highest respect for you," Miceli lied. "But I just think the Satans are pushing us around and we're losing respect on the street. Makes it hard to keep people in line."

Amato, easing his voice, said, "Anthony, there have always been 'other' groups. In the Thirties it was the Irish and their whiskey running. The Jews and bank frauds in the Forties. Negroes with their extortion, prostitution, and gambling lasted to the late Sixties. The Seventies brought Asian Tong gangs, and in the Eighties we have vicious Colombian and Cuban gangs who'd shoot their own mother for a score."

Miceli sat in silence as Amato went on, "The bikers are nothing new, merely a different spoke on the same wheel of greed. They'll eventually self-destruct, they all do. Sometimes we help this process, usually they do it on their own. You see, that's the 'difference' between them and us." He paused to allow the meaning of his words to reach Miceli's brain. "Do you understand?"

"But Mr. A—" Miceli started to say, and by the tone of his voice Amato realized Miceli did not understand, could *never* understand. He had wanted desperately to get Miceli under control; now he knew this would not happen.

Miceli was babbling, "Then we agree, these bikers, it's time we help the destruction."

"I'll tell you what," Amato said, sorry now he had started the conversation. "I give you my word that the Satans will cease to exist in six months. I'll take care of them, my way. If I fail, then you can deal with them—your way!"

Miceli gave Amato one of those "You kiddin' me?" looks.

"I promise," Amato responded to Miceli's eyes.

This was the second time that day Amato had given his word. He had never in his life broken a promise. He had no intention of starting now, even to someone like Miceli.

"You know, Mr. A., I'm glad we had this talk." Miceli sounded as though he meant it.

"I am too, Anthony," Amato said. "I am too."

Miceli stood up and headed for the door. He turned and said, "See you later, Mr. A.," before walking out.

Amato reached inside his suit jacket, pulled out the prescription bottle that he hoped would lower his rocketing blood pressure. The meeting with Miceli had taken its toll. He washed down two pills and slumped back in the big leather chair. The empty room seemed much larger than it had a few moments ago.

He thought, Okay, Michael, it'll work, it's all there. Besides, it *has* to be done. God give me the energy to see it through. If it works, I retire; if it fails, I die. Either way I get needed rest. He smiled at his unintended gallows humor and reached for the phone.

"Let me talk to Lucifer," he said. "This is Michael Amato."

MICELI sauntered down the hall to a working office. Phones, filing cabinets, desk-top computers, and two men wearing wingtips, who had never had their noses broken.

"Marvin, I want a guy checked—all the way!" Miceli said to one of the men playing with an IBM desktop.

"It's Melvin, Mr. Miceli," the man corrected him. "What's his name?"

"Joe Vitali."

"Do you know the exact spelling of his name, sir?"

"The fuck I know," Miceli shot back. "Spell it like it sounds."

"Do you have any other personal identification on him, Mr. Miceli?" Asked with some hesitation.

"A fuckin' white guy!" Miceli screamed. " 'Bout forty-fuckin'-two, probably a rap sheet, dope dealer, Philly house, short dude, probably got a big dick. That enough info, Marvin?"

"Sufficient to get us started." Melvin began to play with access codes. "I'll try for the basics first. DMV, arrest record, citizenship, utility bills, credit check."

"Do it!" Miceli ordered.

The man named Melvin accessed directly into the NCIC, the National Crime Information Computer in Washington, D.C. This international machine contained detailed and personal information on most of America's citizens, whether they wanted it there or not. Tapping into computers was a national epidemic; even Arkansas eighth-graders pirated millions from New York banks. The LCN's money bought the best technicians and equipment; there was no contest accessing NCIC.

"A hit on Joseph John Vitali," Melvin said proudly. "DOB, 12-28-46, POB, Philadelphia, height, five-eight, weight, 175, current address 415 South Third, drives a Mercedes, has two priors for dealing coke, credit's A-1 with six major credit cards."

He turned to Miceli, asked, "You want more?"

"Everything. Including the name of his dog."

Twenty minutes later Miceli left the room smiling. He held a perforated tear-off computer sheet that included Vitali's IRS returns for the last five years, his military records and fingerprints, DEA information, a Philly PD arrest photo and rap sheet, employment and marital history. And that indeed he once had a dog named Alice.

Feeling the neatly printed information in his hands gave Miceli a sense of security—computers don't lie. Melvin had double-checked. Miceli knew all there was to know about Joseph Vitali and thoroughly believed he was a dealer in dope.

7

The Dragon Queen would've loved this joint." Moose surveyed the undercover apartment.

Lerza sank into the plush velvet sofa, stared up through the twenty-five-foot skylight in the roof, then asked, "Who's the Dragon Queen?"

"My second wife. The one with the expensive taste."

Lerza could not resist the obvious. "How'd she end up with you?"

"The bimbo thought I'd stay a CPA and start reading the National Business Weekly instead of the National Enquirer."

"Why the name 'Dragon Queen'?"

"The Dragon Queen had some foul-smelling breath coming outta big red lips, Joey." Moose headed toward the wet bar. "She'd get so pissed at me she'd throw fits. Stand real close, squint them beady little reptile eyes, and call me rich people's names like 'incorrigible.' "

The two men laughed at the image of Mrs. Moose Deuce. Moose asked, "Whatta ya drinking, Joey?" as he poured himself three fingers of Imperial.

"Whiskey and Coke."

"Oh, Jees, I forgot!" Moose screamed in mock horror. "Now, how we gonna scare anybody, bad-assed drug dealers drinkin' a candy-ass drink like whiskey and fuckin' Coke?"

The undercover apartment was top-shelf. Pristine egg-colored walls, twenty-foot ceilings, a bathtub that sat three and bubbled. *And* a uniformed doorman named Bruce who used a dog whistle to attract taxis.

"Just consider it a personality flaw and pour it." An order.

Moose grabbed the Seagrams, filled most of the Waterford, added two ice cubes and a split second of Coke.

He handed the drink to Lerza and asked, "Know what this place is missing?"

"No, but I'm sure you're gonna tell me."

"It's okay as it is, but it'd be a lot more believable if I sent for my velvet painting of Elvis and the Duke. Jazz up these hospital walls."

Lerza took a healthy gulp of his drink and sighed deeply. His shoulders relaxed; his mind began focusing on what lay ahead.

"Let's go over the game plan, Moose," he suggested.

"Go to it, Joey," Moose agreed. "That's what you're good at. Thinking and planning."

"First off, we assume we're being watched," Lerza began. "Visually and electronically. No personal calls from the phone. They can pull tolls or tap as easy as we can."

"Easier, Joey," Moose agreed. "Don't have to go through liberal judges and government typists."

"And we can't forget about the bikers. The minute after

we meet Miceli, they're gonna be real curious 'bout me and you."

"Who'd a thought of the LCN vouching us to the bikers?" Moose said.

"That's the beauty of this operation, Moose. Once we deal with Miceli, the bikers are gonna feel safe about us being legitimate dope peddlers. They know how paranoid the Italians are. They're positive we've been checked and rechecked. Saves us twelve months undercover work."

Moose asked, "How we gonna deal with the bikers?"

"By not getting ahead of ourselves." Lerza emptied his glass. "First off, we get Miceli, and that's gonna be tricky."

"Why?"

"Logistics problems, Moose." Lerza headed toward the bar. "We *have* to record my first conversation or Miceli and the rest of the capos could skate, and we'd end up with some minor-league wiseguys."

"Simple enough." Moose shrugged. "Wire you up with a Nagra and a bellyband."

"Source says Miceli pats down on first meets. Forces the issue. Pants to ankles, shirt out, in the john. We *want* Miceli to deal with us. That's what this is all about. We'll make concessions. *But* I still won't make it easy for him because no self-respecting drug wholesaler'd put up with that kind of shit without *some* facesaving. Which brings us back to the problem of where do we put the mike?"

"That sorta depends on where you have the conversation, don't it?"

"Miceli's a creature of habit and caution," Lerza answered, starting his next whiskey and Coke. "Has first meets at *his* table in the Classy Chassis. Likes the loud background noise. Hard Rock stands ten feet away with a bunch of other apprentice Capones in the area. You, my friend, will also stand ten feet away."

Moose asked, "Why not just bug the table?"

"Not so easy. It's one of those little round cocktail tables with just enough room for two drinks and four elbows."

"Whatta we do?"

"The lovely Miss Masters went to sound school. She'll figure out something. In the meantime get ready for our face-to-face with the source."

Moose guzzled his third shot of Imperial. "How we gonna handle the toss?"

"Don't really know yet. May just have to follow my lead." Lerza added seriously.

"But remember one thing."

"What's that?"

"Under *no* circumstances do I leave your sight!"

Moose poured himself a fourth and fifth shot of the cheap whiskey. "Don't worry, munchkin," he said. "But you better wear your elevator shoes, Joey, 'cause little things tend to get lost easy in dark, dangerous places."

MOOSE had not seen so many titties since his 1968 R&R in Bangkok. He marveled at the different shapes, sizes, lengths of nipples, and the way each bobbed and weaved.

Lerza's libido wanted to take in the boobs, too, but his mind had a different agenda. Cops and agents consider informants necessary evils. Any first-day rookie knows that hard investigation does not put people in jail—informants do. You need snitches to do your job, but they are also major-league pains in the ass. They lie, cheat and deceive, play both ends against the middle, and sometimes get you hurt.

It just is not normal for some civilian to wear a body recorder, buy dope, and eventually put people who trusted him in jail. With a cop, it's his job, it's what he does when he gets up in the morning, it's how he pays the mortgage. But why would anyone else do this double-cross work?

Ever since Judas, who was the first snitch, Lerza thought, there have been only five reasons why one person informs on another. Judas did it for money, followed in no particular order by revenge, elimination of a competitor, saving your own butt, or the obsession of a police buff who failed the academy's entrance exam. That's it—only those five. Contrary to some TV scriptwriters' imaginations, it's never some upstanding citizen who wants to save society. That type of person doesn't know criminals in the first place and certainly won't risk his colonial home for intrinsic reasons.

So it was critical for a UCA to know a snitch's true motivation *before* he met people like Hard Rock in breast factories.

That was what tonight was all about. Meet the confidential source, get acquainted, set the stories straight, have a feel for the way each thought, the meaning of a glance or unspoken gesture, and then decide if each could pull it off. You keep telling your source they're doing the right thing. You use all the standard lines about getting the junk off the street, how it could end up in some kid's arm, how the bad guy is really bad and *belongs* in jail, *but* the bottom line is that most cops can never completely trust someone who is in the process of helping you betray someone else's trust.

That's because most cops and agents are closemouthed by nature. They have an unwritten, unspoken code of honor, sometimes called the blue wall of silence. It means a cop would never dime out a brother cop and is automatically suspicious of anyone who would do the equivalent in his own world. Another one of life's ironies, cops and criminals sharing wholeheartedly a credo: lose your job, go to jail, lie under oath, *but don't rat!* That left informants in some in-between world. Neither side trusting them, *both* sides using them.

"Would you look at that!" Moose pointed to a naked girl doing a handstand onstage.

Lerza looked and realized the handstand was only half her act. The more unique part was the ability to shoot Jergens lotion twenty feet in the air from her vagina.

He said to Moose, "Yeah, she's a certified talent all right. Probably a third-year medical student earning tuition." He thought, Anything's possible in this city of brotherly and sisterly love.

The twenty regulars of the Classy Chassis cheered the Jergens girl, who seemed to have a never-ending supply of lotion in her magazine. Prompted by the crowd, she was only three inches shy of hitting the stage lights and short-circuiting the joint.

"How she do that?" Moose asked.

"Something to do with air pressure."

"I could be in love." Moose sighed.

The two undercover agents found a table away from the excitement and waited until Dirty Denise took their drink order. Denise may have been a headliner in the Fifties, but everything important had long ago sagged two feet.

Lerza asked Dirty, "Will you tell Stormy that Joe Vitali and Russ Napoli are here?"

She nodded and winked at Moose before heading toward the bar.

"This undercover work is tough, Joey." Moose chuckled as he eyed the grandma stripper's rump. "Why Russ Napoli for my monicker?"

"Cardinal rule in the Undercover manual. Don't get too far from the truth."

"But you made me a greasy Italian," Moose teased.

Both men had been to Chestnut Street, where they had spent two grand of the taxpayers' money, choosing from the racks that should have been marked "drug dealers." Actually only Lerza fit the stereotypical bill, with an open silk shirt, melon sports coat, and alligator shoes that hurt. Moose looked more like a down-and-out undertaker.

Just as the Jergens girl started shooting blanks, Dirty Denise returned and placed two plastic glasses filled with a brown liquid, green straws, and red cherries on the table. She said, "Stormy'll see you now." She jerked her head in the direction of a door by the men's room. "In the office."

Moose threw a fin on her tray and said, "Later, Dirty."

Lerza opened the door to the designated room. He was surprised to see a very attractive lady waiting. There was a softness to her face, a gentleness to her look. Not what he expected. He had known his share of topless dancers, with their pencilled eyebrows, blue eyelids, and cigarettes dangling from painted, pouting lips.

The first words out of her were, "I'm really nervous."

"Nothing to worry about," Lerza lied.

"I just can't believe I'm actually doin' it." She sat down on the couch.

Lerza, wanting to start this conversation over, switched gears, introduced himself and the Moose. Spotting the liquor supply, he poured an Amaretto for Stormy and began talking about the weather. This had a calming effect on her. When the time seemed right, he eased back to the reason they were there.

He said in a soothing voice, "The main thing is be yourself. A guy like Miceli will notice anything that don't seem natural. We'll carry the conversation; all you do is a simple introduction, then leave."

"I can do it, don't worry." Defensively.

"Good girl." Approvingly. "Now tell me everything you

know about Miceli. Don't leave anything out. I wanna feel like him and I been asshole drinking buddies our whole life."

When she had finished, Lerza had formed a strong dislike for Anthony Miceli. He now also knew her motivation.

He said, "Okay, be just as thorough and give me a word-for-word on what you told him about me. This is very important, because he's gonna test me. How you and me met, who introduced us, what day it was, have I been to your apartment, if we slept together, am I a user. *Everything!*"

Stormy was good on her feet; she left nothing out, told him exactly what her words had been to Miceli. Lying is an art. Most people cannot do it. Sometimes their egos give them away, sometimes their voices. Psychologists say the people who do it best are diagnosed psychotics, so good they routinely beat polygraphs. The group who do it next best are criminals and undercover agents. Probably has something to do with practice.

Stormy must have picked up the knack, Lerza thought, from her friends. He was convinced she had carried off the lies about him to Miceli. He listened hard for something that didn't jive, a sentence that didn't ring true, but there weren't any.

The most difficult part came next. Lerza never exaggerated, embellished, or lied even to the most degenerate junkie flophouse informant when it came to this part, and he would not start now.

He told Stormy sternly, "You know when this goes down, Miceli will figure out your part. Don't even think about trying to tell him you didn't know we were FBI. You gotta know what happens then."

At this point most FBI agents say the magical words "Witness Protection Program" and expect the snitch to drop to his knees and kiss their Hoover ring. Take someone from the bowels of Philadelphia and deposit them in Ames, Iowa, stipulate they never call or see family again, give them just enough money to eat for a year, provide them with a phone number to call if they are close to death, and you have the Witness Protection Program. Statistics show most people drop out after six months and risk immediate death on their home turf rather than slow decay in Ames, Iowa.

Lerza was on a roll, so he tackled the justice system. He said, "If we nail Miceli on camera in the act of murder, blood dripping from the knife in his hand, giving us a signed confession on the spot, the chances are still fifty-fifty he walks. Good lawyers, bad juries, and soft judges make for a lousy combination. It all adds up to you knowing the score. Pretty dismal picture, eh?"

Stormy stood up, walked over to the room's only window. It was night, and for a moment she stared into the darkness. She finally turned and said strongly, "I'm in."

They talked for another hour, each getting the rhythm of the other's personality, the nuances and peculiarities each individual alone possesses. Stormy talked about her childhood, Lerza talked about Nam, and the Moose contributed tales of his nuptials to Alimony Annie, Nina the Nympho, and the Dragon Queen.

Lerza discussed contact procedures, what to do if things got shitty, and the greatest threat in undercover work—the need to tell someone. Most human beings have an overwhelming urge to share secrets. They rationalize there's no harm in telling just *one* person—their best friend, their mother, their lover. What they fail to realize is that the person they're telling also has the same urge. It multiplies with some kind of geometric progression until everyone in your time zone knows you're an FBI snitch.

Stormy kept nodding as Lerza patiently explained the

do's and don'ts of his world. When there was nothing left to say, he got to his feet and said, "Show us Miceli's table."

She hesitated slightly. He walked over to her, took her hands in his. He said, squeezing her small fingers, "You'll do fine. It's the right thing to do, you know." He realized he had just cliché'd her but also realized that for this one time he meant what he said.

"You don't need to convince me, Joe," she said. "I'm a big girl. I want this to happen. I'm ready for whatever. And—I trust you."

The Moose, who hated anything sentimental that didn't involve war movies or cowboy's horses, bellowed, "Hey, you two, cut that shit out, it's disgusting!"

THEY sat at Miceli's table with fresh drinks. On stage Candy Gram was doing squat thrusts on soda bottles and sticking first-row eyeglasses where the sun doesn't shine.

"We need a key for this place," Lerza said, "and for any alarms."

Stormy slyly pushed a key ring from the back pocket of her tight designer jeans and pointed at two keys. "This one's the front door," she said, "then you got ninety seconds to use this one to shut off the alarm. Box is behind the bar near the bourbon."

Lerza chuckled. "That eliminates the Moose from alarm duty. He'd never get past the bourbon."

"Excuse Santa's helper, ma'am," Moose said, "but you always hurt the one you love."

The three laughed like old friends, comfortable with the meeting and with each other. The Classy Chassis was rocking. Dancers were scattered all over the floor, bumping and grinding to six Sanyo speakers the size of refrigerators blaring at maximum decibels.

"We'll be back after closing," Lerza said. "Place empty at three?"

Stormy nodded yes and sipped the last of her Amaretto.

"Set the meet with Miceli in two days," Lerza said. "In the meantime avoid him. If you deal, introduce someone who does, or even *talk* about drugs on the telephone on any deal we don't control, you're criminally liable." He eased up, said, "I know it's gonna be tough, but there's no choice."

They said their good-byes, giving the required South Philly hugs and kisses. Stormy had passed the test; she was someone you'd trust with your life, Lerza thought.

"Nice bimbo," Moose tossed out as they walked to the car. Lerza did a double take. It was the highest compliment Moose could give a female with only two legs not in a cowboy movie.

The late October air had a bite, but Lerza did not notice. The excitement of the case, of jumping in with both feet and feeling it come together, made him immune to the cold. Then he remembered. Every case had its unexpected downs, when things went to hell, moments the bad guys got the upper hand, split seconds when the good guys almost died. This one would not be any different. It would just be a matter of when.

But for now he enjoyed Thirteenth Street. A carnival of human beings. Men dressed in wigs and miniskirts with better legs than Patty Masters. Big-breasted hookers with enough cleavage to hide Irish wolfhounds. Street hustlers offering everything from counterfeit Rolexs to choice lots in Key West.

"Whatta the Satans' old ladies doin' at the club?" Moose asked innocently.

"What!" a scream from Lerza.

"Saw three of 'em dancing."

"You shittin' me?" Lerza turned to him.

"Thought you noticed," Moose said defensively. "Three hoofers with property tattoos on their right thighs."

"Sure?"

"Positive. All biker ol' ladies have property tattoos. I should know. I dated enough of them toothless wonders with the stringy hair hanging from their armpits and eight-foot platform heels."

"But are you absolutely positive *these* girls were *Satan* old ladies?"

The Moose zippoed a cigar the size of Rhode Island and said, "Hey, munchkin, I may be from Pittsburgh, but I can see. They had a little tattoo of a red devil inked on their butts. I noticed," he went on, " 'cause I love a girl with a tattoo."

"Whatta you make of it?"

"Plain as the genes that make you so short. They're there to keep an eye on the competition."

"That's the obvious part." Lerza then snapped his fingers; something had clicked. "So that's how the bikers know *who* to offer a better deal."

"The plot thickens, eh, Joey?"

"Yeah, Moose, it does that."

They reached the pay phone at the corner of Thirteenth and Bainbridge. Lerza got out and stood, trying to digest this latest development. Did Stormy know? Hell, she had to, didn't she? If she did, did Miceli? Should he ask her? Were they being double-crossed? What did it all mean?

He dropped a quarter in the hole, realized the phone had just been used by a nonfilter cigarette smoker who liked cheap wine. He accepted the foul odor, punched the digital display beeper number, waited until the connection sounded, then followed up with the phone booth's number.

Somewhere in Philadelphia, Special Agent Patty Masters's curvy left hip beeped. She hit the button on the $42-a-month pocket phone, and a seven-digit phone number appeared. It took her three minutes to find a phone.

Lerza grabbed the receiver before the first ring ended. He said, "We scheduled an entry."

"When?"

"Three A.M. Bring your black handbag from Mission Impossible school."

"Where?"

"Meet you at two. Our place."

"I'll be there."

"Drive carefully, Patty. It's a crazy city."

8

The meet," as it was called, took place in the Pacard Park Food Distribution district near the Delaware River. If anybody cared to look, they would be able to see Camden, New Jersey, across the expanse of water. Nobody did.

Billy "One Punch" Averone stood across from and stared hard at Nicholas "Needledick" Jones, Robert "Cement Shoes" Esposito matched up with Henry "Brain Dead" Ward, and so it went. Two rows of organized crime's finest with five feet of Philly asphalt separating them. Looked like the trenches of an old Chicago Bears-Green Bay Packers game.

It was almost midnight, and the deserted waterfront was lit only by the lights of the Walt Whitman Bridge, helped by the moon's reflection on the river George Washington once crossed.

The LCN wiseguys with their vested suits, porkpie hats, and issued .38-caliber Model .49 Smith and Wessons, resembled private dicks from a vintage 1930 movie. The Satans countered with leather jackets, skullcaps, exotic modified M-10s, and butterfly switchblades. Two of society's countercultures in a show of force.

Neither side believed much in "détente"—no unilateral volunteering to reduce the number of silencers in their back pocket. Force is what they knew; violence is what they took for granted.

Amato had attended a dinner meeting earlier that night in the private back room of Salfranco's Restaurant. The eight elderly Italian gentlemen (Miceli was absent) could have passed for two tables of a geriatric bridge party. The menu was pasta, red wine, and a heated discussion on why "the meet" should take place.

"It's wrong to meet with them," said Dominic Costa, almost crying.

"We don't need *them!*" shouted Vito Coliano.

"They're snakes," warned Robert Esposito, "not to be trusted."

Amato met all their objections calmly. He sounded like a heart surgeon trying to convince a patient the transplant would be only an elective minor cut. He could not tell them everything. Not because he did not trust *these* men. They had been his friends since the boat crossing. Two were his kids' godfathers, he himself was godfather to five of their children.

They would *never* betray him on purpose. It was just that they were getting old. Some shouted when they thought they were whispering. Security became a victim to senility. He also knew there would be opposition, and he did not have the time to deal with new factions.

"I say we meet," he insisted. "It will accomplish many things."

Carlo Cicci picked up his wineglass, waving it as he

spoke. He was the eldest mafioso. He started off, "We give these—" then lapsed into Sicilian, calling the Satans a variety of names that questioned their mothers' virtue, ending with "too much respect."

Amato smiled at Cicci and said, "Yes, yes. You are correct, my friend, but it is important to have these scoundrels *believe* they are our equals."

One Punch's cancer medication did not mix well with the heavy port. He begged, in a slow voice, "Explain please, Don. Tell us your plan."

Amato launched into his rehearsed story. It was almost true; in fact there were no lies, just major omissions.

"I will meet with their leader," he began. "I will propose a truce on the trade problem. I will allow them to operate, to sell their poison in a defined territory, in the ghettos. They will make much money without fear of retaliation. I will allow their women to operate as prostitutes in our casinos. I will offer these and other minor concessions. But make no mistake," he said firmly, "the Satans will know these offers come from our strength, our generosity, our benevolence. *Not* our weakness."

"What do *they* give up?" Vito Coliano asked.

Amato stood at the table and emphasized his words. "Freedom," he said. "They will be controlled by us. They will be accountable to us. They will tell themselves it is a partnership, but their hearts will know the truth. *And*"— he paused for effect—"they will be required to give us ten percent of their profits."

This latest bit of information silenced the room. It took several seconds to digest the simplicity, yet enormity, of his thoughts.

"Ah, ah," said an admiring Carlo Cicci. "I now see the wisdom of your plan, Don Amato. They take the risk, we collect the rewards."

"Yes, it is a good plan," interjected Coliano, "but what makes you believe the Satans will agree?"

"I have little doubt they will," Amato said. "As many of you know, I can be quite convincing at times."

There were knowing laughs, loud and genuine. But the laughter ended abruptly as William Averone, waving a hand like a traffic cop stopping a row of cars, asked somberly, "What about Miceli? He'll never go for it."

The room fell silent again, all eyes focused on Amato. He said, "Miceli will embrace this plan. He will protest at first, but in the end he will believe this will make him even more powerful. I will permit him to collect the Satans' money. He will tell the streets the Satans are his. He will claim victory."

Averone insisted, "But what if—"

Amato interrupted, "If he *doesn't* approve, then I will finally concede to Miceli's desire."

After a moment's silence, contented looks replaced frowns. Amato's bluff worked. He had answered their questions, soothed their concerns, ended all further talk of business. At least for the moment.

The LCN hierarchy ate ten pounds of pasta, sixty fried clams, forty-two meatballs, a garden full of antipasta, and drank two gallons of imported wine. They drove from Salfranco's directly to "the meet."

Amato sat next to Lu in the backseat of the mob's finest limo. They were alone. Each sipped a straight Cutty Sark. A small, ten-watt floor light gave off an eerie glow, making the men appear almost headless.

"We're heading toward a war," Amato said, once the small talk ended.

"Yes." A knowing nod of Lu's head.

"You know that you cannot win *that* war."

"Maybe. Maybe not."

"The reality is I pick up the phone and three hundred men come from places like Chicago, Detroit, Cleveland, and Buffalo."

"I know that if you were gonna do that, you'd have done it by now, Michael." Lu's voice was conciliatory.

That Lu addressed Amato by his first name was not lost on the capo. He responded by putting on his most fatherly voice as he said, "Talk to me, Lucifer. Tell me what would make you happy. How can we avoid violence? Tell me."

The Don's quick change in demeanor threw Lu, but only for a moment. He then said evenly, "Michael, you got internal problems named Miceli. I also know your heart ain't really in the drug business. It boils down to a simple matter of money and turf with a little respect and power thrown in."

"Oh? And what else do you know?" A faint smile on his face.

"I know that you're a smart and fair man. So let's cut the crap and get to the reason we're here."

"Fine with me." Amato thought, I have underestimated this man. "You and I are leaders. Men look up to us for guidance, they trust us with their lives. So it is important that you trust my words. That we *both* honor any arrangement." He paused, then asked, "Do you agree?"

"I do." Calmly.

"Good. Now we will *both* dispense with verbal games and be completely honest."

Lu turned in his seat, faced Amato direct. "Go on," he requested.

Amato laid out the proposal, word for word, as he had done for his men earlier that evening. Lu listened, nodded here and there. The Satan president did not offer a word— not a protest nor a counterproposal.

When Amato finished, Lu said the obvious. "Miceli'll

never go for it. And since we're being completely honest, *you* can't control him."

Here is where the boss of bosses deviated from the story he'd told his capos. His longtime friends and associates wanted and even needed to believe that Miceli could be controlled. Amato and this renegade biker knew differently.

"A definite problem," he said. "But you're the solution."

For the first time Lu objected. He said, "I don't like where you're heading."

"Hear me out." Amato's voice was quiet. "You are correct that the old-timers don't like dealing drugs. It's a dirty, risky business, yet one we cannot ignore. You are *also* correct that Miceli can't be controlled much longer; it's just a matter of time before he makes his move."

He stopped for a moment, then went on, "I won't allow that. Here's what I propose. You have a narcotics network in place—from what I hear, a very efficient one. You know the identity of Miceli's major distributors, you have your own street wholesalers." He paused and digressed. "Excuse me if I say that you and your group seem well-suited for this business. Now, what I'm offering you is the chance of a lifetime."

"You got my interest," Lu said after a pause.

"I want you to kill Miceli." In a matter-of-fact voice.

Lu's voice was calm. "Do it yourself."

"That would cause us both problems. A contract released by me would not remain in confidence. It's a small circle in which we exist. I'd lose control of Miceli's band of misfits, and right now I'm the only thing separating them from you. So it becomes important that his men direct their hate toward you."

"I ain't following you." Lu looked puzzled.

Amato poured two fresh drinks and explained, "If we do nothing, Miceli will most certainly succeed me, by force or simple attrition. If that happens he will have at his disposal unlimited money, men, and weapons, all of which will be directed at you. If I let out a contract on him and it becomes known, his men would have to revenge his death, and I would have open internal war. But if you kill him, we rid ourselves of a common enemy which threatens both our existences."

Lu asked, "What stops Miceli's goons from coming at me anyway?"

"Me," Amato said quietly. "With Miceli gone I will again be in total control. A few in his group will be given ceremonies, made street bosses, let them convince the others. Put the word out Miceli was in bed with you, chalk it up to occupational hazard. I let it be known the slate's wiped clean. With Miceli's sleeping in the Yeadon Gardens, nobody would dare defy me."

Lu's mouth formed a grin; then he asked, "Why should I take the chance? I'm doin' okay as it is."

The Don had anticipated this concern. "A fair question," he replied. "I will give you control of *all* narcotics in the city of Philadelphia. You pay me a ten-percent fee to operate. I pass the word on the street to cooperate. The small fee assures that your clubhouse remains intact. Nobody gets hurt, everybody gets rich."

"Sounds too good." Skepticism in his voice.

Amato's next words were measured, almost solemn. "I give you my word."

Lu's mind raced. Amato calculated. Neither spoke for almost a full minute. Like two street brawlers forced to put on gloves and box in a gym with rules and a referee. Nice jab, good footwork, but just a matter of time before one of them low-blows a shot in the nuts.

Lu finally said, "I heard your word is good."

"You heard right," Amato reassured him.

Lu's next words were, "You have a deal, Michael. I'll kill Miceli and throw in that fat piece of shit called Hard Rock."

Amato extended his hand, Lu took it, and this sealed "the meet."

"My word." The Don's final communication of the night.

As Daniel Di Sipio rolled the Cadillac from the parking lot, Michael Amato realized that, for the first time in his life, he had no intention of honoring his word.

9

It was a gaping wound. The blood poured out of Joe Lerza. He thought, God help me, Hail Mary, full of grace.

The bullets were still flying overhead. Didn't they know he was dying? Couldn't they just let him be? It took all his energy to raise his head. The Asian faces with the automatic weapons were contorted, alternately smiling and snarling as they kept shooting.

He screamed, "Fuckin' NVA!" and eased his head back into the creek's water.

When he looked up again the faces had changed. Miceli, Amato, Lu, and Hard Rock had replaced the NVA. He blinked; what he now saw made him welcome death. The people holding the Chinese weapons and laughing were Brad Keenan, Patty Masters, and the Moose.

"No!" he shouted.

He knew what would happen next but also knew he could

not stop it. The ex-Sergeant would walk in the water to save him. Then he would be gunned down. Lerza would again be a helpless, unwilling bystander to his friend's brutal death. He waited. The footsteps could now be heard splashing in the creek. Lerza slowly rolled his face over and out of the water. *No!* It was not the ex-Sergeant. *It was Laura! No! No!*

His screams could be heard two floors away in the luxury apartment building.

"Wake up, Joey, come on, buddy." Moose's voice as he shook Lerza's shoulder.

The undercover opened his eyes and dimly saw Moose's concerned face.

"Bad one," was all Lerza could say.

"Nam?"

"Yes."

"You okay?"

"Yeah."

Moose knew his friend was not okay. He had heard the rumors about Lerza and Vietnam. Something happened over there; something caused that wicked scar on his right temple and the slight limp in his walk on damp days. Lerza never talked about *what* happened, but Moose knew the United States Marine Corps did not give the Silver Star for nothing, and Lerza had several.

"I get 'em myself," Moose said.

"Only when I'm under."

"What?"

"The nightmares," Lerza explained. "I only get them when I'm undercover."

He sat up and flicked on the bedside lamp. The red numbers on the digital clock radio showed 2:30 A.M. He said, "Last time was six years ago in New York when I was playing games with Pauly Contellano."

"With me, the smell of diesel fuel or hearing a helicopter could bring it on," Moose said.

"Believe in that Delayed Stress Syndrome crap?"

"No."

"Me either. Probably just getting worked up over our deal tonight," Lerza said. "Or maybe I just miss Laura and the kids. I don't know. But I do know that when I'm under I start circling the wagons. Trusting no one, looking for bad guys behind every door. Always waiting to get double-crossed. Hearing words that aren't spoken. A guy says 'nice day' and I'm convinced he's got my contract."

He looked at Moose intently and asked, "Ever feel that way?"

Moose said seriously, "Joey, I don't have a wife or kids. My mother and father are dead. I ain't got a steady girl or even a fuckin' parakeet and, to be honest, the FBI has been seriously pissing me off lately. I really don't give a fuck who might want a piece of my ass. I feel like, 'Come on, mutha-fucker, take your best shot.' "

Lerza smiled. "Somehow I don't feel sorry for you." But he understood. He had felt the same way twenty years ago on the flight from a Philippine hospital back to the U.S.A.

"Last thing I want is pity," Moose said. "Want some warm milk or a beer or something?"

"No thanks, big guy. I'm okay now. I'm gonna get some shut-eye. Need to be fresh for our dance with Miceli to-night."

"What time is it set for?"

"Ten, but we see the lovely Miss Masters at seven to field-test the bugging equipment."

"Yeah, well, good night and all that." Moose headed for the door.

"Hey, Moose!" Lerza called out.

"Uh?"

"I like the pajamas."

"Picked them myself."

"I figured." Lerza chuckled. "Good likeness of Hulk Hogan."

"Still some on the rack at K-Mart, Joey."

"Good night, Moose."

"Yeah."

"Moose?" Lerza called again.

"Uh?"

"Thanks."

From the dark hallway he heard, "Sleep tight, munchkin."

PATTY Masters said sarcastically, "Your wife wants to put your picture on a milk carton."

"And why's that?" Lerza asked, knowing the answer.

"It's been three weeks, Joseph."

"Busy setting up the deal."

"That crap might wash with civilians," Masters said, "but not with me. Takes five minutes to find a safe phone and say, 'Remember me, the father of your kids?' "

The three special agents sat in a ripped plastic booth at the Triangle Bar deep in the heart of South Philly. Ten feet away a toothless Rusty accompanied by Shellshock Tony and Cassanova Crown almost made music. The Triangle was a neighborhood bar where the local generations had come to eat the spaghetti, dip their garlic bread in the clam sauce, and listen to Rusty's trio, who had been playing bad music for the past twenty-three years. The pizza boy, a fat kid with greasy hair named Romeo, would grab the microphone every few hours and scream Sinatra songs. Everybody told him he sounded just like "the man," but his was far from Frankie's seductive voice. All in all it was a great place to meet: no one gave a crap who you were.

"Don't go south on me, Joseph," Masters warned. "Let's get our priorities straight, bub."

Lerza swallowed the last third of his whiskey-and-Coke and said simply, "You're right. I'll call tonight."

Moose sat poised with a boilermaker, born knowing not to interrupt important conversations between others.

"Laura and I will *both* count on that, mister," Masters said and picked up her vodka tonic, sipping it slowly.

Romeo now felt the urge to sing-scream.

"That's life!" he shouted, standing in his stained white T-shirt and apron. *"That's what all the people say!"*

"Good voice." Moose was serious.

Lerza and Masters smiled at each other, the tenseness completely gone.

"What'd you decide?" Lerza asked her, getting back to business.

"Our entry the other night convinced me it'd be too risky for a stationary microphone." Masters reached inside the tote she carried and drew out a dime and a man's belt. She pushed the dime in Lerza's direction and said, "Here."

He picked it up and examined it closely. "Hey," he said. "They got it in a dime now?"

"Yep! The dime is actually a miniature mike." There was a touch of smugness in her voice. "Miceli can strip-search you, pat you down, run a metal detector over you, hold the dime in his hand, or even put it under a microscope, and never suspect. It's the best miniaturization the lab has ever come up with."

She went on, "But used alone it's useless. What gets Miceli on tape is this." She held up the fashionable belt. "The Moose puts this around his size-fifty-two waist. The buckle is actually a repeater that uses microwave rays, just like the oven. All he has to do is face you; he doesn't need to be in earshot or even close, it's good up to eighty feet.

"The microwave unit is on a special frequency compatible with a porta mobile radio unit in my car. I'll be six or seven blocks away from the club. I'll plug a special recording adapter directly into the porta mobile. The dime picks up your conversation with Miceli. It hits the belt buckle, which microwaves the sound into my porta mobile and onto the tape recorder. Every word goes down in history, and neither of you run a risk no matter how thorough the shakedown is."

"What about the loud music?" Moose asked.

"Voices are on a different frequency than recorded music," she explained patiently. "The tape is sent to the lab, and they eliminate the background noises entirely."

"I'm impressed," Lerza said.

Moose raised his shot glass for a toast. "May this maggot Miceli spend his remaining Thanksgivings eating prison bird."

They raised their glasses to meet Moose's. Lerza said, "Salud."

Masters added to the toast with a staccato barrage of foreign sounding words.

The two men looked at her as though she had suddenly lost her senses.

She explained, "Korean for 'don't count your rice before it's harvested.' I gotta go set up." She slid across the booth until she was touching Lerza. "Don't underestimate this guy, Joseph," she whispered in his ear. "He's dangerous. Please be careful."

The two stared at each other the way fifteen-year-olds do on prom night. She broke the contact by getting to her feet. "Take care of him, Russell," she said to Moose. Then she turned and walked out of the Triangle.

Lerza avoided Moose's stare. He focused his attention on the screaming pizza boy.

"Got it bad, huh?" Moose asked.

"What?" He turned in Moose's direction.

"Don't bullshit a bullshitter, Joey." Moose chased his whiskey with a beer. "Bimbo fever, when the brain travels south to the dick. The loveboat. You know."

"I'm afraid so, mutant." He looked unhappy.

MOOSE slipped a fin to the parking-lot attendant and told the kid he did not want the Mercedes blocked. He and Lerza walked a short way down the street and into the Classy Chassis, adjusting their eyes to the dim lights.

Lerza spotted the group immediately. Men who spent their lives being bullies have trouble blending into a crowd. Lerza had grown up with these guys. They always looked pissed off, eyes squinting badly. They seemed like hemorrhoid patients.

Lerza knocked on the office door, hoping Stormy was ready, hoping, too, she was playing it straight with them.

"He's here," she said, even before the door had completely opened.

"I know." Lerza's calm voice. "Everything set?"

"He's ready, but *real* hinky."

"No sweat, Stormy," he told her. "Remember, just a simple intro. Hook us up, make some small talk, be your charming, pretty self, then leave."

She smiled. "Okay."

Miceli did not get up as the trio approached. He sat like some third-world dictator greeting his subjects, Lerza thought. Hard Rock mimicked a statue directly behind his boss.

Stormy said, "Tony, this is Joe. The guy I told you about."

Miceli held out a manicured hand. Lerza took it and pumped it firmly.

"And this is my business associate." Lerza pointed at Moose.

The Italian made no effort to take Moose's outstretched paw.

"*My* associate," he said, mocking the word, thumbing toward Hard Rock.

Neither of the Twin Towers made an attempt at amenities. The two heavyweights merely glared as they sized each other up. Hard Rock may have won the tale of the tape, but Moose was the clear victor in the "bad-ass stare" contest.

"I know you two have business to discuss," Stormy said. "I'll get some drinks and split."

Lerza took a seat, but Miceli held up a hand when Moose started to sit down. He said to Lerza, "Private meeting, just the two of us. Any problems with that?"

"None," Lerza answered. He said to Moose, "Hang loose in the club."

Then, staring at Hard Rock, who moved not an inch, Lerza said to Miceli, "I still count three."

The massive Sicilian waited until Miceli raised an eyebrow, then lumbered to the bar and stood five stools from Moose. Miceli's other goons, numbering about six inside and probably a few outside, too, were scattered, Lerza noted.

Stormy returned with the drinks, placed them on the table, then retreated to the office.

The stage was set, the two main players ready to do battle. Each looked for telltale signs of deceit: a twitch of the eye, a word out of context, a tapping foot.

Miceli wasted no time and said, "I understand you wanna do business."

Lerza thought, Shit, he knows all about entrapment, wants me to make the first move, say all the buzz words.

"That's because I hear you're the man with the product," Lerza said.

Miceli reached inside his coat pocket, and Lerza realized he was about to pull the oldest trick in the bad guys' handbook. He watched as Miceli positioned a mirror, small brown vial, and straw on the table, then removed a chain from his neck with a gold-plated razor blade attached. Chopping and forming the white lines of powder on the mirror followed.

When Miceli finished, he pushed the cocaine at Lerza and ordered, "Here, cops can't use dope."

Lerza took the straw and smiled at Miceli. Instead of putting it in his nose, he wrapped his lips around the plastic cocktail straw. Lowering his head until it was an inch from the fine powder, he took a deep breath. Then he blew with all he had. The coke flew in fifteen directions, rising like a cumulus cloud, then settling on the dirty bar floor. About half a grand worth of blow mixed with cigarette butts and spilled beer.

"Real fuckin' bright!" Miceli screamed.

"Send me a bill," Lerza shot back. He stood up and said, "I don't like your style, Tony."

"Whoa, whoa." Miceli realized easy money was about to walk away. "I gotta be sure you ain't the heat. How the fuck I know you—"

Lerza interrupted, "Look, I'm a businessman, not some fuckin' junkie. That shit's only a product, not my god. Besides, I've been vouched for by your own people. You wanna play games, I go somewhere else."

It could have gone either way at this point, but greed won out.

"I like your style," Miceli finally said. "But you ever pull a stunt like that again, and you're dead. That shit on the floor comes outta your first load."

"I can live with that." Lerza slowly sat down once again. "You ready to talk business?"

"Not yet. First we take a piss."

"What?"

"You feel a piss coming on." A nine-millimeter pistol appeared in Miceli's hand, pointed at Lerza's gut.

"Your shot to call." Lerza shrugged, stood up, and started toward the men's room.

They had just reached the empty bathroom when he heard Moose scream, "What the fuck's going on?" Moose pushed into the one-sink, no-mirror, cracked-toilet men's room as if he were the cavalry rescuing a wagon train.

Hard Rock followed three feet behind, waving a gun just like Miceli's. "Couldn't stop him, boss," Hard Rock apologized, pointing to Moose.

The four men barely fit in the strip-joint's john. The two automatic pistols looked like bazookas in the confined space, Lerza thought.

"Easy, Moose," Lerza cautioned. "Let 'em play it out."

"This ain't personal," Miceli said, "but take off your shirt and drop your pants to the floor. *And,* since your *associate* decided to join us, he can do the same."

Five free Bangkok whores couldn't get the Moose to strip if he didn't want to. Lerza could only hope Moose knew how close they were to consummating the deal and would not let bullheadedness interfere.

"Do what they say," Lerza ordered, unbuttoning his own shirt.

Moose glared first at Hard Rock, then at Miceli, finally at Lerza. Two nine-millimeter guns couldn't make the Moose strip; hell, an intercontinental ballistic missile wouldn't even budge his zipper, Lerza thought. But out of his loyalty to Lerza, the Moose finally discarded his wardrobe.

They were made to empty their pockets and place everything including wallets and change on the sink. Being forced to strip at gunpoint, as any rape victim knows, is a humiliating experience, one Lerza and Moose filed away for the future.

Miceli inspected everything, checked ID, even gave the dime a feel. Five minutes later all the players were seated at their original stations. The magic dime and belt buckle had passed the inspection.

The clarity of the voices surprised even Patty Masters, listening nervously in her car six blocks from the action. She heard a satisfied Miceli say, "I deal drugs. Okay, you want drugs. Let's talk."

The pretty dancer onstage with the property tattoo on her right thigh watched as the deal was consummated.

The sparse brown mustache was only noticeable when the old fat lady was shoved directly under a light. The Moose had grabbed her as she was making her way to the toilet, and they'd been dancing ever since. Lerza wondered how, with all the bouncing and beer, she held herself up, but the smile on her toothless face gave the answer. It was the first time anybody had asked her to dance in the last twenty years. If you could call it dancing.

Moose dipped, she giggled, Moose tugged, she twirled, Moose knocked over a chair, she kicked it out of their way. The corner juke box, which blared old 45s, mercifully ran out of quarters.

She went to the ladies' room, and Moose sat down once again next to Lerza. They had decided to stop in at the Dolphin Bar and Grille on the corner of Broad and Tasker, a favorite watering hole for sailors stationed at the Philadelphia Naval Base. After they ordered drinks, Moose had suddenly reached out and grabbed the fat old lady.

Moose was now complaining, as he started to guzzle an eight-ounce beer, "The pretty young ones are all married."

"Oh?" Lerza didn't understand why he complained.

"She's got a husband and six grandkids." Moose chuckled.

He put a large hairy arm around Lerza's neck and planted a kiss on his forehead. Then he slobbered, "We got that guinea bastard, didn't we?" referring to Miceli.

Immediately he apologized, "Oh, I forgot! You're Eye Talion, too. Ever bother you having to say, 'Surprise, I ain't your gumba, I'm the heat'?"

"Never." Lerza then asked, "Where'd you learn to dance?"

"Boot camp."

"And Arthur Murray was your DI." Lerza laughed. He waved at Nicky the bartender and ordered "another round." He held up two fingers. "It went well, but without the powder, all we got is a dry conspiracy."

"Miceli will deliver."

"I think so, too."

Nicky the bartender appeared with fresh drinks, tried to find space on a table already full of empty glasses, chicken-wing bones, plastic baskets holding potato chip crumbs, and a dirty rag he had left behind.

"Hey, Nicky," Lerza said seriously. "Ever make fancy drinks like Banana Daiquiri or Brandy Alexander? Ever put an umbrella in a glass?"

The crusty bartender, who resembled Lon Chaney, gave this some thought, then said, "Two months ago some lady with blue hair come in and asked for a vodka tonic. It broke her heart when she found out the Dolphin got no tonic."

He laughed, grabbed two soggy bills off the wet table, and limped back to the bar.

"*Salud!*" Lerza hoisted his whiskey glass.

"Down the hatch." Moose clinked Lerza's glass with his own.

The liquor hit Lerza's belly. He felt warm. Suddenly remembering something, he got to his feet and said, "Be right back."

The telephone was stuck on the wall by the pool table, and it annoyed him that he had to think about the number. Was it 6785 or 6875?

"Lerza residence." Angela's five-year-old voice.

"It's Daddy."

"Daddy!" she screamed. "When you comin' home?"

"How ya' doin'?" He avoided her question.

"Got in a fight with Tommy Nagy."

"Oh?"

"Yeah." Proudly. "He said Robo Man could beat up FBI Man, so I suckered him."

"I love you, Rocky. Let me talk to Mom."

"I love you, Daddy. Here's Mom."

Lerza had had his share of long-distance telephone conversations ever since he'd gone through a three-week football camp in the ninth grade. Football camp was followed by calls from college, marine boot camp, Vietnam, the FBI Academy, and undercover apartments in New York City and Miami. He handled these separation phone calls poorly. Push your loved ones away, and it won't hurt as deeply. Besides, it makes it easier on the ones left behind if they think you're a son of a bitch.

"Joe, how are you, hon?" Laura's soft, eager voice.

"Okay."

"How's it going? Is it almost over? Are you eating?"

"I'm okay. How's the kids?"

"They miss you."

"Yeah."

Laura searched for some common unemotional ground. "Your sister called, just to say hi. I explained. She said, 'Be careful.' "

"Oh."

"So. How's Moose?"

"Fine." Silence, then, "I gotta go."

"I understand, hon."

"Laura?"

"Yes, Joe?"

A slight hesitation, then, "Nothing."

"You really okay?"

"Just great," Lerza lied. "Having a ball."

"I don't believe you, Joseph Lerza. You have that same voice I heard on the night we met. You weren't all right then."

After hanging up, Lerza just stood there, leaning on the pool table, making an effort to wipe the call from his mind. Two sailors with fire watch ribbons and acne interrupted his thoughts. One of them said, "Hey, mister, you playin' or what?"

Lerza stared at their clean white Navy uniforms and it hit him like a barrel of napalm. Memories of the Naval Hospital, Subic Bay, Philippines, 1968. He had lain in the bed staring at the doctors' and nurses' starched white uniforms as they scurried around the ward. At first they thought he could not talk, but the fact was he had nothing to say. It took all his energy trying to forget that terrifying day and night in Vietnam. The harder he tried, the more vivid the memory.

"Hey, mister," the young sailor said again. "You okay?"

Lerza refocused his eyes, said, "It's yours, Mac."

The two young sailors with fire watch ribbons, who had not even been born when Lerza lay bleeding in the Nam river, smirked at each other. They threw a pitying look, the kind usually reserved for bag ladies, at the strange man with the haunted eyes, as he headed back to his table.

"Hey, munchkin!" Moose screamed. "I'm two ahead of you. Drink up."

Lerza grabbed the whiskey, used it to bring on amnesia. He said to himself, Fuck it.

"Fuck it," Moose said, as though reading Lerza's mind. "What'd the ducks want?"

"Who?"

"The sailors." Moose pointed toward the pool table.

"Nothing."

"We ever that young?"

"Never."

"Hell, Joey," Moose chuckled, "we was both nineteen when we staged for Nam, but I never remember looking so—so—" and he floundered for the word.

"Innocent." Lerza finished Moose's thought.

"Yeah, innocent. That's it."

"Maybe because when we were their age, we had to kill people."

"Or be killed." Moose lifted his beer glass. "To all our nineteen-year-old buddies we left behind."

Lerza bumped Moose's beer glass with his own, adding, "To fallen comrades."

The two undercover agents chugged their Schaefers, well on their way to making a load. Moose tried to get Nicky's attention; when he finally turned back to Lerza, he saw tears flowing down his cheeks like the Johnstown flood. He broke the awkward silence and said in a low voice, "Hey,

Joey, you and me been through a lot. Something bothering you? You can tell me. You don't seem yourself, midget. What's up?"

"Nothing."

"Bullshit!" Moose pressed on, "You're as uptight as a hermit expecting six for dinner."

Lerza thought of telling Moose how he felt after the phone call but decided on the easy way out. He lied, "No problem, mutant. It's this rotgut you make me drink."

At first the two had taken the plunge off the deep end of the pool. They had become accustomed to a certain calm in their daily life that was, in part, unnerving.

But now feelings long ago repressed were surfacing, feelings that Lerza prayed had vanished forever, but had just been lying dormant, slowly eating away at his psyche. Combat veterans and undercovers knew of a strange seduction. A desire to make contact with the enemy, a compulsion to envision the bad guy trying something just so you could pull the Magnum and use it. These emotions were now only like a dull toothache, but it was the kind of ache you knew would get worse.

"Hey, dwarf," Moose said, "remember this one?"

Someone had fed the old jukebox and punched in the number-one hit in 1965, "Shotgun."

The Moose grabbed Lerza and a beer bottle. The beer bottle became a microphone, and Lerza replaced the old fat lady as Moose's dance partner.

"I said 'Shotgun'!" Moose yelled into the beer bottle, mimicking Junior Walker and the All Stars. "Do it for me right now. Do the jerk, baby." He swung his massive hips, and the beer bottle became a saxophone. "Do the jerk now," he said as he dipped.

Lerza smiled, fell into sync with his best friend and heard himself sing, "I said 'Shotgun'!"

They made quite a sight on the dance floor. Big Moose and Little Joey singing and doing a dance that normally brought the rain. Two buddies drunk and on the edge.

"WHO could this be?" Patricia Masters said aloud through the noise of the apartment buzzer that would not stop. She grabbed a terrycloth robe that did little to hide her nakedness and hit the intercom.

"Who?" she asked.

"Me," came the reply.

She pushed the button that released the door latch and waited as Lerza bounced from wall to railing up the stairway, watching him from the open door.

"Everything okay?" Masters asked, concerned because of the late hour.

"Everything's dandy." Lerza slurred the words.

"You're drunk, Joe."

"You're right."

"Sit!" she commanded, pointing to a chair. "I'll make coffee."

"Don't want coffee. Pour me a bourbon."

"The bar is closed, bub." Masters started to boil water.

Lerza did not know why he was there except that at some point in the evening he had thought of her, knew he would end up with her. At first he rationalized why he shouldn't, but each succeeding whiskey wiped out anything rational.

"Get a decent tape?" he asked.

"Dynamite," she said, pouring hot water over instant coffee. "You handled him just right. Any dope delivered and he goes to jail."

"It got interesting," he said.

Her apartment was one of those standard overpriced Center City square spaces. A combination kitchen, dining, and living room with a tiny bathroom and bedroom.

"Typical male bonding," Patty said. "Guns, booze, and bathrooms. You knew it was coming."

Lerza sat on a soft couch watching Patty prepare the coffee. He said, "Snitch called it, but I still don't like his stuff. 'A low class dago,' as my father used to say."

"We get the last word, Joseph. Miceli and Hard Rock will spend their golden years in some federal pen."

"And I get to do this shit again!" he spat.

Patty sensed something wrong. The whiskey was merely a catalyst to some already existing conflict. As his control agent, she had a professional responsibility, she knew. She also had a personal obligation as his friend.

"What's the matter, Joseph?" she asked soothingly.

Lerza jumped to his feet and opened a few kitchen cabinets until he found a bottle of Absolut Vodka. He uncorked it and took a long pull of the clear liquid, then wiped his mouth with the back of his hand.

"Don't you know?" he asked.

"Tell me, Joseph." She looked interested.

He took another healthy gulp of vodka, then headed back to the couch. "Sometimes," he began in a whisper, "I don't like myself very much. Sometimes I can't stop thinking about all those people I left behind in Nam. Buddies rotting under rice paddies, old village men strafed by Phantoms, women and babies napalmed into oblivion. I'm not even sure I always killed the bad guy. Sometimes I wonder what the fuck it all meant. What *this* all means. Our one-act play with the mob. Will it make the slightest dent in the drug trade? Fuck, no. Some other gold-chained punk is waiting in line right now. This shit's just like the Nam, Patty. No real victories. No good guys."

Patty took a seat next to him. She said softly, "It makes a difference. *You* make a difference, Joe. What happened in Vietnam is over. You can't change it. But you can help

≡ 100 ≡

some kid hooked on smack by putting his supplier in jail. You—"

Lerza cut her off. "Bullshit! They're no different than us. Keenan and Amato are two sides of the same coin. It's about power. How you get it and keep it. Our boss would sell us out in a fuckin' second. You think the Bureau really cares about Patty Masters?"

Patty leaned over and touched his hand. "Why all the anger at the Bureau?" she asked.

"Because it's a shit job. Run by a bunch of Ivy League empty suites."

"They're not perfect. They're human, like us."

"Like us," he mocked. "We're out here risking our butts and doing their dirty work—work they *can't* do. But fuck up once, break one of their useless, idiotic rules and—"

He sighed, not needing to finish his thought. Patty was beginning to understand, and it scared her. This wasn't just a drunken binge, a tough guy with a tough job working off some frustration. This came from his heart.

She said, businesslike, "Joe, we got a good first lick tonight. Take a break. You earned it. Let the Bureau buy you and Laura a weekend trip, somewhere with a balcony overlooking some gulf. I'll even babysit."

Lerza ignored her offer. "Goin' the whole twenty?" he taunted.

Patty sipped her coffee and answered, "Been with the FBI fourteen years, Joseph. It's all I know."

He said with an edge, "Gonna be one of those old spinsters married to the Bureau, a BU wife, the kind we made fun of in Cincinnati? Going around the office looking at the desk photos of everybody else's kids."

It took a conscious effort to hide the hurt. "I just haven't met the right guy yet."

"You got guys falling all over you," he countered.

"Maybe. But the good ones are all taken."

"Like me?" he asked impulsively.

"Like you," she answered.

Her response wasn't what he'd expected. It made him uneasy, took some of the venom from his system. He noticed her terrycloth robe slide high, exposing a curvy thigh. She curled up next to him on the couch, one leg beneath her buttocks, the other stretched to the floor.

Lerza pulled back, afraid to be so close. "When this is done," he said, "I'm turning in my creds."

"You don't mean it!" She sounded shocked.

"Never more serious."

"Why, Joseph?"

"I'm tired, Patty. Plain tired."

She sighed and resigned herself to his anger. "Undercover is voluntary, Joseph. Nobody would care if you came in. Let Moose handle the delivery. Introduce another UCA. It's just a case."

"I'll finish my tour," he said, the edge back. "I signed up for the duration. Never quit before, never will. It may be one big cluster fuck, but it's mine. When it's over, I walk. Not until."

"Is that really it?"

"Yeah."

"I don't think so," she said angrily. "I think you're a thrill junkie. You enjoy being under. You *need* the edge. You thrive on danger. You—"

He suddenly grabbed her, pulling her close to him. Close enough to feel the exhale of her surprise. A split second of awkwardness, of not knowing what came next, held them. Both had wanted this for so long, had fantasized about the exact moment. The fatalism of their jobs created a "there's no tomorrow" feeling—the last dance on the Titanic.

Lerza slid his hand down her taut back until he reached

the end of the short terrycloth robe, then continued to the flesh of her thigh. Feeling no resistance, he slid his hand beneath the robe and buried his head into her neck. The smell of sleep was still on her, mixed with her own unique fragrance. It was different from Laura's, he thought, as was the muscularity of her body.

Their lips met with mouths open, tongues touching, lightly at first, almost playful, then fiercely. They stared, open-eyed, kissing. Each wanted more. Joe's hand stroked Patty's silk panties, roamed over her firm buttocks, then onto the bareness of her muscular leg. A finger, then a hand, slid beneath the elastic of the panties, and he felt himself go erect.

He rubbed her bare bottom, exploring her rectal crevass with a finger, sliding it down until it reached her moist, willing vagina. Feeling her wetness, her willingness, he plunged his finger into her, moving it slowly as she responded with a twisting midsection. He then placed a second and third finger deep inside, all the while grinding his manhood from the front. A gasp from Patty, eyes closed, then fluttering, as she met his thrusting body with her own. A moan from somewhere deep inside her.

He wanted to make love to her, almost needed the love, but he knew it would mean the end of two things he treasured—Patty Masters's friendship and his marriage to Laura. He battled the false courage and bad sense that comes with too much whiskey and suddenly pulled his hand away.

"It's no good," he said. "I can't."

The two froze, still locked in an embrace. Suddenly the passion dissipated, replaced by the cold reality of their fate.

He pulled himself together and turned to leave. She grabbed his arm and said, "You're not driving in that condition, mister. The couch and breakfast are included in the price of admission."

He was too confused and tired to argue. He dropped on the couch to await unconsciousness. He felt his shoes being slid from his feet, followed by a blanket gently placed over his body. A kiss to his forehead, and he heard her say, "The good ones *are* always taken."

Alone in her bed, Patty Masters tried to make some sense of what had happened. She knew that Special Agent Joe Lerza *had* to be brought in—that much was certain. First thing in the morning she'd tell SAC Keenan, and he'd rubber-stamp her decision. Wouldn't he? Of course he would. Lerza was dead wrong in his judgment of the FBI hierarchy. They'd do the right thing. They'd never sacrifice an agent to make a case. They'd understand.

An hour later, as she lay awake tossing in her bed, she heard his screams.

Miceli grinned. "You gonna get fat, Hard Rock."

"Gotta keep up my strength," the Sicilian explained, in between chunks of imported Italian cheese.

The Ragni Imported Wholesale Food Company was the front Miceli used to bring in white heroin from Sicily. It was simple. Cocaine from Colombia through Miami, then muled to Philly by flunkies doing fifty-five miles per hour up Route 95. Heroin harvested in Sicily, shipped to Genoa, and placed on wooden pallets marked "tomato paste" and "cheese."

Miceli's Sicilian *paisans* shipped it to Brooklyn, where Ragni's customs broker accepted the shipment, played with the extensive paperwork, then trucked it to the South Philly warehouse on Ninth Street. Not one to waste anything, Miceli removed the horse, then sold the tomato paste and cheese at large profits to the Italian Club and other controlled restaurants. It was another mob success story. An almost legitimate business turned over a legitimate profit besides the main, illegitimate one.

Miceli would sometimes joke with Jerome Ragni, "Hey, Jerry, maybe we stop scoring smack and we all get rich selling cheese."

Ragni, a distant cousin of some chubby aunt, was sole proprietor and owner of the business. At least on paper. He would always chuckle and answer, "Lotta money in cheese, Tony," and they would all laugh, as if it was Rodney Dangerfield's best one-liner.

Miceli snapped his fingers and said, "Reminds me, send some of that cheese to my mother."

"Done." Ragni handed the bill of lading to Miceli as he ran a manicured finger down a row of numbers.

"Get 1658, 1712, and 2397," he ordered. Ragni responded by moving toward wooden pallets stacked twenty feet high. The bogus importer found crate 93, removed number 2397, and cut an opening in the heavy cardboard box. Then he carefully took ten five-gallon cans of Sanuti Tomato Paste, placed them on a metal table, and started opening the cans with an industrial can opener. Miceli and Hard Rock silently watched until all ten cans were open.

"Go to lunch, Jerry," Miceli commanded.

"Want a sandwich or something?" Ragni asked on his way out the door.

"Pastrami on rye with mayo," Miceli said.

"Two hoagies with everything and a six-pack of Piels," Hard Rock ordered.

The two men were now alone. Hard Rock stuck a massive paw into a can of thick tomato paste. A smile came to the fat cheeks as he extracted a heat-sealed plastic packet and wiped it off. It contained eight ounces of 91%-pure heroin.

"What Vitali want?" Hard Rock asked.

"Pound of H and two keys of coke," Miceli said. "Handle it."

"Tomorrow?"

"Yeah, but run him around and clean yourself before the actual hand-to-hand." Miceli paused, "It's his first score. We can't be too careful."

"The usual?"

"Yeah."

Miceli handed Hard Rock a paper towel and asked, "Whatta you make of him?"

"An ounce guy moving up to keys." Then, "He's harmless, but his muscle pisses me off."

"You 'fraid of him, Rock?" Miceli taunted.

"Fuck!" Hard Rock growled. "I ain't afraid of him or any other living thing. I can kick his ass straight up."

"Sure about that?"

Just as Hard Rock was about to erupt again, Miceli held up a hand and said with a smile, "I'm jerking you around." Then he added seriously, "I know you can take him, but remember one thing. *Don't* take him or anyone else for granted, *paisan*, or you'll be sleeping with the fish."

Hard Rock grunted himself calm enough to remove the remaining ten pounds of heroin from the thick Sanuti Tomato Paste.

It was just 9 A.M. but Moose was already working on his third beer as he sprawled out on the gold velour couch. Looked like a beached whale, Lerza thought.

He passed the Moose on the way to the coffeepot. "Yo, mutant," he said. "Little early, ain't it?"

"Trying to get my blood sugar up."

One month had elapsed since their meet with Miceli and no contact; then a midnight call had come from Hard Rock with a delivery set for that night.

"Coffee was invented by God." Lerza took a long sip of the hot brew.

The Moose grunted and let out a fart that was an eight on the Richter scale. "Good one, eh?" Proudly.

"You're disgusting." Lerza laughed.

"Thanks."

"Whatta you think about tonight?"

"Don't trust Hard Rock."

"Good point. But he'll do what he's told, and tonight he's just a delivery boy."

"Still don't trust him."

"You don't trust no one," Lerza pointed out.

"I trust you." Defensively, "And you're just a midget, or is it dwarf? Maybe a little person. I never know what to call you freaks of nature, you're all so touchy."

Lerza moved over to the window and pulled aside the designer blinds. "Three wives, three divorces. *Now* I understand. When this is over *I'm* going to divorce you!" He chuckled and looked down on the street, said, "They're still there."

The Moose hoisted himself off the couch and stared over Lerza's shoulder. He said, "Dumb shits. They either want us to know they're a tail, or they flunked Surveillance 101." Even at twenty floors below, the blue Ford that had been following them for two weeks was unmistakable.

"Who *are* those guys?" Moose asked.

"Smell like us but that just don't add." Lerza was puzzled, too.

"Then who? Greasers? Scooter boys?"

Lerza finished off his coffee and said, "It's time to find out. I'm tired of me and my shadow."

They got dressed and made a plan. Not your classic law-enforcement-academy-approved, strategic, by-the-book plan. This was more your kitchen-table, back-alley plan using salt and pepper shakers, spoons, forks and beer cans to denote men, buildings, and cars. The two Vietnam grunts had made similar plans on the dirt floors of Southeast Asia.

Lerza maneuvered the Mercedes along the up ramp from the underground garage and turned south on Fourth Street. The Ford followed. At Washington Avenue he turned right. Five blocks later he pulled diagonally into a parking spot between two vacant tractor-trailers. Washington Avenue was wide enough to accommodate the eighteen-wheel semis filled with produce to be delivered to the Italian Market. On Sunday the district did not come alive until noon, two hours away.

Lerza cut the engine, exiting on foot and leaving Moose in the passenger seat. A tall, skinny, baby-faced guy in a gray overcoat got out of the Ford trying not to look obvious but doing it poorly. He just didn't belong at Ninth and Washington in the heart of Little Italy.

Lerza gave an instinctive touch to his Smith and Wesson .357 shoulder-packed Magnum. It felt good. He walked a city block, turned right, and repeated the drill three more times, circling back past the Mercedes. The baby-faced kid in the gray overcoat followed him like a bad hangover. The shadow never saw Moose's knee, which shot out from between the semis like a greased switchblade, knocking most of the oxygen from the tail's stomach.

Lerza continued his nonchalant stroll until he stood alongside the blue Ford with its remaining occupant. The guy looked confused. Lerza grabbed the door handle and in a split second was in the passenger seat, pointing Mr. Smith at the driver's belly.

He looked the guy over and realized he was a clone of the first joker. Clone Two and Lerza joined Clone One and

Moose in the Mercedes. Lerza stuck the Magnum barrel into Clone Two's ear. He said menacingly, "Now, the location of any guns, knives, or hand grenades."

"Revolver in shoulder holster," Clone Two said excitedly.

"Ankle holster," Clone One volunteered.

Lerza removed the two .38-mm. revolvers, but kept the chill in his voice. "No bullshit. I ask a question and you give an answer." He gave a slight twist to the gun barrel, causing severe ear pain in his captive.

He then demanded, "Who?"

Clone Two twisted uncomfortably. "Cred's inside suit pocket."

"What?" from an amazed Lerza.

"We're agents, just like you," Clone One explained.

The words rattled around Lerza's brain as he examined the familiar FBI identification credentials. Confusion turned to anger.

"Just like us!" he hissed. "You two back-stabbers are OPR spies. Don't even put yourself in the same sentence with brick agents."

Clone One mustered some instant courage. "We ID'd ourselves, Lerza," he challenged. "Now cut the theatrics or you two'll be in real trouble."

"Shut up, kid," Lerza snapped, winking at Moose. "Now the million-dollar question. *'Why?'* "

Clone One turned to face Lerza in the back seat. He said, "New procedures in undercover cases. Hell, your SAC knew. We're just doing our jobs."

Lerza held up the ignition key to the blue Ford and ordered, "You two are off the case."

"You don't have that authority," Clone One challenged.

Moose grabbed Clone One's fifty-dollar Ralph Lauren silk necktie; the color coordinated with his gray overcoat.

He pulled Clone One's head to within two inches of his own blazing eyes. He whispered, "If I ever see you or your friend again, I'll eat your nose right off your face." He emphasized the threat with a beer belch. Then added to the two agents, "It's Sunday, go golfing. We'll express-mail your weapons to the director's office."

Clone Two pleaded, "You know that'll jam us up."

Lerza opened the car door and said, "Just doin' *our* jobs. Bye!"

The two internal affairs agents glared silently back at Lerza and Moose as they exited the Mercedes. Definitely unhappy campers.

Lerza dialed Brad Keenan's home from the gas station phone. He heard the SAC's voice, "Hello," and Lerza hissed, "You son of a bitch."

Keenan recognized Lerza's voice. "What's the problem, Joe?"

"Trust."

"What are you talking about?" Keenan knew the answer.

Lerza was so angry it was hard to sound calm. "You know what. OPR putting a tail on us. *Why?*"

"To help you." Calmly. "In case you needed a way out. Another pair of eyes to back you on deals. If you knew they were there, it might make you careless."

"*Bullshit!*" Lerza's reply. "Try again, *sir.*"

Normally when an SAC gave an explanation, rare in the first place, it never got challenged, especially by a GS-13. Keenan had a choice. Pull rank and give orders *or* cajole, appease, and back off. He needed Lerza but, aside from that, the SAC recognized the demon in the undercover's voice.

"It wasn't my idea, Joe," came the copout. "New head-quarters' procedures. They're worried, Joe. Too many UCA's crossing the line. Now *I* realize what it's like out there. I know you can't always go by the book. *But* these HQ types live by the book. They don't understand that you sometimes have to bend a rule, write your own rules."

Lerza said calmly, "Call 'em off."

"It's not that easy."

"We got fifty thousand kids reported missing each year," Lerza said. "We got one hundred tons of dope crossing our borders weekly and the fuckin' Russians got more KGB agents employed at *our* embassy than we do *and* we're wasting manpower using agents to follow other agents!"

"Calm down, Joe." A plea.

"Look, Brad," Lerza continued. "These OPR hotshots are parading around out there in three-piece suits, blow-dried hair, and driving cars with blackwall tires and mini aerials. They're not street agents and they're gonna get themselves hurt."

Then fury took over again, and he shouted, "Worse yet, they're gonna get *me* hurt! Either get rid of 'em, or I will."

"I'll take care of it." Keenan relented and changed the subject. "Masters tells me you're making progress."

Lerza took a deep breath, realizing Keenan was just laying some kind of smokescreen. "We're holdin' our own, Brad," he said.

"Keep up the good work."

"Yeah."

"Good-bye, Joe."

"Good-bye, Brad."

Lerza slammed the phone back into its cradle and signaled Moose.

"I don't believe it!" he said to Moose.

"What'd he say?"

The two undercover agents began walking down Wharton Street toward the outdoor market. Moose knew Lerza well enough to know he was both hurt and angry.

"Gave me the expected bureaucratic babble." Added solemnly, "It's what he didn't say that scares me."

"Oh?"

"We're on our own out here, Moose. I don't trust Keenan, which means I don't trust the Bureau. I'm in this thing till it's done, but I'd understand if you'd want out now."

"What's the big deal, Joe?" Moose sounded calm.

"We just hit the trifecta," Lerza said seriously. "We're out here on the DMZ, just me and you. Ten minutes ago it was only the mob and bikers planting punji stakes and laying claymores. *Now* we add the FBI to that list, and the odds get shitty. You got a career and pension to think about. All I'm saying is that I'd understand if you got on a plane back to Pittsburgh."

Moose took a few steps, then stopped and eyed Lerza. There was a weird smile on his face as he patted Lerza's head. He said, a caring quality in his voice, "You're my buddy, munchkin. You're also terrible with your fist, a lousy shot, afraid of spiders, and a midget to boot."

As though it were all settled, he added, "Just think of me as your guardian angel, Joey. Besides, Airborne don't desert in combat—even a marine."

"Touching!" Lerza felt deeply moved but could only manage sarcasm.

"Yeah," Moose agreed. "I am some kinda regular fuckin' Hallmark card."

12

Laura Lerza was doing battle with an oven that was not self-cleaning. She desired the busy work to keep her mind occupied. The odor from the powerful chemicals mixed with her depression of the last few months put her on the verge of tears.

Laura rehearsed the speech to Joe in which she gave the ultimatum "The Bureau or me." She always backed off when his infrequent calls came, though. That was because even Laura somehow unconsciously linked Joe's undercover work with the Vietnam war, and she was not the type to "Dear John" her combat vet while he was overseas. Besides, she never really meant it; she just felt deep frustration and anger at not seeing him for long periods.

Laura remembered to look at the wall clock and said aloud to an empty house, "Crap, already time. No chance to clean up."

The doorbell rang on cue. She removed the rubber gloves, tucked in her shirt, and pushed uncooperative long, blond hair from her forehead. She thought, Of all days to look a mess.

Opening the front door, she held out her hand. "Hello, Patty. It's been a while."

Patricia Masters took Laura's hand and held it warmly. "How have you been?" she asked.

The two women had met several years ago in Cincinnati, when Joe and Patty first became partners. Under normal circumstances, they would have become fast friends. Their demeanors and personalities were much alike, and the friendship would have been warm and lasting. The kind with shopping-mall sprees, aerobics classes, and white-wine conversations about life. That never happened, because of Joe Lerza. Both women recognized somewhere deep within that it would be a mistake to start sharing secrets when, at some point, one or both would have to be dishonest.

"I'm doing fine," Laura lied. "And you?"

"No complaints."

Laura poured coffee, then pushed a plate of pastries toward Patty, and asked, "How's New York?"

"No white picket fence, but you can get Chinese food at three in the morning." Patty smiled.

Laura smiled back; they started the small talk. Ten minutes on fashion, ten on decorating the home, twenty on keeping in shape, five on the latest books they had read, and fifteen on how they could not find the time to do much of the above.

Finally Patty switched to Bureau business. She gave Laura pay stubs, U.S. Savings Bonds, new insurance forms, and other useless government forms already overdue, only useable by the people who created them.

"Joe usually handles all this," Laura said.

"It's a pain in the ass," Patty agreed. Then she asked, "Is there anything the Bureau can do for you?"

"Nothing, thank you."

"Kids okay?"

"Yes. They're great."

"Car and house shipshape?"

"Fine. Good as new."

"You okay?"

"Great."

"Are you absolutely sure?" Patty pressed. "Is there *nothing* you need?"

Laura suddenly heard herself sobbing, "My husband." The first tear to hit her cheek was swiftly followed by others.

Then it all came out, the truth. The kids were doing terribly. Marie missed her father so much that A's and B's had turned into C's and D's at school. Angie had almost become the first child ever expelled from kindergarten for constant fighting. The house was falling apart, the car was making loud noises and leaking oil.

The hardest part, she said, was trying to explain the phone calls from Joe. How do you tell someone that the man on the phone was no longer your husband, not the man who left four months ago. That he had been replaced by an uncaring, distant stranger who frightened her.

Patty walked behind Laura, weeping on the couch, put her hands on shoulders that shuddered between sobs. She waited until her almost friend calmed down, keeping one eye on the kitchen clock. She could not tell Laura she had just enough time to drive to the Triangle Bar and deliver $270,000 to her husband, who would then use it to buy narcotics from a psychotic backed by the Mafia. She could not tell Laura she would do everything in her power to bring Joe Lerza "in" from his undercover role. She could not tell Laura a lot of things but she knew her heart ached for the woman. Patty Masters vowed then and there that she'd do the "right thing." She'd force Special Agent Joe Lerza back to reality. By doing so, she'd save his life.

13

Romeo, the pizza boy, was screaming his third "Old Blue Eyes" in a row. Lerza and Moose sat at a table, waiting for Patricia Masters.

Drug deals excite undercover agents. That's what it's all about, Lerza thought, knowing he felt pumped up. He asked Moose, "What time you got, mutant?"

"Five minutes later than the last time you asked," Moose answered. "I gotta take a leak, wanna hold my watch?"

"Naw, Mickey Mouse would miss you."

Moose passed Patty coming in on his way to the toilet. "Hello, darlin'," he said. "You're lookin' good tonight."

She shrugged and replied, "And you, Russell, look good yourself."

"Does that mean I can tie you naked to a tree and roll hard-boiled eggs at you?"

"Cut the crap." Harshly, "I'm not in the mood."

Feeling awkward, Moose informed her, "I gotta go pee."

He said it like a little boy asking permission; she suddenly felt a strange kinship for this gentle giant.

"Just a bad day." Her voice was softer. "Sorry."

"Go get a drink, you'll feel better."

She joined Lerza at a back booth. He was twirling linguini on a fork. Romeo finished up his repertoire with "That's Life," and Rusty's trio took a break.

"Any word, Joseph?" she asked.

He looked up and said, "An hour ago. Looks like a dance."

"Why?"

Lerza waited for the waitress to take Patty's drink order, then said, "Hard Rock called the apartment and told us to be at a public phone, Broad and Snyder, by midnight."

"A definite dance," she agreed. "They'd never do it on the street."

Lerza caught a glimpse of Moose weaving his way back to the table. He asked in a hurried whisper, "What about the other night?"

"No need to worry," she assured him. "You were very drunk."

"Do me a favor and *forget* it," he said.

She gave him one of those smiles that melt glaciers and said warmly, "You are my friend, Joseph. Friends don't put conditions on their friendship. I—"

Moose interrupted, "I can't fuckin' believe it! Some guy just pissed on my new shoes in the latrine."

"I'll bite. Why?" Lerza chuckled.

"Ever see a drunk try to talk and pee the same time?" Moose asked indignantly. "The son of a bitch was cross-eyed to boot. Add it up and you got acid rain on my Buster Browns."

The waitress brought them fresh drinks and said admiringly of the singer, "That Romeo can sure belt 'em out."

Moose agreed, "I kinda like him."

"This round's on Lester," the waitress said as she placed the glasses on the table.

"Who's Lester?" Lerza asked.

"You seen him around," she said. "A regular here. Little guy, bald. Sits at the bar. Big wart on his nose. Got cross-eyes."

"Lester!" Moose said. "Him and me are buddies. Buy him one on us."

"You got it, honey." She walked off.

"Hope the son of a bitch chokes on it," Moose chuckled.

The three special agents started to sip their drinks. Patricia used the break to get down to business. "The serial numbers are all Xeroxed," she said, sliding a briefcase filled with $270,000 in hundred-dollar bills toward Lerza. "The digital metric scale and narcotics field test kits are inside, too."

Lerza tapped the Samsonite. "Recording equipment okay?"

She nodded. "Checks out fine."

"Good, we'll take it slow. Moose stuck an icepick in the Mercedes' taillight. Make it easy to follow us."

She smiled and said, "I haven't heard of anyone pin-holing a taillight in ten years."

"The ol' gimmicks are still the best," Moose defended himself. "Besides, they work. The problem with the 'new' Bureau is too much technology, not enough sleuthing."

"To you, indoor plumbing is advanced technology," Lerza said.

This triggered an exchange of eight or nine barbs, and when the two men ran out of verbal gas, Patricia said, "You two are worse than an old married couple."

"Bite your tongue, Patricia," Moose said. "I love this guy more than any of my wives."

"I hate it when he gets emotional," Lerza remarked, but with a smile.

Patricia realized the two men really did love each other; the insults were actually signs of affection, a way of relieving the tension that living on the edge brings. The *only* way this type of man could show affection. They were a dying breed, she thought, replaced by pretty boys who ordered the right wines at restaurants and went on Club Med vacations.

"You two do good. I'll see you tomorrow, hopefully to relieve you of the evidence. I got to keep a good chain of custody, right?"

"God forbid some technicality would give 'em walking papers," Lerza agreed. "See you tomorrow."

Masters rose to her feet and said, "We have to talk tomorrow, guys. It's important."

Once Patricia had left, Moose downed a shooter of Imperial and asked, "Tell her 'bout Keenan?"

"No."

"Why not? You trust her, don't you?"

"Shit, yes," Lerza said, almost ardently. "But she don't need the excess garbage. Besides, she's a big fan of the Bureau. I don't wanna break her bubble."

"That's it?" Moose gave his friend a serious look.

"That and the fact I don't want her involved in my—I mean 'our'—problems with the paper pushers."

Moose looked directly into Lerza's expressive brown eyes and asked matter-of-factly, "You don't think she's already involved?"

Broad and Snyder was a busy corner deep in the bowels of South Philly. Even at midnight you had an assortment of types not ready to end the day. Moose checked out the public phone near the McDonald's to make sure it worked.

Midnight came and went.

"Fuckin' drug dealers are all alike," Moose complained. "Should go to jail just for being late all the time."

"Patience, mutant," Lerza reassured him. "Probably got an eye on us right now. Sure be easy enough here."

At 12:33 the phone rang. Lerza grabbed it. "Yeah?"

Hard Rock's voice was unmistakable. "Take the subway north, get off at City Hall, stand on the compass."

"Cut the—" Lerza said, and the line went dead.

"Wants us to subway our way to Center City," he told Moose.

Moose had been chewing on an unlit cigar; now he cursed, "Son of a bitch! I gotta get the Mercedes a new taillight for nothing."

Lerza asked, "Whatta you think, Moose? Carrying more than a quarter-million dollars of taxpayers' money down into the crime pit at midnight don't make me all that happy. We could get ripped off by some innocent street gang before we hit Lombard Street."

Moose shrugged his shoulders and said, "Fuck it."

"Fuck it," Lerza agreed, then spoke for Patty's benefit. "Patty, if you copied our instructions, drive past McDonald's and turn right at Snyder."

The two men tried hard not to look directly at the nondescript Chevy carrying Special Agent Masters past them.

"See you at Billy Penn," Lerza said to her into his dime microphone.

The two undercovers descended the steps into the world of the Philadelphia subway system. Moose punched Lerza's arm, pointed at two hookers going uptown to walk South Street, and said, "Would you look at that!"

The old subway car rocked and rolled, the overhead lights blinking on and off. Their particular car had one of everything the night brings out. Hookers decked in microskirts and teased, multicolored hair. Students from Drexel and Temple. A gang of young punks bent on terrorizing anyone who would let them. Lerza unconsciously clutched the suitcase on his lap until his knuckles turned white.

The young punks stared hard at Moose then made a tactical decision to terrorize another subway car.

The statue of William Penn, founder of Pennsylvania, sat high atop City Hall, easily the most recognizable landmark on the Philadelphia skyline. It had its own subway stop. The complex of City Hall buildings boasted a massive courtyard at street level, with a thirty-foot brass compass denoting the exact center of the city recessed into the sidewalk. The compass was a conversation piece for the thousands of tourists traipsing through the historical city daily. But at 1:06 A.M. the courtyard was deserted, and the undercover agents' footsteps echoed soundly off the tallest structure in the city of Philadelphia.

"I got that old feeling," Lerza said, pacing nervously.

"What ol' feeling?"

"Nam. Night ambush. You know, like when you just knew you'd make contact with Charley."

"They were always out there," Moose reminisced, "with their slope-eyed sneaky booby traps, using our C-Rat cans to blow off a leg or arm. Fuckin' gooks."

"The hair on my neck would stand on edge just right before," Lerza recalled.

"My dick'd get hard," Moose offered.

Five minutes turned into twenty; now they both paced like expectant fathers.

Moose put another stogie in his mouth and commented, "Could be a rip."

"Naw," Lerza said. "Don't feel it."

Ten minutes later they heard it. Faint at first, then louder, as the sound of footsteps echoed in the courtyard and bounced off City Hall's outer walls. Adrenaline surged as the two undercovers placed their backs to the courtyard walls and waited.

Then someone was running right at them. Not an all-out sprint but fast enough, a determined trot. Moose and Lerza pulled their revolvers and sighted in at the footsteps. First a shadow in the dark square, then a definite form. Lerza calculated his leap to coincide with the runner's gait, timing it perfectly.

It all happened in a split second. In a textbook Weaver shooting stance, Lerza gave the runner just enough time to hit the brakes on his Reebok hightops, actually leaving skid marks on the compass. The undercover looked down his gun sights into the face of a scared fourteen-year-old Puerto Rican street urchin.

"Yo, man," the kid said excitedly. "This ain't worth no twenty bucks."

"What?" Lerza asked.

The Puerto Rican teenager grabbed his heart with a hand, flapped it back and forth. "You dudes scared the shit out of me," he said. "Put that piece down."

Lerza slowly lowered his weapon. "Tell me somethin' I don't know," he warned the youth.

"Some dude, a real *big* dude," the kid explained, "give me two sawbucks to deliver this." He handed Lerza a piece of paper.

Lerza took the paper and nodded at Moose to keep an eye on the street kid. He read the note silently, then handed a twenty-dollar bill to the boy and said, "Now get the fuck outta here."

"Ya don' have ta say that again, man." The street kid disappeared into the blackness.

Lerza read the note aloud to Moose: "Cab it to the Airport Sheraton, ask for the key in your name, wait in the room."

"Why all the games?" Moose asked.

"Criminal paranoia. Watching for a rip or a cop tail."

The Moose looked at his watch, finally lit the chewed-up stogie. "Asshole's gonna cost me my beauty sleep," he said.

For Masters's benefit, Lerza spoke into the dime, "Patty, I hope you copied. It'd be too risky to drive by and confirm we're being scoped. Your car could've been seen earlier."

Patricia copied the microwave transmission, on the verge of calling it all off. Whether it was intuition, overcaution, or a premonition, the bottom line was the knot in her stomach. Lerza's behavior and her visit earlier in the day with Laura made her feel like a crew member on the Titanic. She wanted to stop tonight. Instead, she found the entrance ramp to the Schuylkill Expressway and headed southeast toward the airport.

Thirty-five minutes later the two undercovers paced a typical motel room at the airport hotel. They were uncharacteristically quiet, even after checking the room for listening devices.

Lerza jerked visibly when the phone finally rang. He told the caller, "I'm getting tired of this shit."

"Shut up an' listen." The voice of Hard Rock. "Call room service and order a strip steak."

"Room service is closed."

"Just do it!"

"You—" The line went dead in his ear.

Lerza cradled the phone in his hand and said to Moose, "Bastard hung up on me again."

He dialed five; someone said, "Room service."

"This Mr. Vitali, Room 617. Is it too late to order?"

"No, sir." A friendly male voice.

"Two New York Strips, well done, with the works."

"That'll be twenty minutes, sir."

"Make it snappy, I'm starvin'," Lerza said.

Nineteen minutes later there came a rap on the door followed by the same friendly voice saying, "Room service."

Moose held his Magnum inconspicuously at his side as Lerza opened the door. Both agents immediately recognized the wise guy dressed in a bow tie and waiter's jacket pushing a cart topped with stainless-steel serving trays. The gun bulge on his hip and the sleazy stare were blatant.

"You have something for me?" the waiter asked.

"Don't make me laugh," Lerza shot back. "Where's the junk?"

"I think you'll find the steaks done to your pleasure," said the mob guy turned waiter.

Lerza jerked the top off one of the steel trays and saw the clear plastic baggies containing a white powdery substance.

"I'll need payment for your order *now*," the waiter pushed.

"Fuck you, greaseball," Lerza said. "The game ain't played that way. We test and weigh first."

Moose kept a quiet glare fastened on the mob delivery guy as Lerza expertly weighed the packets on the metric digital scale. Extracting random samples of powder from four packets, he placed them into Scott Reageant field test kits, broke the glass ampule, and shook the packet until the powder mixed with the chemical and turned a bright blue.

"It checks," he said, and repeated the process with the heroin.

Lerza nodded at Moose, who stood up and slid the money briefcase toward the waiter.

Lerza pointed a finger at the mob guy and said, "Tell your boss, he ever plays games again, the deal's off."

The LCN waiter did not bother with an answer on his way out the door.

"Now what?" Moose asked.

"Get some sleep. I'll take first watch."

"What?"

Lerza sat down at the round wooden table by the closed drapes. "Our wheels are still at Broad and Snyder. It's obvious we can't trust the hotel phone to get a ride, and we *ain't* gonna carry $270,000 worth of drugs out on the street at three A.M."

"Probably right," Moose agreed. "Besides, they won't risk a shootout in the hotel."

With that, the Moose kicked off his size-thirteen Tom McCann's and stretched out on the flowered bedspread.

"Night," he said and fell asleep in fifteen seconds.

Lerza thought, No conscience. To add insult to injury, his big friend started snoring, chain-saw sounds.

It had been weeks since Lerza had slept for more than a solid hour. He needed sleep but was afraid of it—sleep was his enemy, filled with a private horror. It was as predictable as night following day: sleep triggered the "dream," and the dream meant terror once again.

As the Moose slept, Lerza forced himself to keep awake just as he used to do on perimeter watch in the Nam. He went through the repertoire of tricks that combat vets used to deny unconsciousness. He paced, pinched himself, fantasized. He hummed, doodled, and daydreamed.

Thoughts of Patty Masters, Laura, his daughters, Brad Keenan, Michael Amato, Miceli, Hard Rock, the old policeman, and unknown people flicked through his brain like a damaged movie. The more he thought about it, the angrier he felt. This *wasn't* Vietnam and he *wasn't* in the Marine Corps anymore.

The packets of white powder were neatly stacked on the table where he sat.

He absent mindedly reached for one of the packets of cocaine. At first he squeezed the white powder through the plastic; then he tossed the packet in the air, playing catch with it. He thought, What does this all mean? Why do men worship this? Why are women willing to do anything for a few grams? Are we really doing any good in trying to stop the fire?

Would tonight even make a dent in the drug trade? Did anyone care? Could cocaine really keep you awake?

Before he realized what had happened, the packet was open and the white powder had spilled on the table.

14

Arny Tomossino switched. For three years he had regularly been scoring a key a week from Miceli's operation. At fifty g's a kilo, he could cut it three times then "ounce" it out to the shirt-and-tie crowd on Locust Street, the computer programmers, bank tellers, nurses, and other yuppies who supplemented their health-food diets with cocaine.

Arny conducted a strictly mid-level operation, but he made a good buck with all the trappings. He had the required entourage that ready coke brings, which includes a lot of cleavage and hangers-on. Arny also owned a new Corvette and a snappy apartment with yards of velvet and Mediterranean wrought-iron.

Greed can be a dangerous trait. When the Satans approached Arny and offered the coke at forty a key, Arny said, "You gotta be kiddin'."

But the Satans were not "kiddin'," so Arny said, "You got yourself a deal."

Arny was not the brightest guy in the world. He figured you changed drug suppliers the same way you did dry cleaners. While counting out his fifty thousand to Hard Rock one month, he said nonchalantly, "Hey, Rock, tell Tony this is my last score."

Big Mistake.

The Lincoln was full of Italians. Hard Rock drove; next to him sat Dominic and Norman Ciccini, two skinny brothers standing only five foot, two inches each; members in good standing with the Red Brigade terrorist group in Italy. Known as the "Butchers of Abruzzi," the Ciccini brothers were aficionados of sharp things like knives, hatchets, and razor blades.

The backseat of the Town Car was packed with 773 pounds of cousins from Palermo who specialized in car bombs, shotgun slayings, and bludgeonings to death.

Arny's apartment was one of those steel-and-glass, thirtieth-floor square apartment buildings with doormen sitting behind consoles resembling the instrument panels of spaceships.

"Tell Mr. Tomossino that Mr. Rock is here to pick him up," ordered Hard Rock.

"Yes, sir." The doorman punched buttons.

"Tony wants to see you," Hard Rock told a semi-frightened Arny when he came to the door.

The trip to Ragni's Warehouse was anything but relaxed. During the final five minutes Arny babbled incoherently to the six Italians, who had not said one word.

He kept on babbling as the bludgeoning expert knocked him almost senseless, then positioned him over a drain in the warehouse floor. The Ciccini brothers stripped Arny of his leather jogging suit and started the process of skinning him alive. It was definitely a lost and delicate art, the ability to cut no deeper than the first layer of skin, to actually draw little or no blood as their razor-sharp instruments peeled away what the doctors called epidermis.

Arny's screams were gut-wrenching; he was infinitely better off during his frequent faints. That was when the backseat cousins would shove amylnitrate up his nose, reviving him so he would not miss the precision cut.

Miceli's orders to Hard Rock had been, "I don't want the bastard dead. I want him a fuckin' walking example."

So the Butchers of Abruzzi kept him barely alive, and coup de grace'd the skinning by cutting off Arny's dick.

Arny survived the entire ordeal but never could get his heart back into the drug business.

15

SAC Brad Keenan's calm veneer masked the ulcer dripping inside his belly. Two years to go for retirement and he could pull the pin with a full pension, a paidoff house in Philly, and use all his local connections to land a cushy security job. Screw up, or piss off somebody at headquarters, and life would not be so simple. They would transfer him back to D.C., and he would have to do hard time at the cracker factory with an increased mortgage and zip connections.

He sat at his big desk on a dreary Monday morning feeling in a no win situation. Headquarters had ordered the undercover operation on the LCN and everybody knew undercover agents were time bombs waiting to explode. When the shit bomb did explode, the SAC would take the full blast. *And* with undercover cases, the bomb *always* exploded.

Keenan could see it happening; there had already been

two urgent phone calls from an agitated Patricia Masters, telling *him* to pull Lerza.

"Why?" he had asked.

She had gone into some psychological bullshit; he had stopped her in mid-sentence. "This kind of behavior is to be expected, Agent Masters."

The last phone call was the worst. She announced, "I'm coming into the office on Monday to get this settled."

"That won't be necessary."

"See you at nine A.M." She hung up.

Nine in the morning was fifteen minutes away now as Keenan readied himself for confrontation. The intercom interrupted his game plan.

"Assistant Director Webber on two," Betty Northrup announced.

Deputy Assistant Director Robert Phillip Webber, known also as "Blue Flame Bobby," was in charge of the criminal division of the FBI. He had the reputation of double-crossing his own mother if it meant he would get ahead. Blue Flame Bobby's rapid rise through the Bureau hierarchy was littered with the bodies of agents. His first ten years was an example of "taking credit" for other agents' work.

The FBI was the only law-enforcement agency that promoted without examination. You got ahead by riding in the right car pool or playing in the correct golf foursome. Many supervisors had never worked the streets, had never arrested anyone. It was a Wall Street–type career ruthlessness that Bobby relished. He thrived on veiled threats and enjoyed fits of laughter over a competitor's misery. Nobody liked the Deputy Assistant Director, but everybody kissed his ass.

Blue Flame began without formalities, "Brad, how's the Amato case?"

"The usual problems," Keenan said.

Silence, followed by, "Explain them."

"The undercover."

"There's *always* problems with those cowboys."

"Look, Bob," Keenan said earnestly. "This undercover's no kid. He's been deep two other times, wounded three times in Nam. He's a family man. It could have been a mistake putting him under again."

"What's the issue?"

"I don't have the whole story yet, but it appears he's getting too deep, losing identity, feeling paranoid. Has Vietnam flashbacks, emotional problems. You know."

"No, I don't know," Webber shot back. "Read him the riot act, remind the cowboy who he works for. Tell him to do his fuckin' job, Brad. Understand?"

"I'll try." He winced again.

"Do better than that."

"I'll handle it." Reassuring voice.

"Good." Webber relaxed. "Besides, none of it sounds too bad. You should hear the shit some of these undercover agents pull. Your prima donna doesn't sound too tough. They're all glamour boys, Brad. Out there drinking and screwing every night on Bureau money. Then try and make us think they have it rough."

"This guy's different," Keenan said. He had great respect for Lerza, his honesty and his belief in the work of the Bureau.

Webber's voice turned stern. "All we got now is a 'maybe' conspiracy with Tony Miceli and a one-count delivery charge on some unknown player in a waiter's outfit. Amato, Averone, none of the Satans even remotely tied in. We need three or more distribution counts with an intense white-collar follow-up investigation to indict the main subjects. The Director gets weekly reports on this. I'm telling you as a friend, Brad, don't let *your* undercover star jeopardize the operation or your career. Understand?"

Keenan clearly understood. He said, "It's handled."

"Good, Brad." Webber sounded almost syrupy. "How's that lovely wife of yours?"

"SUGAR and cream, Pat?" Keenan asked.

"Black, sir," Patty replied.

The SAC handed her a coffee cup and retreated to the safety of his massive desk. Patty looked at him, thinking, He's one of those men who always appear perfect, hair precise, trousers creased and unwrinkled, top shirt button secure, shoes shined, handkerchief delicately folded in the breast pocket of the jacket. And just a hint of expensive cologne, the kind that is not sold in drugstores.

She had dated this type, they always made her uncomfortable. French restaurants, weekends in the Hamptons, and high-performance cars. Seemingly perfect, yet somehow their humaneness was missing. On those rare occasions she shared her bed, it was usually with some guy who drank wine from a brown paper bag and cried at sad movies.

Keenan shifted in his large leather chair to sit even more erect. He asked, "So it went well last night?"

"Picked up the drugs early this morning," she reported. "It's been tagged and sent to the lab for analysis."

"Good work, Patricia. Or is it Patty?"

"Patricia," she heard herself say, just to be contrary.

"So, Patricia, what seems to be the problem?"

She leaned forward in her seat. "As I explained, sir, Joe's burnt out. I feel he's a potential danger to himself, and I'm recommending he be brought in."

Keenan said condescendingly, "What makes you *think* that Special Agent Lerza is, as you say, *burnt out?*"

She started at the beginning. She described how he was drinking a little too much. Confusing his identity by using the first person "I" when referring to his drug-dealing cover, and "them" when talking about the FBI. His paranoia of the Bureau. His constant references to Vietnam. Her conversation with Laura Lerza. And, lastly, Lerza's nightmare on her couch, when he kept screaming through most of the night. She knew Keenan would draw all the wrong conclusions about what had happened at her apartment, but that was small potatoes now.

When she finished Keenan said, "That type of behavior is typical, not dangerous. It means he has assumed his role."

Though he mouthed this aloud, little alarm bells went off in his mind. He recalled his recent phone conversation with Joe, the edge to his voice, the uncharacteristic way he spoke.

"I respectfully disagree," Patty said.

"You can disagree all you want!" Keenan snapped. "Who gave you a license to practice psychiatry?"

"Did you hear *anything* I said?" she asked.

"Did you hear what *I* said, Special Agent Masters?"

Masters rose from her seat. She turned her back to the SAC and slowly walked to the far wall. Her silence made Keenan uneasy. It made him think of a seething inactive volcano.

She walked back and said to him, pleading, "We're talking about one of our own. What happened to our one big happy family? Is nailing Amato as important as losing Joe?"

"You haven't said one thing to convince me that Lerza's in any danger. He's out there doing his job. He's a big boy, a good agent. He knew what he was getting into, and I don't want to have to remind you that you should begin to do *your* job."

"I *am*!" she shouted, banging her hand on his desk. "I'm

telling you someone is going to get hurt. I can't control Joe or Moose. I'm telling you to bring them in. *That* is my job, and if you don't act, I'm going on paper."

"Going on paper" was the FBI equivalent of Russian roulette. It was the trump card used as a last resort by underlings who tried to force action on sensitive matters. It meant stepping on heads. You only went on paper when you *knew* you were right, because you would definitely piss off the boss. The loaded chamber was in your hand if it turned out *they* were right, and you could expect transfer orders for permanent night duty in Buffalo. If *you* proved right, the gun went off in their hands, and what you put on paper ended up in the Washington *Post*. But it was a big gamble.

The bottom line was that Patty's concerns would be a matter of record and might force Keenan's hand.

Keenan leaned forward. He rested his elbows on the polished wood of his desk and began in a fatherly tone, "Look, Patricia, I realize you're under some stress, maybe some personal problems. You're an outstanding agent, with valued experience. The kind of agent that makes a good Bureau supervisor. When this case is over, I'm recommending you for a promotion."

Patty was silent, thinking, The bastard's trying to bribe me. "I don't think I'm management material," she told him.

"Why's that?" Keenan asked.

"Because if being a good Bureau supervisor means putting a case before my people, if being one of the boys means letting a life go down the tubes, if getting a big desk means ruining a family, if all of that means becoming like *you*, then I'd rather wash dishes!"

Keenan sighed. It seemed he could not win this week. First Lerza's call, now this G-man with tits talking to him as if he were a first-day rookie.

The edge returned to his voice as he dismissed her, saying, "This meeting is over, Agent Masters."

On the verge of angry tears, she stood up and started for the door. Reaching it, she turned and said in a low voice, "This meeting may be over, Mr. Keenan, but *I'm* just beginning."

I took a contract from Amato on Miceli."

"What?"

"I'm gonna hit Miceli," Lu told Acid.

"Can we trust Amato?"

"No."

"Then *why*?" Acid looked puzzled.

Lu popped two 'ludes and fired up a joint of dynamite Peruvian. He never showed the effects of the pharmaceuticals, the booze and the hallucinogenics he ingested daily.

"The old man thinks he's pullin' our strings."

"What you gettin' at, Lu?"

"Amato's gonna double-cross us," Lu said. "I saw it in his eyes."

"Then why ice Miceli?"

"He's dangerous. One way or another he has to die."

Acid had more questions. "They're gonna come at us,

ain't they? Whatta we get out of it? What about Miceli's goons? What about Amato's lifetime friends?"

Lu sucked in the Peruvian and said, "I smelled fear on Amato. He's a dead man, too. But him I'm gonna scare to death."

"How?"

"When it's time. First Miceli."

"Miceli's gonna be tough," Acid said. "Always surrounded by fat greasy wops."

"Pussy's a killer."

"What?"

"Called Dakota. She's Miceli's type."

A smile showed on Acid's face. He said, "Whew, Dakota! Whatta piece. When do you want it to go down?"

"Do it right," Lu said. "Let her dance a month or so. Get her face known around the club." Then asked, "What about Miceli's new customers?"

It took a moment for Acid to realize Lu had moved onto other business. He said, "Oh, yeah, some player named Vitali."

"Approach him."

"Why?" Acid protested. "Wait till Miceli's dead, then we got a fuckin' monopoly."

"Don't think, Acid, I'll do that," Lu warned.

Acid got the hint and asked, "Who's gonna do the hit?"

"I'll be the last person Miceli sees in this world." Lu's eyes had a faraway look. "In a way, I'm jealous. He gets to go to a better place."

Acid nodded, always uncomfortable when Lu pulled this Boris Karloff shit. On his way out the door, he turned to Lu and said, "I'll get ahold of Dakota, tell her to be cool. Tell her she starts at the Chassis next week."

"That's *all* you tell her," Lu warned.

"What 'bout the junkie?"

"Inform her she's hired a new girl, then give her some of mother's little helper."

Acid left the Satan president surrounded by a cloud of smoke, staring straight ahead but not really seeing. He could have sworn that the painting of Lucifer on the wall moved its eyes.

"GIRLS look at guys' crotches, Stormy?" Moose asked as he gazed up on the stage, which had six naked girls doing a special. Some local guy's birthday, and his buddies had bought him a chair dance, which involved six dancers sticking body parts in the birthday boy's face.

"All the time, Moose," Stormy replied, and lowered her head to give Moose's crotch a blatant stare.

He laughed and said, "Cut that out!" A warning, "I'm gettin' excited."

"Big trouble, Stormy," Lerza said seriously. "Better find a tweezers and magnifying glass."

Hanging out at the Classy Chassis was a necessity. It accomplished many things. Such as stroking the source, because if you ignored them too long, they had a tendency to return to the dark side. Also, most of the players came and went at the Chassis—this guy meets that guy, and you got a new connection.

Undercover work was all about relationships, and there were always surprises, always a new face. Undercover agents had to maintain their cover, play their role, keep their credibility. Some fringe guy sees you twice at a place, and they'll swear on their mother's grave you've been hanging there every night for a year.

In addition, the undercovers needed to find out why Satan's old ladies were employed at the Chassis. And last but not least, the undercovers hung out at this strip joint because it was fun to play grab-ass with naked women and get drunk. Moose had said incredulously on more than one occasion, "We get paid for this shit!"

"Who's the new dancer?" Lerza asked.

"Dakota," Stormy answered. "Damn good, the customers love her."

On stage Dakota begged to be noticed. Long muscular legs, a tight waist, and firm full breasts with protruding nipples. Coupled with this near-perfect body was an ability to dance. She abandoned her soul to the music, allowing the body to respond to some unseen force.

Lerza seized the opportunity to ask, "You check out the girls before hiring them?"

"Not really," Stormy said. "There's no way. I just give them a tryout, count the number of boobs, and watch them dance. If they're standing at the end of a song, I use them."

"Ever hire biker broads?" Lerza asked nonchalantly.

Stormy did not hesitate a second but replied, "*No*. Too much trouble."

"What kind of trouble?" Lerza pressed.

"You know. Bikers bullying customers. Drinking all my booze without paying."

Lerza had difficulty hiding his disappointment. "Never get tricked?" he asked.

Stormy seemed on guard now. "Well, maybe I might take on a girl without knowing she's a biker's old lady."

Lerza wasn't ready to confront Stormy. It was obvious she was lying, so the real issue was *why?* If he could figure that out he'd be able to deal with Stormy the Snitch. There was the slim possibility the Satan dancers had nothing to do with Lerza's undercover operation. After all, he'd never told her the FBI was interested in jamming the Satans. So her lie could be linked to something insignificant. Still, it was a major-league coincidence. The troubled agent sat there milling over the options.

If the Satans didn't make the approach, he'd know Stormy was tied to the bikers and had dimed him out. Yet Miceli had already dealt, so she was straight with him on that account—unless, maybe? Could be Stormy was just being choosy with her snitching. Maybe Miceli knew they were FBI. Maybe Lu knew. Maybe, maybe, maybe.

The combination of possibilities overwhelmed him, so he ordered a double Seagram's. Could be as simple as her being embarrassed she'd hired bikers' old ladies. Could be as complicated as an across-the-board double cross. Could be she was playing them *all* like some Spanish guy on a twelve-string guitar.

His headache was back, a steady throb that had pounded his brain every day since he'd gone under. The medicine came just in time—a double shot of Seagram's with a water chaser. It went down smooth, and five seconds later that great flush to the body and brain engulfed him. The whiskey worked its magic, and the headache started a slow retreat to the back of his brain.

"Hit me again," Lerza told the topless waitress.

He waited impatiently until she returned with the Seagram's, then gulped the shooter in a single swallow. The headache was all but gone now, replaced by that sometimes fatal feeling of just not caring.

"Fuck it," he said to Moose.

"Fuck it," Moose responded.

"What *are* you two talking about?" a totally confused Stormy asked.

Lerza ordered again and answered, "Boy talk."

Stormy said, "Tony's been asking about you."

"Oh?" He tried not to show his interest.

"Wants to know what you said."

"What'd you tell him?"

"That your customers thought the blow was dynamite."

"That all?"

Stormy spoke to Moose, "They worry about you."

"They should." Moose chuckled.

She leaned across the table and placed her small hands over Moose's massive paws. "Look, honey," she said seriously. "Hard Rock's threatened by you. He'd never say it, but he is. He's always got to prove himself, and the only way in his warped brain is to hurt people. I've seen him like this before, all worked up because somebody *could* be tougher than him. It drives him crazy." She squeezed Moose's hands and added, "Stay away from him, he's a time bomb."

The Moose smiled. "When this goes down," he said, "I'm personally gonna put the cuffs on him. Prison is a humbling fuckin' experience."

Dirty Denise interrupted their conversation to call Stormy to the phone.

When Stormy left, Denise asked Moose, "When you gonna take me out, babe, or maybe come to my place for dinner?" She emphasized the offer with a wink of false eyelashes that caused a minor hurricane.

"Pick out the furniture, darlin'," Moose kidded. "I'm the marrying kind."

Dirty Denise giggled like a schoolgirl and tugged at the loose elastic on her skimpy outfit. "Whenever," she said, and waddled away, trying for a sexy walk.

"I'm worried," Moose confessed.

"Why?"

"Dirty Denise is starting to look good."

"She'd be an improvement, big guy. You've been known to mate with creatures from the deep."

"Ugly rumors, Joey," Moose replied. "That one girl hadn't worked in a circus for eight years."

"Can I sit?" a female voice suddenly asked.

The two men turned and came face-to-breast with the lovely Miss Dakota.

Lerza pointed to an empty chair and watched as the dancer slithered toward it. In one delicate hand she held a flimsy T-shirt, which she slowly stretched onto her body. The T-shirt did little to hide world-class tits.

"I'm Dakota," she announced.

Lerza smiled and said, "I'm Joe Vitali, and this is Moose."

"I noticed you two right off." She smiled and looked even sweeter.

"Are we that outstanding?" Lerza asked.

"Let's just say 'interesting.' "

It was rumored at the Chassis that Lerza and Moose were dealing coke, that was their role. Consequently, the dancers were now flirting, trying to score free blow.

"Whatta you drinkin', darlin'?" Moose asked.

"Bourbon, rocks."

When drinks arrived, Dakota told them she had just come in from Los Angeles. She missed the sun, but the East Coast guys tipped better than the cheap West Coast fag freaks. She had always wished to be a dancer, had started out in ballet. She had been a headliner in L.A. And, *no*, she was not involved with any guy at the present time.

Then it was their turn. They were in the import-export business (chuckles all 'round), liked to party, had a lot of free time.

"You get high?" she asked.

"Never!" Their standard reply.

"Word is I could cop from you," she pressed.

"Ugly rumors." They laughed.

Ninety percent of the topless dancers went on stage high, but the FBI did not target users and low-level dealers.

Dakota sipped the bourbon and started playing footsies

with Lerza. It felt good, so he let it happen. They made more small talk before Dakota got down to basics.

"Why pay more?" she said suddenly.

"What?" Lerza asked.

Her foot returned to the floor, her smile disappeared, her voice turned businesslike. "You pay forty a key for coke, already stepped on," she said.

"Whatta you talking about?" Lerza asked.

The rules dictated you never admitted anything to an unknown player. He or she could be a snitch for the locals or even another undercover for DEA. Looking at Dakota, Lerza ruled out the latter.

She continued, unperturbed, "I have some friends who can supply you with pure shit for thirty a key."

"Drugs are illegal." Lerza tried to sound offended.

"I like games." She smiled again. "Let's just suppose, then, that *if* you ever wanted to save a whole shitload of money, there'd be no harm in just discussin' it with my friends, huh?"

"We ain't interested," Lerza said. "But *if* our curiosity gets the best of us, we'll let you know."

"I'm here all the time, cutey."

Lerza, recognizing this for the Satan move they'd been waiting for, asked, "Your friends got names?"

"They're shy." She smiled, then got to her feet. She seductively removed the sheer shirt, exposing those spectacular breasts. Then she threw her shirt at Lerza and said, "Maybe sometime soon *you* can take it off for me."

After she left, Moose said, "Bodacious ta ta."

17

Patty Masters executed a series of karate kicks in an attempt to work out her frustration. Sweat dripped from her naked body onto the apartment floor. Martial arts was much more than self-defense. It was a way of life. A total life-style that included no red meat, meditation, and the ability to quote Far Eastern philosophy when the occasion dictated. Patty often daydreamed of being born in another time and place. A time and place of inner peace, gentility, and spiritual pursuits. Then the reality of her current surroundings would inhibit the fantasy.

Callused heels shot out like laser beams, followed by a series of spins and twists that would put Nureyev to shame.

"Focus," she kept reminding herself. "I have to focus." She wanted to block out mental obstructions and gain perspective.

Masters had called Lerza's undercover apartment four times since leaving Keenan's office. The decision had come easy. She had risked her career to do the right thing. She'd try everything to bring Joe Lerza "in." But the decision was the easy part because, without Keenan's support, doing it would prove difficult.

One last series of intricate moves followed by time-honored Oriental breathing and stretching techniques. Finished, she dialed Lerza's number again.

"Yeah." Moose sounded belligerent.

"It's Joe's sister. Is he there?"

"Hold on a sec, Patty."

Twenty seconds later Lerza asked, "What's up?"

"Grocery shopping."

"Can it wait?"

"I'm out of everything."

This pre-arranged code meant she had to have a face-to-face with him ASAP.

"See you in thirty minutes." He hung up.

"What's she want?" Moose asked.

"Dunno. But it'll give us a chance to run Dakota past Patty." He took time for a quick bourbon and Coke before heading toward the garage. Was he drinking too much, he wondered, and concluded not enough.

Pat's Steaks was a landmark in South Philly, crowded even on this dreary March Monday. Lerza arrived before Patty, ordered "two with to go"—two of the best cheesesteak sandwiches on the planet.

He sat in the Mercedes, watching first- and second-generation Italians stroll around Ninth and Wharton. Patty soon drove past in her Chevy, obviously looking for a parking space. A few minutes later she walked toward him as if she were on an escalator, gliding an inch off the concrete. She wore her deck shoes, sweat socks, jeans, and pea jacket the way other women wore Oscar de la Renta.

"Want a treat?" Lerza pushed a sandwich at her.

"No, thanks."

He sensed her nervousness. "Everything okay?" he asked.

Patty had given a lot of thought to the best way to approach him. But now, sitting next to him, her mind went blank. He finished the first sandwich and started unwrapping the second when he remembered something important.

"Before you begin," he said, "I need you to check out a dancer at the Chassis, street name of Dakota. Could be a snitch."

"What's your read?" she asked automatically.

"Made a pitch to lowball Miceli, so she's either a front for the Satans, a snitch for the locals, or a freelancer."

"I'll check her out," Patty said.

They were interrupted by a couple of twelve-year-old tough guys with leather jackets and cigarettes stuck behind greasy ears. The two delinquents grab-assed around, banging into the Mercedes, laughing and screaming obscenities, mostly for effect. When they got no reaction, they moved on.

Masters thought, Now or never.

"Joseph," she began, "we're friends. Right?"

"Old friends," he agreed.

She looked him straight in the eye. "Friends can be honest with each other," she said. "Even if what they say might offend. Right?"

Lerza said, "Right," again, feeling like a witness on cross-examination.

"Sometimes a person loses perspective, especially on our job, and especially in undercover work."

"I don't like where this is going," he said.

"Hear me out, Joe," she pleaded. "A favor for a friend."

Lerza forced a smile and said, "Go on Patty—friend."

Masters decided to reinforce her own opinion. "I met with Laura recently. She's afraid, Joe, that—"

He interrupted, "Of what?"

Patty spoke calmly, trying to diffuse what she sensed was his growing anger. "She's afraid of losing you. Laura feels this case is affecting you. She's seen you in other undercover cases. This time it's different. Laura said she hasn't seen you like this since you got back from Nam. Your wife is worried, Joseph. Worried that you're taking this one too personally. She's fearful that you won't come back to her the same man. She's pertrified that you may not even come back at all."

"Laura's a civilian, Patty," he said. "She has no idea what we do, the way we have to act to make a case. The way to deal with these scum, the way we talk to them. I've been deep before, and when I surfaced I was fine. Back to being a father, husband, and PTA member. It's no different this time. Laura knows what I do for a living. She better accept it and stop complaining."

"She loves you, Joseph," Patty said, then paused. "I care, too, and I'm not a civilian. You've been under a lot of stress. It's understandable."

"What are you talking about?" Lerza challenged.

She began to talk to him as if he were a loaded gun with the trigger cocked. She needed to deal with the facts and not her feelings. Joe would respond to logic better than emotion. But where did fact begin?

As his control agent, hypothetically she could terminate Lerza's assignment. It was SOP in the Bureau undercover handbook: "If in the opinion of a UCA's control, the Undercover Agent is exhibiting behavior detrimental to himself, others, or the specific case, then, upon concurrence with the Special Agent in Charge, the Undercover Agent will immediately terminate his status role."

But Masters, unfortunately, realized two things. Lerza was not a person to be told anything, especially with his current mind-set; and, second, SAC Brad Keenan refused to concur with Patty. That left her with persuasion, cajoling, and their own personal history—whatever that was.

"I'm asking you to come in," she said.

Lerza pointed an accusing finger at her. "Maybe it's you who's crazy. We got these dope dealers right where we want them. The case is goin' great. *Why* would you ask me such a bullshit thing?"

Masters's voice was brittle. "Because I care. Because you're on the edge. I truly believe someone's going to get hurt, Joe, and it's probably going to be you. Because I don't want to see it."

She watched his face as she spoke. It was an angry, confused mask of defiance. A caricature of the man she knew and loved.

Lerza said, "We're FBI agents, not social workers. You're a control agent, a professional."

"Even FBI agents are human, Joseph." She sighed. "They have problems, they make mistakes, they sometimes need help."

"Problems!" he spat. "Like head problems. You calling me a head case? You sayin' I'm nuts?"

"Come on, Joe," she said softly.

The two old friends fenced verbally for a few minutes. Lerza hoped it was one of those conversations where you just talked through until one person got tired and quit. Masters hoped he'd miraculously agree and resign himself to a graceful exit. She painstakingly explained how they could rationalize Joe's exit to Miceli and the rest of the players: "a bullet warrant," "had to get out of town for a few weeks," "deal with Moose while I'm gone."

Lerza finally asked, "What'd Keenan say?"

"Does it matter?"

"He's the boss," Lerza mocked. "He's also a snake."

"Well, I'll tell you anyway. Our SAC thinks I'm off base, that you're doing a good job. That I'm the one with a problem. But Brad Keenan doesn't care about you, Joseph—I do. You were right about him. He is a snake, a bureaucratic python who'd sell you out the first time the boss mongoose looked him in the eye. You're just a pawn in Keenan's career. A nameless, faceless pat on *his* back at some retirement dinner. Yes, Joseph, our SAC thinks you're doing just dandy."

"Then back off," he snapped.

"I can't!" Sadness in her voice.

"You have to." A demand in his.

She reached across the car and touched his hand. He recoiled as if he'd been stung by a bee.

"I thought we were friends," he said caustically. "Friends don't pull this kinda shit. Career suicide with a push from you."

"Come off it, Joe. This isn't about your career. This isn't even about the Bureau anymore. It's about someone who's lost all perspective. Who's pushed his loved ones away. Who would rather get his emotional rocks off by playing tag with other head cases who at least have the sense to realize their reality."

She was silent a moment, then went on, "I am your friend, Joe Lerza, and that's why I'll risk that friendship if it means saving your ass."

"You know," Lerza said evenly, "I used to think you were one of us. You know, the 'balls to the walls' agents who'd rather arrest people than sit around and talk about what secretary is screwin' what agent. Different than them other petty asshole agents. Someone I'd trust to cover my back. But now," he almost hissed, "it turns out you're some kinda PMS bitch."

Masters reached for him again, but he brushed her hand away and shouted, "Maybe *you* should get off the case. Maybe you're the one on the edge. Or maybe you're just on the rag and need to mother somebody, 'cause the fuckin' FBI can give you everything but kids!"

She kept the tears inside, but the hurt had to show. She had never seen *this* Joe Lerza. An angry Joe, yes. A fearful Joe. An excited Joe. But never a hateful, vengeful Joe Lerza. She had gone for the last resort—a human, direct plea. Without Bureau support, she couldn't force him off the case. Couldn't make him go home and relax. Couldn't get him away from the danger that awaited. Her options were limited. Patricia Ann Masters could request a transfer back to New York. She could even quit the FBI, but that would amount to deserting a friend in need.

Helplessness was a new feeling to Special Agent Masters, and it pissed her off. The only *real* choice she had was to stick it out. Buy a ticket and hope the roller coaster didn't derail.

She grabbed the door handle, jerking it open. "I'll check out Dakota," she said angrily. "If it is a Satan move, when's the meet?"

Lerza recognized his victory and said, "I'll set it up in a week."

She started to leave, feeling totally dejected, the meeting a failure. Lerza asked, "No hard feelings, Patty?"

She stepped on the sidewalk, then turned back for a moment. She said to Lerza, "Sometimes, Joseph, you are a total asshole."

18

So, Michael, what's so important that you had to wake me up last night?" asked One Punch Averone.

"Eat first, then business." Amato poured a generous amount of Vermouth into a cup of espresso coffee. Thirty pieces of rich Italian pastry filled with thick cream lay enticingly on Amato's desk.

The Don's limo had fetched Averone earlier in the morning, following a late-night call and the message, "It's important to see you, William, tomorrow morning." Amato more than just asked, he ordered.

Averone sipped the spiked coffee and devoured the pastries like any terminal cancer patient who had long ago stopped worrying about weight.

"You shouldn't have been so generous," Averone said.

"Why not?" Amato laughed. "Grandchildren marry only once."

"But kids nowadays are handed too much without having to sweat for it."

"You and I know how to sweat, my friend, that's for sure. Remember the restaurant?"

They both chuckled at the mention of the restaurant.

Amato sipped his coffee, said, "Such good times we had at that place."

"You were a terrible waiter," Averone accused.

"And *you* were a horrible cook."

"The good ol' days, eh, Michael?"

"Yes, so simple. When men had honor." The Don almost sighed.

He stood up, went to his desk, unlocked a drawer, and removed a stack of official-looking papers. Motioning Averone to the couch, he fumbled with a pair of bifocals and began unfolding the documents.

He began solemnly, "Very soon we will both meet our maker. I regret little of my life, as I'm sure you do, but it is important that we leave this earth with peace of mind."

"You talk like a priest giving last rites," Averone said. "Please, tell me what is on your mind."

"I need your help."

"Anything."

"Remember the promise I made to you, William?"

"I remember that promise."

"You must help me keep my promise."

"It is done," Averone said with finality.

"You know of our problems," the Don began. "Both from within our own organization and from the persistent FBI."

Averone chuckled. "The feds are like fruit mosquitoes. Always nearby, pestering, sometimes landing on exposed skin, but mainly just threatening to land."

"They are much more than harmless pests," the Don said. "Our photographs sit on their desks. Agents park our cars at restaurants, serve as our waiters. Their surveillance vans sit outside our homes. They attend our daughters' weddings and our brothers' funerals. They put listening devices in our kitchens, offices, and social clubs. They threaten our friends with jail for the smallest detail of our activities. Their undercover agents attempt to find any weakness in our defense. That is why I have not allowed *Coda Omertus*. They are always nearby, my friend. And they get closer each day. This is why I must do something extreme. This is why I need your help."

Averone protested, "But they have always done these things. Occasionally these swine are successful, and a friend goes to one of their prisons. But the code of silence is strong. Our brothers do not cooperate. The feds are angered at their resolve, their willingness to sacrifice. Our men are willing because they know that their families will eat while they rot in jail. Their children will be sent to the finest schools, their wives and mothers will be surrounded by our wives and mothers."

Amato knew it would be difficult. Their world had always been black and white. The "mob family" were the good guys, everybody else—bad. It was a way of life, a total belief in something that should *never* change. *Never* bend. Averone was merely mouthing the objections Amato had already mentally wrestled with in the preceding months. The Don tried again.

He said quietly, "If it was just the feds, but now we have a fight with the deceit from within. From our own. This is unprecedented. I have unwittingly painted the old guard into a deadly corner. Miceli's demise is necessary but tricky. It can backfire. Besides, the Satans are a third worthy opponent that we cannot forget."

"Bums," Averone interjected.

"Yes, but lethal in their own way."

Amato put a friendly hand on Averone's shoulder. His face wrinkled. Deep in thought, he was searching for the right words. He said after a full moment, "I have given this matter much consideration, William. What I ask is not asked lightly. It is time to wipe the slate clean. To eliminate the sickness from within our organization, and the leprosy eating away at our flesh. The world that we knew is over; the times have changed, my friend. We can no longer control the corner store taking book, or the teamster official, or the young slick congressman."

He paused, then went on. "Those days are forever gone. In our twilight time we must think of a peaceful ending. A reward for the years of hard work. We owe nothing to Miceli's generation, and if we don't act soon, it will be him, along with the FBI and the Satans, that will leave us with *nothing*!"

Averone lowered his head and said, "Instruct me, my padrone."

In the next hour Michael Amato, Philadelphia crime boss, asked much of his friend William Averone. He asked him to accept the end of the Philly family. He asked him to trust blindly. In short, he asked him to betray all his instincts. Even with the cancer guaranteeing a eulogy in ninety days, Averone had trouble accepting what his ears heard. But in the end, he knew he would do whatever his best friend asked.

Amato tapped a stack of stocks and bonds. "Sell all at the current value," he said. Then he pointed at deeds to some very expensive real estate. "Liquidate at fair market value," he ordered.

The Don gave similar instructions for the remaining documents, which included the location of safety-deposit box keys; secret bank accounts in Europe and small Mediterranean islands; partnerships with legitimate businesses; assumed-name industries; rights to oil fields in Texas, coal mines in Pennsylvania, and cattle in Oklahoma. Averone was overwhelmed.

Amato tightened his reassuring hand on Averone's shoulder. "I want you to sell *everything*," he said. Take the cash and divide it equally among these men." Amato handed him a list of twenty names. "These men have been loyal soldiers for many years. The money will care for them and their families for life."

"You still haven't told me why?" Averone pressed.

"Because it's the right thing to do," Amato said simply.

19

Patty forced herself to make a conscious effort to keep on the go. She filled her days with busy work—contacting the Philly Police Department, the Drug Enforcement Administration, the Bureau of Alcohol, Tobacco, and Firearms, and even the Sheriff's Department. The conclusion was that Dakota wasn't a snitch.

Finally, when she could avoid it no longer, she dialed the apartment. Lerza answered, "Hello."

"It's Sis."

An awkward silence, then, "Hi, Sis. I've missed you."

"Likewise." She felt relieved. "Just wanted to let you know that cousin George didn't get that job."

"Oh?"

"No. So good old George is unemployed."

"Then I'll make a call and set up a job interview for good ol' George."

"That'd be great," she said. "Call me when it's set."

She did not want to hang up but did not know what to say.

Lerza made the move. "I'm sorry about the other day."

"Me, too."

"Then let's forget the whole thing, okay?" Almost a plea for her approval.

If she said yes, it would mean she agreed that everything *was* okay even though it wasn't. If she said no, this would reopen wounds, which accomplished nothing.

She finally said, "Okay."

Lerza hung up feeling good; he needed Patty for the case and, if he admitted it, he needed her for his sanity. She had become an anchor for him, temporarily replacing Laura, his mother, his fat Aunt Cecelia, and all the other significant females left behind in the real world. Another pitfall of undercover work was the transfer of feelings to the people you lived and played with every day. Basically hookers, snitches, criminals, and other undercovers.

Lerza found the Moose working on a triple-decker sandwich that included assorted meats, cheeses, onions, garlic, olive oil, mustard, and his personal trademark—crushed potato chips.

Lerza said to Moose, "Go to the Chassis tonight. Arrange a meet with Dakota's friends."

The Moose's creation dripped disgustingly all over the table. He smiled. "I can handle that."

"I'll bet you can."

"Girl's got great tits, munchkin."

"World class," Lerza agreed.

"Does this mean she ain't a snitch?"

"Gotta be a Satan slut."

"Maybe we can reform her."

"And maybe Ollie North and Gordon Liddy are fags."

"Whatta you gonna be doin' while I'm getting eye-strain?" Moose asked.

Lerza grabbed a Budweiser from the refrigerator and said, "*If* Dakota is a Satan front and *if* Stormy's in bed with them, as soon as we agree to meet one of two things will happen real soon and—"

"Allow me," Moose interrupted. "One would be either Stormy or Dakota calling them scumbag maggots ASAP."

"Good guess," Lerza said. "The other being only Dakota contacting them. Which'll probably mean Stormy's straight."

"That's gonna be tough to find out, what with phones and all."

"Maybe," Lerza mused, "but I sorta hinted to Stormy that her business phone was tapped. A safeguard. Routine."

"Devious, real devious, buddy. So one of 'em *has* to use a pay phone *or* actually meet with the bikers."

"Right. And since we'll set the meet for tomorrow, they have to get hold of the Satans tonight, one way or the other."

"What's the plan?" Moose asked.

"You tail Dakota. I'll bumper lock Stormy."

"Let me get this straight, Joey. I go to the Chassis and tell Miss World Tits we meet?"

"Right."

"I eyeball the pay phone till closing, then tail her?"

"Right."

"Meanwhile, you watch Stormy to see if she makes a move?"

"Your deductive reasoning amazes even me." Lerza smiled.

Moose ripped open a packet of peanut M&M's and put

enough in his mouth to choke most mammals. "It's got holes," he said. "What if Dakota or Stormy makes the call from their apartment? What if they get someone else to contact the bikers? What if they do it tomorrow morning? What if—"

"Whoa!" Lerza interrupted. "I admit it ain't perfect, but it's something."

"You're right," Moose conceded. "Besides, I hate it when I think too much."

"I'm biting my tongue." Sarcastically.

"You Disney characters are real funny," Moose countered.

"Save any food for me?"

"Made you a sandwich, buddy. Bologna and peanut butter."

Lerza grimaced. "Beats C-Rats."

"Hey, Joey, remember ham and lima beans?" Moose laughed.

Lerza shook his head sadly. "So foul the Vietcong wouldn't even use the cans for booby traps."

"I kinda liked ham and mother's lima beans," Moose said wistfully.

"How come that don't surprise me?"

Moose jumped up, grabbed a broom from the pantry. "The Nam," he said as if remembering something pleasant. "Right shoulder, *Ha!*" He yelled, then executed a near-perfect close-order drill maneuver with the rifle broom, bellowing, "Present arms!"

Lerza got into the act. "Platoon, port arms, double time—huh!"

Moose responded with a slow trot around the kitchen table, singing, "Goin' to Vietnam, Gonna kill some Cong, rifle in my hand, I'm a happy man. Hey ho!"

·　·　·

DAKOTA slithered onstage like the devil himself on the apple tree in Paradise, with Moose in the role of Eve in the audience. She ground her midsection in his direction, simultaneously darting a tongue like an arrow leaving the bow.

Dirty Denise caught the action as she approached Moose. "AIDS," she said.

Moose turned to her and protested, "I only got eyes for you."

"You're full of it." Contempt in her voice.

"I am that, darlin'."

"The usual?"

"A double usual."

He had to wait ten minutes for Dakota to make her move.

"Where's your friend?" she asked, taking a seat.

"You writin' a book?"

"He's cute." She smiled.

The Moose downed a shooter of Imperial and said, "He thinks you got great tits."

"I do."

"He also wants to meet your friends."

"I thought he would."

"Tomorrow."

Moose fired up one of his big, cheap cigars. "Where?"

Dakota could not hide her smile. "Chandy's on the Black Horse Pike in Jersey at midnight."

"Who do we meet?"

She chuckled aloud and said, "They'll find you."

"Inside joke?"

"Sorta. You won't be sorry."

"I'm never sorry, darlin', just careful."

"Tell your friend to call me." She stood up.

"He never mixes business with pleasure."

"Too bad. He's cute." She pursed her lips.

As Dakota headed back into the darkness, Moose said aloud to himself, "Great tits."

She turned, smiled seductively, and said, "I know."

He spent the next few hours slugging shots of Imperial and watching the pay phone. Dakota spent her time hustling drinks and dancing. Lerza was somewhere outside waiting for Stormy, who had been in and out of the office. Closing time in thirty minutes.

Moose spotted them right off and knew it was trouble. Hard Rock and his Red Brigade friends marched through the front door, headed his way. It was not that Moose was afraid, just that he was not in the mood. They reached his table and surrounded it, Hard Rock acting as their point man. Placing both hands on the small cocktail table, the massive Sicilian bent at the waist, his face inches from Moose.

He mocked, "How you doin', tough guy?"

"No way outta this, huh?" Moose said in an inaudible voice, speaking to himself.

Hard Rock was like the feature act at the Copa, playing to his audience of flunkies. "Don't look the same with your clothes on," he said, turning to the Red Brigade guys, who laughed on cue.

Moose instinctively knew not to kiss Hard Rock's ass. If he did that he would lose their respect. And if he tried to leave he would lose self-respect. A definite "no-win" situation.

Fuck it, Moose thought. He hissed, "Hey, asshole, your mother still screwing mountain goats in the ol' country?"

It took several seconds for Hard Rock to digest the words. The only thing really sacred to an Italian man is his mother. It was the worst insult imaginable.

The Rock swung his hardest haymaker at the Moose, who slipped it with ease. The undercover was on his feet, choosing the most available target among the Italians. This only angered the Sicilian more; he responded by reaching for his nine millimeter.

"*Fermata!*" screamed Miceli from somewhere nearby.

Miceli continued with rapid staccato Sicilian, half ordering, half pleading with Hard Rock. It could have gone either way at this point if Miceli had not taken hold of the giant's arm and eased it away from the automatic pistol.

An enraged Hard Rock glared pure hatred at the Moose, who decided to rub the Italian's nose in it. He smirked and said in an exaggerated effeminate lisp, "You're sweet, you really are. But you seem to have a jealous boyfriend. Maybe some other time when he's not around, darlin'."

Moose could have sworn little puffs of smoke came out of Hard Rock's ears. Miceli gave a last barrage of foreign commands before the mob's most violent psychopath turned and left the club.

Even Miceli took a deep breath and said to Moose, "If I didn't need the business, you'd be dead."

"Sure 'bout that?" Moose taunted.

"Dead sure."

"Next time, don't do me no favors." Moose's voice was low and even.

STORMY worked the gears on her Trans Am, weaving the flashy car toward her Walnut Street apartment. It was an easy tail for Lerza because of the late hour. She found a parking space half a block from her place, then disappeared into the four-story renovated walk-up.

Lerza got lucky; there was a convenient fire hydrant. He parked by it, from where he had an unobstructed view of Stormy's front door.

Thirty minutes passed before he decided he was wasting his time. While reaching for the ignition, he saw an old van double-park alongside Stormy's apartment house. The driver cut the motor and stepped out directly beneath a street lamp.

Lerza recognized the face of the Satan vice-president from his Philly PD arrest photo.

Acid strolled directly into Stormy's building.

20

Patty Masters dialed the private number of Dr. Donald Thompson. She was determined to enlist the aid of the Board certified psychiatrist on retainer to the FBI.

"Do you remember me, Dr. Thompson?" she asked, after giving her name.

"Of course, Patty. How are you?" He sounded delighted she had called.

It had been only a few months since their initial briefing by him at the Bellevue Stratford Hotel. Patty vividly recalled Thompson's prophetic caveat in pronouncing Lerza fit for undercover duty. He had said, "Your Vietnam experiences, your personality—someone like you can only take so much, then—" and never finished his prophecy of doom. But the warning was clear, "If you go deep again, you risk your sanity."

Patty desperately needed the psychiatrist's support, his professional detachment from the Bureau, which gave him authority. She couldn't convince Keenan to bring Lerza in, but Thompson could.

"I need your help, Dr. Thompson," she said.

She started at the beginning, careful to avoid opinions and layman diagnosis as she spun the Lerza saga. Thompson interjected an occasional "yes" or an "ahem" but remained uncharacteristically silent. When Patty had finished, the FBI psychiatrist said, "I'll be in Philadelphia tomorrow morning."

Thompson *had* to observe Lerza personally, she felt. Otherwise, it would be that hysterical bitch Masters over-stating the undercover's behavior. But how to get Lerza to sit down with a shrink? Patty's options were limited. Trick him and risk open hostility, or be brutally honest. She decided on honesty.

She dialed his number and at once launched into the reasons why he should see Dr. Thompson. "He'll be objective, Joe," she said. "There's no shame in it. I'll abide by his opinion and get off your ass. You owe it to your family."

Lerza was far from enthusiastic. He said, "I ain't ready for the rubber room. You just do your job, and I'll do mine." Then he added, "Thompson gets paid to see wacko behavior. What's Keenan paid?"

She had no intention of telling Keenan about the FBI psychiatrist's forthcoming unorthodox "house call." This was her limb, and she'd climb out to the end of it and wait for the Bureau's push, but she'd be falling on her own terms.

"Joseph," she sighed, "do it for me, okay?"

"Only if you promise that this ends it," he said. "I see the head doctor, he pronounces me sane, and you *never ever* mention this crap again. Just do your job as a control agent and quit imitating Dr. Freud. Agreed?"

Masters relented. "Agreed."

. . .

"How have you been, Joe?" Dr. Thompson asked.

Lerza answered guardedly, "Dandy."

The two men sat alone in Patty's apartment. The psychiatrist knew it would be a hostile interview, but he was looking for some clue, some sign—a smoking gun—that Lerza was a danger to himself or others.

"I know this is difficult for you," Thompson said. "Just know that I'm not the enemy. It's irrelevant to me whether you continue or not in this operation. I represent your well-being, Joseph, not the FBI, not Patty, not Mr. Keenan."

Lerza did some quick deductive reasoning. If the Bureau shrink pronounced him unfit for duty, then Keenan would have no choice. Joe knew he was perfectly sane and functioning normally in the abnormal world of police undercover work. Whatever normal was. After all, it certainly wasn't normal to pretend to be somebody else twenty-four hours a day, buying drugs from guys that'd cut your nuts off if *they* ever found out you *were* somebody else, and drinking booze with hookers and addicts for recreation until your cheeks hurt.

Did anyone else see the blatant contradiction in this? he wondered. It was almost a Catch-22. Be cool, calm, and collected and the psychiatrist may correctly wonder why you're not cautious, jittery, or edgy in a situation that dictates nervous eyes. Bounce off the wall, and you're Section 8 material.

"Okay, Dr. Thompson," he said. "Whatta you want to know?"

"Just a chat, Joe. Nothing special, no trick questions. Just converstion."

Lerza rose from his seat. He asked, "Want coffee or some tea, Dr. Thompson?"

"Coffee would be fine."

Lerza made a show of grabbing cups, boiling water, and finding spoons as he continued the conversation with Thompson. Patty's small apartment had a combination living and dining area. Joe knew the exact cabinet where the vodka bottle resided. He bent out of sight with a coffee cup in hand and filled it three quarters full with the clear liquid. Next, he splashed two fingers of Kahlua for color, into the vodka. Satisfied with the deception, Lerza made Thompson his coffee.

The psychiatrist sipped from his cup, then asked, "Anything *you* want to tell me?"

Lerza pretended to give the question some thought. "Not really," he finally said. "I'm satisfied with the case. There are the usual ups and downs, but basically everything's okay." He took a long gulp of "doctored" vodka.

"You and Moose getting along?"

"Like an old married couple."

"Sleeping okay?"

"Fine," he lied.

"Eating well?"

"Gained eight pounds on Moose's concoctions." Another sip of vodka.

"Been in touch with your family?"

"Like clockwork."

The psychiatrist recognized the warning signals: the slick answers, the indirect eye contact, the insincerity. He also realized Lerza was getting shitfaced while they sat there and exchanged amenities. Coffee it wasn't.

Two hours and forty-two minutes later, Thompson had seen and heard enough. The vodka and the questions wore down Lerza's early defense systems. His answers lost their zest, and his movements betrayed any grip on reality.

As Thompson stood up to leave, Joe asked, "How'd I do?"

The FBI psychiatrist patted Lerza's shoulder and said, "You did fine, Joe. Just fine."

THOMPSON stared at the red rug in Keenan's office, as Patty Masters sat in silence. Thompson had just described his visit to Lerza. He concluded with the words, "Psychiatry is not an exact science, Mr. Keenan."

The SAC was pacing the floor, glaring at Masters and challenging Thompson's diagnosis. He stopped to say, "I don't have your educational background, Dr. Thompson, but it still boggles my mind how you can predict Lerza's potential behavior based on such a short conversation."

Masters had promised herself she would remain silent. Dr. Thompson would be her point man; she just listened.

"Let me explain," the psychiatrist was saying. "Joe Lerza is basically a good man. I understand he is a fine investigative FBI agent. But I see now that his personality, coupled with his background, make him the worst possible choice for deep cover."

Keenan protested, "His background and personality *are* the exact reason he was selected for this case."

Thompson patiently explained. "Joe was raised in a very traditional family. The son of a policeman and an Italian mother who stayed at home cooking, cleaning, and doting on her son. Joe's early life was black and white with no shades of gray. Good versus evil and nothing in between. Then came Vietnam. A place where life got complicated. A place where ten-year-old kids strapped grenades on and incinerated Joe's nineteen-year-old friends. A place where he was forced to kill human beings who didn't neatly fit into his mold of 'the enemy.' "

Thompson exhaled a long sigh, then continued, "He coped by being a super marine. Three Purple Hearts, two Silver Stars, a legitimate war hero who couldn't figure out why the college students spit on him when he returned home. But Joe Lerza tried again. He tried to get his life back to right and wrong, good and evil, eliminating the big 'maybe' that Vietnam injected in his psyche. Joe joined the FBI. As American an organization as apple pie—truth, justice, and where the good guys arrested bad guys. It was simple again, *until* Joe went deep."

He fell silent, then concluded, "He was rudely pushed back into a world where up was down and where kids were again euphemistically strapping grenades on. The bad guys weren't really that bad once he got to know them, once he lived with them, drank with them, saw them in a different light. So he no longer thought like an FBI agent but as someone who could no longer differentiate where the razor-thin line was that divides good and evil. You see, Mr. Keenan, Joe Lerza's life had become one big shade of gray."

Keenan wouldn't relent. He stated, "I can't jeopardize this sensitive operation because Special Agent Lerza thinks he's back in Vietnam. Talk to him, get him back on the track, make him sane again."

Patty masked her anger with a grimace. Thompson recognized her expression for what it was and gave her a wink. He said to Keenan, "During my talk with Joe, he interchanged his pronouns."

"What?" Keenan asked, not understanding.

"He'd use the pronoun 'I' and 'we' when referring to the mob. He used 'them' when referring to you and the FBI, Mr. Keenan."

Keenan asked, "Are you saying that Lerza thinks he's a mob guy?"

"No." Thompson answered. "Joe Lerza hasn't picked sides yet. He and Moose feel they are out there on their own. What I am saying is this—your undercover agent is suffering from a classic case of Delayed Stress Syndrome, caused by Vietnam and his previous undercover assignments. Leave him out there and you risk losing him."

Keenan looked totally frustrated. He asked, "What happens if I don't heed your warning? What could Lerza do? What is he capable of?"

Dr. Thompson stood up. He looked hard at the SAC and said simply, "Joseph Lerza is capable of anything."

21

The Mercedes's brakes caught, jolting the passengers as the car stopped at the Walt Whitman Bridge tollbooth.

"Aw, Jees!" Moose complained. "I spilled hot coffee all over my pants."

Lerza put three quarters into the toll collector's out-stretched hands and nodded. The bridge connects Philadelphia with New Jersey, a state considered a bedroom community for New York and Philly and the brunt of more jokes than Poland.

"Sorry 'bout the quick brake," Lerza apologized.

"You done it on purpose," Moose complained, rubbing the stain bigger with his hand.

"No," Lerza said, "but I *am* enjoying it."

"All you little fuckers are sadistic."

Lerza and Moose delighted in their pre-game drill of light banter. It was their way of saying, "this ain't gonna be so tough because we're joking around."

Lerza flicked the radio on WFIL, keeping the volume low, and said, "Gotta be the Satans."

"Yeah," Moose agreed. "It's them all right."

"Chandy's a biker's bar."

The Moose opened the car window, letting the cool work on the wet spot on his pants. He snorted, "Patty in place?"

"Yeah." Lerza added, "I didn't tell you, but Patty thinks I'm a head case. Wants to pull my ticket."

"You *are* a head case. That's what makes you a good undercover."

"Thanks!" Sarcasm to hide the hurt. Then, "I'm freezin', shut the window."

Moose opened it wider, letting the winter air blow directly at Lerza.

"Real funny," said a shivering Lerza.

"When did Patty hit you with the wacko shit?" Moose asked, shutting the window.

"Couple of days ago."

"Why?"

"Who knows."

"She think I'm crazy, too?"

Lerza shot him a smile as answer.

"Dime you out to Keenan?"

"Yeah."

"So?"

"Our illustrious boss thinks we're as sane as nuns on a perpetual novena."

Moose laughed. "Now I *am* worried."

"Patty and I made up, but do me a favor." Serious tone.

"What?" Moose asked.

"When we're around her from now on, cut the Charles Manson act, Moose."

. . .

THE two FBI undercover agents entered Chandy's Bar on the Black Horse Pike. They immediately felt like black Catholics at a Ku Klux Klan picnic. Conversations stopped or reverted to whispers; nobody tried to hide his stare.

Lerza thought, Welcome to the world of outlaw bikers.

Sixty or so semi-humans of assorted species, sexes, and sizes were arranged around the front-room bar and back-room tables. The guys had chains, steel studs, and other metal objects hanging off leather vests and jackets. The girls wore tight jeans and combat boots. There was not a bra in the joint, since accessible tits was a requirement of biker broads. Tattoos decorated every visible part of the men's bodies, including eyelids—the agents knew that the decorations extended to testicles and rectal cavities as well.

"Just act natural," Lerza muttered to Moose.

The irony of the words hit Moose; he laughed.

"What's so fuckin' funny?" a Grizzly Adams lookalike asked them.

The natives stirred in anticipation of a confrontation between "Head Case," whose hobbies included putting cats into microwave ovens just to watch them explode, and these two civilians, who had the misfortune of walking into the wrong place.

Head Case was the bar's sergeant at arms, with a job description long in murder and mayhem. He had done ten years at Raiford for the ax murder of his daddy, whose crime had been to tell his sixteen-year-old son he could not go out until he cleaned his room.

Lerza winked at Moose. Moose shrugged, trying to figure out his partner's move. Lerza then took a direct route to Head Case who, like Moose, could not decide what the short guy dressed like a used-car salesman was up to.

There ensued complete silence in the joint, all eyes riveted on the upcoming murder.

Lerza broke the silence. "You a tough guy, eh?" he asked Head Case.

"Fuckin' ay." Head Case added, "And you're fuckin' stupid, right?"

"Let's not get into name-calling." Lerza's voice was serious.

Head Case turned to his audience, smirked, then explained, "He don't wanna be called names. Must be the sensitive type."

A few chuckles sounded from the peanut gallery. Everyone seemed completely fascinated with the scene.

"If I told you we're not looking for trouble would it make any difference?" Lerza asked.

"Fuck no. I'm gonna kick your ass anyway."

"I don't think so," Lerza challenged quietly.

"You gonna stop me?" Head Case shot back.

"Not me." Lerza reached into his pants pocket. "But maybe ol' Ben Franklin can."

He withdrew a wad of hundred-dollar bills and threw a handful on the bar. "Drinks are on me," he said to the audience, "unless you guys don't drink. In that case, there's plenty money left over for other recreational escapes."

Everyone waited for Head Case to react. He stared hard at the money. Then he picked up a bill and held it to the light for examination. The sergeant at arms of Chandy's Bar made his decision swiftly. He smiled like a Cheshire cat, revealed missing and stained teeth.

He put an affectionate arm around Lerza and said, "Welcome to our home, dude." The bar and the crowd returned to their normal chaos.

"Nice move," Moose muttered after they were seated in the back room.

Lerza smiled, "I kinda liked it myself."

"What was Plan 'B' gonna be?"

"Dunno."

"Then we're lucky, I guess."

"Rabbits are lucky, Italians are witty." Lerza laughed again.

"Witless is more like it," Moose shot back.

"Just saved *you* an ass-kicking. Be nice, mutant."

They passed the time downing whiskey shooters and alternating turns at the pool table, playing eight-ball with some bikers. They kicked ass and traded good-natured insults with the pool players.

An hour passed and though there was plenty of barroom conversation, no one made the move to sell them dope. They were getting antsy when suddenly two big-boned biker broads appeared.

"Hi, honey," greeted the blond bombshell bimbo with the skimpy halter, sitting down on Moose's lap.

Moose brushed her 44J cups and announced, "I'm in love."

The other girl, a sexy brunette with a tattoo showing above her halter, took her friend's cue. She straddled Lerza's leg.

Her opening line was, "Wanna see my battleship?"

Before Lerza could answer, she whipped up her halter top, giving him a closeup of the U.S.S. *Missouri* in blues, greens, and reds. The ship covered both tits and went from neck to belly button.

"I'm impressed," Lerza said admiringly. "Nice gun mounts."

"Wanna see 'em shoot?" She pushed her chest toward him.

"No, thanks. I'm nonviolent."

She asked, "Where you guys from?"

"Philly."

The Moose and the blond bombshell giggled at something known only to them.

The battleship female pressed, "Whatta you guys do? Doctors? Lawyers? Cops?"

Lerza jerked a thumb at Moose, asked, "He look like your gynecologist?"

She laughed, and they talked about nothing for thirty minutes. Both lied a lot during that half hour. A few more drinks, and the foursome was cozy. Lerza's girl rubbed his neck and said, "You're all tense, honey. Let me give you a dynamite massage."

Lerza had been wired so many times that his first instinct was to grab her roving hand; then he remembered the magic dime and decided to relax. He realized the girls were nothing more than an advance "pat down" team for the Satans.

He thought, Oh well, better a babe than some hairy biker or a greaseball. He looked at Moose, whose date was less obvious, groping, grabbing, and gobbling at various parts of his anatomy. Lerza's girl chuckled nervously when she reached his revolver but, like the pro she was, knew a gun in this bar was standard equipment. Her trained fingers found no wires, no transmitters, nothing on his body that she had not felt on a thousand other guys.

Finished with her searching, she said, "That's better, now everything's all relaxed."

"Almost everything." Lerza laughed and glanced at Moose, who seemed just shy of intercourse.

The battleship biker broad had completed her job. She told her friend, "We gotta go now, Doris."

Moose's girl seemed genuinely disappointed. "I like him," she said, patting his face. "Can't I fuck him?"

"Later, Doris." The voice firm.

Moose gave a final grope to the Miss 44J cup as the two girls stood up and disappeared into the mob.

"That toss was obvious," Lerza said.

"What toss?"

"You're kidding. You'd screw anything, wouldn't you?"

Moose smiled. "Alive and human is my bottom line."

From seemingly out of nowhere appeared the Satan's commander in chief. He stood in front of them. "Dakota's friend?" he asked, already knowing the answer.

Lerza nodded at an empty chair. Lu eased his large frame into it as Lerza and Moose stared at him.

The two FBI agents immediately noticed a man different from his playmates. Lu's eyes were intelligent, his mannerisms controlled, his demeanor forbidding.

"Nice touch out there," Lu complimented. "Head Case loves to hear the sound of broken bones."

"Use to work in a zoo."

"Ever get bit?"

"Once," Lerza said. "Gotta be careful with snakes."

Lu ordered a Budweiser. He seemed to enjoy the head games preceding drug deals. It was like a military tactics class, trying to anticipate the enemy's move, giving counter measures, then mounting the offensive. With Lu, Lerza sensed, there was no taking of prisoners.

"Dakota tells me you're businessmen."

"So to speak," Lerza said.

"Wanna talk business or continue this bullshit?" Lu challenged.

"*And* who the fuck are you?" A challenge from Moose.

"Name's Lu." He seemed unperturbed. "I'm a distributor of fine powder."

"The kind that lets your brain go on vacation?" Lerza asked. "Or maybe the kind you rub on a baby's ass."

"The cocaine kind." Said with finality.

"We're listening." Lerza sipped at his sixth whiskey.

"You pay between forty-five and fifty grand per key," Lu began. "From the wops. Their shit is overpriced and poor quality."

Lerza was content to let Lu shoot off his mouth. The fact that the Satan was fingering the mob as his competitor was a bonus. It'd play well in court. He took a long pull on his beer and said, "You know a lot, pal. Maybe you also know that our current wholesaler would not like losing our contract."

"They understand business," Lu said. "We offer a better product at reduced cost. It's capitalism, it's American."

"You know," Lerza laughed, "just the other day I heard Miceli say 'Capitalism without bankruptcy is like Catholicism without hell.' An understanding Mafia capo, he is—"

Lu interrupted, "Miceli is not my problem."

"Don't kid yourself, bud," Moose offered. "He's a pepperoni away from turning your clubhouse into Chernobyl."

Lu took another sip of his Bud, leaned forward in his chair, and announced, "Thirty-five a key, at ninety-five percent, with a guaranteed two-day turnaround time."

"What about weight?"

"Not an issue."

Moose, who had been bestowing on Lu his finest glare, spoke directly to Lerza. "We don't know this guy from dog shit. Could be the heat."

"Fair concern," Lu conceded. "Check it out, ask around. In the meantime," he tossed an aluminum-foiled packet on the table, "test the product. It's a free sample."

"Same shit we'll get if it's a deal?" Lerza asked.

"From the mother lode. Always quality."

Lerza stared at the packet and asked, "How come this don't make me feel better about you?"

" 'Cause cops can't give it away." Lu smiled. "Pisses off

the taxpayers if some innocent junkie OD's on government dope."

"What happens if we mysteriously get blue-lighted five blocks away?" Lerza asked. "Or worse yet, at the bridge, which would carry an interstate rap."

"Life's a crapshoot," was Lu's serene answer.

Lerza picked up the aluminum packet with the sample of cocaine, stuck it in his pocket, and said, "*If* we deal, Dakota's outta the middle. I don't trust broads who flash their tits, and I don't like delays."

"Agreed." A half smile.

"Run it all down," Lerza asked.

Lu sounded like a prerecorded message on an answering machine. "One key of blow, thirty-five grand. Two to four keys the price drops to thirty per key. More than four keys, down to twenty grand per key for anything over three keys. Any type of pharmaceuticals like Dilaudid, Valiums, dex's, ice, or 'ludes is available. Any exotic shit, just name it."

"Impressive." Lerza wanted to smile as he pictured the tape replayed for some jury.

The trip back to Philly was uncharacteristically quiet, considering the success of the meeting. It took a full half hour before Lerza spoke.

"Something strange about that guy," he said.

"Whatta you mean?"

"Way he looked at me," Lerza explained. "Like he knew what I was thinking. Like he was inside my mind."

22

Stormy had just injected a load of street-quality heroin into her foot. She avoided the arm because the needle tracks would send Miceli into a frenzy if he found out she was a mainliner. Now she faced the added hassles of two FBI agents who could spot the telltale signs of addiction.

Miceli would not deal with heroin users. He'd often say, "You can't fuckin' trust a fuckin' junkie; they'd dime their own mother for a score."

She thought, Little does he know.

She opened the office door, felt the rush junk brings, spotted Lerza sitting near the stage. He waved her over.

"How ya' hitting them, Stormy?" he asked.

"Just home runs." She laughed. "Our friend's waiting for a call. Needs the business."

"Good. I need to see him."

Stormy sensed something was up and asked, "Anything wrong?"

"Just business. Listen." In a serious tone. "You may not understand this now, so I'll just say we still have your best intentions at heart, but I'm gonna meet with Miceli and call off our deal."

"What?" she screamed.

"Let me explain—"

Before he could utter one word more she shot questions at him like an M-60. She pleaded, "Why, Joe? You know what he'll do? He's gonna be pissed. I mean real pissed. Are you crazy?"

Lerza could not tell her that the master plan was working. Step 1, they scored from the mob. Step 2, the Satans approached them. Step 3, the switch. Step 4, jam up the bikers. Step 5, arrest the lot of them.

Instead, he said, "Hold on. Listen. We know what we're doing. I'll take the heat with Miceli. When I tell him why I'm backing out, you'll be off the hook. Believe me."

"He'll kill me," she said quietly.

"Not when I explain."

She challenged, "Is that why you came tonight? So you could tell me face-to-face that you lied to me?"

"Hold on," a now-angry Lerza said. "No one lied to you. If you want protection, you got it. Right now. But I'm telling you, everything'll be okay. Miceli will deal with me, he'll direct any revenge at *me*."

Stormy relaxed somewhat and ordered a drink. "I got myself into this," she said fatalistically. "I should've known better."

"Believe me, Stormy," he pleaded. "This has all been planned. We know what to expect. We've been through it before. These guys are all alike."

Dirty Denise dropped a double round of whiskeys at the table because they both looked like they needed it. Stormy emptied the glass in one gulp, turned away from Lerza, and stared straight ahead. Onstage a naked dancer went through supposedly seductive motions.

Suddenly Stormy grabbed her refill. "You really don't understand them, do you?" she asked.

"I think I do." Seriously.

"I vouched for you," she went on in a plaintive voice. "I said you were a standup guy. When you tell Miceli the deal's done, he's going to come at me first. It's a personal insult. He can't let it go. Oh, he'll get around to you eventually. But it will be *me* first. He'll hurt me because you *think* you know these guys."

Her voice was now just shy of a shout. "Let me tell you something, Mr. Know-It-All, you're the same. You're *just* like Miceli. And I hope he kills you!"

She shot to her feet and hurled the whiskey in Lerza's face.

His instincts, coupled with lack of sleep, total paranoia, and deep depression, made him react by grabbing Stormy's leopard-skin blouse and backhanding her cheek as he hissed, "You bitch!"

He left the club and drove the Mercedes aimlessly for more than an hour. When his mind finally cleared of anger, he replaced the rage with overwhelming shame. He had not reacted so violently since his return from Nam—it seemed so long ago, yet at times also like yesterday. What was happening to him? When did he lose control?

He looked out the car window and realized he had driven to Veterans Stadium. The massive empty parking lot with its black asphalt and yellow lines loomed like a giant jigsaw puzzle. The tears rolling down his cheeks only confirmed that he had long ago lost control. He vaguely remembered taking the plastic Baggie filled with nose candy from the glove compartment. He had every intention of throwing it away.

• • •

THE two men sat at their kitchen table sipping hot coffee. "I hit her, Moose." Lerza spoke in shame. "I can't believe I hit her."

Moose tried to reassure him, "Don't sweat it, Joey, the bitch probably deserved it."

"She didn't. It was totally uncalled for."

"So it's over. Forget it."

"Not that easy. Aside from feeling like shit, I and you now got a hysterical source who could blow this case, not to mention our butts, right off the map."

"She'll be okay."

"I should call her, apologize."

"Let her cool."

"Maybe you're right."

The Moose had a bottomless pit for a stomach; he made pancakes disappear with the skill of Harry Houdini. Lerza admired the Moose's ability to handle the chaos around him. True, he drank a lot of whiskey, true he was somewhat crude, he had bad table manners, and true he had a short fuse directed at anybody he did not know and love. But the bottom line was that this prehistoric beast with the genius IQ let *nothing* get to him.

He was a total contradiction to the twentieth century. It would all be there when he got up the next morning. There was nothing anyone could do to harm him, because the Moose understood that power is achieved only if *given*, and if you felt things would work out, then they did. What "could have" happened "always" did.

Lerza, on the other hand, sensed he was losing it, whatever "it" was. He was driving his family away, he had put a move on a friend who now thought he was crazy. He had struck an informant who was defenseless and could not or would not strike back. He was losing his battle with booze;

the Vietnam nightmares continued. And he had just done something terrible he swore he would *never* do—strike a woman. As bad as all this was, the worst part was the feeling of not caring any more.

"When you gonna call Miceli?" Moose asked.

"Now's as good as ever."

"You may not want to know this, but Miceli ain't too predictable. He could go jackbatty."

Lerza did not want to hear from his partner that Stormy could be right; he wanted to ignore Moose's caution. He finally said, "Look, mutant, Miceli's just a wiseguy, a puke guido. We've put a hundred like him behind bars, and when I tell him our deal's off, he'll throw his little fit and threaten to do impossible things to my body. But the fact is Miceli'll just go huff and puff until he blows himself down. Then we'll arrest him."

"You're probably right, small one." Moose spoke without conviction.

"Ready?" Lerza asked.

Moose responded by opening a kitchen cabinet and removing a Swedish food-processing machine. It was a plastic-and-stainless-steel contraption capable of frappéing nuts or bolts. The Moose stuck the point of a butter knife into the back plate of the machine, popped off its panel, then removed a suction cup, cord, and microcassette tape recorder. The cream-colored wall phone contrasted sharply with the black suction cup that dangled from the receiver into the microcassette.

Lerza flicked the machine to "record" and gave the preamble: "This is Special Agent Joseph Lerza, the time is eleven A.M., the date is November thirtieth. I am about to place a telephone call to Anthony Miceli at area code 215-555-2206."

He dialed the numbers and watched the tape slowly make

its way around the reel. He thought, I missed Thanksgiving with my family, I even forgot to call.

His thoughts were interrupted by Miceli's voice saying "Yeah?"

"It's Joe V.," Lerza said.

"You ain't supposed to call here, Joe V.," Miceli complained. "Call the Rock if you want the cheese delivered."

"We gotta talk."

"What about?" Miceli pressed.

"Not on the phone."

"It better be important." A warning.

"It is."

"Tonight, eight o'clock, at the Chassis." He hung up.

Lerza took a deep breath and poured a second cup of coffee. He shrugged his shoulders and said to the Moose, "Piece of cake."

"Where?" Moose asked.

"Where else?"

"Good. I get a chance to dress up."

"Not the damn bow tie again," Lerza pleaded.

"Why not? It's suave and debonair."

"On you it looks like a bat died on your neck."

"Fuck you, midget." A soft laugh.

23

Brad Keenan had resorted to marking big "X's" on his calendar. They denoted the time until his retirement. Blue Flame Bobby had called twice in the last ten days, putting on the pressure to indict everyone on the eastern seaboard with an Italian last name.

Keenan was faced with balancing the need to retire before disaster struck while still showing just enough progress to keep the Deputy Assistant Director off his ass. The SAC made the tactical decision not to tell the DADC about Dr. Thompson's diagnosis. It would only be construed as yet another inability to lead.

His desk was littered with potential obstacles to successful retirement right now. For starters, the blistering teletype from the headquarters voucher unit complaining, alleging, and threatening because the undercover agents' expense money did not jibe. It *never did* in undercover cases, since the Bureau required absurd things, like receipts for high-rolling drug dealers.

The undercover agents *never* bothered with receipts but attempted to "balance the books" at some later date by recreating expenses through filling in blank receipts. When the undercover agents would complain, the accounting gnomes in headquarters would quote some regulation and threaten dismissal and criminal charges. This would only serve to further piss off the undercover agents, who would then respond by totally neglecting any receipts or paper trails. In Lerza's case, the money he and Moose spent on paper nowhere near equalled the amount allocated, and the two had ceased writing vouchers altogether.

Blue Flame Bobby had also chewed Keenan's ass out about Patty Masters's blistering memo, which surfaced in headquarters on Bobby's desk. Blue Flame demanded, "Can't you control your people? First the undercover cowboy, now his control bitch causing waves."

Lastly, but certainly not leastly, was the laboratory's report and attached letter. It more than just asked the SAC why the amount of submitted cocaine differed from the promised amount on the recorded conversations between the "bad guys" and the undercover agent.

There was a six-ounce discrepancy that could not be chalked up to spillage or a bad scale. The letter concluded, "Take appropriate action to determine the reason for this difference and submit your findings by COB"—meaning close of business—"14 February."

Keenan thought, Valentine's Day, nice touch, the bastards. He did not want to conduct any inquiry, did not want to ask Masters to ask Lerza, did not want to ask Lerza directly, and certainly did not want to *know* where the six ounces went or *how* it got there. But he had to submit something.

He dialed Masters's number. When he heard her voice,

he said, "Patricia, there's a problem with the drugs you submitted to the lab."

"Oh?" She sounded puzzled.

"Six ounces are missing, and HQ wants to know where it went."

She tried to interpret his question. Was he accusing her or maybe Joe or Moose? Or was it just an oversight, a classic Bureau screwup?

She finally said, with certainty, "It's headquarters' mistake, probably a typo."

"I agree," Keenan said but without conviction. "However, you'll have to run it down and get back to me. And while you're at it, tell Lerza to square away his vouchers."

"Joe and Moose have enough pressure on them." She rose to their defense. "I am *not* going to even bother them with this."

"Do what you have to do," came the SAC's answer.

They both hung up, not wanting to think the worst. It probably was a Bureau overreaction to a typo or an insert error, but in the back of Patty's brain stirred a gnawing doubt about an FBI agent who had recently been acting pretty bizarre.

She knew she had to say something to Joe, but she decided to work it in nonchalantly during a conversation, not make it an accusation. It was a fact that he was not himself, but stealing drugs just did not fit the man she had known in Cincinnati. Had he gone to the dark side? Had undercover work unlocked the combination that snapped not only his morale but his morals?

She jumped at the sudden ringing of her phone. It was Captain Joyce of the Philly PD. He told her that some guy with ties to Miceli's narcotics-distribution network was minus his dick.

The victim's name was Arny Tomossino, and he was not

the most talkative hospital patient the police had ever interviewed. Rumor was that Arny tried to kiss Miceli goodbye, but the Italian did not kiss back and removed his manhood instead. Captain Joyce said he knew Masters had been asking around about Miceli's operations, so perhaps she would be interested.

She hung up, almost relieved. There it was—the smoking gun. Now Lerza had to be brought in before Miceli tried to inflict the same punishment on him for threatening to leave him for the Satans. The case plan openly dictated that Lerza switch drug suppliers. If he did, it looked as if Lerza would end up like Arny Tomossino.

LERZA sat at the kitchen table nervously loading and unloading his nine-millimeter automatic. He said to Moose, "After we tell Miceli to fuck off, we call Lu and set up a ten-key deal."

"Sounds good to me," Moose approved.

The two undercovers were watching a kitchen clock that was still three hours away from their scheduled meet at the Chassis. The newness and excitement of the case had long faded. They were operating on pure adrenaline, fueled by plenty of booze. It was a tribute to Moose that the two men maintained their close friendship. Joe was now moody and irritable.

"We gotta do this just right," he cautioned Moose.

"The Miceli thing?"

"Yeah, the Miceli thing. Let me do the talking. I'll handle it, I know what to say and—" The phone interrupted him.

He heard Patty's voice; she said, "It's Sis."

"Everything okay?" he asked.

"Everything's *not* all right." Her voice was emphatic. "Tonight's got to be cancelled."

"Why?" A protest. "We've been through this before."

"Not on the phone," she cautioned. "See you at our regular place in an hour."

"Okay, but bring the sound equipment anyway, because after we square away whatever's got your bowels in an uproar, we *will* go to the meet." As though nothing could stop it.

Patty knew it was foolish to argue on the phone. It was simple: she would tell him the news, and he would never go near Miceli again. Should she call and tell Keenan? The SAC would finally have to agree and cut their losses. She decided to wait, tell Joe first, then draft an immediate teletype to headquarters, bypassing Keenan, authorizing them to terminate the case. The meeting between Joe Vitali, a.k.a. Joe Lerza, and Anthony Miceli would not take place; the issue now became solely one of how to wind down the operation with maximum arrests and convictions.

As she took a shower her confidence ebbed. Patty could almost hear Joe say, "It won't happen to me." She dressed and grabbed the recording equipment on her way out the door. It was an automatic reaction.

The regular weekend crowd appeared in their accustomed weekend seats, watching the usual Rusty trio and the screaming pizza boy. A typical night at the Triangle. Moose and Lerza had become regulars at the joint, which meant quick service, sincere greetings, and unwanted table visits by people like Lester, the cross-eyed, backslapping shoe pisser.

"Lester, you're full of shit," Moose argued.

Moose and Lester had become friends. The little man followed Moose around like a puppy dog. Undercover work was a bombardment to the senses. The first month or two had a UCA on edge, alert and in his usual role. After a while you settled into a strange type of normalcy. You assumed your new life until it wasn't forced; it became as natural as breathing. You needed relationships with people like Lester because they were not the norm.

Lester had to tilt his short neck upward to talk with Moose. "It's true, Moose," he protested. "I really did serve with Patton in the big war. The ol' man even gave me a battlefield commission for saving his life."

"You're full of shit," Moose said once again, trying to follow Lester's eyes, which appeared aimed somewhere on the ceiling.

"I can prove it," Lester challenged. "Rusty was in Wally Wally II. He'll back me up."

Without waiting for Moose to respond, Lester jumped up and headed toward the stage. Rusty was in the middle of a serious rendition of *O Mine Pappa* when Lester jerked the microphone from his hand. He announced, "Enough of this Commie crap, Rusty. Get your ass over there and tell my buddy Moose how I was a war hero." Cassanova Brown and Shellshock Tony finished the song to an appreciative Triangle crowd.

Moose was about halfway through some cheap stale cigar when he realized Lerza had been gone on a twenty-minute piss. He found the downstairs one-seater and banged on a locked door. "Joey, you okay?" he asked.

Almost a full thirty seconds later a disheveled Lerza opened the bathroom door and said sheepishly, "Some diarrhea, Moose. What's goin' on?"

Moose Knepp knew what was "goin' on" but fought that knowledge with his love for Joe Lerza, his partner and his best friend. The Moose saw all the warning signs even without the fancy psychology degree. Undercover Agent Lerza was in trouble. He was out of control and the trace of white powder on his mustache only confirmed Moose's worst fears.

Moose put an affectionate arm around Lerza and said, "Know something, Joey? I worry 'bout you sometimes."

Lerza asked defensively, "Whatta you talkin' about?"

Moose knew that Joe was on the verge of something bad.

Like the balloon that would certainly burst with one more breath of air.

"I need a break," Moose said, hoping to deflect his accusing finger. "This undercover work burnt me out."

"Bullshit," Lerza said.

"No, Joey, I'm serious," Moose assured him. "Maybe we both need some time away. Let's go to Pittsburgh and drink Iron City Beer till our cheeks hurt. Let's get the fuck away from the wops, the bikers, and the bureaucrats."

Lerza jerked from Moose's arm. "You can quit if you want," he said angrily. "Get the fuck outta here. I don't need you or anybody else. This is the big time, pal, and if you can't hack it, then I'll get a partner who can."

He half ran up the stairs, found a waitress, and ordered a double whiskey. Moose followed slowly, trying to figure out what would be going down next.

Like an omen, Patty Masters appeared. She smiled and said, "Good evening, gentlemen, I have good news and bad news."

Moose grimaced and said, "We sure the fuck need some good news."

"Let's hear it," Lerza said, knowing he wasn't going to like either.

"First a drink to soften the bad news," she said, "then a second to celebrate the good."

Their regular waitress, Tootie, took the orders and returned almost immediately with three shots of tequila, a salt shaker, and a cut-up lemon.

"Must be a special occasion," Tottie said. "This crap is top-shelf Mexican booze; there's even a dead worm in the bottle."

"Only the best, darlin'," Moose said. "Bring three more, Tootie."

As she left to get three more shots of the Mexican booze

with the dead worm in the bottle, the eyes of Lerza and Moose bolted to Patty.

"Well?" Moose asked.

"First, the bad," she said. "One of Miceli's distributors got busted up pretty bad. They actually amputated his penis."

"Oh, Jees!" Moose cried. "It hurts just hearing you say it."

"A Philly cop," she continued, "said that this Arny Tomossino switched coke suppliers to the Satans. He breaks the news to Miceli's goons and ends up skinned alive minus his most vital limb."

Moose begged, "Don't say it no more, I'm having sympathy pains."

"So." Lerza's only comment.

"So!" Patty shouted. "So it's obvious you can't meet with Miceli tonight and tell him *you're* terminating your deal without running the real risk he'll sever your—"

Moose interrupted, "I get the picture!"

Lerza waited until Tootie came and went with fresh shots of tequila. Then he asked seriously, "What's the big deal, Patty? So Miceli screws up some flunky distributor. I never thought we were dealing with the Easter Bunny. That's why they're called criminals."

"You can't be serious," she said in astonishment. "You meet with Miceli tonight, and I guarantee you'll both end up on some coroner's table." Patty Masters's good judgment had been clouded with an unwanted naivete since the case began. Love was the culprit.

"I don't agree." Lerza's voice was defiant.

"And you're full of shit, Joseph," she countered.

"Maybe. But I ain't calling off tonight."

Patty downed the tequila and looked at Lerza in disbelief. She turned to Moose and said, "You can't let him do this."

Moose gave it some thought, then said, "I go where Joey goes, darlin'. I won't let nothing happen to him."

He agreed with Patty, but he couldn't desert Lerza when his friend needed him most.

She said, anger in her voice, "You two are incredibly stupid. You're out of your league with no backup against fifty mob guys who don't have government rules and regulations or even basic morals. They'll kill you both, then go out to dinner."

"We can handle them," Lerza said, matter-of-factly.

"No!" Her voice rose. *"You can't!"*

Even at the noisy Triangle, her cry drew attention from nearby tables.

She said in softer tone, "Look. You two can keep playing John Wayne all you want. I would have thought you'd had your fill of it by now. But I am *not* going to be part of your suicide. I am *not* going to ID your bodies at the morgue. I will *not* be part of your Vietnam guilt-trip death wish. I'm off the case, I'm outta here."

She stood up. As she walked away, Moose called out, "Hey, Cutey, what was the good news gonna be?"

She retraced her steps to the table and bent over just inches from Lerza's face. "The good news was for you, mister," she said to him. "It was that you'd be able to go home to your family." She turned and walked swiftly out of the Triangle before Lerza could form a reply.

"That's one tough bitch," Moose said admiringly.

"Maybe," Lerza conceded. "But she's got a bad case of the 'for reals.' Miceli ain't shit! And we ain't Arny Tomossino."

"Hey," Moose said automatically. "You forgot to give her the coke sample we got from Lu."

"Later," Lerza said. "She wouldn't appreciate it now."

. . .

TONY Miceli lived just eight blocks from the two undercover agents in a remodeled row home on the fringe of Center City. He had installed the best security system money could buy. It gave him peace of mind. Alarms triggered by the sound of broken glass, top-of-the-line dead bolts, intercoms, steel windows, and door gates made to look like animal ornaments.

A virtual fortress. The living room had a twenty-foot mahogany bar stocked with the best imported booze. The bedroom was a shrine to sex, with a round bed, ceiling mirrors, recessed soft-color lighting, and the sound of music from seemingly nowhere.

Cognac filled the French crystal bottle that was poised in his manicured fingers as the intercom did its thing.

"It's the Rock," came the gruff monotone.

A buzzer admitted the mammoth Italian, who checked the door behind him before proceeding up six stairs to the living room.

"Wanna drink?" Miceli asked, tilting his head toward the bar.

The Rock rambled over and poured a triple-decker of Anisette, asking, "What's up?"

Miceli stood silent until the Sicilian indelicately dropped into one of his delicate Italian provincial chairs. The furniture's thin legs groaned and creaked under Hard Rock's poundage.

"Jesus, Rock," Miceli said. "How many times I gotta tell you not to sit on that chair, you fuckin' horse."

Hard Rock started to get up, but Miceli stopped him with a wave. "Forget it now. You're already down." Then, "I want you to get the Ciccini brothers and some of the other soldatos. I gotta meet tonight."

"With who?"

"Vitali."

"Why?"

"Dunno, but I got a hunch I ain't gonna like it. That's why I want you there."

"Follow him from his apartment to the meet?" Hard Rock asked.

"Yeah, and wherever he goes after. I gotta hinky feeling 'bout that guy."

"Me, too. Somethin' ain't right."

STORMY Monday had just eased her anguish with two grams of smack in the vein of her foot. An hour before she had been on the verge of tears and indecision. Men, they're all the same, she thought. This FBI agent is no different than Miceli. All alike with their backhands to the mouth, their bullshit sweet talk. Using me like a piece of trash, none of them really caring about me, only what I can do for them.

Well, lady, what are you gonna do now? Maybe tell Lu? No, he'd kill me quick. Double-cross Lerza? Run away?

She still did not have an answer when the miracle drug reached her brain. But then she no longer cared.

As she left her office she saw Tony sitting alone at his table. She strolled by and took a seat. "Hi, honey," she said.

"Hey, babe, what's up?"

Here was the golden opportunity, the opening, the chance to tell all. But something held her tongue. She said, "Nothing's up. Expectin' someone?"

"Oh, yeah. Your boyfriend Vitali wants to see me about something important. Know anything about it?"

"Why would I?" she lied.

"The fuck I know. Maybe you two are tight."

She grabbed his arm and said coyly, "He's just a guy who comes here and drinks. A doper. Nothing like you, Tony. You're the real thing, babe."

She knew Miceli was a typical Italian man who basically believed females were useful for cooking and screwing. Whenever one flattered him, his libido would kick on automatic and he would actually be nice without realizing it.

"Yeah," he agreed. "Vitali's dog shit. Just a lowlife druggie."

"I don't like him, Tony," Stormy said. "He put the move on me once."

"You want me to mention it to him?" He emphasized the word "mention," meaning something else.

Stormy gave it thought, then said, "Naw, let it go. But if he tries it again, I'll let you know."

HARD Rock and the Ciccini brothers tailed Lerza and Moose from the undercover apartment to the Triangle. They may not have had college degrees and FBI surveillance training, but they lived the streets and had something much more valuable—instinct and common sense.

The Rock weaved the Lincoln in and out of the narrow South Philly streets, never getting closer than three cars from Lerza's Mercedes. The Ciccini brothers maneuvered their Oldsmobile several blocks ahead and criss-crossed streets perpendicular to the two agents. The Italians communicated by modifed CB's with private frequencies, compliments of their electronics computer whiz, Melvin.

Waiting outside the Triangle, Hard Rock noticed the pretty lady leave with a pained expression on her face. He thought, Nice bod, looks like my type.

• • •

LERZA and Moose left twenty minutes after Patty for their meet with Miceli. The two undercover agents were both in a sour mood, saying little on their ride to the Chassis. Lerza had never felt more alone—without Patty, without the Bureau, without his family, and without that bottom line of morality to which he had clung for the past fifteen years. He had lost his anchor to life and seemed to be floating aimlessly in a sea of deadly mines.

The Chassis was rock-and-rolling, with all systems on go. For some reason an emotional electricity filled the air. Miceli's goons were spread among the middle-class voyeurs. You could almost touch the tension.

Miceli sat at a table with that thousand-yard stare that marine recruits had perfected over the years. Looking, but not really seeing.

The two undercover agents entered and decided to piss off Miceli further by ignoring him. They headed straight for the bar.

Miceli stared holes in their backs as they ordered shots of Imperial, refusing even to acknowledge the mob chieftain.

"You think this is wise?" Moose asked.

"He's gonna be pissed off anyway," Lerza said. "Let him get good and lathered."

They re-ordered shooters of Imperial in water glasses with no chasers. Adding insult to injury, they did three "Imps" over an eighteen-minute period before heading Miceli's way.

They faced him as he said, not offering a hand, "You fuckin' guys are real game players."

Ignoring the reprimand, Lerza said to Moose, "Say hello and good-bye to Mr. Miceli."

The Moose grunted something unintelligible and headed back to the bar. There he came face-to-face with his nemesis, Hard Rock. They glared their greetings, then fixed on each other the unblinking stare of two boxers receiving prefight instructions. Moose thought, My eyes are starting to hurt, this is ridiculous.

At Miceli's table the mob guy wasted no time. He said to Lerza, "So you got me here, what's so fuckin' important?"

"Business." Grimly.

"Yeah, what about it?"

"I'm cancelling our agreement."

Patty heard the words over her porta mobile radio. She felt like an eavesdropper; her mind told her not to be there, but her heart would not listen. She was unable to stop two hardheaded Vietnam grunts. She was just along for the ride, to pick up the pieces of a man she cared too much about. Miceli would go for the throat; it was merely a matter of where and when. She prayed it would not be now, although it really did not matter, since she had long ago lost any control.

"That'd be a fuckin' mistake," was Miceli's reply.

Lerza protested innocently, "Hey, I can get this shit a lot cheaper. I'd thought as a businessman you'd understand."

Miceli was so furious he could only repeat, "That'd be a fuckin' mistake."

Lerza said calmly, "Well, that's the way it is. No hard feelings, I hope."

"Listen, asshole," Miceli shouted. "You made a deal with me, a business deal. Nonnegotiable, set in cement, get my meaning? There *ain't* no backing out. Understand?"

Lerza smiled, serving only to infuriate Miceli further. He said quietly, "Threaten me all you want, but I'm buying my dope someplace else."

Miceli shot to his feet, flipped the table over, then kicked it two feet in the air. Miceli's goons waited, tensed, as their boss pointed a finger at the mid-level dope dealer and threatened, "You're a fuckin' dead man!" then marched angrily out of the room.

Twelve guys, including Hard Rock, followed the mob boss; their exit looked like a mother duck and her ugly ducklings.

Moose rejoined Lerza as he was righting the table. "You handled that well," he chuckled.

"All in the approach."

"No need to ask what he said. I heard."

"A little mad."

"Just a little." Moose chuckled again. "What now?"

"Let's get drunk."

"Here?"

"Why not?"

They settled down not just to a little, but a monumental drunk. Sometime later in the evening Lerza and Stormy got together. He apologized over and over, repeating himself the way drunks do. She welcomed his symbolic return. It always amazed Moose how two drunks made sense, communicated with coherent sensitivity while in the throes of a major load. The booze somehow tied Stormy and Lerza together as they talked about things that really meant something to them.

The next morning, the evening was a big blank spot to Lerza. Moose helped fill in the missing parts. A major-league hangover only intensified Lerza's feeling of doom.

He could have sworn at some point in the evening he ended up alone with Stormy on her office couch, a vague remembrance of lines of cocaine and playing kissy-face.

As faint as that memory was, more disturbing was a flicker of remembrance somewhere in the deep recess of his brain that Stormy confessed something about "not being completely honest" with him.

24

Amato had not felt this good in a year. He was tempted to ignore his four-a-day blood-pressure pills, trade them for a bagel with cream cheese, then decided on both. What the hell, the pill would counteract the effects of the cream cheese.

Since he had made "the big decision," his life seemed calmer. Like a man on a cruise ship destined for some final warm paradise port. Knowing he would get there but not knowing when and, in the meantime, just enjoying the cruise.

The conversation with One Punch Averone had gone well; it was all a matter of execution now, so to speak.

His thoughts were interrupted by the intercom chime. The voice announced, "Mr. Miceli to see you."

This news soured his mood. He said, unhappily, "Send him in."

Miceli swaggered into the room and took a seat opposite

Amato without offering the respect of a handshake to the capo who had sworn him in as a member.

He began, "Mr. A., how ya feeling?"

"Fine, Anthony." A truthful answer. "And you?"

"Like a million bucks." He laughed.

Amato waited, knowing Miceli was not there to inquire about his health. Unless, of course, it was for a pre-funeral diagnosis.

"Hey, Mr. A.," Miceli said, waving a hand, "I—I mean *we*—got a problem."

"I figured *we* did." Sarcastically.

"Yeah." Miceli looked a little nervous. "I roughed up Arny Tomossino 'cause he started copping from the Satans."

"Roughed up? You almost killed him," Amato objected.

"He deserved it. But that's not why I'm here."

"We've had this talk before."

"Yeah, well we gotta have it again. I want your permission to make a hit."

"Who and why?" In a controlled voice.

"Some mid-level distributor. Got zip connections, not wired to nobody. The reason is he broke our contract and wants to deal with the Satans."

Amato was silent, and Miceli went on in an excited voice, "Hey, Mr. A., I'm looking like some kinda wimp skirt on the street if we don't make a statement. You know, blow somebody away or something. Our business interest will go belly-up. We gotta do something. *Now!*"

Amato's good health was short-lived. His stomach prepared to drip acid, his head began a dull throb. The two men started a heated discussion, hands waving, fingers pointing. Amato realized that with each succeeding day Miceli became bolder, consumed more of Amato's power.

He thought, Let me give him a bone, what difference

does some drug dealer's life mean? I'll give the permission for a hit, maybe it will keep Miceli happy for a few weeks.

Amato wanted this madman gone, so he conceded, "Okay, make the hit. What's the guy's name?"

The corner of Miceli's lips formed the slightest of smiles as he said, "Joe Vitali."

"I T S time," Lu said.

Dakota smiled, crossed her long, slim legs, and said, "I'm glad, I'm getting bored."

"You'll be back in L.A. soon," he assured her.

She smiled again, an automatic, practiced, insincere smile. One that pretty girls get away with because they are pretty. It sailed right past the Satan president.

"Listen and listen good," he commanded. "Just get him to his place, fuck him if you want, but make sure he's alone and the alarm system is off."

"No problem." The password of the twentieth century.

"Better not be any."

"Ease off," she said, then regretted it, knowing you did not talk to Lu in this manner.

She tried to use her physical attributes to disarm him; after all, he was a man, and no man could resist her when she displayed her charms. She went through her entire repertoire: licking full lips with a seductive tongue, spreading ever-so-slightly those gorgeous limbs, willing her nipples erect and visible through her cotton T-shirt.

"You and I ever gonna get together?" she asked seductively.

Lu fixed his best glare on her and retorted, "I don't fuck pigs."

Dakota gave up trying to seduce him and concentrated on just staying alive. She said in a serious tone, "I'll handle Miceli. Don't you worry."

"I'm not the one who should worry," Lu said. "Go do your thing."

Dakota left the Satan clubhouse feeling like a school-girl just chewed out by the principal. She thought, Well at least he didn't use a ruler on my knuckles, and smiled to herself.

Lu ground the dilaudid into dust, added water to the syringe. A powerful narcotic prescribed to deaden the pain of terminally ill cancer patients, one dilaudid could almost sedate an elephant. He shot three into his vein, added crack for dessert. He locked the office door to prepare himself for the evening.

He replaced the overhead lights with candles, took off his street clothes, and donned a black robe. He knelt before a makeshift altar and started a rhythmical chant: "Prince of darkness, hear my plea."

Stormy instructed the girls to be especially seductive in honor of Anthony Miceli's forty-fifth birthday party. "Shake those titties," she ordered.

Dakota was decked out in a new G-string and a black nightie that pushed and shoved in appropriate spots as the birthday boy walked in with his entourage. The jukebox blared "Happy Birthday" by Martha and the Vandellas, the cue for balloons to float down from the ceiling. Six tables were pushed together with twenty mob guys seated around their boss shouting lewd and lascivious comments to the girls.

"Happy Birthday, honey," Stormy said, and handed Miceli a small box containing a twenty-four-carat-gold, wrist bracelet worth a bundle. "For you. Maybe it's not too late for us."

Miceli opened his gift and bestowed a peck on her cheek.

He said, "You shouldn't of," and placed the bracelet on a wrist already littered with gold.

The party was monumental; naked girls, booze, lines of coke, dancing, and false bravado filled the Chassis. Dakota teased Miceli with dirty dancing by the best body in the joint. She was not ready for the overt move—the booze and drugs had to take hold first.

Hard Rock suddenly screamed, "Quiet! *Shut up!* I want quiet!"

He stood up, held a glass of Scotch in the air, and said, "A toast to the best friend and boss on earth, Tony Miceli." The liquid disappeared in one gulp; the guests followed suit. The group stood with all eyes on Miceli.

Tony began formally, "I'm honored to have such good friends. You people stick with me, and I promise you'll be taken care of. But"—menace now in his voice—"if you ever double-cross me, I'll piss on your grave!"

An awkward silence followed this strange birthday speech. He smiled, then yelled toward the bar, "Another round here. *Now!*" He sat down as the mob guys returned to their individual conversations.

Hard Rock shifted close to Miceli. He said, "They went from their apartment to the Triangle and met some broad. Could've been just pussy. Then they came here."

"After?" Miceli pressed.

The Rock inched closer to Miceli's ear. "Never left. Got ripped here. Fucked around till closing. Vitali got cozy." He hesitated, then repeated, "Vitali got—" and stopped.

"Talk to me, Rock!" Miceli ordered.

Hard Rock squirmed uncomfortably. "Stormy and Vitali, boss. They were a big item. Closed doors, plenty of gabbing and grabbing. I know you and Stormy are tight, but I don't trust the bitch. I think she's a track junkie."

Miceli gulped three inches of straight Scotch as an initial

response. Then he said, "The ol' man gave the okay for a hit."

"Who?" the Rock asked.

A small smile came to Miceli's tight lips. "Vitali," he said.

"When?"

"Real fuckin' soon."

It proceeded as a typical birthday party, with games of pin-the-tail-on-the-dancer, speed drinking, and blowing out the candles held in the vaginas. Around midnight Miceli was doing the Tarantella with some broad when Dakota made her move.

She walked over to him and said admiringly, "You dance good."

"I dance great," his voice slurred.

"Dance with me," Dakota said. "Dance with me— slow."

She grabbed him away from his partner, and they did a slow grind around the floor as her sensuous, active tongue flicked in and out of Tony's ear. Miceli felt in love. He asked all the standard boy-meets-girl questions.

"Why does a fuckin' good dancer like you work in a joint like this?" he said.

She just smiled. She groped him as he went on, "I'm an important man, you know. You belong in the movies." Then, "I'm gonna take care of you."

She smiled again; then she said, "Why don't we go to your place, and I'll lick whipped cream off your dick."

He asked, "We ain't there already?"

Miceli staggered to his Lincoln, supported by Dakota. She rubbed his thigh along the way.

"I'm gonna make you a star," he babbled as they drove along Broad Street.

The loving couple reached his house and tripped up the

steps; they headed for the bar and additional fortifications. Miceli leered at Dakota as he poured Amaretto into two tumblers.

She took a seat on a bar stool and opened her legs wide. He could not resist the invitation; he positioned himself between her knees, and stood with his zipper open. A rough jerk on her belt buckle and a pull of the tight jeans revealed her bare waist. She shifted on the chair and raised her legs high in the air, allowing Miceli to slowly peel the Jordache over her rump. Just the Frederick's underwear left.

"Not here," she said. "Let's go someplace comfy."

Miceli led her to his mirror-walled bedroom with the round water bed, recessed lighting, and elevator music. Dakota watched as he stripped down to purple mono-grammed shorts, then lay his tall, lean body on the heated, wave-resistant water bed.

"Come to Papa," he ordered, adding, "and hurry the fuck up."

The sexy, classy, Chassis dancer stood at the foot of the bed doing a slow, enticing striptease. Down to lace bra and filmy panties, she said, "Be right back, honey. I gotta pee."

She ran off before he could protest, heading for the front door. She disengaged the alarm system with a flick of the switch, then released the dead bolt. The thought crossed her mind that she might actually have time to fuck the Italian before Lu got there to kill him.

She asked aloud, "Why not?" and raced back to the bedroom.

In the middle of a downstroke Miceli suddenly was seized by the feeling someone besides Dakota was in the room. It was far too late for him to react swiftly. He turned.

"What the fuck you doin' here?"

Lu stood silent. Miceli continued with the voice of a man

who knew he was swimming in treacherous waters, "You know who the fuck I am?" Almost a plea, "You're a dead man, you know that? A fuckin' dead man, comin' in my house like this."

Lu had a weird, out-of-this-world smile. He pointed at Miceli with a high-powered weapon that had an unmistakable silencer on the end.

"What the fuck you gonna do?" Miceli cried. "Look, maybe we can talk. You know, make a deal. I'm an okay guy, generous—"

There was a sound like somebody spitting watermelon seeds. Miceli felt a bullet smash into his left kneecap, crushing the bone, ripping through tissue, muscle, cartilage, and ligaments. He screamed. Then a second bullet hit his right kneecap.

Lu walked nonchalantly over to Miceli, now grabbing his new pain with both hands, watching his own blood drip freely between and around his palms onto his white satin sheets.

Dakota stood naked off to one side, watching in quiet fascination. Lu turned to her and ordered, "Leave!"

She gathered up her clothes, gave Miceli a last look, and made a quick retreat. She had debated whether to say something like "good-bye" or maybe "see you around," then decided on silence. Acid was waiting for her. As she entered the living room, he slit her throat, thereby eliminating the only witness.

Anthony Miceli, made mob guy of the Philadelphia crime family, died a slow, painful death. It culminated in Lu cutting off Miceli's ears and shoving an Ace of Spades in his mouth. The last two acts were the unmistakable signature of a Vietnam combat death.

· · ·

THE two undercover agents were just waking from their late-night binge as Miceli's body lay lifeless, in a state of semi–rigor mortis. The corpse would not be found until the next day because Hard Rock and his friends had been given further work to do. The Rock had his orders for that night. They included a sanctioned hit on one Joseph Vitali and his muscle, the Moose.

Lerza waited impatiently as the Mr. Coffee did its thing. Moose sipped a beer, smoked a big Parodi cigar. It was six in the evening.

Moose asked, "What's on the agenda for tonight?"

Lerza poured a cup of java, added two sugars, and took the chair next to Moose. "The call to Lu to set up a deal," he said.

"When and where?"

"Chandy's in two days. I like the place; besides, it'll be a nice touch having them cross the bridge with the dope."

"Is Lu actually gonna deliver?"

"Don't think so. Probably use a mule."

"Whatta we gonna do 'bout Miceli?"

There was an edge in Lerza's voice as he said, "We do squat, 'cause Miceli ain't no threat. We'll take two, three scores from the bikers, then I'll call Tony, sweet-talk him and order up some real weight for the grand finale. That okay with you?" Almost a challenge.

"Sounds good to me."

"Look, partner," in softer voice, "trust me on this Miceli thing. Even if he wants a piece of us, it'll take a lot of convincing to get Amato's okay. We got three, maybe four weeks. In the meantime we jam up the Satans."

Moose did not sound too convincing, however, when he said, "Yeah, Joey, whatever."

Winter was appearing full force, tossing wind and snow around, registering a wicked windchill. Philadelphia was one of those eastern seaboard cities, like New York, Baltimore, and Boston, whose sheer mass of people, cars, and buildings crippled it with only an inch of the white stuff.

HARD ROCK sped up Sixteenth Street toward the Chassis, followed by the Ciccinis in a Buick, the Palermo cousins in a Caddy, and assorted other mob guys in assorted other big cars. They had the look of men with a mission—frowns, grimaces, and puckered assholes.

Stormy was not exactly glad to see Hard Rock and his friends, although she smiled and poured drinks for them in her office.

She asked sarcastically, "Where's Tony? Haven't seen him or Dakota since they left last night."

"You jealous?"

"No, honey. He's over twenty-one, white, and free."

"I hear you're tight with that Vitali creep."

"Where'd you hear that?"

"The wall's got fuckin' ears." Hard Rock stood up and walked over to her. "You two got close here the other night."

"Just some drinks," she protested.

"The fuck you kiddin', slut!" he shouted.

"Come on," she said, "you know—"

His arm shot out; he slapped her hard on the right cheek.

Stormy felt the blood trickle down her lips onto her knee as she landed on the office floor. Her mind raced, trying to figure out what was happening. Even for Hard Rock, this was strange behavior. Miceli had to have known of and okayed this beating, which meant he'd ordered it.

She relaxed, thinking the worst was over. Just a little roughhouse to show her who was boss—Italian payback for getting drunk with Vitali. Miceli's way of putting her in her place.

"Listen and listen good, bitch!" Hard Rock grabbed her by the hair, jerking her to her feet. "You're gonna make a call."

The worst was just beginning for Stormy Monday.

As he answered the phone in their hotel apartment, Moose asked himself, Who could this be?

The voice was Stormy's; she announced her name then said, "Gotta see you and Joe."

"No problem. We'll be at the Chassis around ten."

"Not here." Stormy sounded excited. "Fairmont Park, midnight, by the boat dock."

"You all right?" Moose asked, sensing something different in her tone.

"Fine," she lied. "But it's important that I see you and Joe. Okay?"

"We'll be there, darlin'," Moose said. "Don't you worry your pretty head."

"Please, Moose, tell Joe, both of you gotta be there."

A small voice of warning stirred in Moose's head as he thought, trap. He assured her. "We'll be there."

She hung up. Moose made a beeline for Lerza and found him behind a closed door. Moose banged his massive hand against the wood, saying, "Open the fuck up. We got trouble."

When they sat down at the kitchen table, Moose told Lerza about Stormy's unexpected call. They reviewed the options and reached the conclusion they *had* to go to Fairmont Park at midnight. It probably was a trap but, as Lerza said, "It's like a movie, Moose. Can't walk out in the middle, gotta see how it ends."

"It's like a horror movie," Moose countered, "and they *always* end shitty. Let's call Patty."

"No!" Lerza was adamant. "What can she do besides give her little hysterical speech and tell us not to go."

Moose smiled and said, "We gotta go, Joey, I know that. But maybe we should tell someone. Keenan or maybe get back in touch with Stormy. Tell something to someone."

In the end they spent the hours before the meeting drinking vodka and talking about Vietnam. Their conversations of late usually included memories of the Nam. Around 11:30 P.M. Lerza announced, "It's time."

As they entered the elevator, Moose hit the "Open Door" button and told Joey he forgot something and would meet him in the garage. Back in the apartment he dialed Patty's number.

"Hello," a sleepy voice finally responded.

"Listen up good, I gotta hurry," he said.

He told her that Lerza and he were on their way to meet Stormy at Fairmont Park. No, he did not know why. Yes, he knew it could be a trap. No, he could not talk Joey out of it. Yes, they were just leaving and *yes*, he, Moose, wanted her there.

The Mercedes carrying the two FBI undercover agents rolled slowly through the acreage of Fairmont Park. This was a massive area near Center City with ponds, lakes, horse trails, picnic grounds, and lots of spots for Mafia ambushes. An abbreviated graveyard shift of city cops patrolled the park but at the moment were downing thermos jugs of coffee at the park office.

A night ground fog rolled in, limiting vision, adding to a sense of doom. Moose said, "I don't like this," as he checked his ammunition, playing with ejector rods and safeties.

Lerza had a resigned look in his eyes. A condemned man just turned down by the governor.

"See anything?" Moose asked.

"Trees, bushes. Lots of places to hide."

"What's our play gonna be?"

"I go in first, you lay back, wait and see their move. Cover my ass." Lerza chuckled. "Just like the ol' days."

"You'll be a sitting duck," Moose protested. "I don't like it."

"Got a better idea?"

"Yes," Moose said. "Call in the cavalry, don't go anywhere near the boat dock."

He grabbed Lerza's shoulder, pleading, "You don't wanna hear this, but Stormy ain't completely trustworthy. She's a snitch, Joey, been lying her whole life, don't know how to tell the truth. She sells out to the highest bidder, got Satan ol' ladies working for her and Miceli's dick in her pussy for years. Why believe her now?"

Lerza stopped the car and then explained, "We call the troops and the case is over. Besides, I don't trust the troops, don't even know who they are anymore. Who's gonna come? Keenan, maybe our OPR friends, Frick and Frack, the PD? *We* gotta do this, Moose, *we* gotta play it out, just like Nam." He repeated slowly, "Just like Nam."

The Moose was a victim of too many late-night war movies, when two buddies go down in a blaze of gunfire and background music. He looked Lerza in the eye and said, "Let's do it, munchkin."

They had no way of knowing that Hard Rock, Stormy, both Ciccini brothers, the cousins from Palermo, and half-a-dozen other mob guys waited behind the storage building at the boat dock. Stormy was on the verge of tears, afraid of Hard Rock and ashamed of what she had done. Knowing what was going to happen but rationalizing she had to save herself, didn't she? After all, she barely knew this Joe Lerza and his friend, Moose. They certainly weren't worth her life.

Lerza stopped the Mercedes a hundred yards from the dock. Moose got out and worked his way around on foot. Then Lerza checked his revolver and rolled the car to a stop in the parking lot adjacent to the boat-dock ramp.

He waited in the car for a moment, allowing Moose to get in position, then opened his door and slowly walked toward the building. A few overhead lights were positioned among the tall trees, but the moonless, foggy night was still virtually pitch dark.

The FBI undercover agent grabbed the butt of his revolver, pulling it from the shoulder holster. It felt good. He quickly surveyed the killing zone, as he had done so often in Nam. He did not like what he saw.

A wooden ramp with water on both sides led to a combination storage and boat-rental building. No cover, no concealment, no chance if it *was* an ambush. The building doors appeared closed and padlocked. If he retraced his steps it would place him back in the dimly lit asphalt parking lot. A quick calculation on ways of strategic retreat brought the sad conclusion that there weren't any.

He thought, Fuck it, and started toward the wooden ramp.

The sound of heels on wood broke the late-night silence. Stormy appeared from behind the storage building, and even at thirty yards Lerza could see the swollen lip, the terror in her eyes.

"You okay?" he asked.

She continued a slow walk toward him and whimpered, "Fine."

The hairs on the back of Lerza's neck suddenly stood on end. He asked, "What's the emergency?"

Stormy hesitated slightly, groping for words. Her mind raced on a moral pendulum back and forth, between setting up Lerza and saving herself.

Although Hard Rock had not said the words, she knew Lerza would die, probably viciously, slowly, but what could *she* do? Maybe nothing, maybe something. All of this flashed through her brain in a split second as she wrestled with her conscience. Stormy judged the distance between herself and Joe at thirty yards.

Now or never. Before she realized what she was doing, Stormy Monday, former topless dancer, drug-dealing FBI snitch, heard herself scream, *"Go back, it's a trap!"*

Lerza watched in horror as automatic gunfire ripped into Stormy's brain, tearing chunks of scalp from her head. His first instinct was to run and help her, the way he had done in Vietnam for the ex-Sergeant. But the bullets that sprayed at his feet made him jump off the wooden bridge into the shallow water.

A round of bullets from one of the mobsters' guns hit his thigh before he completed the leap. A check of the damage showed he had been hit in the exact spot where the NVA's AK-47 round had struck in 1968.

He lay in the shallow water for a moment, as he had done in Nam, before the flashback hit him like a sledge-hammer to the mouth. Bullets flying overhead, blood oozing from his body, totally alone in the killing zone, and hopes for escape rated "shitty" at best. It was a bad case of déjà-vu and the worst was yet to come.

Muzzle flashes were everywhere, instinct told him he was in a cross fire. He thought, Return fire. He put out four rounds in the direction of the supply building.

He heard Moose long before he saw his best friend coming to save him. He screamed, "Go back!" but there was no retreat in the Moose.

"Hold on, munchkin!" he shouted. "I'm coming, I'm coming!"

To Lerza, Moose seemed to be in some kind of slow

motion. He watched, knowing already what had to happen. It was his dream, his own personal nightmare come true. A twenty-year-old replay of the night of horror his brain had told him could never happen again.

He tried to stop it, screamed, *"No!"* But Moose ignored his protest and kept moving closer. The sound of feet splashing through shallow water told Lerza that Moose was almost beside him. The massive agent reached his prone friend. He fired five rounds at the mobsters before kneeling and asking, "Where you hit, Joey?"

"You shouldn't have come," Lerza protested. "I'm okay."

"You look like shit." Moose laughed. "I'm gonna get us outta—"

Four bullets hit Moose's chest before he could complete his sentence. Four steel-jacketed .38-caliber *Plus P* rounds could down an elephant, but Moose just stared at the holes in his body and returned fire with four of his own nine-millimeter rounds. Then two bullets hit the big FBI agent in his arm and leg, which only seemed to step up his rage. Three more hits put Moose prone in the water as he slowly fell alongside Lerza, who noticed the blood spreading over Moose's tan coat until it was all but red.

Lerza screamed once again, *"No!"* as though to protest the attack on his buddy. He grabbed at Moose, who was barely conscious.

"You okay, buddy?" Moose whispered.

"I'm okay," Lerza said. "How 'bout you?"

"Been better, Joey."

Lerza held Moose's limp head out of the water, keeping one eye on the storage shed. He said, knowing it was an impossibility, "I'll get us out of here. Hang in there."

Moose chuckled. "You're full of shit, pal. We're in the trick bag."

Lerza thought Moose was correct, but his combat experience demanded that he return fire or the bad guys would soon be standing six inches away, emptying guns at them like they were ducks in a barrel.

He boosted himself up to return fire and was greeted by a bullet that glanced off his skull, making a two-inch crevice in his forehead. Blood poured into his eyes, causing him to fire wildly in the direction of Miceli's men.

The blood triggered his final break with reality. Something deep in his psyche snapped. Joseph Lerza, former Vietnam veteran, FBI undercover agent, father and husband, finally went over the edge. He jumped to his feet and a strange animal-like sound erupted from within.

He screamed, "Fuckin' NVA!" and charged the storage shed, as he had the jungle full of enemy soldiers in Nam.

Sirens pierced their late night terror. Patty and six Philadelphia PD cruisers had just red-lighted their way to the parking lot as Hard Rock and most of the mobsters were bolting into their cars and high-speeding out of Fairmont Park. Three mob guys were taken into custody. (None did any talking during their interrogation, all made bond.)

It was the worst possible night Patty could imagine. Moose lay bleeding and unconscious in the shallow water with nine bullets in various parts of his body and seemed doomed to die. Stormy Monday was stretched out prone on the boat dock, extremely dead. Lerza was screaming like a madman and firing his weapon wildly at the now-vacant boat dock supply building.

He kept shouting, "Corpsman, *up*! The sarge is hit. Corpsman, *up*!"

PART 2

25

The NVA's fist crashed into Lerza's head with tremendous force. It hurt, but he would not give his enemy the satisfaction of showing pain.

"Fuck you, gook!" he spat in the North Vietnamese face.

This time it was the butt of the AK-47 that hit the festering wounds on his thigh bone, causing him to lose his balance and fall facedown on the dirt floor. His resolve was even stronger as he snarled again, "Fuck you!"

The NVA gave him one of those smug smiles, left the room, and returned ceremoniously pushing the unconscious body of the ex-Sergeant into Lerza's view. Blood seeped from his chest, but a slight movement indicated life somewhere deep inside his best friend. The NVA removed a sixteen-inch killing knife from a brown leather sheath and put it to the ear of the ex-Sergeant. With the precise movements of a surgeon the NVA—

Lerza awoke, smelled "hospital," and heard the jargon. A voice said, "A hundred milligrams Demerol."

He forced his eyes open but they took a few moments to focus on the IV's and other hospital paraphernalia attached to his body. A twist of the head allowed him to recognize the emergency-room chaos, six or seven people surrounding some poor soul on the next table. It did not register that the Moose was being worked over by the "Almost Dead" hospital blue team.

An attempt by Lerza to raise his head caused excruciating pain. He gave in to his body's warning signs, lay back and watched in silent fascination.

"Don't look good," an authoritative voice said at the next table.

"Damage to lung, kidneys, and intestines," somebody reported.

Finally a gray-haired nurse noticed Lerza's open eyes and approached him. She said, not too sympathetically, "Oh, so you're awake. I'll get doctor."

A young man with long brown hair, a sparse beard, white coat, and a stethoscope hanging around his scrawny neck, appeared at Lerza's table. "How you feeling?" he asked gently.

"You tell me," Lerza replied.

"You'll live, but you got some serious mending to do. A head wound caused a bad skull fracture, and the thigh is more than just superficial. We'll probably keep you here a few weeks."

A light went off in Lerza's brain. He raised himself to a sitting position, ignoring the pain.

He asked worriedly, "What about my friend?"

The young doctor put on his most serious face and said, "Bad news. She's dead."

"She?" He thought a moment, then said, "I mean Moose."

"The big guy brought in with you is critical. It's touch and go," the doctor said.

"Don't bullshit me. What are his chances?" Lerza demanded.

The doctor gave it some thought. "Not good. Twenty percent at best. His insides are like scrambled eggs."

Lerza slowly began pulling the IV's from his arms and painstakingly managed to dangle his legs down to the hospital floor.

"What are you doing?" The doctor asked.

"Leaving."

"Oh no, you don't. You are in no shape to go. You can't. I won't let you."

Lerza placed his unsteady feet on the tiled floor, grabbed his coat, got his bearings, and ignored the young doctor's protest. As he started for the door, the physician actually blocked his path.

"You can't leave!" he ordered.

Lerza grabbed the lapels of the starched white coat and hissed, "Get the fuck outta my way. I'm gonna go kill that scum."

"What? Who?" the startled doctor asked.

"That bastard Miceli is as good as dead." Lerza tossed the doctor aside and limped out the door.

He took a taxi to the apartment, slowly making it to their quarters. He removed his coat and dragged himself to the phone. He called Keenan, told him what had happened, and said he was going to get revenge on what the Italians had done to Moose, especially Miceli. "He's a fuckin' dead man," Lerza put it. "You understand me, Mr. SAC?"

Keenan tried to dissuade him, saying, "Joe, it's over. Come in. The case is finished, do you understand?" The SAC knew instinctively that his career was intertwined with Lerza's acts.

"Fuck you, too," Lerza said. "It ain't over until Miceli dies. The sarge is hurt bad, Miceli has to pay."

The dial tone buzzed in Keenan's ear, signaling upcoming doom, dread, and disaster. Blue Flame Bobby had been right when he said, "These undercover agents are nothing but prima donna cowboys."

HARD Rock made good his escape from Fairmont Park and headed straight for his boss's house to give a report on "the meet." He found the front door unlocked. In the living room Dakota's spectacular naked body, spilled blood from a slit throat. Miceli's body lay on the floor of his bedroom, minus his ears, the Ace of Spades stuffed in his mouth.

At first even the conscienceless Hard Rock was aghast at this sordid display of death. But then he felt a certain exhilaration. He was now in charge; his boss lay at his feet in a river of blood. He walked around wiping fingerprints off things he might have touched and left the apartment.

The next day the Rock placed an anonymous call to the cops. What the hell, he thought, I can't let him rot there like an antipasto salad.

PATTY tried to fight her urge to say "I told you so" as she gave her oral report to Keenan at his home. The Fairmont Park Massacre, as she nicknamed it, seemed suddenly to pique Keenan's concern for Lerza and Moose.

"How could you let this happen?" Keenan challenged her.

"Me?" she said incredulously.

Keenan paced nervously in his sterile living room filled with modern expensive bric-a-brac. Fear and indecisiveness were etched on his handsome face. It was damage-control time, and the SAC needed a fall guy—or "girl," as the case might be.

"Did you know about the meeting at Fairmont Park?" Keenan pressed Patty.

She refused to sit even after repeated commands from the SAC. She zigzagged a crossing route with Keenan over the plush pink carpet. "Well, I knew," she began. "Not really," she corrected. "Moose called as they were leaving. I couldn't stop them. I tried."

"Why couldn't you stop them?" he asked.

"Because they were out of control," she said. "You knew it. I told you to pull them. *You* could've prevented this."

Keenan knew Masters was correct in her assessment of the entire affair. He also knew that an inquiry would signal the beginning of his end. There was her memo that predicted the night's doom, coupled with Dr. Thompson's clinical evaluation of Lerza. The kind of smoking gun newspapers doubled their circulation with. He could see it now. The bespectacled psychiatrist staring sternly at the cameras, saying, "Yes, I did recommend case termination prior to these killings." "Yes, the FBI was aware that Agent Lerza was no longer fit for undercover duty." "No, my recommendation is not binding on them; I am merely a consultant with no official government capacity."

Keenan finally slumped into a highback chair and decided on charm and tact.

"Please sit, Patty," he begged. "Let me pour you some coffee."

She reluctantly took a seat opposite Keenan, wary of his sudden attitude change. The SAC poured two cups of blended java from a hand-painted china pot. He handed Patty her cup, smiled, and said, "I probably should have listened, Patty, you were right and I—" He purposely didn't say the words, admitting his guilt.

Masters didn't respond. She knew the SAC wasn't finished. He was in the middle of bobbing and weaving an alibi—a way of keeping himself administratively pure.

He sipped his coffee and asked, "Did you interview the doctor at the hospital?"

"Me and three city detectives. The doc was scared shitless. He called the cops. I was on the phone to you when Lerza ignored the doctor and checked himself out."

The SAC didn't like what he was hearing. Another law-enforcement agency, the Philadelphia police, now enjoyed this blemish on the the face of the supposedly lily-white FBI. Denial would be more difficult.

"They know Lerza's an FBI agent?" Keenan said, already knowing the answer.

Patty nodded, adding, "They also know he threatened to kill Miceli."

"What?" Keenan sounded horrified.

"Lerza told the doctor that he was on his way to kill Miceli. The detectives copied every word for their report."

Keenan visibly sighed, "Joe called me and said the same thing. He sounded strange, Patty. Like a different person. Like someone who'd—"

Masters interrupted, "He'd just been shot! How'd you expect him to sound?" There was anger on her lovely face.

"Of course," Keenan said, to calm her. "It's just that we need to limit Joe's exposure. Find him before he does something foolish. Any ideas on where he's headed?"

She did not want to admit it, but Joe Lerza was, in all probability, searching for Anthony Miceli as they spoke. Should they call the Mafia and warn them? She dismissed that idea and decided on her own course of action.

"The doctor said that Joe was loaded up with Demerol, and he'll have trouble just staying conscious in the next eight hours. But if he isn't found soon, infection will set in, and there's no predicting what can happen then. Delusion, gangrene, death. Wherever he's going, it won't be far."

"I'll have to let the Assistant Director know," Keenan said.

"I wouldn't," Patty warned.

"Why not?" he asked, clearly indecisive.

Masters placed her coffee cup on the nearby table. She leaned toward him and explained. "He'll try and run this thing from Washington. He'll order you to cough up Lerza to the headhunters." She smiled, then continued, "I'll have to tell him about my warnings, about Dr. Thompson's visit."

Keenan received her threat loud and clear. "We'll find Joe first," he said. "Maybe Moose will rally, and then we have good news to report, not just bad. I'll wait, but you've got to find Lerza fast!"

J O E Lerza was a walking time bomb. He'd been seriously wounded, suffered severe blood loss, was filled with a pain-killing narcotic, and had a terminal case of anger and paranoia. The former undercover agent had left the hospital obsessed with the idea of killing Anthony Miceli. But his body had a different agenda, one that included blackouts and delirium.

The cab driver looked at his fare in the mirror, shook his head, and said, "Hey, buddy, you don't seem too good. You okay?"

"Just drive," Lerza commanded.

"Where to?"

The question confused Lerza until he got his bearings. Then he began, "Left here, straight, a right at the light." Eventually he found Miceli's apartment. He threw a Ben Franklin at the cabby, insuring he'd be remembered. "Thanks, Mac," the grateful driver said. "You want some help or something?"

Joe dragged himself from the cab, forced a smile, and said, "Wait."

"Till the sun don't shine," the happy cabbie assured him. "As long as you want."

Taxicab drivers were like priests and bartenders in some ways, Lerza thought. They daily observed the varied peccadillos of humanity, and none of it could arouse surprise or shock. There was a strange confidentiality between a driver and his passenger. Privileged communication, like doctor-patient. The hundred bucks helped.

Lerza staggered up the front steps to Miceli's row home without a plan. He was minus a weapon, sanity, and physical strength. All he knew was that he would kill the man who had hurt his friends. Images of Stormy's shattered head and Moose's bloody chest festered in Lerza's psyche.

The front door opened to his touch. Even in his condition, alarm bells went off in his head. He took a few steps inside the vestibule and waited, listening for some sign of deceit. A familiar smell filtered through his deadened senses. At first he couldn't identify the odor, but it didn't take long to recognize death.

He entered the living room and saw Dakota lying naked and seductive, even in death. The clean, neat slit on her neck and dried blood resembled a pretty brown necklace on the sexy topless dancer. Joe noticed a half-filled glass of Scotch on the bar. He gulped it empty, then headed for the bedroom.

Before his eyes lay Anthony Miceli, made mob guy, dope czar, Don Juan—dead. There was a surprised expression on his frozen face. Lerza approached the corpse and took in the nasty handiwork on the body. Knees, ears, balls slashed, and the Ace of Spades shoved in his mouth. Joe instinctively grabbed the card, pulling it from Miceli's teeth, studying it like it was some kind of pop quiz. He replaced it inside the mutilated face and found himself suddenly filled with rage.

Someone had deprived him of his kill. Someone else had

taken his satisfaction, his vengeance, his retribution. He began savagely kicking Miceli's face, stomping on it repeatedly until his own pain became excruciating. Lerza fell to the floor beside Miceli, gasping for air. Eventually he regained enough strength to get to his feet and shuffle out of the deceased man's home.

The cabbie dutifully waited for his big tipper, watching in amazement as Lerza half stepped his way to the car. Opening Joe's door, the cabbie asked, "Where to, pal?"

Joe directed him to the one safe place on this earth— the last refuge for wounded, half-crazed undercover agents, a sanctuary from NVA savages and mob hit men—Patty Masters's apartment.

PATTY left Keenan's house with a plan. She didn't want to believe Lerza would actually kill Miceli, but nothing in her present life made sense. So she headed for Miceli's house, deciding on some surveillance. Operating on pure adrenaline, Patty had not slept in forty hours. She drove in an unfeeling daze through the Philadelphia weekday streets and the city's routine activities. Businessmen and women, coffee cups in hand, laughing and ready for the beginning of their *normal* work day. "Normal" was no longer in her vocabulary, and she felt jealous of the peaceful surroundings.

Patty found a parking slot directly across from Miceli's home, hoping Lerza would show but praying he wouldn't. She reviewed the possibilities. Lerza couldn't go home to his family, couldn't go back to his undercover apartment, and wouldn't involve civilian friends in his work. Killing Miceli was a long shot, but Patty was down to deuces.

She glanced at her *New York Times* at about the same time the first police cruiser pulled up with its siren blaring and overhead lights flashing. It was followed closely by an ambulance.

She flashed her tin following the Philly cops through Miceli's front door. "Call homicide," an old grizzly uniform told a rookie.

Twenty minutes later the homicide dicks had Miceli's home looking like the textbook crime scene. An M.E. bent over a corpse, lab guys took photographs of the room and dusted for prints, a chalk outline of the two bodies and yellow plastic tape proclaimed "Official Police Business."

Patty approached the homicide lieutenant, a twenty-eight-year veteran of the Philadelphia mean streets. She asked, "Whatta you got?"

"A corpse," was the succinct reply.

"Time of death?"

The grizzly veteran of a thousand homicides looked at her for the first time and asked, "What's the FBI's interest in this?"

She decided on a version of the truth. "He's a made wise-guy. The Bureau is always interested in organized crime."

The old lieutenant chewed on a stogie. Usually a pretty girl could soften his gruff personality, but this was an FBI agent, and all FBI agents thought their shit didn't stink. He snapped, "Cut the fluff. This is my jurisdiction, and unless you wanna fill out twenty request forms in triplicate, then ante up with some truth."

Patty Masters had little fight left. She told Lieutenant George Lanuti about their undercover case gone bad. It was important to determine time of death since it could eliminate Lerza as a suspect. He'd been a memorable hospital patient, and the time of his premature exit had been dutifully noted on his chart. But fate was playing dirty tricks on the good guys. The temperature in Miceli's house was sixty-one degrees, and the dead man had consumed a fifth of hard liquor prior to his execution. Both these factors would make a coroner's already-difficult estimate on time of death equivalent to a rookie weatherman's prediction of a sudden tropical typhoon.

A lab technician interrupted their conversation. "We got plenty of prints, Lieutenant," he said. "Even one on the Ace of Spades in his mouth. That has to be the killer's."

"Get elimination prints from the corpse," the Lieutenant ordered.

The small group was again interrupted by a detective. He said, "Lieutenant, a neighbor saw a yellow cab parked outside for about fifteen minutes yesterday."

Lieutenant Lanuti automatically barked, "Get your ass to the cab company, find out who drove that shift, check their trip sheets. Anybody don't cooperate, arrest them as an accessory!"

"Yes, sir!" The detective raced out the door.

Patty studied Miceli's body for the first time, noticing the killer's peculiarities. She asked, "What's the significance of the knees, the ears, the card in the mouth?"

Lieutenant Lanuti twirled the cigar in his mouth, and said, "Yes, lady, the guy who did the hit was a real pro. He'd also been in Nam."

"Why's that?"

"Grunt outfits in Vietnam, around 'sixty-seven, 'sixty-eight, usually Marines, liked to cut off an ear, carry it around like a trophy, put the card of death in NVA's mouths as a warning, their own personal greeting. Let the enemy know not to fuck with their outfit."

"A pro," Masters said, almost to herself.

"A real pro," Lanuti agreed. "Like a guy who'd been wearing a gun his whole adult life."

She stared at Lanuti. The description fit Lerza, but she would not believe he could kill anyone, except perhaps himself with drugs and alcohol.

26

Michael Amato sat across from Hard Rock looking every bit the dapper aging crime boss. A snappy tan three-piece pinstripe suit, matching silk tie, and gold pocket watch enhanced the Don's quiet authority. It was critical that this scene unfold as planned.

The Rock's violent nature had to be neutralized. Amato was in the seventh-inning stretch of his perfectly executed game plan. The score—a few dead, a few wounded, and the best yet to come. Definitely a high-run contest.

"So, my friend Miceli is dead," Amato began. "He was the son I never had."

"It had to be those scumbucket Satans," Hard Rock said. "I got the boys ready to hit their clubhouse."

"We must wait." Amato's voice was soothing. "It is not certain who killed Miceli. I will know very soon who will pay the price of his death. Very soon."

The Rock had never been privileged to attend such a high-level meeting and did his best to act human. "Had to be the Satans," he said. "Nobody else has the balls."

Amato kept eye contact with this psycho, treating him like a loaded shotgun with a sensitive trigger.

"I agree with you," he said sincerely. "And I want *you* to be the person to avenge our friend's death. When the deed is done, it is you who will direct Miceli's operation."

Hard Rock, puffed like a peacock at his newfound respectability, nervously twisted a massive gold pinky ring while trying to form a reply. "Me?" he said, pointing a fat finger at himself.

"You," Amato replied. "But first we must wait. As you know, my friend, leadership is complicated. Decisions made only after each obstacle anticipated. Every complication foreseen and planned for. If the feds think we have declared war, their attention may prove smothering."

"Don't we do nothing?" Hard Rock asked.

"Share a plan."

The two men sat in Amato's plush office at the Italian Club. Amato gazed out the window. Winter's gray was evolving into spring green. The old Italian looked forward to its warmth. His bones needed the sun's energy to turn more fluidly toward the fruition of his revenge.

"As long as Miceli's killers end up dead," Hard Rock said.

Amato smiled and assured, "They will, and it will be at your hand, my new capo."

"You making me a boss?" Hard Rock asked directly.

"Yes," Amato lied. "A pledge of Coda Omertus. My successor."

"I'm honored, Don Amato," the Rock said, eager to please. "What is your plan? How can I help?"

"In due time, my new friend."

"You won't regret the decision, Mr. A.," Hard Rock said, smiling.

"I'm sure I won't." Amato smiled back.

PATTY Masters activated her digital pager and the SAC's private number appeared. Her first instinct was to ignore Keenan, but she realized that any official word on Joe would come through FBI channels.

Deputy Police Commissioner Salvatore Rigosa paced the SAC's office, chain-smoking nonfiltered Camels. Balding, portly, and politically connected, Rigosa had the smug look of a man holding a royal straight flush to his opponents six high. The two men had already exchanged the opening verbal barrage in a conventional war about to turn nuclear. Now they waited in stony silence for Special Agent Masters.

Rigosa clutched a handful of official-looking documents like rare stamps in a windstorm. Patty was ushered into Keenan's office and introduced to the deputy commissioner.

"Patty," the SAC said, "this is Commissioner Rigosa of the Philly PD. He's got some questions and, I'm afraid, bad news."

"About Joe?" she asked immediately.

"Sorry to say." Rigosa took a deep drag on his cigarette. "But first, some questions."

Keenan approached Patty. "I've briefed the Commissioner about the undercover case. Don't hold anything back, Patty. The Philly PD wants to help. They understand our predicament. They realize the potential embarrassment."

Patty was livid at Keenan's choice of words. "Embarrassment," "predicament." It was clear that the SAC had already sold Joe Lerza out.

Rigosa began by reading portions of Masters's own

memo. The one she'd sent to headquarters in an attempt to force Keenan's hand. It had been intended to help Lerza, to bring him back from the undercover work destroying his life. Now, in the hands of Rigosa, it was nothing more than "evidence" against a murder suspect—Joseph Lerza.

Rigosa started with the descriptive terms of "time bomb" and "potentially dangerous," then advanced to adjectives like "uncontrollable" and "destructive," ending with the ever-damaging "capable of violence."

Masters had purposely laid it on heavy, and now her words backfired. She didn't have to ask how Rigosa got a copy of the smoking-gun memo.

He waited for her to respond. Rigosa's practiced silence was guaranteed to elicit fear in his subordinates. Patty wouldn't give the bully his satisfaction. "You making a point?" she asked sarcastically.

Rigosa had all the cards and was enjoying the FBI's collective discomfort. "Yeah," he said. "Let me make the point, Patty." He shuffled the papers in his hand, then slapped a sheet triumphantly. "Fingerprint report," he began. "Got two latents that match with Agent Lerza's knowns. One off a Scotch glass in Miceli's house." He paused for effect, slapped his report again, and added, "The other from an Ace of Spades card stuck in Miceli's mouth."

The words hit Masters hard. Scientific evidence was the most difficult to refute. A murder-scene print of the accused was a sure conviction. It made all other evidence pale. Defense attorneys would beg "plea bargain" when their client's print ended up as Government Exhibit One.

She tried anyway. "What's that prove?" she said. "Just that Lerza was in Miceli's house. What about the murder weapon? What about an eyewitness?"

Rigosa gave her a wicked smirk. "We'll find the

weapon," he promised. "And we've got an eyewitness that puts Lerza on the murder scene at about the same time the M.E. fixed death."

Keenan finished Rigosa's litany of hard evidence. "It seems," he began, "that a taxi driver took Lerza to Miceli's apartment yesterday afternoon. The M.E. had trouble on time of death but fixed it at sometime between two A.M. and five P.M. yesterday. Cabbie said Lerza was acting weird, mumbling something about killing someone. I'm sorry, Patty." His tone held no sincerity.

"Why am I here?" Patty demanded.

"Because you are still an FBI agent assigned to the case," Keenan said sternly. "You know the players and Lerza's hangouts. This office will cooperate fully with the police on the murder investigation because we *are* the FBI."

She knew Rigosa wasn't bluffing with his evidence. That meant Lerza was as good as convicted of Miceli's murder. A first-year law student could win the case. The evidence was overwhelming. There was Lerza's bizarre behavior, his vow to kill Miceli made to Keenan and the emergency room doctor. The cabbie placing Joe at the murder scene at the time of death and, finally, the irrefutable fingerprints. Her memo would also make interesting courtroom testimony. In addition to the memo, the Freedom of Information Act guaranteed the prosecutors every document written on this case. In her mind, she heard the prosecutor:

"Did you write the memo, Agent Masters?"

"Yes, sir."

"Did you believe what you wrote?"

"Yes, sir."

"So you believed Lerza was unbalanced, dangerous, and capable of violence?"

"Yes, sir."

"Did you ever find the missing cocaine?"

"No, sir."

"How about the missing money, unvouchered expenses?"

"No, sir."

"Is it at all possible that Lerza kept the cocaine and stole the money?"

"He wouldn't."

"Is it possible, Agent Masters—remember you are under oath and you testified that Lerza was unbalanced and should be suspended from the case—if he didn't keep the cocaine, then where is it? Is it not true that your own chain of custody shows the cocaine discrepancy with Lerza?"

"Yes, sir."

Following her testimony on the witness stand, she saw Dr. Thompson summoned, who would substitute clinical terms for her lay description of an insane Lerza. An open-and-shut case if ever there was one. She might concede bizarre behavior, but her heart firmly believed Joe Lerza was not a common killer.

The final piece of paper Rigosa tapped was an arrest warrant for Special Agent Joseph Lerza. When she saw this, Patty pleaded directly to Keenan, "You can't let this happen. He's innocent."

"I'd like to agree with you, Patty," Keenan said. "It's difficult when one of our own goes bad, but the facts speak for themselves. He's out of control and *may* kill again. He's capable of it and dangerous. Lerza's killed before in Vietnam. He's a highly trained assassin who needs help. The FBI will support Joe, plead insanity, get treatment."

"I've got to go," Rigosa announced. "Can I assume you will effect Lerza's arrest, if given the opportunity?"

Keenan answered for Patty. "Of course, Commissioner. We are sworn to uphold the law." He glared at her and asked, "Correct?"

She was silent. She stared in pure hate at Rigosa as he left Keenan's office. The two FBI agents were now alone in a room filled with tension and treachery. She tried a last plea.

"Lerza didn't kill anybody," she said to Keenan. "He's not capable of murder."

"Men do strange things under pressure, Patty."

"I suppose *you're* off the hook." There was anger in her usually soft voice.

"What do you mean?" He looked startled.

"Lerza's the scapegoat, the sacrificial lamb headquarters dissects. You offer him up to the public, saying, 'See, we clean our own house, dirty agents do go to jail.' It all ends at Joe, and you get to retire to some golf course in Jersey. Only you're in this up to your blow-dried hair. You ignored my warnings, caring only about your own career. Joe and Moose are pawns in your power games. You're just as guilty, Mr. SAC, and if Joe Lerza goes to jail, you should go to hell!"

Masters started for the door. "We just had our last meeting." She spat.

Keenan stood up and asked, "Are you quitting, Miss Masters?"

She turned and said, "Not hardly, Mr. SAC. I'm just beginning."

LERZA lay on Patty's couch, alternating consciousness with unconsciousness, reality with flashbacks. During his more lucid moments, he would go through the full range of emotions, starting with self-pity and ending with fury. During his less lucid moments, he tried to ease the pain of his ongoing torture at the hands of the ruthless but skilled NVA interrogators. He ripped off the head bandage, causing the crusted, coagulated blood to flow freely from his scalp wound onto his face.

"Kill me instead!" he screamed at his imaginary nemesis.

"You mother fuckers!" he cried out, trying to free himself from imaginary bonds on his legs and hands.

Patty, who had not slept in fifty hours, was on the verge of nervous exhaustion as she drove to the apartment. Her world was in a shambles with Lerza a fugitive, Moose all but dead, and her own FBI career one big question mark. She opted now for sleep, if for no other reason than to avoid passing out.

Perhaps it was the lack of sleep, perhaps the conflicting moral messages her brain was sending to her heart, but the fact was that she was not sure if it were day or night, summer or winter, Philadelphia or Mars. The daughter of a conservative New York stockbroker, her education had been carried out by Immaculate Heart nuns, Jesuit priests, and Sunday-school pageants. She was a product of steep tradition, the values molded by a mother baking cookies and a father who sat by the fireplace smoking a briar pipe, reading novels by foreign authors. This turbulent period in her life was unprecedented. She sometimes wondered why she had wanted so desperately to be a member of the FBI, but she knew it was her way of trying to make the world a better place.

As the Chevy rolled to a stop in front of her door, Patty noticed the digital dash clock showed 1:30 P.M. She dragged herself up the two flights of stairs and inserted the key in the door. Immediately, she sensed something wrong. Even in her exhaustion, her instincts took over, pushing the alarm button in her brain.

Something was out of sync. She removed her revolver, suddenly alert. She slithered silently across the room.

"Put that piece away," said a familiar voice. "I've already been shot this week."

She gasped as the overhead light went on, illuminating Lerza's battered body. They stared at each other for a moment, neither sure of what to do.

She slowly went to him, reluctant to touch him, not sure where the bloodstains originated. Patty brushed his dark hair away from the jagged, ugly crease.

She said in a soothing voice, "What am I going to do with you, Joseph?"

"I'm hurting, Patty." He sounded like a little boy telling his mother he'd fallen.

"I'll call an ambulance."

"*No!* No hospitals, no doctors!"

"But Joseph—" she started to protest.

"Promise me, Patty," he pleaded. "Just promise me you won't call anybody. I don't trust one soul. Promise me or I go."

She suddenly remembered that the man she held in her arms was a fugitive wanted for murder. A trip to the hospital would end with Lerza in the prison ward. So she did the best she could. Iodine, warm water, compresses, old antibiotics from a bout with bronchitis, clean bandages, and soothing words. Lerza lost consciousness then regained it in the middle of a nightmare, grabbed her by the collar, and screamed in pain before passing out again.

She decided to tell him later he was a fugitive. For now, she feared for his life, so she cradled him in her arms, comforted him, tried to make rational decisions about irrational thoughts. Should she take him to the hospital? If she did, he'd be arrested. If she did not, he might die; the wounds seemed serious. Should she tell someone he was there? Tell his wife he was okay? Tell Keenan? The FBI had always stood for fairness, and integrity, but in the last eight months, listening to Lerza and watching Keenan, a serious doubt had persisted. Like the black shadow of a tumor on the X-ray of a formerly healthy lung.

The six o'clock news as well as the morning newspapers would carry banner headlines about the FBI agent wanted for murder. Lerza's house would be under surveillance, his daughters watched as they went off to school, Laura followed wherever she drove.

Lerza was screaming, "Don't! No more!" Then lost consciousness again.

She held him until she could no longer keep her own eyes open.

"I love you," she whispered to the unconscious body just before she fell fast asleep.

27

Di Sipio thought he heard the words "federal building" but wasn't sure. His hearing aid needed a new battery. The Don was not the type to joke around, although Di Sipio could not remember a time he had seen Amato so happy.

"How's the grandkids? How's the wife? Nice weather." Followed by a joke with a punchline. The Don laughed, Di Sipio laughed. Who would believe they were headed for the FBI office?

Jees, Di Sipio thought, something's up.

Now the Don was humming. Strange. Di Sipio twisted his head toward the backseat. "Where to?" he asked, needing to see the Don's lips form the words.

Amato did not hesitate, did not seem embarrassed. He smiled as he said, "The FBI office, Daniel, is on Spring Garden Street."

The loyal driver almost asked why they were going there, but in the four decades he had worked for the Don, he had never questioned a business decision. Di Sipio instinctively knew this was business. As he drove, he tried to think of one earthly reason why the head of the Mafia would be visiting the Federal Bureau of Investigation. It was like a Ku Klux Klan member going to a bar mitzvah.

Di Sipio finally decided it had to be some scam the Don had devised to throw the Bureau off. Misinformation. Or maybe something as innocent as signing some Social Security forms, though the FBI didn't do Social Security—they put Italians in jail.

The black Cadillac turned right onto Spring Garden and slowed as morning shoppers darted across the street. Three ladies from the suburban womb. Spoiled kids off to school. Breakfast for some husband wearing a Robert Hall suit and carrying a leather briefcase he'd received for Christmas. The girls from the neighborhood meeting for a trip downtown to the wicked city. Comments on the winos, homeless, and bizarrely dressed teenagers. Sneers at the handsome businessmen followed by shopping at boutiques that were not in their suburban malls.

Di Sipio thought about it all and decided he hadn't missed much. He eased the limo to the curb and felt Amato's hand on his shoulder. The Don said, "Don't bother with the door. Go to Enrico's and get some lunch, be back here in two hours."

The receptionist noticed the impeccably dressed elderly gentleman enter and walk with purpose to the bullet-proof glass at the reception desk. All he said was, "Brad Keenan."

"Yes, sir, is he expecting you?"

"Not exactly. Just tell him Michael Amato."

"One moment, sir." The nineteen-year-old punched the button to the SAC's office. A mere thirty-eight seconds elapsed, then she said, with newfound respect, "Someone will come for you immediately."

The two men acted like whooping cranes during mating season, mentally flapping wings and circling each other to get a scent. Keenan's brain did somersaults. This was unprecedented—a Mafia Don voluntarily coming to an FBI office. Mafia Dons had been present before but only after United States Attorneys issued warrants, subpoenas, and other legal papers that commanded their presence. And then they came accompanied by high-priced attorneys who did all their talking.

"Coffee?" Keenan offered.

"Black with one sugar, please."

Amato's eyes took in the SAC's office with its flags, plaques, photos, shelves of legal-looking books, and other trappings. He realized it wasn't much different from his own office. With power comes a need for confirmation in the form of relationships with powerful people, captured on film, displayed on "I LOVE ME" walls, accompanied by letters of appreciation, certificates of awards, and other useless mementos in frames—brass, glass, and gold-plated trinkets.

Keenan thought about making small talk, knowing the Don would not let a secretary with a tray of coffee interrupt the purpose of his visit. But he could not think of a thing to say, and it was Amato who finally chose to break the awkward silence.

"Nice view," he said. He sat back comfortably in the highback leather chair, crossing his legs in a relaxed manner.

"Uh-huh," Keenan replied.

The SAC was standing awkwardly by his desk looking down at the Mafia chieftain, who did not seem nearly as uncomfortable as his host. The SAC sat, he rose, he paced. Finally the coffee arrived, and the two men sat facing each other with Amato ironically holding a coffee mug emblazoned with the FBI logo.

Amato enjoyed Keenan's discomfort as he slowly sipped the coffee. Finally the SAC could not take it any longer and asked, "How can I help you?"

Amato leaned forward in his chair, pointed a finger in the air, and said graciously, "I'm here to help *you*."

THE newspapers loved it, playing to the masses with ten-inch headlines: FBI AGENT BELIEVED TO KILL MOB BOSS— POLICE SEARCH FOR RENEGADE AGENT. The Philadelphia Inquirer, considered conservative by some, ran the story with the zeal of a cheap supermarket tabloid. The juicier excerpts read: "According to an arrest warrant filed in Common Pleas Court, Veteran FBI Agent Joseph Lerza is suspected of the bloody murder of Anthony Miceli, an alleged Philadelphia Mafia crime boss. Lerza should be considered armed and dangerous."

Patty forced herself to read the entire story. She felt the morbid fascination of a churchgoing housewife from Duluth unable to look away from a bloody highway accident.

She had no intention of returning to New York and was not sure what, if any, authority she now had in Philadelphia. Disobeying the direct order of two SAC's would mean some kind of disciplinary action—brick agents always get in trouble.

"What's next?" She reviewed her limited options. She had to prove Lerza did not kill Miceli. Great, but how?

Find the murderer. Who did kill Miceli? Was it an inside mob job? After all, the old guard wanted him dead. Did Amato order the hit? Maybe the Satans? Certainly plenty of motivation there. Perhaps even a dope connection gone bad? Hell, it could be nothing more than a jealous boyfriend of one of the dancers Miceli had seduced.

Arresting Lerza was not one of the options. She had

enough proof of the system's injustice, of its disloyalty, of its need to eat its own.

When she entered her apartment, she knew instinctively that Lerza was gone. A note on the purple couch made her already tough day much worse. It read:

Patty,
    I can't just sit here and do nothing. The TV said I'm a wanted man. What irony—*Me!*—the hunted, no longer the hunter. I don't know what I'm going to do, I just know I have to do something. You're a hell of a friend. Fuck the Bureau.
I love you.
Joe

Tears of frustration filled Patty's eyes. The sound of the phone startled her.

It was Keenan's voice. "Agent Masters, come to my office immediately."

"Can't." Defiantly. "On my way back to New York."

"If you want to save Joe Lerza's life, you'll get here immediately." Keenan hung up before she could reply.

LERZA had felt better, but the fractured skull gave him blurred vision, like a screen out of focus. His brain seemed to be on a three-second delay, which made his movements slow, almost mechanical. His sense of reality went, and scenes from Vietnam intertwined with flashbacks of the Moose, the Sarge, NVA, Patty Masters, Hard Rock, Miceli, and other players he did not recognize. He had a plan but first he had to find out about Moose, or was it the ex-Sergeant?

The phone booth inside Angelo's bar was the old-fashioned kind, with the glass-and-wood door moving uncertainly on shaky tracks as it closed. Lerza wrestled it shut and looked under the "H" in the Yellow Pages.

"Jefferson Hospital," the girl said.

"Russ Knepp."

A short delay, followed by, "That patient is still in intensive care, sir. Are you a relative?"

"Yeah, his brother," Lerza lied.

"I'll connect you with the nurses' station."

He heard clicks followed by two rings; then an efficient voice said, "Intensive Care."

"How's Moose? I mean Knepp. I'm his brother."

"Mr. Knepp is very critical, sir," the nurse replied. "I would suggest you contact the rest of your family and come here immediately." A pause, then, "Your brother may not make it."

Lerza hung up, shaking his head. The Moose did not have any family. Didn't they know? No brothers, sisters, mother, father, children, only three ex-wives who wouldn't give a shit if he lived or died. His friend would have little proof he had existed on this earth if the bullets did their ultimate damage. Just a green plastic body bag, extra large, zipped up and disposed of like Wednesday-morning trash at the curbside of suburbia.

Lerza sat unsteadily on the bar stool and ordered a shooter of whiskey from Angelo. The liquid felt warming as it reached the brain, dulled the pain. He asked for two more glasses.

Thoughts flickered in and out of his head. He had told Patty he had to do something but he did not remember exactly what. It was all confused, facts merged with fiction. Where did fiction end and facts begin? There were also suppositions, hunches, and intuitions.

Fairmont Park, that was a fact. Lerza had personally watched Hard Rock kill Stormy, shoot him and Moose—

all facts. But who killed Miceli? He didn't, that was a fact. Or was it? Maybe Hard Rock or even Amato killed Miceli. It wasn't uncommon to knock off a member of the home team. Hard Rock may have wanted a promotion, and Amato could have sanctioned the hit, figuring it was a lot easier to control a moron like Hard Rock than a ruthless Miceli. Just hunches.

There were so many unanswered questions that his forehead started to throb. Why the Fairmont Park massacre? Did they know he and Moose were feds, or was it as simple as a pissed-off drug dealer making an example of another errant doper? An Arny Tomossino, minus his prick and a layer of skin.

It was obvious where Keenan stood on all this. The newspapers had quoted the SAC: "It's a sad day for the FBI when one of its agents commits such a heinous crime as murder. As the leading law-enforcement agency in the United States, it is our duty to assist the Philadelphia Police Department in the hunt for the fugitive, Joseph Lerza, former Special Agent of the FBI."

"Former Special Agent." The reference to his status as lost hurt more than Lerza cared to admit. It was classic Keenan. Probably said the words as he washed his hands in a bowl of water like Pontius Pilate denouncing Christ.

Lerza found himself back inside Angelo's decaying phone booth, punching in Patty's pager number. He sat slouched over a whiskey glass, waiting for the phone to ring. She answered immediately.

"Patty?" Lerza's voice was hesitant.

She tried to remain calm. She said, "Just listen, Joe. Just listen. Amato's trying to make a deal with us right now. He can prove you didn't kill Miceli. He can clear your name. Lu killed Miceli. Amato can prove this. Go back—"

The line went dead in her ear; she knew Lerza was going to get himself hurt. Probably killed.

"Hey, Angelo," Lerza said. "Call me a cab."

Angelo looked at Lerza, smiled. "Okay, Joe, you're a cab."

Then Angelo laughed, his filthy apron heaving up and down, pushing back a belly resembling the Goodyear blimp. Laughter revealed all of his remaining, cigar-stained teeth.

Lerza stared hard at Angelo and for the briefest moment forgot he was a half-dead, psychotic, unemployed fugitive. He could not help the laugh that erupted from somewhere deep within him. He laughed and laughed with Angelo, the bartender. It was certainly not the quality of Angelo's jokes; it was the fact that life could not get any worse, so nothing mattered any more.

The yellow cab arrived three whiskeys and five bad jokes later. The bartender was on a bad-joke roll, sorry to see Lerza leave.

Lerza said to the driver, "The Satan clubhouse," and patted the nine-millimeter Angelo had formerly kept wrapped in a towel behind the bottle of vodka.

ENJOYING the ride, Lu kicked his hog into fifth gear. The business was better than ever. New customers, plenty of dope, the money rolled in. Miceli was dead, Amato was scared shitless, and the ten-percent operating fee would soon be a thing of the past.

The plan was simple: take over the remaining mob drug customers—with the Don's blessing. From there the Satans would offer loans at less juice than the mob, more and better-looking whores at reduced rates, vending machines with only thirty-percent setup fees and, finally, infiltration into the labor unions with their millions of dollars of kickbacks, raped pension plans, and no-bid contracts. Lu smiled, feeling the wind on his teeth.

Amato was old and would welcome Lu's offer of one million dollars cash stapled to a one-way airline ticket to Sicily. Lu practiced what he would say: "A well-earned retirement, Michael. You deserve it, relax your last few years." What he *wouldn't* say, but would be as clear as ravioli and meatballs, was that Amato *had* to leave, *had* to give up the mob's business, *had* to get out of town.

Lu understood people, and he knew Amato was aware he was a defeated man. The old man's eyes told the story of too many confrontations, battles won and lost. Of accumulated emotional scars, of life-and-death situations. Of too many ghosts that haunted sick old men.

This had all taken its toll on Amato, whose biological clock was slowing, ticking away at 11:51 P.M. on a cold, dreary spring day.

Lu could not quite figure out the newspaper headlines that proclaimed Miceli had been whacked by some FBI agent. Brilliant move by the Don, who was as guilty of Miceli's murder as if he had pulled the trigger. Fuckin' "conspiracy." That legal mumbo jumbo had equaled the electric chair for both the shooter and his string-puller. Put two guys remotely together in a conversation, instant fuckin' conspiracy and jail for a long time.

Amato had ordered the hit. If Lu went down the tubes, the old Italian would be strapped to the next chair waiting for General Electric to deep-fry his ass, which would probably smell like burnt garlic. How the Don had framed some fuckin' fed was pure irony, a final masterpiece of poetic justice, a Picasso painted by numbers. It served two purposes—it took the heat off Lu, and it blackened the lily-white, pristine reputation of the FBI.

Amato had enough judges, cops, and newspaper editors

in his pocket to orchestrate a rape case against the Pope. Framing some slob FBI agent must have been first-grade shit.

The Satan leader downshifted his hog—squeezing the hand brake while simultaneously foot-braking his scooter to a stop at the clubhouse. Once inside he asked Acid, "Is everything ready?" as he slipped on a black robe.

Acid, already dressed in hooded black regalia, nodded, and said, "They're waiting in the chambers, along with a goat and three chickens."

Lu said in singsong fashion, "Next month our Archangel will be delivered by the flesh of an intelligent soul. A living, breathing organism that communicates. One that thinks. A human!"

THE old man's eyes were clear and intense. They engaged the SAC's in such a direct, controlling manner that Keenan began to fidget; he tapped his government pen on his government desk, keeping time with his government shoes. He stared at a spot above Amato's head.

"I'm willing to make a deal," Amato said.

Keenan squinted, leaning forward in his seat as if to hear better. The word, "What?" was all that came out of him.

"I'm offering a proposition of mutual benefit," the Don said in an even voice. "Are you interested?"

Keenan was speechless, which seldom happened to the Special Agent in Charge of the Philadelphia office of the FBI. Mafia chieftains did not offer deals. On those few occasions where the Bureau amassed enough evidence for a conviction, the chieftains shuffled off to federal pen with their lips so tight a hydraulic jack could not pry loose the glimpse of a single gold tooth.

Keenan rose from his desk and began to pace. He certainly could not make a decision right away; he would need to talk it over with an aide, maybe a higher official, get recommendations.

He thought, Patty Masters knows the situation. She would be able to figure out a double cross, she would know if the Don was telling the truth. She was the only remaining agent of the three who was not lying, near death or a fugitive; she had an operational knowledge of the case.

He would order her to come to his office at once to hear Amato's deal, ask for her recommendations, then decide. It would be his decision, maybe after a call to Blue Flame Bobby to get final approval of an agreement. A deal with the *capo de tutti capi* would certainly redeem Keenan's status with Washington. They would now have to allow him to remain in Philadelphia until his retirement. Maybe even an incentive award, probably a cushy retirement job.

He dialed Masters's number, used Lerza as his carrot to persuade her to head immediately for the federal building. Then he said to his guest, "Have another cup of coffee, Mr. Amato. I've called an associate to listen to and evaluate your offer. It won't take long."

Amato immediately understood that Keenan was a lightweight, a bureaucrat with no balls. When the "associate" turned out to be a female, Amato at first felt insulted. Italians *never* involved women in business. Women had big mouths and could not be trusted to know the details of men's work.

But Patty had been in the office only a few minutes when Amato reluctantly observed her beauty, noticed her long, muscular legs and taut shoulders—he always evaluated his enemy. The initial exchanges between Keenan and Masters seemed strained, he thought. Since he was an expert on human behavior—a Ph.D. of conflict—he picked up the hidden meanings of their words, their body language, the animosity just below the surface that he would use to his advantage.

Patty took a seat perpendicular to both Amato and Keenan. She swiveled her head as each spoke, like an avid fan on the fifty-yard line of a playoff game. She was determined to keep quiet, listen, and consider, give Keenan no satisfaction, no help, watch him squirm.

He positioned himself at his desk and folded his hands. He finally asked Amato, "What is it that brought you here?"

Amato was silent. He removed a legal-looking document from his breast pocket, got to his feet, and placed the paper ceremoniously on Keenan's desk. Keenan read silently for a while, shaking his head.

He finally said, "No way! This is ludicrous. The FBI will never approve such an agreement."

Amato, seated again, merely shrugged and said, "It's a small price to pay for the results you will achieve."

"I can never get this approved," Keenan explained. "Headquarters will reject this entire offer. You'll be subpoenaed before a grand jury, and we will learn the truth without agreeing to this—blackmail."

Patty could restrain herself no longer. She did not know exactly what the document contained but she did know it affected Lerza. She bolted from her seat and was at Keenan's desk in one step. She pulled the sheet of paper from his hand the way a magician does a tablecloth topped with dishes.

She read the document quickly, pivoted toward Amato, and stood excitedly waving the paper in his face. She said, "We'll accept your terms."

Keenan, barely able to control his voice, ordered, "Sit down, Agent Masters. *I* will make the decisions affecting this office of the FBI."

She ignored Keenan and spoke directly to Amato. "How will you give us Miceli's killer?" she asked.

"In due time, Miss Masters," the Don said quietly. "First, the agreement must be signed. Then I will give you the proof of Miceli's murderer. I can tell you this. It wasn't your agent Lerza. I will also provide you with Dakota and Stormy Monday's killer, plus a list of every major drug dealer and importer on the East Coast, the names of every crooked labor official, along with written records of their criminal activity, and assorted other details concerning extortion, prostitution, and unsolved homicides."

Keenan repeated, as though to himself, "We can never agree to your terms."

"Then I shall go home and eat my lunch," the Don said.

Patty pressed, "Who killed Miceli?"

Amato smiled at her for the first time. Then he slowly rose to his feet. She recognized the smile as a "kiss-off." The smile of a man with a full house to your eight high. The capo of the Mafia could legally walk out of the door, and with him would go Joseph Lerza's future, his life.

The old man buttoned his jacket, put on his expensive heavy winter coat, and started for the door.

Patty shouted, "*Wait!* Allow Mr. Keenan and myself a few words. Give us a minute." Her eyes held a plea for the saving of an innocent man's life.

Amato frowned, then said, "I'll wait five minutes in the outer office, no longer. After that, my offer will expire."

He left the combatants and closed the door behind him.

A CID led the reluctant goat to the basement of the Satan clubhouse, pulling it by a rope. On these special nights Lu worked himself into a lather, assuring himself of even the smallest details. Members were required to bathe before donning black ceremonial robes. In the hour before dusk, dilaudids dipped in PCP were downed with a fruit juice laced with phenobarbital. Meditation was followed by Satanic readings in which the power of the devil was extolled.

Give your soul to Lucifer, blindly believe in his almighty power, reject God, offer Satan living sacrifices, and perform other insane acts involving violence, and you can receive any wish, any desire—money, girls, whatever. Just believe in the guy with the red suit, pitchfork, and horns.

Basically, the general members of the cults were born losers, with bad self-concepts. They were natural followers, who did not realize they *never* got what they wished no matter how much dope they ingested, no matter how often they chanted, no matter how many chickens they sacrificed. They merely enjoyed the pomp and circumstance involved in belonging. They did not have an original thought in their burnt-out brains—exactly what the leaders needed. Blind obedience—kill for me and I will love and accept you. The goat was mildly protesting, digging in its small hoofs as if it knew its fate.

The Satan clubhouse basement had been transformed into the basic devil-worship lore room. Walls, ceiling, and floor were painted dull black with candlelight providing the shadowy illumination of satanic props: an altar of marble, incense burning, devil symbols hung on walls, assorted statues of the Fallen Angel, Lucifer, in different artistic interpretations.

Twenty Satans formed a semicircle near the altar, each holding a candle, chanting rhythmic, foreign-sounding words over and over.

Acid appeared, half-dragging the goat to the altar. The animal stared up at Acid with mournful eyes, reminding the Satan vice president of a collie he owned as a kid. He had loved that dog, named it Laddie, sneaked it into his bedroom every night. Cried for a week when the produce truck had crushed Laddie. Ever since, he was never completely comfortable with this part of Satan worship. On the few occasions they had sacrificed humans, Acid had not felt nearly the same pangs of guilt.

As Lu arrived, all chanting ceased. His eyeballs seemed vacant, replaced by dark pools, slitted eyelids illuminated by shades of red. The hood attached to the robe surrounded and extended over his head. It made the flickers of the candles dance on his already demonic face.

The ritual was written in stone, long-practiced over a period of centuries by satanic cults who never deviated from the original ceremony. It was believed the Devil himself dictated the contents of the worship ceremony, passing it on to his own apostles; it was later refined by the black witches of England.

Lu stepped up onto the altar, faced his flock, and began: "Disciples of the Archangel Lucifer, the Almighty Lord originally on the side of God, father of Jesus the traitor, we worship your omnipotence, we ask that you come to us tonight, we ask that you give us the power to do your work, we pray that you grace us with your presence, and offer a living sacrifice to bleed and die so that you may continue to live."

Lu raised his arms upward, fingers spread to the ceiling. A guttural chant emitted from deep within him. The congregation knelt, then bent at the hips, placing their heads on the floor. All echoed the chant in Lu's melodic rhythm.

Suddenly the hands of the Satanic Priest dropped, signifying the end of chanting. He turned to face the altar upon which the goat tentatively stood. He leaned forward until his head was only inches from the animal. Slowly, Lu began kissing the goat, starting at the forehead, then gently, almost erotically, the eyes, nose, lips, and slowly down the body to the goat's genital area. There he massaged the penis with his lips. Lu then retraced the kisses back up to the neck area. The goat seemed pacified by all the attention; it stood motionless.

The disciple of the devil then grasped the head of the goat with his hand as he continued to tongue the neck of the goat. The farm animal suddenly flinched.

Almost as suddenly, a dead goat fell hard on the altar, blood pouring from the gaping hole in its neck. Lu chewed the goat's neck arteries, swallowing pieces of them as if they were a delicacy.

The fun was just beginning. The goat's heart was cut out, chopped into bits, and passed out to the faithful, chased by a cup of goat blood. The group was like a pack of sharks at a feeding frenzy. More chanting, worshipping, and cannibalism followed.

About an hour into the feast, the only door to the upstairs opened. The participants froze. The door to the upstairs never opened during a ceremony.

Two heavily armed Satans appeared, dragging a man down the steps. Lu approached the steps just as the man hit, face-up, at the bottom of the steps. Lu stared at the motionless body on the floor.

Goat blood still stained Lu's mouth. He smiled and said, "Special Agent Joseph Lerza, I presume."

28

The fat, wailing Italian ladies surrounded the bed with rosary beads clicking at the speed of light.

"Hail Mary, full of grace—"

Billy Averone lay in his last moments of life, semi-alert, observing the ritual. Present were his wife, two sisters, three sisters-in-law, and one old two-hundred-fifty-pound broad with blue bouffant hair, who was somehow related to him. She only appeared at family weddings and funerals, she was the key. When the fat, blue bouffant lady showed up in his bedroom, he knew he was a goner; she was a specialist in death.

The cancer had eaten away most of his stomach, part of his liver, and assorted other organs. Averone had almost prepared for death as he carried out his last assignment on earth. The meeting with Amato had been sacred, and his impending death merely served as an unnecessary obstruction to fulfilling promises made at that meeting.

He would gladly die following the completion of his mission. Also, he was curious. Amato had told him much of his plan but not all of it. Curiosity killed the cat, was it killing him? The dying man smiled to himself and tried to figure out what Amato was up to. He knew it was monumental—the end of the Philly mob, the end of the Satans, the end of Hard Rock's group.

The smile deepened as he thought of Miceli's decomposing body with his balls severed. The symbol of a man's machismo, his manliness. At least *he* would die with dignity, as the fat, blue bouffant lady of doom stood nearby. He would be wearing his favorite pajamas, lying on clean sheets in his own bedroom.

Why had the papers blamed the FBI agent for Miceli's death? Averone had attended the meeting where Amato gave the Satan, Lu, the contract. More questions than time to answer. The knock on the bedroom door interrupted his musings.

He said, seeing the familiar figure, "Glory Be to the Father!"

Amato entered, kissing the ladies, including the lady of doom. In return they pulled the godfather to their big bosoms, asking about his health in whispers loud enough to be heard in Trenton.

Averone listened from his bed as his wife Concetta sobbed, "He's so frail." She grabbed at Amato's sleeve and wailed, "Why him? What am I going to do without him, Michael?" She made the sign of the cross, and this cued the remaining fat ladies to do the same in a supporting role.

Amato touched Concetta's cheek. This had a calming effect on her; after all, he was the padrone. His touch was considered magical by the people of South Philadelphia.

Concetta and Amato spoke, and in an instant the mourning crew left the bedroom single file.

Amato approached the bed, bent over to kiss Averone's cheek, and asked, "How are you, my friend?"

Averone smiled, answered, "I feel great. Want to play some bocce?"

"I could never beat you," Amato admitted.

"No, but it's only fair to tell you now that I cheated all those years."

Both men laughed; then Averone coughed.

Amato said, not too convincingly, "You'll feel better."

"You are my best friend, Michael, and also a horrible liar." A sad tone.

"Have you made your peace with God?"

"Yes, my padrone. I examined my conscience. I have no regrets. God has not judged my actions as sins but merely as men doing what they must to survive. Business. God understands, and soon I will get the chance to discuss it with Him face-to-face. But don't worry," a faint smile, "I will put in a good word for you."

Amato and Averone again chuckled. Amato then touched his friend's hand, and asked, "Who will make me laugh?"

"Perhaps Hard Rock. I always found him amusing."

"That beast with the brain of a peanut does not amuse me."

"Then how about that filth, the Satan called Lu?"

"Another problem, and also not very funny."

"I know," Averone said. "I have heard that the FBI can make you die laughing."

The capo gently squeezed Averone's hand. "It's obvious from your comments that you have unresolved matters on your mind. Can an old friend ease this burden? What's troubling you?"

Averone shifted his weight, slid his feet beneath his legs, and, with the help of Amato, boosted his upper torso almost to a sitting position. He said, "Well, since you ask, I cannot meet my maker until you tell me everything."

"Everything?" Amato teased.

"Tell me what you intend to do with Lu and Hard Rock. Tell me why this FBI agent is accused of a murder he did not commit. Tell me why you will sell off our properties, which took blood to obtain. And why a list of our lifelong friends sits in my safe, which says also they will radically change their few remaining years on earth. Tell me all of this *now*, or I will surely die immediately and you will have this guilt to contend with." One Punch finished out of breath.

"Where shall I begin?" Amato asked. "Such a demanding dying person."

"Begin. My time is scarce."

Amato lowered himself gently on the bed next to Averone, shifted the vest of his three-piece suit, and said, "Within the next sixty days, several of our enemies will die violently."

PATTY turned on Keenan like a she-devil protecting her newborn. She demanded, "What are you thinking of?"

"What do you mean?" answered the SAC.

"Amato's deal. We have to take it."

Keenan rose to his full height, pointed a finger at her, and announced, "You are in no position to demand anything. Besides, why do we have to take it?"

She tried to control the rage inside, to keep calm, and said slowly, "Because Amato is the only one in the world who can clear Lerza besides the actual shooter."

Keenan was silent for a moment, then said thoughtfully, "His price is too high."

"Not for what's at stake. Moose is on the critical list and may not make it. Lerza is out of his mind. Stormy Monday is dead. They can't prove squat. We need Amato. He is the key. Turn him down and Lerza remains a fugitive, Lu continues to rise as a major dope dealer, and Hard Rock takes over Miceli's operation."

Keenan protested, "Amato has to go to jail. He has directed a major crime family in this city for thirty years. You want me to give him immunity? Immunity for him and thirty of his friends, with the blessing of the FBI?"

"Listen to me closely," she almost whispered. "Stormy Monday's killer cannot be charged unless the lone eyewitness testifies. That eyewitness is Lerza, and he can't testify unless he is cleared of Miceli's murder. The only person that can clear Lerza is Amato. You have to let Amato prove Lerza's innocence and by doing so, it will set a chain of events into motion that will send Lu and the Satans, as well as Hard Rock and his renegade stallions, to jail for a long time."

He was silent; she went on, "And this is only for starters. Amato is also offering a major seizure of cocaine, labor racketeers, identities of corrupt public officials, unsolved murders, and assorted other solutions to crimes that apparently are beyond your comprehension."

Keenan hesitated slightly; he was starting to understand the intricacies of Amato's offer. But the SAC could not or would not give his authority away so easily. He said, with newfound confidence, "We still have the drug buys from Miceli and Hard Rock. That means Amato and the rest of the Philadelphia LCN goes to jail for drug distribution."

Patty shook her head. "Who's your witness?" she said sarcastically. "Joe Lerza, the psychopathic killer, or the comatose Moose?"

"We have tape recordings of conversations, drugs in the vault, meetings. You were there, you can testify."

"You have nothing!" she said angrily. "Hearsay evidence is inadmissible in a trial, something about the Sixth Amendment, face to face with your accuser. I never *saw* Lerza and Moose meet Miceli, Hard Rock, or Lu. I never personally witnessed the drug deals or the Satan conspiracy to sell cocaine. The drugs and tapes are worthless without Lerza or Moose."

The SAC's face deflated visibly; his eyes looked like a sad basset hound's. He said, "Are you telling me there's no case against any of them? Not the Italians, not the Satans? All this work, all this time, all this misery and death, and no one can be prosecuted?"

"A weak case at best."

"Weak?"

"Let's say nonexistent."

He sighed and asked, "What's the risk factor if we deal with Amato?"

"He can always double-cross us," she replied. "He's smart and probably keeping some of the truth in reserve. I don't completely trust his motives, but we have nothing to lose. Our case is blown, we have corpses lying all over the city morgue. One FBI agent is about to die and another is being hunted like an animal. The Satans are poised to take over the city. Hard Rock and his crew will probably go on a killing spree if not restrained by Amato. Are you getting the picture?"

Keenan stood up and slowly crossed the room until he stood inches from her. He asked sincerely, "If we are successful, do you think the Bureau will let me retire in peace?"

For the first time in months, Patty actually smiled. She said "Fuckin' Ay."

. . .

THE plastic flex cuffs cut into Lerza's wrists, but he was semihappy for the small things, like being cuffed in the front instead of the back. A leg chain fastened him to a makeshift metal railing. He still felt dizzy from the Fairmont Park wounds and the bumpy trip down the Satan basement stairs.

How long had he been unconscious: one, two, four days? What was going on? Why hadn't Lu killed him yet?

Lerza took inventory of his battered body. The head wound had crusted into a newborn scab, making it itch uncontrollably. His right thigh bled slightly as it rubbed on the floor. The little finger on his right hand probably was broken and his left eye about swollen shut, compliments of a Satan fist. All in all, not too bad. He would miss this year's Philadelphia marathon but with any luck be ready for the prison softball season.

He focused his eyes on the surroundings, took in the basement with its altar and devil trappings. He had heard about satanic cults. Almost always drug-related, which had compelled his curiosity and resulted in some research at the FBI archives. He found it disgusting but also fascinating that the worship of Satan was steeped in tradition. It usually involved killing in the form of sacrifices to the Devil. There was a strong leader in the form of a high priest. Its members were totally obedient and ruthless. They believed the living sacrifices shielded them from harm. Mind control at its worst.

Surprisingly, Lerza was more angry than scared. A swollen tongue forced him to breathe irregularly through his mouth, which was as dry as sandpaper. He desired water desperately and realized he needed it soon. In Vietnam he had disciplined his body to require few fluids by a slow process of using less and less of the scarce drinking water.

Over a period of time he was able to fill his mouth with warm canteen water, swirl it to touch each cavity of his throat, and slowly, very slowly, swallow minute amounts, thus being able to function for long periods in the jungle. But this wasn't Nam—or was it?

The upstairs door was opening. Footsteps on the old wooden stairs indicated someone descending but not in a particular hurry. He caught a peripheral glimpse of the large figure as it stood silently watching him.

"Thought you'd die," Lu said matter-of-factly.

"That'd ruin your day," he shot back sarcastically.

"I've been fuckin' with you since the first day we met," Lu said. "You amuse me."

"You're an asshole, Lu, you know that? A total fuckin' asshole, and there ain't nothin' you can do to me that hasn't already been done."

"Sure about that?" Lu taunted.

"Fuck you," Lerza said.

Lu slithered to where Lerza sat and stood over him intimidatingly. He said, "Don't be so angry at me, Joseph Lerza. You and I are not that much different."

Lerza grunted a sarcastic laugh. "Ha! That's really funny. Maybe we can get together for my birthday and do lunch." He spat and went on, "You're the scum of the earth, pal. With your pack of zombies you wreck lives, terrorize innocent people, sneak around in darkness. You follow them to do harm and worship the devil in your filthy clubhouse filled with its garbage."

Lu stared with dead eyes, then said, "And are you so different, Mr. Special Agent of the repressive FBI with its police-state mentality? I worship the Archangel Lucifer, you deify that queer Hoover as your god. You and your pack of KGB clones also follow people to do harm, no less harm than mine, because, my friend, pain is pain, whether it's a bad load of dope or fifteen years in your federal prisons. And my home is no different than your FBI office."

Lerza kept silent as Lu continued, "So you see, Joseph Lerza, a thin line separates us. Separates good and evil. Separates Satan and FBI agent. Besides, if the newspapers are accurate, and we both know newspapers don't lie, then you, my Vietnam comrade, are a fugitive. Wanted for murder."

Forgetting his bonds, Lerza jerked toward Lu and screamed, "You fuckin' creep! *You* killed Miceli. Not me."

Lu said calmly, "Then maybe I should just call the cops and confess. You can be my character witness. Or maybe they'll just cart you off to your own jail."

"I wanted to kill Miceli," Lerza admitted. "I would have but—" and he stopped.

Lu recognized the small hole in Lerza's armor. He said, "Those big black bucks will love to see an ex-FBI agent in their jail. Maybe I can go to your wedding."

Lerza shouted again, "You killed Miceli!"

"Just like in Nam, Joe," Lu admitted. "I shot his kneecaps, then cut off his prick and balls. You've probably done that, haven't you?"

Lerza reached for Lu but was again restrained by his leg shackles. He said officially, "You are under arrest for the murder of Anthony Miceli. I'm fuckin' arresting you *now*. Put your hands on the wall, you got the right to remain silent, you got the right to an attorney, you fuckin' scum!"

"You are no longer amusing me, Joe," Lu said, ice in his voice.

Lerza spit in Lu's eye. "Fuck you!"

Lu merely smiled and said reprovingly, "Such behavior from a marine Nam vet. I read the newspapers, Joseph Lerza, FBI agent, former war hero. The papers are quoting some government shrink blaming your stint in Nam as the reason you went berserk and killed Miceli."

Lerza again spat at Lu and said, "I am a United States Marine. The meanest fighting machine on earth. Joseph Lerza, Lance Corporal, United States Marine Corps, serial number 2374824."

Lu stared at him solemnly and said, "We're fraternity brothers, Joe. Parris Island graduates with Nam as our finishing school. Same year, both I Corps. Resident blood-brother marines, Joe, you and me. Semper Fi, buddy."

Lerza looked at Lu but saw the NVA captain, a skilled interrogator—the enemy. He repeated, "Joseph Lerza, Lance Corporal, United States Marine Corps, serial number 2374824."

Lu bent down, produced a glass of water, and offered it to Lerza. He recognized the water, understood he needed it badly. He also understood that taking it would represent a victory for his enemy and a personal defeat for him, a prelude to cowardice. But his body decided on survival. He hungrily grabbed the water glass, gulped it with one long swallow. Suddenly Lu appeared, replacing the NVA captain, Nuey Ye.

Lerza tried to sit up straight, restore some dignity. Stop Lu from making them the same side of a bad coin. A trick coin with two evil heads facing each other with smiling, sinister profiles. He was different, he was an FBI agent, trained by the United States Government. A person with status, a person the public respected, a person associated with good. He had decided in his torment that he had had enough of verbal warfare; he wanted to return to the familiar ground of a law-enforcement official.

He boosted his torso against the wall and attempted to rediscover the authority in his voice, the way he had interrogated a thousand other bad guys. Many FBI agents reported that Lerza could make the hardest head case crack with his interrogation. The bad guys said he made them nervous, scared; they knew he was as tough as they were, his toughness made even more intimidating by the utter control of fingerprinting his captives. Having your hands twisted at his will as he roughly manipulated their fingers which, in turn, twisted hands, arms, shoulders, and entire bodies twirling in ink. All the while staring and letting them know their only option was to do whatever Joseph Lerza wanted.

He yearned to regain his interrogation mentality, and then Lu would realize it was hopeless to continue his captivity. Laura had chided him when he occasionally came home with his interrogation voice intact. "What did you do today, Laurie?" sounded like a demand to confess a triple homicide. She would smile, and he would laugh and give her a hug. That signalled the real end of his work day. Cops and agents always had a tough time "turning off" at the close of a shift. It was hard to go from a high-speed car chase with a drug dealer to playing bridge with suburban neighbors who had returned home from their safe desks and elevator music.

"I want some answers," Lerza demanded.

"Anything you wish." A mocking reply.

"Did Stormy tell you we were FBI?"

"That whore was Satan property. She sucked my dick in between diming you out."

"Why?" Lerza already knew the answer.

"Because I told her to."

"Why?" Lerza repeated.

In a flash Lu moved at him, backhanding Lerza's remaining open eye with knuckles flexed and extended for maximum hurt. The knuckles caught Lerza's bone over his eye and struck it like a Mike Tyson uppercut. Blood gushed out.

Lerza spat the red liquid at his nemesis. "Fuck you—"

Lu tensed, flexed his powerful hand, and Lerza involuntarily jerked backward to avoid the knuckles. The solid mass of hand stopped a fraction of an inch from Lerza's nose. Both men realized that the Satans were one-up on the visiting team: namely, a one-eyed, overweight, psychotic former lawman.

Lu eased his large frame onto the basement floor, comfortably crossing his legs just inches from Lerza's. His voice was far softer, almost conversational, as he reminisced, "Remember Parris Island, Joe? During the first week of PI every boot was positive he would die before getting off that island. Then just when you hit rock bottom, after the DI's beat the shit out of you, after you couldn't do another push-up, you realized you *could* get off that island, but only with the help of the other guys in your platoon?"

He went on thoughtfully. "You remember, Joe, they let you know you were a human being with worth and not the piece of worthless shit the DI's told you that you were. When graduation day came, you felt closer to your boot-camp buddies than you did your own mother. So you see, Joe, you and me are blood brothers. Parris Island, Vietnam, Philadelphia. Linked together by fate, by history. Talk nice to me, and your old marine buddy'll take care of you."

In one last moment of internal personal protest, one last attempt to maintain his unique identity, his last shred of dignity, Lerza let out a bloodcurdling scream. It started at his toes and ended at his curly Italian hair.

"Eee yowwwwww, ee yoww. Fuck!"

The Satan honcho watched in silent control until Lerza had exhausted himself and lay with nothing left—no breath, no freedom, no dignity.

Almost a full moment passed before either combatant spoke, and when Joe did, the mood had changed. Every man has his breaking point, and Lerza's had come and gone. He was a physical and emotional vegetable, about to rot on the vine. Under ideal conditions he needed a two-month hospital stay, followed by a year or two on some shrink's couch.

Lerza suddenly asked, like a man seeking directions on a summer vacation, "What about Dakota?"

Lu replied, "She met with an accident. She was eye-witness to a murder."

Lerza mumbled, "Waste of tits."

"What?"

"Broad had great tits." Lerza switched gears like a de-railed Amtrak. "Where were you in Nam?"

"Hotel 3/6," Lu answered. "Khe Shan, Conthien, then Hué during Tet." He fell quiet, then added, "I know you had an ugly time of it, Joe. Won three Purple Hearts and two Silver Stars. You're a tough marine, Joe, a real war hero." The Satan had become strangely sympathetic.

Lerza shifted again, more alert, and asked, "How do you know all this?"

"I know a lot about you, Joe. I know about Laurie and your two daughters. I know about your girlfriend Patty Masters. And your best friend Moose. We all had a beer at Chandy's, remember, Joe?"

"How's Moose?" Lerza asked.

"Bad. Real bad. Most men would be dead."

Lerza seemed to accept this, and asked, "You at war with the mob yet?"

"No, not yet. When things work out the Italians will be a greasy memory, lots of dead wops, lots of spaghetti funerals, and the end of an era, Joe. The guidos are about to be a thing of the past."

Lerza stared absentmindedly at the ceiling, then asked, "You the drug czar yet?"

"That I am, Joe," Lu said. "I'm the only game in this town—importer, cutter, and distributor. A fuckin' monopoly, buddy. And in case you don't know, Joe, there's a whole lot of money in dope."

"You really in Nam?" Lerza asked, changing subjects again.

"Yes, Joe."

"A marine?"

"Like you."

"What's going to happen to me?" Changing back to the black, menacing present.

"Depends on you."

"Whatta you mean?"

Lu rose to his feet and removed a dark brown glass vial from his pocket. He unscrewed its cap, tapped a small amount of white powder on his thumb, raised this to his nose, and inhaled deeply as the powder disappeared. He placed the vial with the remaining powder near Lerza's face, and said, "You know a lot, Joe. You can school me on all of the FBI's investigative techniques. Where they hide their microphones, how they tail people, mark their buy money, what's in their files, and who their undercover agents and snitches are. I want to know all this and more, Joe, as your marine buddy. Understand?"

"What's in the vial?" Lerza asked, already knowing.

Lu smiled and said, "You've been through a lot lately, Joe, banged up pretty bad. Lots of stress. They say cocaine'll mend your body and mind, relax you."

"But you worship the devil. The SAC, I mean, my boss, told me you practice Palo May—" He forgot the word.

"Palo Mayombe," Lu finished. "Cambodian cult, evil for evil's sake, Joe. The human sacrifice, the big 666. The

≡ 273 ≡

power of the Devil is unlimited. Give yourself to it and your troubles end." He added ominously, "And you, my friend, have troubles."

"And what if I don't go along with you?" Lerza challenged.

"You'll die a slow death within a week in a ceremony where I'll eat your still-beating heart."

At this Lu stood up and quickly walked up the steps that led from the basement to the first floor before Lerza could say another word.

Lerza sat staring at the brown vial containing the bright white powder. Like a wounded animal, the special agent of the FBI crawled on all fours to the powder's promise of making him whole again. Making the hurt stop, mending Moose, dropping the murder charges. Allowing him once again to feel his daughters' arms around him and Laura's lips on his.

MICHAEL Amato shifted and said, "It's uncomfortable."

"After a while you'll forget you're even wearing it," Patty assured him.

She twisted the expensive Swiss tape recorder into the bellyband, positioning it in the small of Amato's back. Two wires originating at the recorder went up the Don's back, over each shoulder, and down again in front, about chest high. At the end of each hung a microphone so small, yet so sensitive, it could detect a pigeon feather hitting a down pillow on a water bed.

The dime microphone would be used only as backup, due to the need to capture every word, every sound, every nuance as evidence. This Swiss recorder, about the size of a cigarette pack, cost $4,000 a unit at government discount and was considered state of the art.

As Patty finished taping the wire to the capo's Italian undershirt, she said, "Done. Do a test count."

The Don reluctantly started, "One, two, three, four—okay?"

Patty studied a multicolored electric sensing meter and said, "Fine. Let's go over the plan."

Amato complained. "Again? I know my role in this Greek drama. Just be sure of yours."

Patty paused before saying, "You came to us, now it's our show. Unless it's done right, unless the evidence is gathered in a way a judge rules legal, then none of it is any good."

Amato was not used to a female giving him orders. Yet this female with a badge, an FBI agent, seemed self-assured, he thought, someone who knew her job, a professional. Amato respected a professional.

The old man sighed and said, "I summon Hard Rock to my office, I go over in detail the shooting at Fairmont Park, especially the part where Hard Rock admits his role as shooter, plus the names of everyone else present. I request the identity of all drug distributors supplied by us, controlled by Hard Rock."

Another sigh, then, "I instruct him to order fifty kilograms of heroin from Sicily, tell him I will be present at his secret warehouse when the shipment arrives. We take the fifty kilograms and rent a second warehouse in which you will place cameras. I ask Hard Rock to tell his fifty main distributors to come to this warehouse to pick up 1 kilogram each at an especially good price."

He paused again, went on, "Each will be caught both on film and by your agents, losing both freedom and ninety thousand dollars per kilogram. The FBI will be able to balance their budget by seizing four and a half million dollars in drug money, plus the actual fifty kilograms of heroin, while jailing fifty of the biggest drug dealers in Philadelphia. They will also learn the heroin route from Sicily, not to mention charging Hard Rock and twenty-five of his men with murder and drug conspiracy."

The Don paused, sighed, and asked, "Is this satisfactory?"

Patty was grudgingly impressed with the old man but would not admit it. She said, "You forgot the Satans."

"Ah," the Don teased, patting his forehead as though he were an imbecile. "Yes, the Satans. And the proof that your friend, Joseph Lerza, is not a killer."

He sighed and continued, "I contact my associate Lu and arrange a meeting wearing your microphones which, I might add, feel the size of a 1956 Buick on my back. At this meeting I review our previous meeting in which I ordered Miceli's murder, offering drug trade in return. I confirm the hit, let Lu speak, make the admission in his own words, talk about his drug business. Then I meet you so you may relieve me of this tape recorder which puts people in jail."

Although Amato knew his role, Patty did not completely trust him, but she also realized there was little choice. The man was holding back something; a glint in the wrinkled eyes hinted of untold motivations, of his own agenda, of simply being deceitful.

But she smiled and said, "Very good, Mr. Amato. Now if it will just work."

"It will," he assured her.

"Thanks." She looked at him with a friendly expression.

As Patty listened, she thought she heard her own seven-year-old voice. Amato was her father, comforting her following a scraped knee after a roller-skating fall. The head of the Mafia had the same tenor in his voice, that of a man who could control conditions, even those normally reserved by nature. "Make the rain stop so I can go out and play." "Beat the TV monster up!" "Ask the ocean waves to stop before they buckle my knees."

Patty desperately needed Amato who, aside from being a likeable old man, also was a violent career criminal. A man who killed many people, ordered the deaths of many more. A man who extorted money from the innocent, who used women as objects of prostitution and, most of all, *the* man who allowed Stormy Monday's death, Moose's critical wounds, and Lerza's status as a fugitive.

But this was also a man who could save Lerza from a premature death, find Stormy's murderer, and put desperate criminals in jail.

These moral contradictions grated on Patty, whose life, until a year before, had been an orderly progression from birth to the FBI. No glitches, no major interruptions of moral expectations. Since this case, "up" was "down," Lerza was accused of murder, and she was exchanging pleasantries with and actually liking a Mafia chieftain. Gee, Toto, this can't be Kansas anymore, she thought.

"Tell me about Joe Lerza," Amato asked, sensing her affection for the agent.

"We were partners a few years ago," she said. "He's an outstanding man. The type of person who'd do anything for a friend, give you his last dime, care if you're hurting. He'd push you away from a bullet knowing he'd take it." She hesitated, feeling awkward, then said in an official tone, "Also an excellent FBI agent."

Amato listened to Patty's tone and words, which confirmed his suspicions about their relationship. He said, "Sounds a lot like you."

She blushed. "Joe's one of a kind." In softer tone.

"Any idea where he is? The papers said he's running, that he's dangerous."

Patty realized she should not tell Amato anything about Lerza's situation, but she possessed an overwhelming need to talk to someone. You couldn't have a heart-to-heart with Keenan. Before she realized it, the words spilled out of her mouth and she told it all—when the undercover case began, the sour period, things going completely to shit, Lerza's drinking, his flashbacks. His hiding out in her apartment, her relationship with Keenan, career doubts, and her favorite flavor of ice cream.

Amato listened like the grandfather everyone wished they had, and when Patty had nothing left to say, her breath gone, the tears dried, the Mafia capo stood up. He placed his fatherly arms around the FBI agent and said, "I will make everything right."

And she believed him.

29

The young United States marine walked in torn jungle utilities for eighty-three miles, making the westward trip, following the setting sun out of Vietnam and into Cambodia. He negotiated rice paddies, low flatlands, gentle rolling hills, valleys and jungles so dense he could only manage one hundred feet per hour among animals, insects and other living things imagined by science-fiction writers.

The young leatherneck's name was Raymond Edward Hatchinson. He had a reputation as one of the toughest marines since Chesty Puller. He also was considered strange. At this time he was leaving the U.S. Marine Corps, South Vietnam, and the United States, giving up everything he had ever known—shopping malls, Christmas trees, little league, automobiles, and round-eyed girls with names like Betty, Darlene, and Susan. Raymond was going AWOL into Cambodia. He had had enough of the war; there was nothing left to prove since winning all those medals. Also, he had never liked shopping malls or girls named Darlene.

The marine called Raymond walked methodically, in no hurry, barely perspiring even in the one-hundred-degree heat. He had no idea where he was heading, only that it was out of Vietnam. Raymond used his marine K-Bar to kill and skin critters; he recognized edible plants; and even without salt pills, malaria pills, and purification pills, drank the jungle water and did not get the runs, pass out, or become delirious. He prided himself as some kind of man, an outstanding marine.

On the seventh day of his trip, Raymond came upon a mountain village. Instead of first determining the village's preference between vegetarianism or cannibalism, he walked to the campfire in its center and asked to speak to the leader.

He was not exactly greeted by the village welcome wagon. Instead, he was stripped naked, shackled by crude hemp ropes, and left for three days. At the end of the third day a rather distinguished-looking savage entered Raymond's hootch and did things to his body that the marine found amusing, at least at first.

The savage colored Raymond's body a deep purple with wet roots. His feet, testicles, earlobes, and forehead were probed with a thorn-like twig, never too deep but deep enough to draw blood. A greenish liquid burned at his feet like the eternal flame at Arlington. Then the body parts of animals were sautéed with the green liquid, marinated with the thorn-like twigs, and offered to Raymond as his only choice of indulgence. Chicken livers, monkey's eyes, lizard tails, and the ever-popular water buffalo heart were devoured by Raymond like an Ethiopian at a French restaurant.

Six days into his ordeal they cut his hemp ropes and ceremoniously bathed him and gave him a clean white robe. White to signify his purity, his virginity, his newborn status.

At the end of the evening, Raymond surrendered his white robe for the black robe, signifying a full-fledged disciple of Satan—rookie edition.

Over the next four years Raymond became a quick student and was awarded a Ph.D. in Devil worship, working his way up to High Priest. The former marine, since he had long ago been court-martialed for desertion, became an expert in mind control, narcotic synthesizing, reducing a pulse rate to one, killing with a fingertip, and sucking water through his rectum. When he had learned all he could, he returned to the United States with a new outlook on life and a new name—Lu. Lucifer.

He accepted the words of the poet Milton, that it was better to reign in hell than serve in heaven.

Two days before Lerza was scheduled to have his still-beating heart eaten, his Vietnam flashbacks reached an all-time high. He had spent more mind-time returning to the jungles of Southeast Asia while in the basement of the Satan clubhouse than in any previous period since he'd come back to the United States.

He began to look forward to his many conversations with Lu with a pleasant anticipation; they became, for him, almost a necessity. And Lu seemed to enjoy exploring Lerza's brain as it alternated between different time- and land-zones.

"Got any heat tabs, Lu?" Lerza asked.

"Trade you two heat tabs for your B-3 can."

"Throw in a cookie and some toilet paper. These C-Rats suck."

"See any VC?" Lu asked.

"They're out there, I know, waiting for dark. They'll probe our lines, find a weak spot, and cut our sleepin' throats."

"Stay alert, marine."

"Fuckin' ay," Lerza said; then his brain slowly faded to black and refocused on the present. He snarled, "I ain't tellin' you nothin'. No FBI information, no undercover names. I can't do it."

Lu smiled slightly, said, "You'll feel better tomorrow, Joe. Just tell me something, anything. Something simple like how many FBI agents in Philadelphia. That's no big deal. Tell me just that, and I'll give you a sandwich and some more of that nose candy. Your escape from this basement."

"Fuck you, Lu!"

"I'm disappointed, Joe," Lu said, like a jilted high schooler. "We're supposed to be Marine Corps Vietnam buddies, and you keep telling me to get fucked."

"I ain't no snitch."

"I know that, Joe, you're a marine. A point. The gyrene that leads the pack, a magnet to NVA booby traps and bullets. A leader. You ain't no snitch."

Lu knew exactly why he was saying what he did. The mention of Vietnam, point, NVA, and bullets triggered Lerza's flashbacks. All calculated to weaken his resolve, a form of intense behavior modification using sensory deprivation. A slow trickle of water on the forehead, a blindfold and loud noises, little sleep, water or food. A classic Stockholm Syndrome where the victims begin identifying with their captors.

Lu screamed, *"Incoming!"*

Lerza flattened out in an attempt to avoid the imaginary shrapnel and waited. When no hot metal ripped his flesh, he straightened up and saw Lu smiling.

Lerza sat upright, trying to regain his dignity. He held his head high, looked Lu in the eye, and said, "Why do you want this information?"

Lu spoke patiently. "I'm about to be the new drug czar,

Joe," he explained. "With your help, no undercover agent or snitch can buy my drugs and arrest my runners, my distributors. I can laugh at their surveillance, block their wiretap transmissions, and get inside our enemies' brains."

"Our?" Lerza asked.

"Yes, Joe," Lu went on. "Yours and mine. As we talk, the FBI is searching the city for you. Not to save you from me but to arrest you and put you in prison for the rest of your life. They are as much your enemy as mine. They are a danger to you, to us. They will destroy us. *Now* how many of them are here in Philadelphia?"

Lerza was silent for several minutes. When he finally spoke it was a simple number—"Four hundred and sixty-five agents."

H A R D Rock got the message from one of the fat Palermo cousins: "The ol' man wants to see you now."

The Rock puffed up his greasy black hair like the NBC peacock being wooed by a stud eagle. He said, "Probably wants to ask me about something. Business, you know."

Hard Rock had had a higher status in the mob since his meeting with Amato following Miceli's death. The new guard was bullied, and the old guard treated the Rock like a root canal. The Don had given him some minor-league collection jobs requiring little brains, tact, or finesse.

Rock now climbed into the backseat of his new black Cadillac, because mob bosses had wiseguys drive. Typical south Philly wopmobile with gold trim, fur seats, car phone, and a St. Christopher magnetic statue next to a nine-millimeter magazine holding twenty rounds.

The trip from Ninth and Carpenter was short. Rock and his entourage, which included the Butchers from Abruzzi and the Palermo brothers, entered the Italian Club at a whirlwind pace.

"Go get a drink," the Rock ordered his men. The fat mafioso then climbed to the third-floor offices, breathing heavily but high on the excitement of a private meet with the old man.

Amato sat behind his mammoth, shiny desk in a high-back leather chair looking like an ethnic Judge Wapner on "People's Court."

"Sit," the Don commanded.

"How ya doin'?" Hard Rock asked, adding, "Sir."

"Never better."

An awkward silence followed before Amato straightened his vest and spoke officially.

He said simply, "It's time."

"What?" The Rock wondered, Time for what?

"Our big move. A multi-kilogram heroin deal."

The large psychopath leaned forward, realizing something important was being described.

"I want fifty keys imported from your supplier in Italy, shipped to our warehouse."

"No problem," said Hard Rock. " 'Cept the Satans are operating with your blessing."

"No longer," Amato said. "Remember when I promised you a time of revenge?"

"Yeah, boss."

"It is time, my large friend. After our deal you may eliminate our competition."

Hard Rock said emphatically, "I'm gonna enjoy wasting every last one of them pigs."

"But only on my orders," Amato warned. "And only after our fifty-kilogram deal."

Hard Rock grunted assent.

Amato continued authoritatively, for the moment of truth had arrived, and he could not allow Hard Rock to continue Miceli's practice of keeping drug connections from him. "I will be present when the shipment arrives," he said.

The Rock hesitated only slightly and said again, "No problem."

Amato, in control, continued quickly, "Where is this warehouse?"

"Ragni's, over on Second Street."

"How much per kilogram?"

"I'll need seventy thousand dollars per key to import. We sell it here for one hundred and thirty thousand dollars."

"See Dominic for the money."

The Rock nodded.

"Contact our fifty best customers, offer them a special, only ninety thousand dollars a key."

Hard Rock protested, "Too cheap! We take the importation risk, we gotta pay the shippers to sneak it over, we got a lot of overhead."

Amato pulled rank. "Just do it, and after it's set, I will rent a second warehouse for the actual deliveries. You contact our fifty best customers, no deadbeats, no mid-level operators, only the top legitimate heroin people in the city, let them know it's a blue-light special at K-Mart."

"You got it, Mr. Amato."

"Good. Now onto other business, my capo," Amato said. "I'm getting heat from the politicos in this city over your actions in Fairmont Park. I'm attempting to put out the fire but I must be armed with all the facts so that I may manipulate them to our advantage."

"Three of my guys already got indicted on that," Hard Rock complained.

Amato feigned support, looking sympathetic. "A shame, and I am also working on their release. But I want you to tell me every detail of that night. Who was present, what cars were used, where your men were positioned, where the murder weapon is, how you escaped."

For a split second Amato thought he could actually feel the reels of the FBI tape recorder slowly revolving their way in an inevitable circle, imprinting Hard Rock's words. Also, like every other person, whether undercover agent or FBI snitch, who had worn the secret recorder, he became absolutely positive the small device was as visible as a Motorola Home Entertainment Center complete with forty-two-inch TV.

The look on Hard Rock's face could have been mistaken for pain but he was merely trying to think with his peanut-size brain. His usual answers were monosyllabic grunts, and the need to bring several sentences together had him worried.

He began, "There was Rocco and Vita. I did the hit on the broad myself with a Beretta I got stashed at Ragni's warehouse. Blew her head apart." He chuckled and went on. "Then we beat feet in cars we leased from Fasulos under John Does."

The Rock told Amato every detail. Once he started he could not stop. He confessed to four other homicides, eight aggravated robberies, and gave his own educated guesses on who kidnapped the Lindbergh baby and where Jimmy Hoffa's skeleton lay buried.

Amato had to halt the Sicilian an hour into his nonstop recorded confession just as the Rock was giving the gory details of how he tortured a cat when he was eight years old.

On his way out the door, Hard Rock turned and said, "Sorry about Billy Averone. The big C ate him up, huh?"

"Yes, a terrible death."

"Who's gonna take his place?"

Amato knew he was expected to designate the Rock to replace Averone as the family *consiglieri*.

He smiled slightly and said, "I am hoping *you* will follow William."

≡ 286 ≡

. . .

PATTY guided the Chevy into a spot under the neon sign, "The Triangle." Pure irony, meeting Amato at the same place where she had planned and plotted against the Don with Lerza and Moose. The fat pizza kid, Romeo, pulled a large one with pepperoni out of the oven, and looked up at Patty as she glided past the counter.

"Hey, hon!"

"Hey, Romeo," she said. "Gonna do Sinatra?"

"You bet. I'm gonna dedicate 'Strangers in the Night' to you." He winked a fat eyelid.

"Better not," she teased. "I may not be able to resist."

He laughed. "That's what all the girls say."

She saw the old man sitting in the rear booth, looking as natural in the South Philly bar setting as garlic bread in gravy.

Amato slid over to make room for her next to him. The Don had taken off his suit jacket. His tie was slid an inch below the top button, his sleeves were rolled up. This gave him the appearance of a man getting down to hard work, and ready for it.

He sipped a Cutty Sark, asked, "How are you?" and placed his hand on her shoulder in a comforting way.

"How did it go?" She got right down to business. The old Italian knew business could not be rushed, should not be conducted until it was time. First, the amenities of small talk, health, family, the weather, then food and drink. Then, and only when the time was right, did business begin. At that point it was attacked with the ferocity of marines at boot camp, life-and-death decisions made with the flick of a hand, lives altered forever with a nod of the head.

"Have a drink," he said. "Some clams and spaghetti. I already ordered."

The waitress appeared. Patty asked for a double vodka, straight up with a twist of lemon. She sighed deeply and started to relax. They ate clams and devoured spaghetti, a side order of pizza, antipasto salad, Italian bread and cheeses, topped off the meal with spumoni ice cream.

Then Amato took a green tape-recording reel from his vest pocket and handed it to her. He said, "I'm sure you will find this to your liking."

"Did you cover everything?" Her voice was excited.

"All and more." His voice was calm.

"What about the heroin?"

"Ordered."

"When? Where?"

"It seems that Ragni's warehouse is the importation point of the city. Soon. Fifty kilograms. I will be present, I assume, with your federal tape recorder."

"Correct assumption." She sipped her vodka. "You have to take possession of the fifty keys from Hard Rock. That's important because once the government has custody of the heroin, it's our ass if some junky OD's. *And,*" she emphasized, "once *you* have custody of the heroin, then *we* have custody."

Amato leaned toward her and said softly, "I understand, Patty. I will personally take the heroin and place it in my safe at the club."

"Can't work that way," she corrected. "You must get the heroin to me as soon as you leave Ragni's. The FBI will repackage it with just enough heroin in each kilo to make the case. Then I will bring some fifty sham packages to you just prior to 'D' day—Delivery Day."

Amato sighed and said, "As you wish. When I leave here I will rent a warehouse on Third and Oregon. A key to that warehouse will be delivered tonight by messenger to the

FBI office. This will allow you to place your cameras and microphones tomorrow."

"Layout?" she asked.

"Excellent. The fifty heroin distributors must enter and exit through the front door. An old, empty tenement house directly across the street allows for suitable camera angles to capture faces, vehicles, even license plates. Third Street is a one-way street, so they must leave the area driving south. This will allow your agents to make the arrest discreetly at Packard Avenue, without incident. They will find one kilogram of heroin in each of the fifty vehicles."

"What about the inside?"

"Twenty feet inside the front door will be a counter. I and Hard Rock will be behind the counter with the heroin. We will take their money and hand them the heroin. I suggest a camera situated over the door pointing at the counter. This will capture the entire transaction. As the buyer leaves he will walk directly into your camera."

She said admiringly, "You have a flair for this."

"I'm a businessman, Patty. These are merely the details needed to complete a deal."

Then he asked, "Just curious, Patty, but what will the prison sentence be for one kilogram of heroin?"

"Ten years mandatory. No parole."

She shifted in her seat and faced him directly. "Just you and me, Michael," she said seriously, "drinking booze and trusting our lives to each other. *Why?*"

He paused, chuckled, and said, "You wouldn't understand."

"Try me," she challenged.

He gave it some thought, then said slowly, "You just might understand, at that. As I said, this is business, and business has rules, whether written or unwritten. These men, who will go to jail at my hand, have violated *our* rules. Hard Rock, Miceli, Lu, and the rest have taken our business and insulted our intelligence by hurting innocent people, showing lack of respect to our authority and, most important, cheating, lying, and stealing business profits.''

He hesitated a few seconds and went on, ''That all boils down to honor. You may say honor among thieves, but honor is a virtue that does not judge its possessor. Only if one practices it does one treasure it. I do what I do so I may restore honor—to them, to me, and to you.''

Patty listened to the old man and believed him. But she also knew there was still something ambiguous. The hidden motive, the missing ingredient to the Amato puzzle of unexpected cooperation.

She asked, ''What about Lu? When is the meet that will get his confession to the Miceli murder?''

''And the clearing of Lerza,'' he added.

She blushed and said, ''Yes, and the clearing of Lerza.'' Patty paused and added hopefully, ''Can't you use your resources to find Joe?''

''First Hard Rock and the biggest fifty heroin dealers in Philadelphia.''

He smiled at her, almost a wistful smile, as though he wished he were young again and could be her suitor.

JEROME Ragni was excited. Never before had his warehouse imported over twenty keys. Hard Rock had been almost solemn as he said, ''Jerry, it's the big fuckin' one. 'Fifty' big ones and the ol' man and *me* put it together. I pray to God it goes well, Jerry, 'cause if it does, you may be looking at the new *consiglieri*.''

The Sicilian exporter was the only one in the meeting who was calm. He did not blink an eye. Their Philadelphia cousins were money in the bank. The opium was harvested in the fields by squat ladies with no idea what destructive effects their efforts in Italy had in the schoolyards of America. The raw opium was then processed into the finished product by skilled men whose cousins, brothers, and uncles were also skilled men, only they were shoemakers, cement men, and carpenters.

Opium was just another skill to the poor hill people who considered the heroin trade as just another business. A way of putting bread on the table. It was packaged in red opaque plastic bags, heat-sealed in clear plastic packets by the village bosses, who took the largest share of the profits simply because they had the American market. The heat-sealed packets were carefully placed in tin cans half full of tomato paste. They were sealed and cartoned in cardboard boxes marked "Sanuti Tomato Paste, Palermo, Sicily."

The village elders took the cardboard boxes to the seacoast and watched as the valuable cargo was loaded on ships that had Swiss registry and Italian crews. The captains were paid in gold and threatened with death should the shipment not reach its destination.

The heroin was due to arrive at the Philadelphia port on Wednesday morning, and Hard Rock was so excited he held a party Tuesday night at the Chassis, now under the management of Wicked Wanda, the Rodeo Queen. The fat Sicilian exporter could not sleep and stayed up all night enjoying sex with two dancers who took turns playing Hard Rock's favorite game, "Squeeze the salami."

The Don's instructions to the hungover Rock had been simple and nonnegotiable: "Be out front at nine A.M. Just you. No mopes."

It was a career comedown for Hard Rock to chauffeur himself, but he popped three pink benzedrine tablets, and chased them with a swig of Cribari wine. When the amphetamine hit his brain, the Cadillac took on the aspect of a jet-propelled NASA rocket hurtling through the narrow streets of South Philadelphia.

When he arrived at the Italian Club, Amato's limousine with Di Sipio behind the wheel was already waiting. The Rock took a seat next to Amato, inspected the luxury car, and said, "Nice ride."

Amato grunted and ordered Di Sipio, "Drive." The limousine turned right on Lombard, heading east to the river and Ragni's warehouse.

Amato's blood pressure had skyrocketed, causing light-headedness and irritability. When he felt in better health, he thought, he could put up with the moronic Hard Rock, but today it took all of his acting ability to treat the man civilly. Ever since his best friend Averone had died, Amato had felt his own mortality. A slight upset stomach mushroomed in his mind until it threatened like impending death.

Amato's intellect knew death was not close, but his heart made it feel as immediate as stepping in front of a high-speed Mack truck. Too much confusion. Too many unnatural acts. The irony was not lost on him. Perfectly natural to order a brutal killing, but very unnatural to cooperate with the feds.

"Shipment still expected at nine-thirty?" he asked Hard Rock.

"Should be on the shelves by then."

"Have you contacted our wholesalers?"

"They're comin' all over their pants," Hard Rock said, "getting a key of heroin for ninety thou."

"You must arrange for pickups on the same day," Amato cautioned, "every fifteen minutes starting at eight in the morning. You *must* emphasize that they are to be prompt and you *must* demand that the price of ninety thousand dollars is only good that day. The next day the price doubles. Of course, they must have cash."

Hard Rock twisted in his seat. "Maybe we'll have too much activity and draw heat, boss," he said.

Amato dismissed this, explaining, "It's a warehouse. Besides, only one or two people will be present at a time. They will enter, hand you the money, you will give them the heroin, and they will leave immediately. Understood?"

"That's what I've been tellin' them," Hard Rock agreed. "None of them got any problems with paying ninety grand for one hundred and thirty thousand worth of heroin. Hell, I could tell them to wear a Santa Claus suit and stick a rotten orange up their ass, and they'd do it."

Di Sipio maneuvered the large vehicle into one of those very small parking spaces so common in South Philly. The chauffeur reached Amato's back door as fast as his old legs would let him and strongly considered slamming the door in Hard Rock's face. He had never asked Amato why such a low-class pig was awarded such respect. He never would, but he still resented it.

The large steel-accordion warehouse front door was positioned down and secure. The side door, protected by seven-foot iron bars, bore the large red-lettered sign, CLOSED.

As the two men approached, the iron bars miraculously opened. Jerome Ragni stood there smiling. The curly-haired third cousin of the deceased Miceli seemed in awe of Amato. He took his hand and kissed it the way a Peoria nun would the Pope's.

"Don Amato, a pleasure. How are you?" Ragni said solemnly.

"Never better," Amato lied. "And you?"

"Seven children, very little sleep."

Amato smiled, reached into his pocket, extracted a hundred-dollar bill, and pushed it into Ragni's hand. He said, "A Christening gift for the last born."

Ragni almost bowed. "Thank you, padrone, thank you. God bless you." He stuck the C-note in his pocket.

Hard Rock interrupted, "Yo, Jer, did it come in?"

Ragni grabbed a clipboard from a nearby stack of boxes, ran a finger down a row of numbers, and said, "Yeah, Rock, the carton numbers match the ones you gave me—7218, 7315, 7408, 7418, and 8643."

"Get 'em," Hard Rock ordered.

Jerome Ragni started pushing a small dolly around the warehouse until he had five cardboard cartons filled with Sanuti Tomato Paste and China white heroin. The warehouse man quietly placed the cartons in front of the two mafiosi.

"Open 'em," Hard Rock said.

Ragni cut the boxes with the carton knife, removed ten cans from each carton, and placed them in front of Hard Rock. He started opening each individual can with an electric can-opener. He had opened only two before the impatient Hard Rock stuck a meaty paw inside the tomato-paste can, spilling the thick gravy onto the counter, and removed one kilogram of heroin wrapped in a heat-sealed package.

The Rock smiled and started to hand the dripping package to Amato before he caught himself, wiped off the red sauce, then repeated the gesture. Amato took the heroin in his hand, felt its weight, its texture, its fiber, tried to understand its enormous power. He grunted approval. "Does it meet *your* approval?" he asked the Rock.

Hard Rock beamed. "Looks good to me, boss."

"Pack it up."

Ragni and Hard Rock went about the business of removing and wiping off fifty packets of heroin from tomato-paste cans, then placing them in two large canvas bags until each was full.

When they finished, Amato told Hard Rock to take the bags to the limousine and wait. Once the Rock had left the warehouse, Amato put a hand on Ragni's shoulder and said, "The heroin trade will be slow for a while. Can you survive on the legitimate business of this warehouse?"

"It will be difficult, Mr. Amato, the volume of imports is—"

Amato cut him off with a wave of the hand, said, "No need to explain. You will receive twenty-five thousand dollars within the next week. Do not discuss this with anyone. Do you understand?"

"Yes, my padrone." Ragni beamed.

"No one," the Don warned again.

"No one," Ragni repeated.

"Now give me all the paperwork on this heroin shipment," Amato commanded.

Without hesitation, Ragni did as he was told.

Amato said, "Good-bye," and walked to his car.

He dropped Hard Rock back at the Club and ordered Di Sipio to drive toward the Italian Market. When they reached the corner of Ninth and Wharton, the Don stepped out, carrying the two canvas bags with the one hundred pounds of heroin. Amato handled the weight easily despite his age and health. His raw strength and sense of purpose eased the burden.

Di Sipio asked, "What time do you want me to pick you up?"

"Go home, Daniel, I will take a taxi," the Don said. "Go home to your grandchildren."

Di Sipio protested, "It's not safe on the streets. Your heart. What if—"

Amato interrupted, "Go home. I have walked these streets for the last fifty years. My heart will last the day."

Di Sipio drove off, leaving the old man alone with his

thoughts and the two canvas bags. He began walking, carrying the bags easily. He talked to outdoor vendors who hawked everything from hot peppers to tuxedos. One offered three cantaloupes for two dollars as the booth next door screamed three for one dollar and eighty cents.

The Don had shuffled only about a hundred yards when he saw him. With the death of Averone *he* was now his most trusted friend. The exchange was quick and covert; then his friend left, leaving the old man alone again.

Amato smiled and spoke staccato Italian with the vendors, some of whom recognized him; most did not. This raucous outdoor market resembled turn-of-the-century Rome, with barrels burning wood for warmth, live chickens running in the streets, and everything for sale and negotiable.

The Philly crime boss walked slowly for three blocks until he reached the Triangle Bar for his meeting with Special Agent Patty Masters. She sat at "their" booth in the back, sipping a vodka and tonic, chomping, not too delicately, on a slice of anchovy pizza.

She watched the elderly man carrying the two large canvas bags enter and walk purposefully toward her. She appreciated the raw physical strength of Amato. She did a quick calculation: one kilogram was 2.2 pounds, and this sick old man in his seventies was carrying 50 kilograms as if they were plastic lawn chairs.

"A double Cutty," Amato said to the nearby waitress. "And an extra plate for that anchovy pizza."

"Hello, Michael," Patty greeted him warmly.

"A wonderful day," he commented.

She was starting to understand the old man's quirks and held off on asking about the deal. Her FBI background demanded she immediately determine if he got the heroin, who was at the warehouse, how it was packed, where the shipment originated, what vessel transported the heroin, and a thousand other questions.

The canvas bags were a hopeful sign, but her previous dealings with the Italian crime boss dictated that she wait. First report on each other's health, the weather, argue about the sanitation strike or the Phillies' losing streak. Then it was time to discuss business.

They ate, they drank, and they shared words, looking more like father and daughter at a leisurely lunch than an FBI agent and a mob crime boss.

When it was time, Amato tapped on the canvas bags, handed her the papers Ragni had provided, and said, "All there, fifty keys. Ragni's Warehouse on Second Avenue. A ship named *Ollie Olson* delivered the heroin wrapped in Sanuti Tomato Paste cans shipped from the village of Abrumi in Sicily. The exporters are part of the Nardinio family."

Patty noticed a trace of pride in Amato's voice. She said, approval in her soft voice, "Excellent."

"Just a day's work," he kidded.

"When is the delivery set?"

"Day after tomorrow, starting at eight A.M."

"What about the meet with Lu?"

Amato's tone changed, became serious. "When fifty or so heroin dealers get arrested leaving my warehouse, the word will get out that I am no longer trustworthy. I will have to meet with Lu the next day so that the Satan is candid."

"I understand."

"You worry about Lerza?" He sounded concerned.

"Yes." Her voice was low.

"I understand." Sympathy in his voice.

30

Patty briefed the one hundred agents in the Situation Room at the FBI office. She stood before a blackboard dotted with X's and O's—a layout of the warehouse, the tenement across the street that would act as the Command Post (CP) and the location of the fifty arrest teams a block away. Keenan watched her like a theater critic watched a star on opening night.

Pointing at a square on the blackboard, Patty said, "Bubba Nite will coordinate the arrest here. I'll call out a number, the description of the vehicle, and its occupants from the CP. Remember the numbers because each two-man arrest team will also have a number. Arrest team number three will arrest the third group of bad guys. Arrest team number four, the fourth group and so on. Any questions?"

"Everybody in the car gets cuffed?" Reginald Bubba Nite asked.

"Everybody gets arrested," she said. "It's critical to this operation that no bad guy is allowed to reach a phone. Also, timing is everything. The arrest teams have to do a felony car stop, ID themselves, arrest and secure the occupants of the car, and get them and their car out of the area in ten minutes."

Bubba Nite, who wore a perpetual smirk, chewed on a cheap stogie. He was in trouble with the front office most of the time. He was a compulsive gambler who drank beer the way most people drink water. But he was an efficient FBI agent, which was why Patty chose him to coordinate the arrests. He knew the streets, and the other agents respected him.

"Just a day's work." He laughed.

"But we can't forget these guys are extremely dangerous," Patty warned. "They're going to be carrying heavy heat, transporting heroin worth half a mil once their chemist cuts it up in grams."

Keenan asserted his authority. "Once the arrests are made, transport the prisoners directly back here for processing. Their cars will be taken to the naval base and forfeited to the government."

Patty sighed, finished the briefing, and warned, "Remember, everyone must be in position by seven A.M. tomorrow morning; check your car radios. Communication on A-2. Wear your protective vests and know your arrest-team number."

The roomful of FBI agents closed notebooks, stood up, and shuffled their way to the door. Keenan got the last word, calling out, "Remember—be careful!"

When the room emptied, he asked Patty in a whisper, "Will it work?"

She shrugged her shoulders, "No guarantees."

He did not like that answer. He wanted reassurance.

Wanting to hear something positive, he asked, "When is Amato's meeting with Lu?"

"Day after tomorrow."

Keenan actually bowed his head and said, "I pray to God the old man gets that Satan to confess to Miceli's murder. I want to clear my agent. I want Joe Lerza back alive, safe, and healthy."

"Do you?" A challenging tone.

"Yes, Miss Masters, I do. Do you think I enjoy reading about the FBI killer in the newspapers? Do you think I relish the calls from Laura Lerza? I lie in bed at night hoping Lerza is alive and won't do something that can't be undone. *Yes*, Miss Masters, I care."

She felt moved and said, "Look, Brad. You and I don't particularly like each other, and maybe it's me." She walked out the door, leaving further thoughts unsaid.

She punched the first-floor button on the elevator, exited the federal building, and felt the bite of late March night air. She drove her Chevy south on Broad Street, her mind racing, her adrenaline high with the anticipation of tomorrow. She looked at her watch and realized visiting hours at the hospital would be over in forty-five minutes.

She left the Chevy in front of a fire hydrant beneath the statue of St. Agnes. As she passed the nurses' station, Sister Alberta Maria smiled at her.

"How is he?" Patty asked. The plump nun said, "Better, much better. Still comatose, but the vital signs are strong. The Good Lord isn't ready to take the likes of Moose Knepp."

"Thank you, sister." Gratitude in her voice.

"God bless you." The nun smiled. She had seen Patty several times on her way to the small room Moose occupied.

Patty entered Moose's room feeling low. It was dark except for a recessed light that shone somewhere beyond the still patient. Moose lay peacefully on his back with tubes, IV's, and other paraphernalia hanging from a tall rack like Christmas decorations on a blue spruce.

The Moose had been comatose since the nine bullets found their mark during the Fairmont Park shootout, and each day that passed made the unhappy diagnoses of brain and kidney damage, among other injuries, more likely. That prognosis, however, seemed to be for average beings, not for physical specimens like Moose.

Patty sat on the empty bed next to him and gently held his hand. She asked softly, "How are you doing, you big lug?"

The Moose lay motionless, eyes shut, huge chest gently rising and falling with each breath.

"We got big problems," Patty talked on. "Our good friend, Joe, is bonkers and a murder fugitive. Stormy's dead—murdered. I'm all but washed up in the Bureau. Persona non grata. And you're lying here like a vegetable." She was silent a few ticks of the clock, then asked, "What do you think? What's the matter? Cat got your tongue?"

She didn't expect a reaction but just talking matters over had a peaceful effect on her. She went on, "We did an absolutely shitty job, you know, all except for you. You were the Rock of Gibraltar in this whole mess. I let my ambition, my desire to get ahead in the Bureau, interfere with doing the right thing, like bringing Lerza in and ending the undercover assignment."

She sank into private thought a moment, then went on. "Joe acted like a sophomore at a fraternity party and all the criminals acted like criminals, but you, Moose, you were outstanding. You were there when it counted. You stood by Joe and me when we were out of line, when we were downright shitty to you. You never judged, you never sec- ond-guessed, you just loved us. With no strings. Just loved us—" She stopped as tears came to her eyes, and then she started to sob, "Oh, Moose, don't die! You can't die!"

"Who's gonna die?" Moose's deep voice.

She stared dumbly at the moving lips of a friend medical science said shouldn't be talking.

The Moose's brown eyes were now wide open. He gave Patty one of his classic shit-eating grins and asked, "What day is it?"

She gulped in amazement and stammered, "W-Wednesday."

"What day was Fairmont Park?"

"On a Saturday."

He asked incredulously, "You mean I been out cold for four days?"

She gently squeezed his hand, smiling. "Moose, you've been in a coma for seven weeks!"

Without hesitation he said, "I need a beer."

"No way!" she said. "Nurses won't allow it."

"Then I need sex if it's been seven weeks."

"It's been seven years since you had sex." She laughed softly.

"Take off your clothes, Patty, or I'll go back into a coma," he threatened.

She laughed, this time a louder laugh, a hearty laugh, something she had not done in a long time. She leaned over, kissed Moose on the forehead, and said, "I love you, you animal."

She spent the next hour explaining to Moose what had happened since Fairmont Park—Keenan's behavior, Amato's deal, Lu's hit on Miceli, Lerza's fugitive status, and the recent Italian deal.

Moose wanted at once to leave his deathbed, find Lerza, beat the shit out of Keenan, shoot Hard Rock, bugger Dirty Denise, and drink Imperial Whiskey at the Triangle. But

Sister Alberta Maria, tougher and meaner than Moose, ordered him to remain horizontal. As Patty left, the Moose and the Nun were engaged in a serious quarrel as to when he could leave his bed and what he could eat to gain the strength to walk out.

"I wanna meatball hoagie," he was insisting.

"No solid food until the doctor says so."

"Call the sawbones then." A disgusted tone.

"Now you listen here, Mr. Moose—"

Patty was out the door and smiled all the way to her car, which now had a seventy-five-dollar parking ticket for having been left in front of a fire hydrant. She crumpled the ticket into a ball, tossed it in the gutter, and thought of the nasty legal threats she would get in the mail from the Philadelphia Police Department.

Her dream that night was jumbled and disjointed, but on waking she vividly recalled the frightening scene where the bullets hit the good guys.

THE staging area was the parking lot of a third-rate diner eight blocks from the warehouse. In the early-morning dawn Patty, Keenan, and Bubba Nite were huddled in a group, going over their checklist. It promised to be a warmer day with the hint of a March sun cutting into the chilly morning's bite. Nondescript government cars were neatly stacked in rows, some with engines running, their heaters warming half-awake agents sucking on hot coffee.

"All arrest teams present," Bubba said, adding, "Radio checks completed, support people ready to transport vehicles and process prisoners."

"Good," Patty said approvingly. "The CP camera is loaded and tested, Amato is ready. I've already left the sham heroin in the empty warehouse behind the counter. It's being surveilled now."

Keenan stood ramrod-straight, impeccably dressed in a three-piece black suit sans overcoat despite the thirty-one-degree temperature.

He asked Bubba Nite, "Are the men ready?"

"Overripe," Bubba shot back.

"Very good." The tentative tone belied his words.

"Let's get it on," Patty said anxiously.

She and Keenan drove to the tenement building across from the warehouse, left the car, and tiptoed up the three flights of creaky wooden stairs to the front room apartment. It was empty except for the closed-circuit television equipment and two metal chairs.

Patty strode over to the equipment, flicked switches, and checked batteries, monitors, and camera angles. The inside warehouse counter slowly appeared on one monitor; a second focused on the street and outside door. When she was satisfied the equipment worked properly, she pushed one of the chairs close to the window and looked out onto the street through a small slit in the shade. She was trying to avoid any small talk with Keenan in the thirty minutes remaining before Amato's arrival.

Several moments passed before either combatant made an attempt to speak. It was Keenan.

He said seriously, "You don't like me, do you, Patty?"

She shrugged her shoulders. "Is it important to you that I do?"

Keenan sighed and said, "Not really. But it *is* important that you follow orders. That you respect the chain of command. That you do things the Bureau way."

She said sarcastically, "The Bureau way! It's the Bureau way that has created this mess. I'll make this operation a success not because I want to endear myself to you or the Bureau. Not because I want to be a Bureau supervisor. But because it's the right thing to do at this time."

She looked him straight in the eye and said, "The Bureau's mystique is more than just a little tarnished. I don't give a rat's ass whether you or all those other empty suits at headquarters like me, my methods, or my FBI monogrammed lace panties. Because when this is over and Lerza is cleared of Miceli's murder, my creds will be on your desk with my legal handbook and my popgun."

Her outburst assured the room's silence until she spotted Amato's limousine on the outside CCTV monitor. Then she said, squelching the hand mike to a porta mobile radio, "Signal twenty-five to signal ten."

"Ten, go ahead." Bubba's voice.

"The old man and the Sicilian just arrived."

"Ten four, signal twenty-five. Notify me when the first subjects arrive."

With Keenan standing by her shoulder, Patty observed Amato and Hard Rock enter the warehouse through the side door and make their way to the counter. The camera was located directly over the inside door, aimed at the counter, giving her an unobstructed view. She watched as Amato ducked under the counter, grabbed the two canvas bags, and placed them on the counter. With Amato now facing the CCTV, she saw him open both canvas bags, check the fifty heat-sealed plastic jackets, and replace the bags on the floor behind the counter and out of the camera's view.

The audio was as clear as the video. She heard Hard Rock ask, "All there, boss?"

Amato responded, "Yes, and are you certain that each customer knows his pick-up time? Knows the price and the importance of punctuality?"

"Called them again, boss." Hard Rock's defensive voice. "They know they're gettin' a bargain. They'll be here."

At exactly 8 A.M. Vinnie "The Stiletto" Garbonito arrived with his driver, Tommy "Six Toe" Nardi. The black

Buick parked across the street from the warehouse. Vinnie, who had gotten his monicker by shiving eight guys to death in his youth, walked out of the Delta 98 carrying a blue nylon gym bag. Six Toe, born with an extra little toe on his right foot, followed him.

"Signal twenty-five to signal ten," Patty repeated into the hand mike.

"Go ahead twenty-five."

"Advise team number one that their package has arrived. Get in position. Their target is a Buick, 'eighty-eight, black in color, four-door, Pennsylvania license 68R25."

"Ten four," Bubba Nite said, repeating her description of the vehicle and then alerting her that team one was now in position.

"Further advise team number one that there are two subjects, both white males, approximate age mid-forties, identified as Vincent Garbonito and Thomas Nardi," she said.

Twenty seconds later the radio crackled, "Ten four, signal twenty-five, arrest-team number one has been advised."

Patty picked up a clipboard, put a large X beside the time, 8 A.M., wrote "team number one." She added the words "two males and black Buick" to the chart. Then studied the monitor as The Stiletto and Six Toe walked to the counter, their backs to the camera.

The Stiletto said, "Mr. Amato! A real surprise. Also an honor."

The old man glanced at his watch, calculated how much small talk he could allow before the 8:15 A.M. heroin dealer arrived. He said, "Vincent, how's your uncle Sal?"

"Arthritis got him planted in a wheelchair, but he still eats solid food and pinches the nurse's ass." The Stiletto laughed.

Amato smiled. "Tell him I send regards." Then, brusquely, "Now on to business." The old man pointed to the Rock, who leaned behind the counter, retrieved one kilogram of heroin, and handed it to Vinnie, The Stiletto, who said "Good shit!"

"No complaints yet." Vinnie pushed the blue nylon bag at Amato. "All there, Mr. Amato. Wanna count it?"

Amato feigned surprise. "No need. We are businessmen. Mutual trust, mutual benefit."

The Stiletto started to say something, but Amato cut him off, "Good day, Vincent." The Stiletto and Six Toe got the message, turned toward the door to face the FBI camera, which photographed a Pulitzer Prize shot of the two heroin dealers. No jury in the world could mistake those faces in a courtroom.

"Signal ten, be advised the first package is leaving and about to enter their vehicle," said Patty.

"Ten four," came Bubba's response.

FBI arrest-team number one consisted of Daniel Estreb and Kevin Burns. Estreb, a former Detroit cop, chewed on a toothpick and belched the chili he had eaten at midnight. Burns, a twenty-five-year-old first office agent and former third-grade teacher, thumped a hand nervously on the steering wheel.

Estreb said, "All right, kid. We block the subjects' vehicle from the front, Bubba pulls behind them in his car so we don't get in any high-speed chase. You run out and go to the passenger side and ID yourself loudly. I go get the driver. Get 'em out of the car, a quick pat down, cuff 'em, throw 'em in the backseat of the backup car, and get the fuck outta here. Got it?"

Burns looked straight ahead and said apprehensively, "Got it, Dan."

It took The Stiletto and Six Toe forty-two seconds to drive the city block and reach the intersection where Estreb and Burns waited.

"Now!" yelled Estreb.

The young agent pulled out from the intersecting street and positioned his Bureau car just two feet from the black Buick and perpendicular to it. Simultaneously, Bubba Nite pulled out of a parking slot from behind. His bumper locked The Stiletto's rear fender.

Burns jumped out of the bureau car, weapon drawn, and started racing to the passenger side of the Buick. Estreb did the same, aiming an old .38 police special at the driver.

The Stiletto yelled *"Rip-off!"* He pulled out an M-10 automatic machine pistol and pointed it at Burns's head just as the young agent was mouthing "FBI."

Burns could actually see the Italian's finger starting its trigger squeeze. As he closed his eyes in anticipation of his impending death in a hail of nine-millimeter slugs, the sound of gunfire reached his ears. His last logical thoughts were that (a) there was no earthly way he could avoid the bullets, and (b) he would surely die.

He heard the sound of several shots as they rang out clear and loud in the early morning. When he finally opened his eyes, he saw The Stiletto and Six Toe slumped in the front seat of the Buick, their blood running over the expensive plush upholstery.

Bubba was smiling at Burns, his pop shooter smoking in the frosty March air. The black Buick's windshield was in slivers. Estreb had axed the driver just as Vinnie bent over to get his .44 Magnum under the seat.

"I hate it when they don't listen," Estreb said serenely.

Bubba cautiously approached the passenger side of the car and assured himself its occupants were no longer a threat. As he opened the door, Six Toe fell out onto the pavement.

Bubba looked at him, then glanced at The Stiletto, also lying silent, shook his head, and said, "Okay, Agent Burns, you got six minutes to remove this mess and clear the street."

THE remaining forty-nine customers bought their dope and were arrested without incident. All but one were armed with everything from two-shot derringers to an M-79 grenade launcher.

The assembly-line arrest at the corner of Third and Christian went off like a day at a Toyota factory in Tokyo. Bubba Nite coordinated each arrest and acted as the rear-blocking car.

Throughout the long, tedious day fifty of the most hardened Philadelphia criminals were arrested with a kilogram of sham heroin on their person. Intent to buy heroin, even a sham product, amounted to a conspiracy rap. This guaranteed them each ten years behind bars without parole. No high-priced lawyers would find the minutest legal technicality in the arrest. Nor would five F. Lee Baileys dispute the videotape, which showed, in living color, their clients handing over the money in return for the heroin. There could be no bullshit defenses like, "My client was in Florida that day, your Honor, and I have fifty eyewitnesses to prove it."

The other delightful part of the operation, a street cop's poetic justice, was the fact that, in addition to putting Yon Yon Carbone, Richie the Stick, Matteo, Monster Riccolboni, and Psychotic Barlone behind bars, the government also received four and a half million dollars in its bank account. A virtual public-relations dream of being able to tell America how the FBI gave them a bang for their tax buck.

The success of the operation was not lost on Keenan, who strutted around the command post gaining macho bureaucratic bravado with each subsequent arrest. At the thirty-eighth takedown he announced, "I better call the deputy assistant director to brief him on the status of this operation."

Patty said nothing, which permitted Keenan more of a chance to gloat. "What a coup!" he exulted. "Fifty of the most hardened criminals we've targeted for years. Four and one half million dollars in seizures, the retirement of the Philly LCN bosses and, if all goes well tomorrow, the end of the Satan Motorcycle Gang."

He added, "No FBI operation in recent history can claim these stats. No SAC since Prohibition will get more press coverage."

His voice turned solemn as he said to Patty, "You may want to reconsider resigning. There's been some bad blood between us, I know, but *now*, what with me—I mean us—turning everything around in this case, I'll certainly let it be known in headquarters what a fine agent you are. I'm almost positive I can get you transferred to Philadelphia on a permanent basis. I'll make you a supervisor and, who knows, maybe you and I can become friends."

Patty looked at him in amazement but said not a word. Here was the major reason the case had gone sour now taking credit for its newfound success. Keenan hadn't listened to her about bringing Joe in, had not supported him, Moose, or her when things got shitty. Initially, he had rejected Amato's offer to turn things around. Now he conveniently contracted supervisor's amnesia and would actually receive the credit for wiping out crime in Philadelphia.

Her initial reaction was rage. She wanted to tell him what she thought, rip into him as she had done before. But it did no good then, and a confrontation at this moment would not accomplish anything. So she smiled and said, "First things first. Let's wrap up today and get a good tape tomorrow between Amato and Lu. Once Lerza is cleared, well, we'll see."

Her words seemed to appease Keenan; he started to pace the small command post like Jack Nicklaus walking up the eighteenth fairway with a two-shot lead in the Masters.

It was almost midnight when the Don's limousine rolled to a stop outside the Triangle. Amato had a spring in his step and a canvas bag in his hand that contained four and a half million dollars in cash. He was late for his appointment with Patty due to the brief meeting with *his* friend, the same old trustworthy friend he had met at the Italian Market, and with whom he once again exchanged canvas bags.

Romeo, the fat pizza kid, pushed a broom across the dirty plank floor, yawning. There were only five other customers in addition to Patty. Five drunks arguing about the merits of oral versus anal intercourse with fat girls.

Patty felt good in spite of her confrontation with Keenan, in spite of the day's shoot-out, and in spite of the fact that Lerza was still missing. Things seemed on an upbeat, Moose was out of danger, her career could be salvaged. She had played a large part in taking out fifty of the most violent criminals in Philly and seizing fifty kilograms of heroin. The vital meet tomorrow night between Amato and Lu would clear Lerza. The cherry on top of the chocolate sundae was the canvas bag Amato would now hand her, containing four and one half million dollars in cash.

Amato smiled at her and said, "A major success. Champagne is in order."

He raised his hand to draw the attention of Thelma the waitress, then ordered the Triangle's current bottle of champagne. One was always kept on hand for weddings, funerals, births or if Don Amato requested it.

"Did you know Vinnie the Stiletto and Tommy Six Toe bought cemetery plots today?" Patty asked.

Amato waved a hand, dismissing the seriousness of her statement, saying, "Vincent and Thomas are more likeable dead, my dear. Vinnie always smelled of garlic, and I once saw Tommy's extra toe. Quite disgusting."

She laughed, he laughed even louder. Their relationship was becoming easier, more relaxed. It troubled her that she looked forward to their meetings, depended on him.

"It went well," she said. "Keenan's happy, Headquarters's happy, you're happy. Why is it I am the only unhappy person involved?"

"Tomorrow is your day," he assured her. "Tomorrow I will get Lucifer to admit to Miceli's murder, and then even *you* will be happy."

Thelma arrived with the bottle of cold duck and two water glasses and poured the cheap bubbly. Amato seized a glass and held it high. "A toast to you, Patricia Masters, to your health, to your happiness. If I was a younger man and you weren't a fed, I would marry you, my dear."

They drank, and before she knew it, Patty kissed his cheek, overwhelmed by the emotions of the past twenty-four hours. They laughed, talked, and when the bottle of cold duck was empty, Amato handed Patty the canvas bag.

"I almost forgot," he said. "Here's the money. All there."

The money was important, she thought, but it was the least of her concerns.

31

Acid shuffled the papers, smiling at all the black ink. The Satans' profits resembled a successful NASA rocket launch going almost vertical. Stocks, bonds, real-estate holdings, T-bills, CD's, Ginny Maes, even United States Saving Bonds, all reaping the benefits of unlimited cash earned via the drug trade. This allowed bold and inventive speculative investments by the Satan vice president, whose pharmaceutically damaged brain had shown moments of the J. P. Morgan syndrome.

"We're fuckin' liquid, bullish, and more than marginally profitable." Acid beamed.

Lu sat behind the big desk, feet up, on the third floor office of the clubhouse. He pointed at Acid. "Only the beginning. Chicken shit compared to what happens after the wops yell 'uncle.' "

"When will that be?" Acid asked.

"Tomorrow. I give the old man a million in cash and a one-way ticket to Garlic Land." He smiled.

"Tomorrow?" A question.

"It's time," Lu said with conviction. "The Don's best friend croaked with cancer. Hard Rock is running the streets fuckin' up what remaining scams they got. And Amato himself is feeling his age. Seems his doctor told him to slow down."

"You sure do your homework, Lu." Admiringly. "Think he'll go for it?"

"Does he really have a choice?" That smile again.

"What about the FBI agent in the basement?"

Lu eased his legs off the desk onto the thick burgundy carpet. He instructed, "Acid, I want you to schedule a ceremony for tomorrow night. A celebration in honor of the Satans' new status in the world of crime. This will be a special ceremony. One in which the Archangel demands a particular sacrifice. A sacrifice that will protect us from Amato, protect us from the pigs, protect us from everyone."

He looked directly into Acid's eyes. Eyes that were mere slits. "A human sacrifice. The FBI offering has a dual symbolism. One, that it's a human, and second, it's a destruction of authority, of its supposed power. Tomorrow night we will cut the heart from the FBI Agent Lerza and drink his blood."

"I'll arrange it," Acid said.

"Get hold of Amato, my friend," Lu ordered.

Acid dialed the capo's private number from a computerized Rolodex.

The old man's voice answered, "Yes?"

Acid said, "Lu wants to talk to you," and handed the phone to his boss.

"Hello, Michael," Lu said. "How are you?"

"Fine. A pleasant surprise. I was just about to call *you*."

"You first, Michael."

AMATO could have predicted Lu's game; he knew it was critical to play him right. It would take all his energy, all his acting abilities and part of his soul to be subservient to anyone, let alone a killer like Lu.

He thought hard of his ultimate goal, visualized the picturesque countryside. He thought of Angelina and of his deceased friend, Averone. Then he plunged ahead.

"We must talk," he said. "It's very important."

"Another coincidence, Michael," Lu said cheerfully. "Tomorrow, ten in the morning. The Lakes. Its Archway."

"Whatever suits you." Amato's voice was suddenly feeble.

"You seem out of breath, Michael. Feeling okay?"

"Just got in, my friend. A late night."

"And I thought I'd woke you up," Lu taunted. "It's past one A.M."

Amato knew that if the conversation continued he would break character and tell Lu to shove a stromboli in the tail pipe of his Harley.

"Tomorrow," he said. "Ciao," then hung up.

The Don had just returned from his dinner with Patty at the Triangle; he was about to call Lu to arrange their meet. It had been a long day distributing fifty kilograms of heroin, very tiring. Lu was up to something, and he feared it had to do with eliminating him. A hit? Maybe, but more likely a 1980s-style takeover, like General Motors buying out Chrysler. Only if Chrysler did not accept, did not agree to the price and to every condition, then General Motors would bomb Lee Iacocca's top-of-the-line Chrysler with him in it.

Amato climbed the steps to his bedroom, removing his clothes in the old tiled bathroom to avoid disturbing Angelina, though he knew she was awake. She was always awake when he came home after his eleven o'clock bedtime. She would be lying on her side of the bed, wearing that damn flannel nightgown that started at the bottom of her chin and ended about six inches below her heels.

He tiptoed into that chamber sacred to old Italian ladies—the bedroom. It was a shrine to everything from ironing and sewing to sedate Bible reading. Everything except sex. That was a function, a duty, a requirement of the marriage vows made before God and a craggly-faced monsignor.

"Is everything okay?" Her voice was aimed at the wall.

"Fine, Angelina, just business."

"Good night, Michael," she said, reassured now that he was there.

"Angie?" He needed to talk.

"Yes, Michael?"

"Would it bother you if we moved? Moved away from Philadelphia? Far away?"

"As long as I'm with you, Michael, I wouldn't mind. My home is with you."

Amato smiled in the dark and said, "Good night, Angie."

"THIS thing again," Amato complained.

Patty struggled with the expensive Swiss tape recorder, trying to tape down the wires to secure them under Amato's dress shirt. She smiled and said, "Quit complaining. I'm doing all the work."

"Must it be so large?" he asked.

"Yes." She finished her taping and did a battery test with the main unit. Then explained, "The bigger, the better. Now give me a count."

"Uno, duo, tre," Amato said.

"That's very funny, Michael." Her voice held an edge. "Maybe we can talk in Polish and get the Pope to translate the tapes."

He sighed. "Smile, Patricia. Life's too short, and you are too young to have such a heavy heart."

She apologized, "You're right, Michael. Sorry."

Amato stood erect, struggling with his suit jacket. She helped him with a sleeve. The old man turned to face her and said, "I know what pressure you've been under, Patricia. I know how important this meeting with Lu is to you and to Lerza. I promise it will go well. My word."

She forced a smile and said, "Let's go over what we need from Lu before I hug you and start calling you Dad."

"I've been called worse."

Patty laughed and said, "Life's really playing a dirty trick on me. With my FBI boss I'm nervous, tense, and void of respect, but with the head of organized crime I laugh and feel good. And believe me, Michael, 'good' has been a rare commodity in my life lately."

The two were in Amato's private office at the Italian Club, taking care of business an hour before the meet with Lu. A variety of omelettes, ranging from cheese to shrimp, along with ham, sausage, bacon, waffles, fruit, hot coffee, orange juice, tomato juice, and Bloody Mary's, sat neatly on white china. But neither the capo nor the agent was hungry.

"Speaking of your boss," Amato said, "was he satisfied with the fruits of yesterday?"

"More than just pleased. He's delirious. Thinks you're his ticket to a cushy retirement job. Maybe a book about how he kicked the mob's ass. The lecture circuit, fame and fortune, and the adoration of a grateful public."

"My, my!" Amato sipped a glass of tomato juice. "Am

I such an important person? Who knows, perhaps your Mr. Keenan can be the Eliot Ness to my Al Capone."

"Enough of this." She sounded impatient. "Let's go over the play with Lu."

Amato put down his empty glass and began, "I engage Lu in conversation about the Miceli hit. He must acknowledge his role in the murder, whether as an active participant or the man who ordered it. He must say the words on your recorder. He must describe the scene, give information only the shooter would know. Tell who else was present. Then your Joseph Lerza will be free of the charges that haunt him."

He continued solemnly, almost afraid to ask, "Patty, tell me again about this man Lerza. Tell me why he is deserving of such fierce loyalty from a person like yourself. Talk to me."

And she did. Patty told Amato about the first day she met Joe Lerza. About his unique qualities, how he picked her as his control agent, her visit with Laura Lerza. Then Joe suddenly drinking too much, his flashbacks of Vietnam, the night in her apartment. She told him everything and felt better for it.

It was necessary she talk about something so emotionally devastating as these last ten months. When she said the words aloud, the realization hit that she had no confidant, no girlfriend with whom to share her secrets, to giggle with about her love life. No next-door neighbor to gossip with over white wine in the afternoon, no sister, cousin, mother, or even a willing stranger to tell her troubles to. All because of the career she had chosen. A career that demanded secrecy, eliminated or diluted friendships, and forced relationships based on random assignments, all night stakeouts, or chance office liaisons.

Now she was spilling her guts to the enemy, though she no longer thought of him as such.

When she had finished describing her relationship to Lerza, Amato said, "This Joe guy is special. Affairs of the heart are never simple, my dear. Sometimes there is no solution, and you must go forward with your life, trust in yourself, in God. It sounds as if your Mr. Lerza is a survivor, and though the present appears dark, I trust things will clear. Then you must make decisions or react to the decisions of others."

"I love him," she admitted, "but—"

Amato finished her sentence, "But he's married with kids."

"Yes," she sighed. "Two beautiful children. My heart wants him, but my conscience wouldn't allow it."

Amato stood up and said with energy, "First things first. We will remove the black spot from Special Agent Lerza's name; then you and he will have choices."

"That's if . . ." She hesitated. "If he's still alive."

"Your Mr. Lerza sounds hardy enough."

"Right." She switched back at once to business. "What do you make of the choice of location?"

Amato said thoughtfully, "Well, the Lakes provide Lu with a tremendous amount of privacy. Also great opportunity for treachery, but I do not sense a trap. Why risk violence if Lu no longer perceives me as a threat? I could tell from his voice that all respect for me is gone. No, he will not physically harm me, but he is going to make some kind of move."

"No matter," Patty said. "The important thing is that he confess to Miceli's murder. After that, Lu and his lieutenants go to jail. Hard Rock and his men go to jail. The fifty biggest heroin dealers are already in jail."

She went on, "The Bureau has recovered fifty keys of smack, four and one-half million dollars, and you retire from crime. A neat package. The only downside is that bastard Keenan becomes an American hero all because he screwed up. The irony of government." She gave a scornful laugh.

Amato smiled, also without mirth, and said, "Maybe a hero. *Or* maybe a goat."

Patty felt a chill in her spine. She asked, "What do you mean by that?"

Amato, still smiling, said, "It's time for Lu."

KEENAN wore that wide smile that turns women's heads at the supermarket. A real pretty-boy. Betty Northrup remarked that morning, "Something's up. Last time I saw him like this was the day after a date with that Channel Three weather woman."

The intercom buzzed on Keenan's desk. Betty said, "It's Deputy Assistant Director Webber on two."

Keenan beamed, said, "Bobby, how are you?"

"Fine, Brad. And you?"

Keenan knew he was hot shit—he intended to milk his praise from Headquarters.

"The sun is shining, and by tomorrow we will have eliminated all organized crime in Philadelphia," he announced.

"A job well done, Brad. Very well done." Webber sounded sincere.

"Thank you, Bobby." So did Keenan.

'"And don't think the Director isn't pleased," Webber continued. "I just left his office. He wanted me to personally congratulate you."

Keenan's fixed smile broadened. "Just doing a job, Bobby, that's all," he said.

"Nonsense, Brad. It was a masterpiece of investigation.

What with that bitch Masters, that head case Lerza, and that barbarian Moose Knepp. You held things together, you kicked ass, that's what the Director said. You kicked a *lot* of ass."

"Lerza's still missing, but if things go good today we'll eliminate that blemish from the Bureau," Keenan went on. "Amato's going to get a confession from the Satans' president that he killed Miceli. That will clear Lerza and the Bureau. Then I'll get murder warrants for the Satans and Hard Rock, for Monday's killing. Amato and his mob faction retire. And—"

"And," Webber interrupted, "you seized fifty kilograms of heroin with a street value of twenty million dollars and four and one-half million dollars in actual cash. You ol' war horse!"

Keenan mumbled, "A little luck was involved."

"Nonsense," Webber said. Then, "The Director wanted me to sound you out about an assistant director's slot here in Headquarters."

"Assistant director?" Keenan whistled. "Really?"

"Look, Brad," Webber reassured him, "you're ninety percent there. Just clear Lerza, the black spot on the Bureau. Arrest all those motorcycle types and young Sicilians. Retire Amato and, along with the recovery of heroin and the millions in cash, I'm certain there's an office next to me, Director Keenan."

When Keenan heard his name preceded by "Director," he almost had an erection. An assistant director of the FBI was more than just a title, more just a function, it meant status, national television interviews, testifying before Senate subcommittees, regular meetings with the Director, luncheons with the rich and powerful. A continual smorgasbord of flash and life in the fast lane of government operation.

Webber continued, "Of course, I'll come in for the grand finale. The arrests, the search warrant for the Satan clubhouse. The newspapers will have a field day, Brad, positive press. I'm flying out in two hours; have a car at the airport by four this afternoon."

"I'll come personally," Keenan promised.

"See you at four." The Assistant Director of the FBI hung up.

Keenan strutted to his outer office and ordered Betty, "Page Masters now. Put her right through."

"Yes, sir."

He returned to his desk, still aglow from his newfound career status. He could not decide if he should brag to his wife, girlfriend, mother, or third-grade teacher.

The intercom dictated his decision. Betty's voice said, "Agent Masters on one."

He picked up the receiver and said in friendly tone, "Patricia, how is it going with Amato?"

"Just wired him up," she reported. "The meet's in an hour."

"Excellent. Is he still a team player?"

Patty did not want to tell Keenan she thought Amato had more integrity in one finger than the SAC possessed in both manicured hands. She said simply, "A fine snitch."

"What of your suspicion about some kind of scheme? Amato holding back something? Not totally truthful?"

"I misjudged him," Patty lied. "The old man is totally ours, no hidden agendas. Just wants to do his thing and get it over with."

She did not believe a word she said. She liked the old man, found him charming, sensitive, and gentle. He appeared actually to care about her and her problems. But she also knew in her gut that Amato was up to something. With him she felt like the potential victim of some prank, like on a sorority pledge night. You knew it was coming, he knew you knew, and it was just a matter of *when* and *what*. Patty also felt in her heart that he would never hurt her, whatever the treachery.

Keenan pressed, "What about the arrest warrants?"

Patty sighed and said, "Federal magistrate signed the arrest warrants for Hard Rock and eight of his men for Stormy Monday's murder. As soon as Lu confesses to Miceli's hit, I'll get those warrants."

"Excellent," Keenan said. "Assistant Director Webber will personally supervise the arrest. He is flying in today."

Then he added, almost a plea, "Patty, let's make sure things go smoothly. The Bureau way. No surprises, hon."

She fumed in her heart but said coolly, "Things will go just peachy."

32

The Lakes," as it was known in South Philadelphia, consisted of a few acres of sparse grass and a few scraggly trees amid solid concrete. A dirty body of water technically classified as two lakes and not for the faint of heart. An old canoe could be rented for maneuvering around discarded tires, sneakers, and an occasional corpse. At the Archway newlyweds took photographs after church to prove South Philly had a countryside.

Patty was uptight because she had replaced the magic dime transmitter with the larger tape recorder and could no longer monitor the conversation. She did not completely trust Amato, and she certainly did not trust Lu in any respect.

She found a surveillance spot across an open field with a clear view of the Archway, approximately two hundred yards away. She checked her Timex, noticing that the meet was set in ten minutes.

Amato showed first, in his limo, with Daniel Di Sipio at the wheel. The chauffeur/bodyguard scanned the area as well as his old eyes would allow. The car came to a stop partly on the grass portion of the road about fifty feet from the Archway. Amato stepped out of the rear seat and slowly, almost at a crawl, headed toward the Archway. A passing car would assume that some rich old man, with too much time on his hands, was appreciating the only patch of grass in South Philly.

Patty focused the Nikon 35-millimeter camera with zoom lens on the old man. She snapped away as the automatic forward made its zipper sound. She barely noticed the old tan van roll by Amato's limousine and stop before making a U-turn. It settled with its front bumper almost touching the Cadillac's front bumper.

Patty tensed and focused the camera on the passenger door. She was not disappointed. Lu slithered out and headed toward the Archway. The suitcase in his hand was not lost on Patty.

Acid and Di Sipio sat behind the steering wheels of their respective vehicles, staring hard to see who would blink first. Di Sipio's recent cataract surgery guaranteed him a permanent squint, a win by default.

Lu spoke first. "Michael, how's the health?"

"I could attempt to deceive you," Amato said meekly, "but your eyes would see through my lie."

"That's tough. Old age is something we all face, Michael. No one escapes." He towered over the Don.

"Yes, my friend, even you will feel its tentacles some day. First an involuntary twitch, a thickening of the middle, a slight hesitation when once there was none. And, finally, you are no longer invincible."

Amato was laying it on thick, hoping Lu would appreciate and believe the performance of Amato's lifetime. The mafioso chuckled inwardly, thinking an Academy Award would not be out of line.

Lu said reassuringly, "A state of mind. That's what old age is. Feel old, you *are* old."

Amato sighed. "If it were only that easy, Lucifer." Then, in a slightly stronger voice, "But we are not here to discuss such a depressing topic on such a lovely day."

Lu sat on the concrete steps that were part of the Archway. He said, "Business, then. I won't insult you by beating around the bush. I wanna buy you out of the dope business. No more ten-percent operating fee, just a one-time buy-out price."

He tapped the suitcase at his side and continued, "One million bucks and you retire, but you must leave the city so your ghost don't haunt me. Before you go, you sanction me with the rest of the city's Italians. In return we stick just with dope. We leave your other action to whoever you designate. We all live in peace, everybody gets rich."

Amato was not surprised, but he forced his eyes to show shock. If he accepted too readily, Lu would be suspicious. If he did not accept at all, Lu would also be suspicious. As the lead character in this modern Greek tragedy, he was asked to be believable, stay in character, make the audience cry and laugh on cue.

After an appropriate silence, he said, "What if I don't accept?"

Lu smiled sadistically. "If you want to hear the words, I'll say them, but I'd rather not. So let's just describe it as a business deal of mutual benefit. In your case, a million mutual benefits."

Amato said slowly, "Ah, the price. They say everyone has one. The going-out-of-business, bargain-basement price. One million dollars to take over a sixty-million-dollar business. A rather good business transaction on your part, I'd say."

"You had your day in the sun, Michael. It's my turn. That simple." He looked the Don straight in the eye.

"Do I have a period of time to think it over?"

Lu smiled wickedly, and said, "No."

Amato dropped his head, allowed his eyelids to droop, tried in his heart to show the defeat he did not feel. The old master let an appropriate amount of time slip by, then said sadly, "Perhaps it is time for my retirement. My wife agrees with you, so one of you must be right." A hollow chuckle.

Lu pushed the suitcase over to Amato and said, "A wise decision. A happy retirement, maybe a few good years left."

Patty was watching through her zoom lens as Amato took the suitcase. She tried to figure out what could be in it and why Lu would give whatever was contained there to the mob chieftain. She didn't come up with the answer.

Amato started to walk away from Lu, took a few steps, and stopped suddenly. He turned back and said, "I should get a bonus."

"Why's that?"

"Threw the cops off."

"Whatta you talkin' about?" Puzzled expression.

"Miceli."

Realization hit the Satan; he spoke before he thought. "Oh, yeah, Michael. You mean getting that FBI agent fingered for Miceli's hit?"

"That was some hit," Amato said admiringly.

"I used a Walther PPK with a silencer," boasted Lu. "Shot his fuckin' kneecaps before I cut his ears off."

"Did you discard the murder weapon?" The question of questions. As Lu was making his confession, Amato noted the FBI recorder seemed lighter and lighter. It matched his spirits.

"Threw it right there." Lu pointed a finger at a spot in the lake about fifty yards from the Archway. "Nobody would ever fuckin' find it in that slop."

Amato noted the position of the murder weapon in the dirty lake as best he could and said, "I hope there were no witnesses."

At this Lu became angry. He said, "Listen up, Michael. I don't like being second-guessed. My men are trustworthy, not like your soldiers, who steal your money and call you an old fart behind your back. My men are stand-up. Acid, Sperm Whale, K-Bar, and Head Case were there to see the fun. Even let Acid put a slug in Miceli's brain and slit that bitch Dakota's throat."

Amato had heard enough; he was pleased with Lu's loose lips, more than ready to leave and stop his one-act play as a washed-up, pathetic crime boss. But Lu had not finished.

"And tonight I off the FBI agent," he announced.

The capo tried hard not to appear interested and started to leave again before turning a second time. He said, "Perhaps this is not wise."

"I don't need your permission," Lu challenged.

Amato shrugged his shoulders. "Just the advice of an old man who has ordered his share of murders *and* had to deal with the results."

Lu gave Amato a long, hard look and announced with finality, "Our business is done. I expect you out of Philly in two weeks. I expect you to vouch for me to your gumbas. Happy retirement, Michael."

The Satan president strode defiantly past Amato, entered his van, and left the Lakes in charge of the dope business in the fourth-biggest city of the United States.

* * *

AMATO met Patty for lunch at the Triangle. He now was all business, forced to make serious decisions he had not counted on until his meeting with Lu. Like what to do about Lerza. Should he tell Patty? Did he owe her that much?

The old mafioso measured each word as he said to her, "The tape should get you a murder conviction."

"That good?" she asked.

"Lu was most cooperative. He gave a convincing confession, complete with the names of his assistant killers and gory details that only someone present could know."

Patty tried to hide her joy and asked, "And the tape got it all?"

"Here." He passed the FBI tape recorder to her. "A belated Christmas gift."

She took the device, checked the battery and the amount of tape used, comparing it with the length of the meeting. Satisfied the recorder had operated properly and more than likely contained Lu's confession, she placed it in her bag.

"Oh, one additional Christmas Club bonus for the pretty lady from the FBI," Amato remembered.

She waited in anticipation as he said, "Lu let it slip that the murder weapon lies at the bottom of the lake, about fifty or so yards from the Archway."

Patty smacked the table with her hand. "Fantastic! Michael, you're great. We drag the Lakes, retrieve the piece, run it for prints, trace the weapon, test-fire it, and compare it with the slugs we pulled from Miceli. All that, with his statement on tape, and he may as well start his life sentence."

Amato smiled, said, "It's good to see you happy, Patty. What next?"

"I take the tape back to the office and give it to a steno who types out a rough transcription. Then I'll listen to the tape and finish off the report, make corrections. Next I'll take a copy of the tape and the transcription to a federal magistrate as part of an arrest-warrant affidavit. The magistrate signs the warrants, we round up the troops and raid the clubhouse. We arrest Lu and his four other co-conspirators for the murder of Anthony Miceli. We'll even get a search warrant for the clubhouse while we're at it. If we find any other contraband like weapons, stolen scooters, drugs, or hot jewelry, then we'll arrest the whole lot of them."

"Will all of this happen soon?" Amato asked anxiously.

"Could be tomorrow," she said.

"Sounds as if the end is near for Lu, the Satans, Hard Rock, his group, and most prematurely, the end of our meetings," he said, sounding a bit sad. "Our sharing of good will and delicious meals. Our planning and scheming. And the end of a friendship, if I may be so bold."

Patty blushed and said simply, "A real friendship. Too bad it has to end, Michael."

They talked on, each afraid to say good-bye, knowing it would be the finale. If they were to meet again, it would take place in courtrooms, with Amato testifying and Patty sitting at the government table. They both knew the mafioso's agreement with the government included his willing exit from his adoptive city in return for immunity.

When it was finally time to say good-bye, Patty stood up and said, "I better get this tape transcribed. See you, Michael."

Amato kissed her cheek and said, "And a good-bye to you, Patricia Masters."

She turned to leave, then suddenly remembered an important thought and asked, "Almost forgot. What was in that suitcase Lu gave you at the Lakes?"

Amato did not hesitate. "A symbolic going-away gift," he lied. "A headless cat surrounded by fish."

Patty gave him a questioning look.

Amato clarified his statement. "If I don't leave Philadelphia, Lu will behead me and dump my parts in the Atlantic Ocean."

THE FBI diving team had a rough time with the muddy lake waters. They needed special equipment such as a Sub-Strobe, a combination strobe and laser light, that could penetrate the murky waters at thirty feet.

Terry "Sea Hunt" Nelson was the team leader of eight diver agents. They systematically searched the area Amato designated. Each was assigned a grid square, starting at the shore by the Archway and progressing outward.

Sea Hunt actually found the Walther PPK three hours into the search, with the silencer still attached. A plane was waiting to jet the pistol to the FBI laboratory in Washington where latent prints would be lifted and compared with Lu's known prints from the Marine Corps records. Then the Firearms Identification people would test-fire to check markings on the rounds unique to each weapon and compare those markings with the bullets retrieved from Miceli's corpse.

Finally, an agent familiar with weapons would trace the gun from its serial numbers to determine every owner who had possessed it. A few threats to owners, starting with the original gun shop. Pegging them as murder accomplices would loosen the lips of tough guys when they were asked who bought the weapon.

Patty rushed back to the office to get the tape transcribed.

Deputy Assistant Director Webber had called, ordering Keenan to arrange a press conference at 9 P.M. in anticipation of a "significant massive arrest." Hard Rock and his Fairmont Park accomplices, as well as Lu with his Miceli co-conspirators, would be arrested before a media circus of UPI, AP, Channels 3, 6, 10, 17, and the Tokyo *Morning Chronicle*.

Blue Flame would officially lead the raid, which meant the brick agents would actually knock the door down, exposing themselves to Satan bullets. They planned to enter the building and secure it, inch by inch, until each room was cleared, all occupants cuffed, and every closet and corner searched. Then and only then would Blue Flame Bobby safely stroll through the premises followed by the press entourage, recording his heroics. The headlines would read: G-MAN ARRESTS EIGHT IN DOUBLE HOMICIDE.

At three in the afternoon Patty handed the tape to a steno, saying, "Get it done right away. I'll be in the bullpen dictating warrants."

AMATO now made one of the fast, hard decisions that had earned him the title "boss of bosses." He mentally ran through the options, the consequences of any actions—the risk, the odds, the rationale. He thought, Lerza is about to be murdered by the Satans, so what? Lerza is an FBI agent, and one less FBI agent is a good thing. That was how Amato should have felt, how he formerly felt. But ever since meeting and knowing Patricia Masters, it was not how he felt now.

The risks of trying to save Lerza were phenomenal. Amato's wife, his friends, his freedom, his life. Serious potential losses because of newfound loyalty to a friend who might eventually arrest him. All to save a man he did not know and who had done his best to put him in jail. And a dangerous group led by Lu might kill him in the attempt.

The old man returned to the Italian Club and started to make his calls. First to his wife: "I want you to get ready for a long trip. You will not return. Have someone pack our photographs, jewelry, clothing, and other treasured things. You know, Angie, the kids' drawings, my first-anniversary gift to you, stuff like that. Leave everything else. Be at the Atlantic City airport by ten tonight with just the clothes on your back."

He then dialed the rest of his Geriatric Group and ordered them to the Italian Club by five o'clock. He said: "Bring your guns. Bring your knives. Bring your St. Jude medals."

The capo thus carried out the last arrangements he would make in this room, in this city, in his adoptive country. All because of a decision he knew was stupid.

A decision based not on sound business but on emotion. A decision, he felt, he might always regret.

Lu was feeling pretty good, even for Lu. The meeting with Amato had gone well, though there was a nagging feeling deep within the Satan president that Amato had surrendered a little too quickly.

He had been too willing to accept defeat, too ready to give up what had taken a lifetime to acquire. Lu thought about this, then decided it did not matter what Amato's deception might be, what trick was played, because Lu was in control, protected by the Power of Lucifer.

He now faced the sacrifice of a human being, of an FBI agent who represented "good," the antithesis of evil. Who also represented the law, the antithesis of chaos, and whose death at the hands of Satan, the Fallen Angel, would infuse Lu and his men with a supreme Shroud of Power.

Nothing could harm them—no wop, cop, or god could stop the Satan Express. That evening, Special Agent Joseph Lerza, FBI, would be ceremoniously sacrificed, his heart cut out to represent the basic life taken, and the basic life would be given to Satan—the heart that signified life. This act would also cement the Satans' hold on the drug trade in Philadelphia.

It was now five o'clock, and in three hours the ceremony would begin. Black robes, candles, and scalpel-sharp knives, thirty disciples, and the main course—Joseph Anthony Lerza.

PATTY ran from the federal magistrate's office, arrest warrants in hand. An arrest warrant for Hard Rock Mastrograrani and one each for the rest of the mafiosi at Fairmont Park, charged with the murder of Stormy Monday and assaults on federal officers Lerza and Knepp. Patty also held warrants for the arrest of Lu and the Satans for the murder of Anthony Miceli and Dakota.

The fingerprint boys at headquarters had called that morning, sounding as excited as lab people could. They told Patty three latent prints lifted off the Walther PPK found at the Lakes were those of Raymond Edward Hatchinson, also known as Lu, formerly of the United States Marine Corps.

Patty rushed to review the typed transcript of the taped conversation between Lu and Amato—the smoking gun! The phone interrupted her reading. The SAC's secretary, Betty Northrup, announced, "Patty, the boss wants to see you immediately."

Patty protested, "Betty, I'm in the middle of reviewing the transcripts. I can't—"

"Mr. Keenan said 'immediately,' Patty," Betty interrupted. "The deputy assistant director is waiting to see you."

Patty sighed and started to put down the transcript when certain words caught her eye:

LU: I wanna buy you out of the dope business. No more ten-percent operating fee, just a one-time buy-out price. One million bucks and you retire.

AMATO: Perhaps it is time for my retirement. My wife agrees with you, so one of you must be right.

The mystery of The Suitcase solved, she thought: "One million bucks and you retire." She read the words again, mentally replayed the suitcase scene at the Lakes. She re-read the words for a third time, hoping the stenographer had made a mistake, knowing she had not. The lie!

Patty felt betrayed, because Amato had deceived her. Though it was not a surprise. She had expected some kind of double cross. But the real knot of fear in her stomach was becoming aware that the "suitcase" was only the known "lie"—the tip of the iceberg, the lie Amato was caught in. The indisputable lie, but *not* the one that stuck in her gut of instinct. That was yet to come.

The phone again interrupted her thoughts. Betty now sounded very nervous. "Patty, the boss is having a seizure. Come on, girl, he's making my already miserable life unbearable."

Patty locked the transcript in her desk and marched toward the SAC's office. After calming down Betty, she entered the inner sanctum. She immediately noticed Deputy Assistant Director Robert Webber, Blue Flame Bobby, sitting behind Keenan's desk. The term "Blue Flame" in FBI jargon meant someone so ruthless, so career-oriented, that the blue flame of ambition cascaded out of his asshole.

Webber looked older than his fifty-one years. He was at least two inches shorter than the five foot, seven inches minimum height requirement. He had a potbelly, compliments of an insatiable appetite for junk food, beer and chocolate covered pretzels.

Blue Flame did not wait for introductions. Keeping his seat, he said, "Agent Masters, sit. This talk is overdue."

Patty reluctantly placed herself in a nearby chair. She watched as Blue Flame sucked in his gut and squinched his eyes in an attempt to look stern.

"I'm not happy," he began. "I'm not happy at all."

He waited for his prey to fidget, squirm, and start stuttering an excuse in the presence of such raw power.

Patty looked squarely into Blue Flame's gray eyes and said, "I'm not concerned about your happiness."

He turned livid, sputtering, "Hold your sarcastic comment, Agent. The way you handled this whole undercover case borders on incompetence. I've got one of my agents lying critical in the hospital, another technically a fugitive, two corpses at the morgue, and bruised feelings with the Philly PD. All of which could have been prevented by you."

She shot back, "You also got the fifty biggest dope dealers in Philly, four and a half million dollars in cash, fifty kilograms of heroin, the *capo de tutti* as an FBI snitch, and in three hours you'll have the Satans and mafiosi in custody on murder and other assorted federal charges. By tomorrow *your* agent will be cleared, but I suppose it was *all* my fault." She turned to stare at Keenan as she finished, as though he were an imbecile.

Keenan recognized the same tone in her voice as when she previously ripped him as an asshole. The SAC also knew that this conversation would eventually lead the finger of blame to be pointed squarely at him.

"Did you get the warrants?" Keenan changed the focus of the discussion.

"All signed and ready to go." Her voice was cool.

Webber whined, still speaking to her, "*I* will lead the raids. You will assure all legal papers are in order. You will assist in processing the prisoners. And then tomorrow you will get on an airplane and return to your duties as a New York agent."

Another moral contradiction hit Patty Ann Masters like a cherry bomb in a tin can. Amato had a million dollars of Satan money in a suitcase, and it was drug money for sure. She was an FBI agent in the presence of two high Bureau officials. A few short months ago she would have immediately told them of her discovery on the tape, then led an arrest team of FBI agents to seize the money and cuff both Lu and Amato. But that was a few months ago.

Blue Flame said, with undeniable venom, "Is there anything else, Agent Masters?"

"No." A quiet voice, an answer without hesitation.

She stood up and returned to her desk to finish reading the transcript. She didn't feel guilty about her silence; in fact she felt strangely serene. One thing for sure, when tonight was over she gladly would leave Philadelphia and return to New York City in an attempt to restore some sanity in her life. Pure irony, heading to Manhattan for sanity.

She unlocked her desk drawer and removed the transcript of the Amato-Lu conversations. The phone would not cooperate.

"Agent Masters?" An official voice.

"Yes?"

"This is Headquarters again. I'm afraid I have some real bad news for you."

Masters endured the pause until the voice continued. "The heroin you submitted is actually confectionary sugar; your money, a high-grade counterfeit."

She listened as he further explained the confectionary sugar, the counterfeit money. The shock of his news left her cold.

She hung up and thought of the saying, "Things can't get any worse." Pure bullshit. She tried to calm herself, totally confused about what to do next.

Absentmindedly she read the final lines of the transcript. What she saw made her blood run cold.

LU: And tonight I off the FBI agent.

She looked at her watch. It was now 5:45.

33

Lerza had all but healed, physically. Emotionally, he was still caught between Vietnam 1967 and South Philadelphia 1989. With each passing hour he became convinced the FBI was as much his enemy as Lu; at times he even thought more so.

The footsteps he heard above indicated some type of activity. That and the fact that Acid had come and gone after preparing the Devil's altar for ceremonies. New candles, incense, shiny steel utensils, and other accessories not sold at K-Mart.

Lerza strained and scraped his flex cuffs against the cement floor and brick wall. Instead of breaking them he merely reduced them to jagged shreds of sharp plastics. Food had been more plentiful the last few days, giving him needed strength. During his more lucid moments, he had a clear sense of right and wrong. He even formulated an escape plan contingent on a few thoughts that came together. Reality now reminded him of his fugitive status, the loss of Moose, his own family, his friends, his sanity, which was his bottom line to life.

Then, suddenly, he'd lose his resolve and regress to a happier, safer time. He was a young boy, watching with adoring eyes as the old policeman removed the bullets from his antique .38. Still in dark winter uniform with a heavy wool greatcoat hiding his thick neck, the old policeman towered over the boy, appearing giant-like. The long overcoat met the back of his cap. He had cop's eyes. Eyes that struck terror into the soul of the most hardened criminals.

The young boy watched this sacred ritual every evening—the old policeman was his father. Aware of his son's eyes on him, when the weapon was empty, the old policeman would always turn and smile at the boy. Fleeting as it was, that smile lifted the boy's spirits, making him feel safe, secure, and loved.

For many years the nightly ceremony took place in the dark dining room with the somber flowered wallpaper and heavy wood furniture. The man didn't have hobbies, nor did he play games or enter into conversations with the young boy. But the boy was sure of his father's unconditional love.

Then the old policeman died. Not a glorious death in a hail of bullets, as would befit the essence of the man, but the slow, sure, inevitable death of cancer. He shriveled from two hundred and ten muscular pounds to ninety-seven pounds of bone and internal bleeding. He died with dignity, in his favorite chair, surrounded by the people and things that made him comfortable. Just before he died the old policeman motioned for his son to come to his side. The boy tiptoed over and heard his dad whisper in a low, sick voice, "I have to leave you, son."

"Don't go, Daddy," the young boy pleaded.

His father smiled weakly. "I'll always be with you, Joe," he said.

This confused the boy. "But how—?"

"Never fear life, Joey," the old policeman commanded. "Remember me and be bold. Be loyal. Be bold."

"I love you, Daddy."

The boy remembered those words as the years passed. For a long time they were merely the words of his dying father. He recalled his father as physically strong, mentally tough, able to handle any situation, able to change the worst happening into something good. He remembered his father's intense loyalty—to his family, to his fellow police officers, to himself.

In later life, the young man did those things expected of him. Little Joey Lerza married, volunteered for war, then joined the FBI. It was an American dream.

The cellar door opened. Lerza immediately recognized Lu's footsteps. The big man appeared before him wearing a black robe. There was an especially glazed look in his eyes.

He announced, "Judgment Day."

"What?" Lerza did not understand.

Lu spoke without emotion in a monotone. "You've disappointed me, Joe. You wouldn't help a friend."

Lerza realized something significant was going to happen to him. He said quietly, "I wouldn't give you the names of our undercover agents or snitches. I wouldn't tell you how we wire people or tap phones. I *couldn't* do any of that. I'm not evil. You're evil. I know I've done some shitty things, but I'm not you. I never betrayed anyone. Except myself."

"Touching. But now you must pay the price for your newfound morals."

"Whatta you talking about?" Lerza challenged.

"You must die for the glory of Satan."

Lerza sighed. "You wanna kill me? Then do it. But don't give me the crap about how the Devil made you do it."

Lu smiled. "Oh, but the devil *does* make me do things. In his honor, for his glory. In return, Satan gives me power. That's why you're lying there like a dead pig about to be roasted. Tonight, my marine friend, my Vietnam comrade, tonight you will die a slow, painful death for the glory of Lucifer!" He sounded triumphant.

Lerza recognized someone crazier than himself. He shrugged and said, "Fuck you."

PATTY grabbed Bubba Nite's arm. "Come on!" she ordered. She sounded desperate.

"Just follow me." She sputtered out the story as she force-marched Bubba toward the door.

"Whoa!" he protested. "Let me at least even the odds a little."

He trotted to the gun vault and twisted the combination lock unsealing the heavy steel door. He entered, exiting within a minute carrying a black, short-barreled weapon: one-third pistol, one-third rifle, and one-third machine gun. Officially labeled the Garnett P-2-28 Modified Colt, it had a banana clip with eighty rounds of forty-five caliber ammunition. Affectionately referred to as Multiple Orgasm by the agents, it could penetrate bad guys hiding behind cars, trees, drywalls, metal doors, and probably plutonium. In addition to old Multiple Orgasm, Bubba grabbed Special Agent Dan Estreb, and the three of them went off to save Joe Lerza.

Bubba and Estreb failed to convince Patty about the need for reinforcements. She no longer trusted the FBI or the Philly PD, since both agencies had orders to arrest Lerza. She couldn't risk an overzealous bullet in the name of "resisting arrest." Besides, Blue Flame and Keenan would probably screw up any rescue.

MICHAEL Amato, Daniel Di Sipio, Dominic Costa, Vito Coliano, Rocco Donati, and ninety-five-year-old Carlo Cicci met a few blocks from the Satan clubhouse with their gamefaces after Amato had called them together. Donati even left his cane in the car; adrenaline had eliminated his limp.

Plenty of Parodi cigar stogies stuck cockeyed in old purple lips. They had met this way often in their youth but now admitted those days were long gone. Call it one last act of defiance, a recapturing of past bravados, of victories, of testosterone run amuck.

Amato spoke officially. "Tonight, my friends, is strictly a gift. From you to me. I will not think less of you should any of you leave. I will still love you."

They stood in the schoolyard at Bok Technical High School, six old Italians in a huddle of blue and gray overcoats on a cold March evening.

"What is this talk of leaving?" spat out Carlo Cicci. "Run from these young whores? I will personally kill seven of them myself." The oldest mafioso kicked at the schoolyard cement to emphasize his intentions. The others chuckled, careful not to let Cicci see their smiles.

Costa spoke for all. "Don Amato, we have followed you

all these years, and we have no intention of deserting you now."

Coliano added, "This is the most fun we've had in a long time."

The comment brought genuine laughter. When it ended, Amato said, "I'm honored by your loyalty, but make no mistake—there will be blood, some of it ours. These men are totally ruthless and will not hesitate with their exotic weapons. Besides, what I ask of you is of a personal nature to me. It has nothing to do with—"

Cicci interrupted. "*So?* Cut the speeches and let's go have some fun before I die of old age instead of on a field of honor. Dealing with Hard Rock tonight has served only to whet my appetite for violence."

There was laughter again; then the Don said, "We are ready. But before we leave the schoolyard, it is important that I know that your travel arrangements are made, because tonight we all leave the world we know. One way or the other."

PATTY, Bubba Nite, and Estreb blue-lighted their way to the clubhouse area, then stopped a block away to make a battle plan. They knew the clubhouse had a lookout on the roof and was protected by a sandbag bunker emplacement, reinforced steel doors, and barred windows, in addition to a collection of weapons that rivaled what the U.S. gave the Contras.

The three special agents concocted a quick operations plan. Their goal was to enter a house defended by armed psychopaths and extract Lerza. This operation was not taught at the FBI Academy nor was it in the Law Enforcement Playbook.

Bubba Nite and Estreb had knocked down more than their share of doors but never such an imposing fortress.

And never with so few agents and so many bad guys. Both Estreb and Nite had resigned themselves to no reinforcements, no proper entry equipment, and no SWAT team.

What could three special agents do against thirty well-armed men, most of them former veterans with automatic weapons?

They would know the answer soon enough.

34

Lerza fought the best he could, but in the end the three 270-pound Satans forced him into a white robe, then injected a massive dose of Demerol into his flailing arm. The basement was candlelit with red-waxed luminaries and filled with satanic accessories. The imposing altar stood ready for its unwilling sacrificial victim.

Fueled by the Demerol, Lerza made sick jokes and sarcastic observations, like, "Am I the main course?" and "I'll taste like shit without salt." But the closer it got to dinner à la Lerza, the less he joked. Lu supervised the preparations, which included rhythmic chanting to work the troops into a lather followed by prayers to the fallen angel Lucifer.

Lu suddenly grabbed a rough stone and expertly flicked the Marine Corps K-bar knife back and forth until the blade was only a few millimeters thick and capable of cutting a Goodyear snow tire in half.

He approached Lerza. "Ready for the glory, Joe?"

"I'm ready for death." Lerza's voice was defiant.

"You are fortunate to have been chosen, Joe," Lu continued. "It is an honor to die for my god, Joe, because you will live forever. For infinity."

"Ain't I lucky?" Lerza slurred his words, then laughed ironically.

The Satan president nodded, cueing the three Satans to drag Lerza over and half drop him in front of Lu. As he stood on the first step of the altar area, Lu seemed larger than life, more omnipotent than ever. He raised his arms and the ceremony began.

First came a sermon, similar to those given by every priest, minister, and rabbi from the pulpits of America. A message to be heard by willing parishioners and taken to heart, aimed at making them better, more productive people.

Lerza was reluctantly positioned on the marble altar as Lu continued the sacred ancient ceremony. The rest of the Satans performed on cue in anticipation of the grand finale—a human sacrifice. For many of these violent criminals it would be their first such sacrifice, causing the same anticipation as for sharks at a feeding frenzy.

The room reeked of strange smells, incense and evil. The participants were aware of the ceremony's ultimate conclusion. Lerza's still-beating heart would be cut out and each Satan required to digest a coronary chunk, chased by the special agent's blood. The anticipation was contagious.

Lu took hold of the K-bar and held it high to allow the members a glance at its deadliness. He turned toward Lerza. It was time!

AMATO'S band of geriatric bandits did not have much of a battle plan of their own. In the old days they would wait until their prey hit the streets; then some wiseguy would put out fifty bullets sprayed in the direction of the target, knowing one or two would hit a vital organ. Rarely did they go inside a structure to do the business of murder. All this ran through Amato's brain as they drove toward their destiny.

The Satan sentry on roof duty was nicknamed Deranged. In and out of mental hospitals, he had earned his name by raping, torturing, and murdering two Drexel coeds, then beating the rap with an insanity defense.

Deranged actually had enjoyed his time in mental wards and had requested to remain inside the state hospital. But the system, in its infinite wisdom, released the vicious rapist against his wishes, forcing him back into society. The Satans had embraced Deranged and made him permanent roof sentry. His strict order was that there be no disturbances during ceremonies. He was backed up by two Satans at the front door who were given the same orders.

The FBI agents arrived first, tires screeching to a halt in front of the clubhouse. Deranged stiffened and chambered a round in his Uzi. Then the insane Satan pressed a buzzer, alerting the two men at the steel-reinforced door. They also chambered rounds with similar automatic weapons.

Bubba Nite jumped from the backup car with Multiple Orgasm in his hand. Patty and Dan Estreb took cover behind their car, facing the clubhouse.

Deranged yelled down at them, "State your business, pigs!"

"FBI. We've come for Joe Lerza."

"Ain't here!" he shouted.

"We wanna look for ourselves," Bubba demanded.

"Gotta warrant?"

Masters was quickly tiring of the word games. Under normal circumstances, the FBI had a standard operating procedure (SOP) for this type of situation. Call up a hostage negotiator, the SWAT team, half the office agents for perimeter duty, a few ambulances, and a priest. However, this was anything but normal. Patty felt an urgency, mixed with frustration and insanity.

She yelled, "We're coming in, warrant or not!"

Bubba cautioned, "Stay put, Patty. We need reinforcements."

"But, Joe—"

"We can't save Joe," Bubba interrupted, "if we're dead."

On the rooftop Deranged made some quick decisions. If anybody approached the clubhouse, he'd shoot the Uzi. The pigs didn't have paper, and without that he'd be legally protecting his property. The roof sentry's finger tensed on the automatic weapon and his eyes widened in anticipation.

Dan Estreb rose from the concealment and safety of the Bureau car. His intent was to reach inside the vehicle, grab the radio, and call for the troops.

Deranged mistook the movement for aggression and squeezed off a burst of nine-millimeter rounds. Estreb's forearm shattered, along with the Bureau radio. End of communications. The wounded special agent fell backward and muttered, "Shit."

The Uzi's retort triggered a reaction from the two downstairs Satans, who fired wildly in the direction of the three agents. Masters crouched her way over to the profusely-bleeding Estreb, shouting at Bubba to return fire. Satan bullets ripped into the low-bid Chevrolet and sent glass, vinyl, and rubber airborne. Bubba pointed Multiple Orgasm toward the clubhouse. The Bureau superweapon did things its manufacturers said it would, knocking chunks of the brick building into the night. For a split second the Satans' guns fell quiet.

Masters tried to stem the bleeding from a major artery in Estreb's arm with the palm of her hand. She propped him in a sitting position behind the wheel well, which offered some protection. "Hang in there," she pleaded.

The sound of the gunfire alerted the remaining Satans, who grabbed weapons and joined the fight. Hundreds of bullets rained on the helpless trio. Bubba would occasionally sneak a burst of rounds at the clubhouse, but even Multiple Orgasm couldn't match the sheer number of bad guys.

Patty realized their predicament. Estreb was losing a sea of blood and was on the verge of going into shock. He couldn't survive much longer, nor could they hope indefinitely to avoid the indiscriminate bullets. Even if neighbors had called the police, it would be several moments before they arrived. She judged it would be mere seconds before their thin cover disintegrated or bullets ricocheted around it.

Estreb smiled weakly and asked, "How we doin'?"

"We'll be outta here soon," Masters lied, feeling responsible for his hurt. Frustrated, she raised herself and emptied her .38-caliber pop gun toward the fortified building. It was about as effective as darts on a stone wall. Patty slumped back behind the car and automatically reloaded her weapon. She had all but given up hope when the cars filled with Italians arrived.

The old men positioned their cars skillfully, giving the Satans severe angles to their targets. They did things naturally, almost gracefully, without the need of Amato's instruction. Their U-shape formation offered the best line of sight and eliminated cross-fire problems.

Ninety-five-year-old Carlo Cicci pointed a three-inch .357 Magnum barrel over the hood of the car. Only five feet, three inches tall, Cicci barely cleared the windshield but held the weapon as steady as a vise. Vito Coliano and Rocco Donati fired steadily into windows and doors.

The new arrivals temporarily confused the Satans, who could no longer concentrate their attention on the helpless agents. Dan Estreb was in the first stages of shock as his body temperature dropped dramatically. Michael Amato hustled his way over to Masters and Estreb.

"Good evening, Patricia," he said calmly, taking in Estreb's bloody arm.

"You're a welcome sight." She was happy to see him.

"We must act fast," the Don said.

She told him, "Door and windows are fortified, but the roof sentry is the biggest problem."

She was correct in her evaluation. The roof position was death from above, a perfect offensive position. It was infinitely easier to shoot down than up.

"I've anticipated this particular problem," Amato said, putting a hand into his large overcoat. Looking at Bubba, he asked, "Ever play baseball, young man?"

Confused at the irrelevancy of the question, Bubba nodded lamely. Amato pulled a military fragmentation grenade from his coat and handed it to Bubba. "Here, should be an easy toss for you," he said.

Bubba palmed the grenade, then handed Multiple Orgasm to Patty. Amato instructed Bubba, "Throw a strike on the roof. My men will heave similar devices at the doors. Then we will enter."

"Whoa!" Patty protested. "You and your men are civilians. I can't allow you to—"

A barrage of Satan bullets interrupted her protest.

The Don said softly, "We will discuss our status at a later date, Patty, but for now there are higher priorities."

She relented, telling Bubba, "I'll cover you with this thing when you throw the grenade."

Everyone nodded, knowing the shit was about to really hit the fan.

Bubba pulled the pin on the grenade and threw a strike that blew Deranged back into sanity. Simultaneously, Patty aimed Multiple Orgasm at the front door, handling the recoil like a pro. Her fire, coupled with the grenade, produced a barrage of return fire from the clubhouse.

The old mob guys reacted instinctively, shooting their peashooters with amazing accuracy at the reinforced windows. A few Satans bought head and face shots. Two additional grenades blew the heavy front doors from their hinges.

"*Now!*" Patty screamed.

She and Bubba broke cover, heading toward the front door. As they did, they noticed blue lights approaching and heard the FBI sirens. Already in motion, the two agents continued to the Satans' front door, one on each side of the opening. Before they could enter, Amato and Di Sipio flashed past them and into the inferno.

Bullets flew in every direction. Patty saw Di Sipio take one in his left shoulder. The chauffeur/bodyguard kept moving and shooting, killing two Satans on his way to the back of the building. He was looking for the captive FBI agent he had never met. The fighting was ferocious. The old Italians moved like young bucks in October.

Rocco Donati caught a round in his ass; Vito Coliano took three slugs in his already crippled legs; and Di Sipio was felled by another round in his calf.

Patty changed magazines on Multiple Orgasm just in time to mow down a squad of oncoming Satans. She pointed the weapon at a seriously bleeding biker. She asked, "Where's Lerza?"

The Satan looked into her eyes and knew she would kill him if he didn't answer. He blurted out, "Basement."

She and Amato headed toward the basement door. It was open. The pitch-dark stairway offered only the promise of death. The basement smelled of doom, reeked of evil. Lu waited somewhere down there, symbolic of hell.

They rushed below to Lu's inferno. Gunfire could still be heard above, and screams of "FBI," which meant Keenan had arrived with his troops.

Amato tried to push ahead of Patty on the steps, saying gallantly, "The dark is a friend to these old eyes, allow me." But she would not budge.

"I'm in charge, Michael. Stay behind me."

They reached the bottom of the steps and stopped. Patty felt an overwhelming urge to turn to her right in the darkness. It was more than an urge; it was an ultimatum from her brain. Every one of her senses ordered, "Turn right!" As if something or someone had entered her body and taken total control.

She did not *want* to go to her right, but in the end she did. As she pivoted into the open area, a strobe of light caught her eyes and she saw him—the most evil face she could ever have imagined. Patty Masters was staring at the Devil himself.

At the same split second she felt Amato's strong hand jerk her violently behind the cement post just as the executioner's knife struck where she had stood.

Amato now shoved her around the pitch-dark room in search of safety. When it felt right, the two paused and waited. Not knowing Lu's location filled them with a silent terror. It seemed as if the Satan could *see* them, was toying with them prior to their certain death. They listened but heard nothing. Even the commotion upstairs faded into their unconscious as they focused their wills on some sensory clue to survival. A sound, a smell, a movement—something!

The two didn't have to wait long. A swooshing sound

similar to an eighteen-wheeler truck whizzing past a pedestrian on an interstate preceded Multiple Orgasm's abrupt separation from Patty's grip. Her involuntary scream punctured the dark. Amato pulled Patty hard to the rear.

"I still have two rounds left, Patty," he reassured her.

They waited for the next pass of doom, assured of its inevitability. Amato's old eyes and ears were useless in the dark, but his years of instinct were their most valuable commodity. Again, something was directing Patty to move—to the left, this time. "This way," she whispered.

As she began to move, Amato once again tugged at her arm. Also in a whisper, he said, "He waits there."

The aging Don pirouetted her to his rear and waited a split second, then immediately took two steps to his right. The unlikely pair moved like competitive ballroom dancers on a warm June evening.

A voice boomed from the darkness. "You are quite good, Michael," Lucifer said. "A strong mind. Able to resist my will."

Patty cringed. The voice wasn't quite human. Its timbre sounded evil—pure evil. Amato whispered, "Be still, my dear. Breathe shallow."

The old man felt a responsibility for their movements. He was operating on an instinct tested over many decades. A wrong move would end in a cruel death.

The unlikely twosome crept back until they touched a wall. Amato felt the two adjacent walls and was struck with despair. They were in a corner with no way to go but forward. Could it be that Lu had controlled their movements after all?

Slowly, ever so gently, Amato moved in front of Patty, protecting her with his old body. He mouthed the Act of Contrition. It was the prayer said to cleanse a soul of its sins.

An animal-like howl erupted from the darkness. The origin seemed inches from them. Masters froze in total fear, her body rigid.

A swishing sound followed, the sound of something moving quickly in the darkness. The movement started to their left, ended on their right. A second blood-curdling scream assaulted their ears. Masters involuntarily cringed, attempting to curl herself into a protective ball position. She felt Amato's strong body shielding her.

The swishing sound was repeated with regularity, seemingly coming closer and closer. Suddenly Patty heard the sickening thud of metal striking bone and flesh. Amato's body jerked violently away from her as the old man gasped in pain.

Amato fired his two remaining bullets into the darkness. It was the futile attempt of a desperate man. He was now totally disoriented, down on his knees, bleeding from a gaping shoulder wound.

The old Mafia survivor was defiant to the end. He spat out, "You'll have to kill me, Lucifer!"

A voice boomed from the darkness, "But you are already dead, Michael Amato!"

Amato could never accept Lu's control of their final parting. The old man was determined to dictate the terms of surrender, even if they were his own. He knew from the pain and the feel of blood that his time was short. The sharp blade of Lu's had ripped open Amato's right shoulder. He could not survive a second blow.

Masters reached out in the dark toward Amato. She felt exposed bone and a river of blood. She pulled the Don to her bosom, like a mother holding a hurt child. But he resisted that indefensible position and staggered to his feet.

He hissed at Lu, "You son of a bitch." Amato could hear his own heart beat like a drum in his ears.

The third and final plunge of Lu's instrument of death began its arc. Amato could not see it, but he felt it directed at his neck.

It began its descent. Amato wanted to move and save his life but couldn't. He was frozen to his destiny, he thought, would have to accept the end of this tiresome, threatening game. The only thing required of him now was to die.

Amato flinched, thinking this was his last second on earth. Suddenly he heard a grotesque scream that he thought must have erupted from deep within his dying self.

Almost a full moment passed before Amato realized he was holding his breath. He exhaled deeply, then asked Patty, "Do you feel it?"

"What?" she whispered.

"Evil," he said.

"Evil?" she repeated, still a whisper.

"Evil has gone," Amato said with a sigh.

Bright law-enforcement flashlights weaved their way crookedly down the basement steps. Voices screamed, "FBI!"

Patty called out desperately, "It's Masters! Find the lights! Come quick."

Within seconds the overhead lights illuminated a scene she would never forget. Only inches from her and the bleeding Amato lay Special Agent Joseph Lerza.

His hands still clutched the razor-sharp Marine Corps K-bar that now protruded from the heart of Lu.

PATTY hopped into the ambulance carrying the semi-conscious body of Joseph Lerza. She held his hand, watching the reflection of the blue and red emergency lights bounce off the ambulance walls.

Joe stirred and squeezed her delicate hand. Then he asked, "Is it over?"

"Yes," she said. "All done. Everything's okay, Joe."

"How'd we do?"

"The good guys won."

"You takin' me to jail?"

"Lu confessed to Miceli's murder, Joe. You're cleared."

Lerza's lip curled ever so slightly into a smile. "I saved the government a trial, didn't I?"

"You were magnificent." She smiled back.

An awkward silence enveloped the ambulance as each searched for the right words. Both knew there would be no more stolen moments at Patty's apartment. Unspoken commitments had to end. But at least they were together, even though it could never be the same. Careers had been in jeopardy; mental and physical health were still fragile for Lerza, who had existed months near the edge. They were now two old friends, not sure of what came next in their work.

Joe said, "We have to talk."

"Later," she said. "There'll be time later."

"No," he protested. "We both know there may be no later."

Patty hesitated a moment, then said, "I love you, Joe Lerza, always have and always will. Loved you from the first moment I laid eyes on that chip on your shoulder and your crooked-tooth smile. But I have buried my feelings, pushed them deep inside my heart because you're someone else's husband, someone else's vacation partner, someone else's breakfast companion. I'd go on, but you get the picture."

Lerza tried to raise his battered body. He needed to explain his feelings toward Patty. He wanted to tell her that he loved her; he had to justify all his bizarre actions, apologize for hurting her, and thank her for saving him. Most of all he wanted to hold her in his arms. He wanted to do all of this but couldn't. Because Patty was right—he was married to Laura Lerza, and that was irreversible.

The words of the old policeman, his father, stuck in his brain: "Be loyal. Be bold."

The ride ended with the paramedics carting Joe through the double doors to the emergency room. A young nurse started her routine, asking Joe questions, not getting easy answers. Patty's last sight of Joseph Anthony Lerza was seeing him disappear behind the hospital door.

She packed her bags that night and headed north on the Jersey Turnpike. The ninety-mile trip from Philadelphia to New York, through cities like Trenton, Morristown, and Red Bank, revealed an industrial wasteland littered with hundred-foot electrical transformers, smokestacks spitting toxic waste, and cyclone-fenced factories.

Time passed like a blur as she drove on. She was lost in a scrambled vignette of bizarre, isolated incidents of the past year. Joe, drunk at her apartment, starting to make ardent love then deciding against it. The massacre at Fairmont Park. Michael Amato and his deceit, as well as his compassion and heroism. Moose and his loyalty to Joe. The villainous Lu. Joe's question played in her brain. "Is it over?" "Yes," she said to herself.

Patty feared she was in for her own personal bloodbath. She knew she was an accomplice in Amato's escape with fifty keys of heroin and millions of dollars in government money. Her bosses would be out to torpedo her, and the man she loved was about to return to a world apart from hers. Not your typical day at the office.

35

The Sicilian villa offered a spectacular view of the ocean from its vantage point atop the plush green hillside. The four old men sat on homemade wooden chairs sipping red wine, talking eagerly. The villagers had welcomed them home with open arms.

Angelina hollered, "Michael, it'sa dinner time."

Amato laughed and said, "I'm coming, Angie, put on some extra for Daniel, Carlo, and Vito."

She protested mildly, "Let them eat somewhere else tonight. I cooka for them all the time. Makea them go home."

Cicci shouted in Sicilian, "Shut your mouth, woman, and do what your man tells you. Go cook."

As Di Sipio rose, he favored the leg that had been ripped by the Satan bullet. Coliano would be on crutches for his remaining years, but his sense of humor was healthy and whole as he asked, "Our usual soccer game after dinner?"

Amato laughed, then grimaced from shoulder pain. His artery had to be sutured where Lu's blade had cut into him, then reconstructed. They raised their glasses in a toast.

"To honor!" Amato proclaimed.

"To peace in our remaining years," Coliano added.

"Peace is boring," Cicci said. "I'm bored already. When are we going to kick some ass?"

The three mafiosi realized that ninety-five-year-old Cicci was serious, which made it all the more amusing. They laughed and touched wineglasses.

The five and a half million American dollars went a lot further in Sicily than it would have in South Philly. The fifty kilograms of heroin translated into another five million dollars. All of which was more than enough to support Amato, his loyal men, their families, and their families' families for generations to come.

Amato's health had even improved since the stress of meeting with a Miceli, a Hard Rock, and a Lu had disappeared. He admitted to himself that he missed Patty Masters. He longed for her humor, her independent assuredness, her vulnerability, her warm smile. He hoped that his deceit would not be taken personally by Patty. He even toyed with the idea of sending her $250,000 but, knowing her, rejected the idea, believing she would feel insulted. She would understand why he took the cash, the dope, and killed Hard Rock. He knew she was grateful for his helping her to keep alive in that terrifying basement.

It had all been planned long ago. His master plan had hatched slowly, fueled by his failing health, Miceli's aggressive takeover bid, and Lu's demonic violence. The plan had worked, and now he was alive in his native Italy with its temperate climate, lovely landscape, and beloved Angelina.

The former mob chief was content to die where he was and know it would be of natural causes, in peace, not in a war with other mobs.

KEENAN was held in disgrace. It was a dark day when the hot teletype from the FBI Director arrived. It demanded immediate answers from the SAC as to how he could allow Amato to give the FBI fifty kilograms of sugar instead of heroin. And why the FBI received four and one-half million dollars in counterfeit paper instead of legal tender.

The FBI also wanted to know how Keenan permitted Lu to pay Amato one million dollars in cash while under surveillance by FBI agents at a meeting arranged by the Philadelphia office of the FBI. And why Keenan ruined relationships with federal prosecutors, who had to release fifty heroin dealers and fifty-eight additional accomplices unjustly arrested by the Philadelphia FBI—many of whom were now suing for false arrest, since they had only transported sugar, not heroin.

The FBI asked why nine subjects were killed and one agent seriously wounded in an arrest situation that was not executed properly. They could not understand how the SAC could allow the one main subject in the case, Amato, to escape, thereby wasting a one-year investigation of minor-league arrests, great expenditures of money, needless injuries, and a tremendous amount of negative press.

Deputy Assistant Director Webber was transferred to 'Ident' Division and assigned to shuffle papers containing fingerprints all day. A real comedown for a power broker. Blue Flame had a nervous breakdown, spent six weeks in a D.C. rubber room before being released, and then was medically retired from the Bureau. Last heard from, he was teaching arts and crafts at a nursing home.

· · ·

PATTY did not suffer. She strode purposefully down the wide halls of the FBI headquarters as the new Supervisor in Charge of Undercover Operations. Her duties included monitoring all undercover cases in the Bureau to assure integrity and sanity. She worked sixteen-hour days, weekends, and holidays, earning the nickname of Ice Bitch, since she spurned practically every male agent at headquarters.

She discreetly checked on Lerza regularly but purposely avoided direct contact. Her fragile emotions would not allow her even to hear his voice. Moose would call occasionally with outrageous requests like, "Got any loose girlfriends at Headquarters that wants to meet a love god?"

She would ask, "How you feeling, Moose?"

"I'm okay, darlin'," he would say seriously. "The doc says I'll recover and can go back to work in a few months."

"I miss you, Moose."

"I miss the shit outta you, Patty."

"When will you get out of the hospital?"

"The doc promises within a month. I think he's sick of me. I sure am of him."

"Call me and let me know when you leave, will you?"

"I promise, Patty darlin'. I'll never forget you." Love in his voice.

"Nor will I forget you." Love in her voice, too. He had saved Lerza that night at Fairmont Park.

THE Atlantic City sand had long ago turned into a brownish, debris-ridden mush. The gambling casinos, coupled with Mother Nature's clock, had turned the once-popular family beach into a playground for raucous teenagers, beer bums, Frisbee players, and *loud* music fans.

Reinstated Special Agent Joseph Lerza lay on a terrycloth towel watching Laura and their two daughters dance along the tide as it hit the beach. Laura did not laugh as often as she once did, but the FBI psychologist told Lerza time would help.

Moose said, "Pass me a beer."

Lerza took a can of beer from the white Styrofoam ice chest, handed it to Moose, and grabbed a Pepsi for himself. Moose lay on a cabana chair, stretched out in a Hawaiian flowered shirt, purple bathing trunks, and straw hat. He was just fresh from the hospital and looked like his old self.

He asked, "How much time before we gotta report back to work?"

Lerza took a sip of his soda and replied, "We got time. I'm recovering from thirty days sitting in circles with other abusers at the la la farm, where they detoxed my ass."

He added thoughtfully, "It's never going to be the same, Moose."

"What isn't, Joey?"

"The Bureau. You. Me."

"It sure ain't, munchkin. And maybe that's good." Moose smiled.

Lerza realized that on the undercover assignment he had acted out some of his earlier terrors. Nothing could have stopped him, especially the use of reason, from daring Lu to kill him. His drinking had been excessive, as though he wished to escape the world of reality. All this he understood after the Bureau sent Dr. Thompson to the hospital. Lerza was glad to see the psychiatrist, who now helped him to understand why, unprotected, he had raced into Lu's vicious arms and sought death in the enemy camp.

Dr. Thompson had said to him, in his always quiet voice, "You unconsciously sought punishment for the death of your faithful ex-Sergeant in Vietnam. You believed your partner had been killed protecting you, which meant you were the murderer and deserved to die."

He added, "You are a superb FBI agent, but you should try to get rid of this inordinate, unreal guilt. A guilt that first started when you were a little boy."

Lerza felt a kind of elation in the thought that his "unreal rage," as Dr. Thompson had called it, even though it had almost led to his death at Lu's maniacal hands, had rid the nation of two terrifying murderous creatures—Miceli and Lu. They were savages from the dark ages, when men had no conscience and murdered another man for food or because they wanted his wife or daughter.

Lerza lifted his head to the sun and said earnestly, "You know, Moose, you and I sent those bastards to a hell they deserved. With an assist from Amato."

He added, "And, of course, Patty."

He wondered wistfully how she was, where she was. He thought, We will see each other again. Somehow I have to repay her for that final rescue. Without her, there's no doubt that I'd be floating in hell.

Moose said, actually blushing, "Glad I could be of some help to you, Joey. I love to work with you."

"Wait until our next undercover case," Lerza said, excitement for his work once again stirring in his breast. "Save your energy so we can give them another good show."

The old policeman would have been proud of him.